The Anticipation
Novelists of 1950s French
Science Fiction

CRITICAL EXPLORATIONS IN SCIENCE FICTION AND FANTASY
(a series edited by Donald E. Palumbo and C.W. Sullivan III)

1 *Worlds Apart? Dualism and Transgression in Contemporary Female Dystopias* (Dunja M. Mohr, 2005)

2 *Tolkien and Shakespeare: Essays on Shared Themes and Language* (ed. Janet Brennan Croft, 2007)

3 *Culture, Identities and Technology in the* Star Wars *Films: Essays on the Two Trilogies* (ed. Carl Silvio, Tony M. Vinci, 2007)

4 *The Influence of* Star Trek *on Television, Film and Culture* (ed. Lincoln Geraghty, 2008)

5 *Hugo Gernsback and the Century of Science Fiction* (Gary Westfahl, 2007)

6 *One Earth, One People: The Mythopoeic Fantasy Series of Ursula K. Le Guin, Lloyd Alexander, Madeleine L'Engle and Orson Scott Card* (Marek Oziewicz, 2008)

7 *The Evolution of Tolkien's Mythology: A Study of the History of Middle-earth* (Elizabeth A. Whittingham, 2008)

8 *H. Beam Piper: A Biography* (John F. Carr, 2008)

9 *Dreams and Nightmares: Science and Technology in Myth and Fiction* (Mordecai Roshwald, 2008)

10 *Lilith in a New Light: Essays on the George MacDonald Fantasy Novel* (ed. Lucas H. Harriman, 2008)

11 *Feminist Narrative and the Supernatural: The Function of Fantastic Devices in Seven Recent Novels* (Katherine J. Weese, 2008)

12 *The Science of Fiction and the Fiction of Science: Collected Essays on SF Storytelling and the Gnostic Imagination* (Frank McConnell, ed. Gary Westfahl, 2009)

13 *Kim Stanley Robinson Maps the Unimaginable: Critical Essays* (ed. William J. Burling, 2009)

14 *The Inter-Galactic Playground: A Critical Study of Children's and Teens' Science Fiction* (Farah Mendlesohn, 2009)

15 *Science Fiction from Québec: A Postcolonial Study* (Amy J. Ransom, 2009)

16 *Science Fiction and the Two Cultures: Essays on Bridging the Gap Between the Sciences and the Humanities* (ed. Gary Westfahl, George Slusser, 2009)

17 *Stephen R. Donaldson and the Modern Epic Vision: A Critical Study of the "Chronicles of Thomas Covenant" Novels* (Christine Barkley, 2009)

18 *Ursula K. Le Guin's Journey to Post-Feminism* (Amy M. Clarke, 2010)

19 *Portals of Power: Magical Agency and Transformation in Literary Fantasy* (Lori M. Campbell, 2010)

20 *The Animal Fable in Science Fiction and Fantasy* (Bruce Shaw, 2010)

21 *Illuminating Torchwood: Essays on Narrative, Character and Sexuality in the BBC Series* (ed. Andrew Ireland, 2010)

22 *Comics as a Nexus of Cultures: Essays on the Interplay of Media, Disciplines and International Perspectives* (ed. Mark Berninger, Jochen Ecke, Gideon Haberkorn, 2010)

23 *The Anatomy of Utopia: Narration, Estrangement and Ambiguity in More, Wells, Huxley and Clarke* (Károly Pintér, 2010)

24 *The Anticipation Novelists of 1950s French Science Fiction* (Bradford Lyau, 2011)

25 *The* Twilight *Mystique: Critical Essays on the Novels and Films* (ed. Amy M. Clarke, Marijane Osborn, 2010)

26 *The Mythic Fantasy of Robert Holdstock: Critical Essays on the Fiction* (ed. Donald E. Morse, Kálmán Matolcsy, 2011)

27 *Science Fiction and the Prediction of the Future: Essays on Foresight and Fallacy* (ed. Gary Westfahl, Wong Kin Yuen, Amy Kit-sze Chan, 2011)

28 *Apocalypse in Australian Fiction and Film: A Critical Study* (Roslyn Weaver, 2011)

29 *British Science Fiction Film and Television: Critical Essays.* (ed. Tobias Hochscherf, James Leggott, 2011)

30 *Cult Telefantasy Series: A Critical Analysis of The Prisoner, Twin Peaks, The X-Files, Buffy the Vampire Slayer, Lost, Heroes, Doctor Who and Star Trek* (Sue Short, 2011)

The Anticipation Novelists of 1950s French Science Fiction

Stepchildren of Voltaire

BRADFORD LYAU

Foreword by George Slusser

CRITICAL EXPLORATIONS IN SCIENCE FICTION AND FANTASY, 24
Donald E. Palumbo *and* C.W. Sullivan III, *series editors*

McFarland & Company, Inc., Publishers
Jefferson, North Carolina, and London

LIBRARY OF CONGRESS CATALOGUING-IN-PUBLICATION DATA

Lyau, Bradford, 1953–
   The Anticipation novelists of 1950s French science fiction: stepchildren of Voltaire / Bradford Lyau ; foreword by George Slusser.
       p.   cm.
   Includes bibliographical references and index.

   ISBN 978-0-7864-5857-8
   softcover : 50# alkaline paper ∞

   1. Science fiction, French — History and criticism. 2. French fiction — 20th century — History and criticism. 3. Progress in literature. I. Title.
   PQ637.S34.L93   2011
   843'.08762090914 — dc22   2010038851

British Library cataloguing data are available

©2011 Lyau Bradford. All rights reserved

No part of this book may be reproduced or transmitted in any form or by any means, electronic or mechanical, including photocopying or recording, or by any information storage and retrieval system, without permission in writing from the publisher.

Front cover art ©2011 Wood River Gallery

Manufactured in the United States of America

McFarland & Company, Inc., Publishers
   Box 611, Jefferson, North Carolina 28640
       www.mcfarlandpub.com

To my mother and father,
who put up with their son's strange reading habits
and even weirder career choices.
Thanks for your understanding
— and for all other things.
And to
Leonard Krieger (1918–1990),
historian, scholar, and mentor.

Table of Contents

Acknowledgments ix
Foreword by George Slusser 1
Introduction 7

One. Background 11
Two. The Moderates 31
   F. Richard-Bessière 31
   M.A. Rayjean 59
   Kemmel 73
   Chapter Summary 75
Three. The Extremist 76
   Jimmy Guieu 76
Four. The Conservatives 94
   Stefan Wul 94
   Maurice Limat 115
   Peter Randa 126
   Kurt Steiner 132
   Chapter Summary 139
Five. The Radicals 140
   Jean-Gaston Vandel 140
   B.R. Bruss 169
   Chapter Summary 182
Six. A Last Word 183
   Gilles D'argyre 184
Seven. Conclusion 193

Chapter Notes 199
Bibliography 211
Index 225

Acknowledgments

As I did in my dissertation, the basis of this study, I begin my expressions of gratitude by acknowledging my head advisor in graduate school in the Department of History at the University of Chicago, Leonard Krieger (1918–1990). His patience and faith as a mentor to me remain a source of inspiration. This is why half of my dedication belongs to him. I know he would have approved heartily of this project. I can only hope he would have thought likewise of the result.

George Slusser, a friend and colleague for over a quarter of century, deserves much recognition for reading the whole manuscript and giving his advice. His insights into French literature, popular literature, and philosophy have enabled me to clear more easily the usual obstacles inherent in studying a different culture. I have asked him to write the preface to this study as I cannot imagine a more fitting person to do so.

Marie-Hélène Huet, Jean-Marc Lofficier, and Laurent Genefort each read a chapter and gave invaluable perspectives (as well as priceless boosts of confidence when I got it right). Lofficier also provided much appreciated background information throughout the writing of this study.

H. Hilliard Gastfriend edited the whole manuscript, helped me avoid embarrassing mistakes, and made sure that what I wrote was what I meant to say.

The community of participants, organizers, and supporters of the J. Lloyd Eaton Conference, the annual academic conference on science fiction centered on the J. Lloyd Eaton Collection of Science Fiction, Fantasy, Horror, and Utopian Literature at the University of California, Riverside, deserve mention. Since I left the academic world, these gatherings kept me in touch with the latest research in the field and provided me with many ideas that resulted in publications, including this study.

The staff of the Eaton Collection has helped me immensely through the years on this and other projects. Particular thanks go to Clifford Wurfel and Melissa Conway, past and present heads of the collection.

I would be remiss if I do not mention Michael Murrin, who sat on my dissertation committee. His comments and advice from back then still apply today. Thank you.

Two people who are no longer with us should be acknowledged as early inspirations for this study. Jack Williamson (1908–2006) needs no introduction to those at all familiar with the field of science fiction. His study on H.G. Wells as a critic of progress helped me focus my theme in my dissertation and this study. He also willingly gave of his time by maintaining a twenty-plus year correspondence with me. Forrest J Ackerman (1916–2008) generously opened his personal collection and archives to me during the early phases of my research. Thank you, Jack and 4E.

Special mention should be given to the "Whensday" writers' group centered in Silicon Valley. They critiqued an early version of a chapter and provided much needed advice for my writing. Thanks for pointing me in the right direction.

This being my first book, I want to take the time and acknowledge those family members and friends who not only encouraged me before, during, and after the composition of this study, but also supported me in the other aspects of my life. Among my immediate family, a special salute goes to my sister and brother-in-law, Kathleen and Paul Price. My recognition also goes to my brother, Bruce Lyau, and his family, May, Brian, Jeff, and Brandon Lyau. Among my friends, a special hello to Paul and Ellen Alkon, Karen Anderson, Linda Austern, Dave Barr, Tom Becker, Gregory Benford, Don Bradley, Mark Budz, Gregg and Elonda Castro, Terisa Chevreaux, Brian, Aleli, and Raphael Colón, Don Coombs, Carol Courtney, Lynx Crowe, Frank Dalton, Richard Dutcher, Anthony Elmendorf, Jan and Ernst Epstein, William Filter, Marina Fitch, Karen Joy Fowler, Nancy Gage, The Honorable John and Patricia Garamendi, Stephen Goldin, Marty Grabien, Michael and Peri Harrington, Howard and Laurel Hendrix, Pamelya Herndon, David and Karen Hinckley, Bettina Hoven, Elizabeth Anne Hull, Yvonne Jaeckel, Ed Kennedy, Michael Kerpan, Katharine and Howard Kerr, Stuart Kisilinsky, Jay Koch, David and Irene Leiby, the Hon. James B. Lewis, Steven Lillard, Jack Little, Claudia Macdonald, Patrick McGaugh, Seethambal Mani, Mary Mason, Alfred Mathewson, Joe Miller, Spike Parsons, Richard and Angelica Plass, Frederik Pohl, Eric Rabkin, Patricia Rogers, Bill Rosenberg, Jack Rosenstein, Allen Sault, M. James and Kay Sawyer, Samuel and Judy Scheiner, Amelia Sefton, Amir Shahvar, Dory Shonagon, Danielle Slusser, Patricia Suhrcke, Michael Tallan, Pascal Thomas, Sabine Thuerwaechter, Steven Walsh, Tina Walsh, Jonathan Weiss, Thomas and Marta Whigham, Walter John Williams (who has actually heard of one of the writers I cover in this study), Leonard and Robbie Winogora, Richard, Ingrid, and Allison Wong, William F. Wu, and the Honorable Leland and Maxine Yee. I hope I remembered them all; my apologies to anyone missing who belongs on this list. Thank you, one and all.

To Poul Anderson, Matt Chevreaux, James Killus, Frank McConnell, and Dave Monroe, I wish you were here to read your names on this page.

I close my acknowledgments by thanking my mother and father, who make up the other half of my dedication. While school was teaching me the Three Rs, my parents impressed upon me the equally important Three Ps—patience, perseverance and perspective. As always, my utmost thanks and appreciation.

Foreword
by George Slusser

I am glad to see Bradford Lyau's work on French science fiction come to print. It is an extremely important book in the cultural history of science fiction, and I applaud McFarland for publishing it. In terms of science fiction, France is the "other shore," and its tradition of science fiction is easily as old and rich as the Anglophone tradition, in fact more so. We may no longer be at the stage where "Joolz Verne" is thought to be an American writer. *Science-Fiction Studies,* under the impetus of Arthur Evans, has published several excellent special issues on francophone SF. But most of the texts discussed remain unavailable to Anglophone readers. Only a scant handful of more recent French science fiction texts have been translated. And, as Lyau points out, only one of the novels he discusses was translated into English. Still today, Anglophone critics pay precious little attention to French SF. It remains common wisdom among them that Mary Shelley's *Frankenstein* (1817) is the first work of SF. In asserting this, they ignore the work of Cyrano de Bergerac, or of Sébastien Mercier and Restif de la Bretonne in the last half of the 18th century. What is more, Balzac's *Le Centenaire,* written four years after *Frankenstein,* is much closer to what we call science fiction today than Shelley's novel.

Science fiction is often referred to as a literature of ideas. In fact, one might argue that many science fiction stories and novels are philosophical tales. Lyau agrees and focuses on a culturally specific form: the 18th century *conte philosophique* widely practiced by Montesquieu, Voltaire, Diderot and other writer-*philosophes*. The essence of these tales, through the "adventures" of two-dimensional, often frankly allegorical figures, is to comment on philosophical, moral, and religious issues of the time, not the least of which was the impact of the material sciences on ideas and institutions. One preferred device was social satire, which is not evident in the novels Lyau covers. The other device however — intercultural comparisons, often revealing what is lacking in a French society that held itself up as paragon of virtue and progress — is easily adapted to science fiction extrapolations, where in comparisons between "worlds," Earth and humanity are often found lacking. Lyau finds plenty of evidence of this device's use. The time of the *conte philosophique* was a time of social and cultural ferment, which led to the French Revolution. It is only natural then that, in the crucial decade of the 1950s, which led in France to profound social change in the wake of post-war American influence, that the French would adapt the science fiction story—a significant American import—to a medium that comments on, and judges, the ideas it conveys. Lyau has hit upon the idea at the core of 1950s American SF—progress as scientific and technological advancement.

Lyau will be examining an important part of French science fiction that emerged during the 1950s: the Anticipation imprint, or series, published by the Fleuve Noir publishing house. Fleuve Noir began publishing its Anticipation series began in 1951 and ran continuously until 1997. The final issue, #2001, was a novel by Roland Wagner, entitled *L'Odyssée de l'espèce* ("A Species Odyssey," the title being a play on words alluding to Arthur C. Clarke's better known book and film, *2001: A Space Odyssey* [*espace*/space vs. *espèce*/species]—as will be shown later, there is also another play on words involved here). It began as a genre line, with a number of "house name" writers—the writers Lyau deals with. Beyond Lyau's cutoff date—1960—it attracted a number of new writers, who continued to turn out the large number of novels needed for a growing reading public. Some of the best writers of the 1970s generation—Michel Jeury, Serge Brussulo, Jean-Pierre Andrevon, Daniel Walther—each wrote dozens of novels for the series. The series in fact has served as a training ground for nearly all the major French science fiction writers of the post-war generation. Yet its reputation as a "pen-for-hire" operation was established early, as Lyau explains, by Gérard Klein, who wrote several Fleuve Noir novels under the pseudonym of Gilles d'Argyre, or Gilles Money. The influential French science fiction magazine *Fiction*, which in its editorial pages sought to elevate science fiction to a legitimate literary genre, follows Klein's lead in relegating Fleuve Noir to the pulp cauldron. The truth is however that this series continued to produce the sort of fiction Lyau describes—space opera plots with serious commentary on political, social and philosophical issues both from a French and an increasingly international perspective—throughout the 1980s and 1990s. One suspects that Roland Wagner, a serious writer with a strong satirical bent, is tweaking the somewhat disingenuous snobbery of Klein, who after all wrote excellent Fleuve Noir novels all the while claiming they were mere toss-offs. Wagner, who wrote the aforementioned *L'Odyssée de l'espèce*, could also have intended his book's title to translate as "The Odyssey of Cash" (*espèce*/cash) as a reference to Klein's d'Argyre/Money pseudonym. In any event, Lyau's analysis of these Fleuve Noir novels proves their complete seriousness. These Anticipation novels are a gold mine for a critic seeking to understand the development of both post-war French science fiction and the fortunes of the *conte philosophique* in France.

In France, in fact, it might be said that there really is no "popular" literature as we understand it. Unlike the Anglophile world, with its strict borders between "high" and "low" literature, in France all literature has the potential of becoming serious literature. Science fiction, in 1950s France, was just another new form of artistic expression vying for a dominant place in the cultural establishment, alongside jazz, the comic book, and American film noir, which the *nouvelle vague* of Truffaut, Godard and company elevated to the realm of art through their sophisticated pastiches. Science fiction had during these years powerful proponents such as Michel Butor and Boris Vian, but somehow did not win the culture wars. It is not therefore a contradiction in terms to see obviously sophisticated writers like Stefan Wul and Kurt Steiner working within what seemed a pulp genre, seeking to adapt its formulas to serious social and philosophical commentary. The 1950s Fleuve Noir Anticipation novels were produced on cheap pulp paper. But their cover art was highly inventive space art, for the most part done by a phenomenal artist, René Brantonne, who began his career doing movie posters for American films. Brantonne, along with Jean-Claude Forest (who worked for *Fiction* in the 1950s) were the ancestors of the great Francophone tradition of the *bandes dessinées*, now considered the "ninth art" in France. So Lyau's thesis, that these pulp paperbacks were in fact complex *contes philosophiques*, addressing the most serious issues of the time in which they were published, is right on the money. His highly detailed analyses of a large number of these works, drawing connections between their plot situations and current events, make it clear we are not dealing with commercial space opera, but with a literary form that demands a well-educated and thinking public. Lyau strengthens his argument by making comparisons and contrasts with American or British science fiction novels of the same period, which demonstrates how a like theme or plot line can be used to very different ends— for entertainment, for didactic purposes, or as in the case of Fleuve Noir, to stimulate reflection on the role of tradition and transformation in French society and culture.

Lyau invites us to consider who in fact were the readers of these Fleuve noir novels. Unlike American culture, French culture is (or at least was until recently) a highly homogeneous culture, based in the rigors of a classical education, where everyone at the *lycée* level (the cutoff point before specialized higher education) had some contact with Racine, Corneille, Descartes, memorized lines from poems and plays, and picked up enough cultural baggage to recognize references to writers, thinkers, and artists. Only in France could you have a phenomenon like the San Antonio novels, a long-running series of what appear to be pulpy detective novels (written by Frédéric Dard), but which in fact are highly literate parodies of the genre, full of verbal invention and play, with sophisticated references to classic works that had to resonate with the larger body of literate readers, otherwise they would not have continued to buy and read them. It is clear from Lyau's analyses that these Fleuve Noir novels developed a like readership. Sold in train stations, supposedly to pass the time between Paris and Marseille, or other points on the map, they in fact provided much food for thought for a readership able to see beneath the surface of genre convention. For example, Lyau gives a fine analysis of a novel by Maurice Limat, *Les Enfants du chaos* (1959) in which he shows how Limat, citing Voltaire's Pangloss from *Candide*, who sees Leibniz's "best of all possible worlds" in the worst places, creates a subtext of conservative commentary on the role of religion in the liberalizing movements of 1950's France. Such intertextual activity demands a high level of cultural awareness on the reader's part. Lyau also demonstrates how Stefan Wul, in his fine novel *Oms en série* (1957), uses the classic plot of small race (the "oms" or "*hommes*"— the race of men) against large race, to engage in ongoing commentary on issues of the time — France and its colonies, *dirigisme*, nationalism versus internationalism, and the need for a strong leader (De Gaulle). Given the subtle interweaving of space opera and current events, the reader of this novel, in 1957, would have to be as well a reader of *Le Monde* or other intellectual newspapers in order to catch all the subtleties of the novel. Certainly, the success and longevity of Fleuve Noir had much to do with the pool of educated readers it continued to attract. In this case, pulp reading matter supplemented daily editorial commentary.

Lyau's study brings to light a whole series of interesting authors, indeed a whole cultural movement within the larger umbrella of science fiction. To do this study, he had to sit down and read 131 French primary sources alone, as well as many other secondary texts in French and English, then sift through this data, make connections, formulate hypotheses, and draw conclusions. A massive amount of "spade work" went into this book. The result is a detailed analytical portrait of what is a seminal publication in modern French cultural history, and a unique literary and cultural artifact. His method is the classical one of intellectual history. This kind of hard and vital academics has, with the advent of (essentially French) theory, fallen into disrepute, as if the study of history were not intellectual. Replacing it is a good deal of *a priori* reasoning on a limited body of texts, based on some theoretical idea that pre-judges the fact of history or literature it pretends to analyze. Lyau's method on the other hand is empirical: the idea of progress was a much debated subject in 1950s France. Through close reading of these contemporary texts, thematic and structural elements are found repeated which point to a common interest in the question of progress, and to a common medium (the culturally identifiable *conte philosophique*) in which to raise and debate this issue from the spectrum of viewpoints then being expressed in France.

One should say, in conclusion, that French intellectual historians studying the second half of the twentieth century have themselves overlooked science fiction. Lyau's study should surely set the stage for further study of this genre in relation to the culture that produces it. His study, focusing on France, should show the historian and the science fiction critic alike that the themes and subgenres of science fiction can be put to very different uses in different cultures. Science fiction studies have generally been parochial, when in fact we seem to be dealing today with a world-wide or "global" phenomenon. Lyau in his study proves a thorough knowledge of English-language as well as French-language SF. Thus he can make the sort of comparisons necessary if we are ever to gain a broader, transcultural perspective on SF. Let this study be a harbinger of things to come.

George Slusser received his Ph.D. in comparative literature from Harvard University and is professor of comparative literature emeritus and curator emeritus of the Eaton Collection, University of California, Riverside. The longtime coordinator of the Eaton Conference and editor of its volumes, he built the Eaton Collection into the world's largest research center of science fiction, fantasy, and utopian fiction.

... [S]cience fiction — even the corniest of it, even the most outlandish of it, no matter how badly it's written — has a distinct therapeutic value because *all* of it has as its primary postulate that the world *does* change....
— Robert A. Heinlein, "The Discovery of the Future"[1]

Science fiction is in any case a reflection of a world which threatens to slip through our hands and to turn man the creator into a victim.
— Hans Küng, *Eternal Life?*[2]

Introduction

> "France throughout her existence has passed through periods in which the general progress of evolution demanded a regeneration on her part, under penalty of decline and death.... This is certainly the case today, for the age in which we are living—marked as it is by the acceleration of scientific and technological progress, the need for social betterment, the emergence of a host of new states, the ideological rivalry between empires—demands a vast regeneration both within ourselves and in our relation with others. The problem is to accomplish this without France ceasing to be France."
> — Charles de Gaulle, 5 February 1962[1]

When he spoke these words, Charles de Gaulle (1890–1970) was responding in part to France's problems with Algeria. However, this statement can also stand as a succinct summary of the dilemmas facing French society in general during the first fifteen years after World War II. France had a lot of work to do. Though it counted itself among the victors in the war, France found itself needing to catch up with the world's leading nations in the emerging new world order. France wanted to reclaim its status as a first-class power. And France must do so without ceasing to be itself.

So France had to modernize, especially in the fields of scientific research and technological innovation. Its resulting policies presented an idea of progress that aroused many debates and caused much anxiety as the welcoming of new ideas and methods often meant a permanent farewell to an old way of life that had supplied France with a kind of social stability which lasted for the better part of a century.[2]

As one would imagine, the concerns over modernization found expression in all venues of French culture. Of course this observation signifies nothing new. Far from it. People's worries over the impact of new science and technology in particular and the depth of social transformation in general have accompanied the march of modern times for the past two centuries if not longer.

A most interesting treatment of this theme can be found in the long-lost first completed novel written by Jules Verne (1828–1905), *Paris au XXe siècle* ("Paris in the Twentieth Century," 1860), which was recently discovered and published in 1994.[3] Verne projects a modernized but bleak Paris a century hence, characterized by what one would ordinarily think of as wondrous technology—including automobiles, fax machines, electric-generated machines, etc. But this progress comes at a price. Verne's protagonist feels alone and depressed. France in the year 1960 has stopped being France. Hints of an Americanization of this future society surface in the novel. French language, literature, and arts have been submerged, if not removed, in the midst of an emerging world culture.[4]

Many readers of the above paragraph may be surprised at the negativity of Verne's vision. In the English-speaking countries, Verne has been stuck with the reputation of being just an adventure writer who should be given credit for writing seminal science fiction stories. He is usually viewed as an optimist and one not given to deep examination of character and social consequences. British-born William Butcher, a leading Verne scholar, proves Verne to be a much more interesting and complex writer. Unconscionably sloppy translations[5] and horrific editorial policies comprise the main two reasons for Verne's sullied literary reputation.[6] In spite of these handicaps, Verne's works — in no matter what form — continue to sell.

Ninety-one years later a group of French writers of popular genre fiction emerge who can be said to continue this discussion about France trying to retain its true self in a time of great modernization. Like Verne, these storytellers are usually given short shrift and dismissed as adventure writers who were merely adopting the idiom of American genre science fiction and writing big-selling products for the postwar French masses. Though these writers nowhere reach the level of literary expression or significance of Verne, they should not be cast aside as second-rate descendants of the French master. They are more than that. They still present ideas worth discussing — ideas concerning the fate of France, its culture, and even its very existence.

This book will examine a little-known, especially in America, cultural expression of France's attempt after World War II to come to terms with modern times: the French writers who appear during the years 1951–1960 in Anticipation, an imprint — or line — of science fiction paperbacks released by Fleuve Noir, a publishing house specializing in popular genre fiction, especially the ones modeled on those imported from America.

On first appearance to the casual reader these writers' stories will seem rudimentarily constructed and containing simplistic, often preachy expression of ideas. Their stories will not contain the realistic extrapolations in science, technology, or society that have become identified as the hallmarks of the best in British and American science fiction. Their characters will seem to be one-dimensional, representing stereotypes — or sometimes even caricatures — instead of fully developed and examined persons as expected in modern fiction. In fact, much of the writing style in their stories will share a kindred spirit more with the stories found in American science fiction pulp magazines[7] from the 1920s and 1930s than with the publications of their contemporary French mainstream literary practitioners — i.e., simple emphasis on action and predictable plots as opposed to literary experimentation in form, character, and theme.

Besides being literary heirs to Jules Verne, these writers also belong to two

Introduction 9

other traditions—one old, the other new. The old is a literary form from the eighteenth century French Enlightenment, the *conte philosophique*, or philosophical tale, primarily associated with its famous developer, the French philosopher and writer Voltaire (1694–1778). The new is the imported genre of American science fiction.

Of course not all of the novels from the Anticipation imprint possessed noticeable philosophical discussion in them. But a significant number of them did, while the others at least showed — however briefly — concerns beyond plot and character. Furthermore, when examining these writers, their differing philosophies and ideas about the situations in both France and the world can be discerned.

Due to the dual literary influences behind these writers, this study will become an exercise in intellectual history, a branch of history generally described as the study of the development, impact, and spread of ideas in society and its culture.[8] More specifically, this study will focus on the idea of progress and how the various writers respond to the idea. Due to the nature of both the industrial world and of science fiction, the main ingredients of progress turn out to be the new developments in science and technology. The writers will take on other aspects of progress, but their concerns will always fall back to these two fields of endeavor. Other approaches of examination do exist. But since the ideas the writers are trying to convey to the reader in large part drive their stories, examining the writers in light of their ideas and their ideas' influences makes the field of intellectual history a most appropriate venue.

The eleven French writers who wrote for the Anticipation imprint during the 1950s will comprise the subject matter of this study. Examining their views on the idea of progress and its application to post–World War II France, the writers are to be divided into five categories of response:

The Moderates: F. Richard-Bessière, M.A. Rayjean, and Kemmel
The Extremist: Jimmy Guieu
The Conservatives: Stefan Wul, Maurice Limat, Peter Randa, and Kurt Steiner
The Radicals: Jean-Gaston Vandel and B.R. Bruss
A Last Word: Gilles d'Argyre

These categories should not be viewed in strictly contemporary political terms. Rather, though the political beliefs of some of these writers do match the labels of the categories, these categories should be viewed in light of how these writers react to idea of progress. What aspects of progress do they emphasize in their concerns? How do these writers apply their views of progress to society?

Before examining the writers, some historical background will be presented for those readers unfamiliar with various aspects of this study's subject matter. The next chapter will do so in three parts. The first briefly surveys the intellectual and cultural situation in 1950s France in light of the idea of progress.

The second describes the nature of science fiction, outlines its development in France and America, and introduces the publisher Fleuve Noir's Anticipation imprint. The third explains the nature and history of the philosophical tale and how it has been resurrected in these stories.

Though some French science fiction writers, especially the major ones such as Jules Verne, have been translated into English, most have not been — and certainly nowhere near to the degree that their English-language counterparts have been translated into French. With one exception,[9] all of the Anticipation novels covered here have never been translated into English. All titles and text quotations have been translated by me, to be referred to in this study as the author. Translations of all other materials will be referenced in the usual manner.

CHAPTER ONE

Background

France faced problems everywhere. Difficulties experienced in rapid urbanization, creation of new industries, replacement of obsolete industries, slowly adjusting political institutions, new centers of power in the international scene, new demographic shifts, the emergence of new and powerful forms of energy, adjustments to defense policy (especially in relation to atomic weapons), and other developments caused many to question the wisdom of government actions during the Fourth (1946–58) and early Fifth (1958–present) Republics. Did the people who experienced the drastic changes arising from modernization policies think the price of progress was justified? Did France truly improve itself, or was it just exchanging one set of problems for another? Such questions remained in the forefront of many people's concerns during the Fifties.

The Idea of Progress

What was France to do? What constituted the best course of action for adjusting to the situation after World War II? The general answer became: France had to change significantly in order to improve itself. The idea of progress and its applications became the central concern for France.

Many took their turn at analyzing the triumphs and traumas of the Fifties and offering their particular solutions to the mounting problems of modernization. France's leading thinkers had written down for posterity their opinions on this period and much has been studied and written about them. However, there were others whose expressed concerns and opinions were aimed at the popular level but without the same amount of scholarly attention paid to them.

Among the intellectuals confusion reigned. The unity in the Resistance that existed during World War II between Catholics, Marxists, and Existentialists disintegrated soon after 1945. Overwhelmed by the problem of social rehabilitation as well as the divisions over how to evaluate Stalin's rule and the Cold War, the intellectuals permanently split up into, roughly speaking, three groups: the Gaullist Right (represented by Raymond Aron [1905–83]), the parliamentary democratic Center supporting—however begrudgingly—the West (represented by Albert Camus [1913–60]), and the divided Left (represented by

Jean-Paul Sartre [1905–80], Existentialists, and Communists). Bitter struggles followed. These various groups could not agree on what really was the surest path to social progress. Even when France overcame the worst of its postwar difficulties by the mid–1950s, intellectuals still fought among themselves, remaining in this state well into the next decade.[1]

There also existed much disunity and anxiety over the nation's modernization policies at the popular level. The parliamentary divisions of the Fourth Republic perhaps best reflected this situation. As British historian David Thomson noted:

> The multiple fractures of French opinion, and the lack of firm correlation between party alignments and social divisions, meant that in a parliament designed to reflect, with considerable accuracy, the state of opinion in the country, a differently constituted majority had to be found for settling each issue that arose.[2]

Worries over what makes true social progress permeated through all segments of society.

The idea of progress certainly did not constitute a new concern for France. Thinkers from the eighteenth-century French Enlightenment produced early systematic studies identifying what they thought represented realistic measures of social improvement. Fontenelle (1657–1757), Saint-Pierre (1658–1743), Voltaire, Turgot (1727–81), and Condorcet (1743–94), with their new views of rational knowledge providing the bases for their plans, emerged as the most notable early thinkers. This trend of speculation continued through the first half of the nineteenth century with Saint-Simon (1760–1825) and his hierarchical society centered on science and technology, Fourier (1772–1837) and his phalansteries of labor and love, and Comte (1798–1857) and his progressive view of knowledge. In the latter half of the nineteenth century and early part of the twentieth century, the idea of progress became the concerns of Pierre Lafitte (1825–1903), who continued the ideas of Comtean positivism; Leon Bourgeois (1851–1925), who applied the ideas of Solidarism to politics; Alfred Loisy (1857–1940), who examined society in light of modernist theology; and Henri Bergson (1859–41), who expounded on the transcendent side of cosmic evolution.[3]

This concept had also appeared in French literature, and in science fiction in particular, for almost as long a period of time. Writers such as Louis-Sébastien Mercier (1740–1814), whose utopian work *L'An 2440, rêve s'il en fut jamais* ("The Year 2440, If There Ever Was One," 1771) can also be considered an early milestone in French science fiction; Jules Verne, the primary influence of science fiction in France and — along with H.G. Wells (1866–1946) — a giant presence in the world via translations of his works; Albert Robida (1848–1926); and J.H. Rosny aîné (1856–1940) produced works which speculated on the possibility of a better future.

By the immediate post–World War II years, however, the idea of progress in France had to change dramatically. The new geopolitical situation left few doubts about France's reduced status. Despite its colonial possessions, which were to be relinquished within a generation, France's claim to power and global respect rested more on past accomplishments than on present capabilities. No longer could France claim a leading role in contributing new approaches to the idea of progress. Other nations, especially the United States, had taken charge. And so progress for France now meant the formulation of policies that helped maintain French influence in a highly competitive world.

If France wanted to re-enter the circle of important world powers, it had to transform its society — and do so quickly. The top priority became the creation of a modern industrial base. France still possessed much of its nineteenth-century rural, small-town society in the late 1940s. Thus, a level of social planning unprecedented in French history became a necessity.

France imported a whole range of new ideas and methods from other countries — especially from the United States with its innovative techniques in business, industry, and research — to facilitate its catching up. The famous series of *Les Plans* ("The Plans," a series of five-year plans by the government), which were implemented to oversee and give guidance to long-term developments, demonstrated how driven the French were in returning their nation to the rank of a world leader.[4]

Popular Culture in France

The postwar years also signaled a new era in French literature. In high literary circles the late Forties and early Fifties witnessed a new generation of writers replacing the one whose practitioners were born around the year 1870 (Alain, Claudel, Colette, Gide, Giraudoux, Saint-Exupéry, and Valery) with those born around the turn the century and later (Blanchot, Butor, Camus, Gadenne, Gracq, Robbe-Grillet, and Sartre). The emphasis had changed from pure aesthetics to social reality and experimentation. Coming to grips with the events of World War II and afterwards also became a preoccupation. Literary life at this level became centered on small coteries, groups based on political affiliation, and past friendships.[5]

On the popular level fundamental changes occurred. Foremost was the introduction of American mass-marketing techniques. This new way of distribution accompanied France's paperback revolution, where this type of publication would eventually saturate all markets. The book became more and more a commodity for mass consumption and, as a consequence, popular fiction was being divided by content into readily identifiable specialized genres. Soon those familiar American genres — mysteries, detective stories, westerns, horror tales, and science fiction stories — started making their presence known to the French public.[6] Of course the French already possessed their versions of these genres, so a mixing among the genre variations occurred as well. The science fiction novels released under the Anticipation line by its publisher, Fleuve Noir, represented part of this phenomenon.

―⚬⚬⚬―

The field of popular culture, for the sake of analysis, can be divided into three categories: folk, popular, and mass. Folk culture focuses on local and unlettered societies; popular culture concentrates on artifacts of a preindustrial social system where interactions between the oral and literate traditions take place; while mass culture deals with commodities distributed throughout an industrialized society.[7] The French Anticipation writers to be examined in this study obviously belong to the final category. In order to be consistent with conventional usage of terms, hereon mass culture shall be referred to as popular culture. If popular culture of the preindustrial era is discussed, it shall be referred to as traditional popular culture.

Popular culture since the nineteenth century has certain characteristics that must be taken into account if it is to be appreciated properly. First of all, it is a product of universal literacy. When more and more people begin to read, the cultural exclusivity of reading held by the upper classes starts to crumble. Literary appreciation is no longer an activity that distinguishes the upper classes from the middle and working classes. Maybe the type of literature preferred by each group could create separations between these groups, but even those distinctions can easily be blurred. The affordable paperback makes both classics and popular literature available to all. Class preferences aside, new forms of literature did appear to meet the tastes of the emerging masses of new readers from all walks of life. Soon different standards and tastes emerged that often ran counter to the aesthetics of high culture.

Second, modern popular literature is part of the industrial revolution. When books start to be mass-produced, the needs of a new literate class can be quickly fulfilled. Immediate publications, not long-awaited masterpieces, become more and more the rule for the practitioners in these new markets.

And third, popular literature provides a function that differs from what literature in high culture has to offer. While the latter implies a connection to the traditions of past ages, the former attempts to share a common experience with the present.[8] Of course this does not preclude popular writers borrowing from past literary forms and traditions, as will be shown in this study.

Of the varieties of popular culture that flourished, the American brand dominated the European scene during the years following World War II. Two major reasons can be given. The first consists of the simple fact that the United States was at the peak of its economic, military, and political influence in world affairs. Along with American ideas and techniques, many items of American popular culture also found their way into Europe. And so the concerns of the present and the goals of the future dreamt by America's masses quickly entered into the homes of their counterparts living in faraway lands.[9]

The second reason involves the nature of American popular culture itself. The United States possesses a young culture when compared to those of European countries. America's literary traditions go back a couple of centuries, while France's alone stretches back to the time of Charlemagne if not earlier. As C.W.E. Bigsby notes:

> The United States was ... the first nation whose institution and cultural identity had been forged almost wholly in a technological era.... A move to the United States was precisely the exchange of a rural for an industrial system and the life-style and cultural ethos which ... developed there was necessarily a response to that situation.... It remains true that, as (F.R.) Leavis had suggested, America's present is Europe's future and the consequences of industrial society immediately observable in the configurations of American life.[10]

As a result, the centuries-old traditions of European countries often ran counter to the development of a modern popular culture created during the Industrial Revolution. The United States by comparison experienced very little resistance since its history is almost coterminous with the Industrial Revolution. Though America also possessed both its high culture and traditional popular culture, neither of them did not prevent its popular culture from reaching the rapidly expanding reading public. Thus, the United States after World War II had in hand a whole system of popular expressions ready to be exported to a world experiencing the growing pains of a modernization increasingly characterized by advances in science and technology.

Science Fiction

Science fiction is a term familiar to most, but one that is also very difficult to define. The term itself first appeared in America in 1929, emerging from a community of writers, editors, and readers created by the specialized pulp fiction magazines of the time. More specifically, Luxembourg-born American editor, writer, and publisher Hugo Gernsback (1884–1967) can be credited for not only popularizing the genre, but also for making this term the preferred one.[11]

However if science fiction is to refer to the U.S. genre only, then so much of science fiction's diversified world would be missing. Just taking into account the United States for the moment, this very strict definition would mean writers from the American literary mainstream who engaged with the themes of science fiction would not belong. Such a list of the missing would include Edgar Allan Poe (1809–49), Mark Twain (Samuel Langhorne Clemens, 1835–1910), Edward Bellamy (1850–98), Jack London (1876–1916), and Sinclair Lewis (1885–1951), all of whom contributed a highly respectable tradition of speculative fiction.

These writers' works definitely belong in the canon of science fiction. As for the writers from rest of the world, they become even more invisible.

So how does one define science fiction in a fashion that is neither too inclusive—to the point where people have included *Gilgamesh* (c. 2000 BCE) and Lucian of Samasota (2nd century CE)—nor too exclusive—where E.L. "Doc" Smith (1890–1965) counts, but not Aldous Huxley (1894–1963) and George Orwell (Eric Arthur Blair, 1903–50)? Some scholars, both fan and academic, have attempted to employ dictionary style definitions in which the term is defined by theme, usually that of science and technology, and in one to three lines. Some writers define science fiction by how they think while writing it. A notable example would be the attempt by American writer, editor, and critic Algis Budrys (1931–2008): "Drama made relevant through social extrapolation."[12]

This being a historical study, an attempt to define science fiction will be made as a type of literature which emerged in a certain place and time. The central concern here is the word "science." In the broadest sense of the word, one could go back all the way to the beginning of literary history. Using the modern sense of the word, however, a historical starting point can now be identified. With this last point in mind a working definition can be made.[13]

Science fiction can briefly be defined as a cultural reaction (whether in literature or later developed media) that (1) is a product of the cultural climate produced by the seventeenth-century Scientific Revolution in Europe, promoted by the eighteenth-century European Enlightenment, and provoked by the late eighteenth/early nineteenth-century Industrial Revolution in northwestern Europe; (2) arose from eighteenth/early nineteenth century literary forms; (3) deals with non-existing, but possible phenomena and their impact on humanity in a manner involving a critique of the type of human reason and ability that emerged from the above described cultural climate; and (4) whose central theme is that of humanity continually attempting to enlarge its horizons in a manner inspired by the above described cultural climate.[14]

This definition attempts to include literature from all traditions while maintaining a starting point in a particular place and time. Even then the western–European orientation of this definition could be debated. For the sake of avoiding a book-length discussion that this matter would require, this particular definition will be used since it describes what is at present the dominant mode of science fiction. When discussing science fiction from non–Western countries, most of these countries will describe their origins of science fiction as taking place when stories by such writers as Jules Verne or H.G. Wells were introduced into them.[15]

Of course other approaches and methods to defining science fiction exist, but it is hoped that the above attempt will suffice for one examining this branch of literature in a historical and ideological context.

Science Fiction, French and American

Obviously science fiction existed in France long before 1945 and the importation of American genre science fiction. Writers to be considered as significant figures include Cyrano de Bergerac (1619–55), Restif de la Bretonne (Nicolas-Anne-Edmé Restif, 1734–1806), Louis-Sébastien Mercier, Félix Bodin (1795–1837), Jules Verne, Camille Flammarion (1842–1925), Albert Robida, J.H. Rosny aîné, and Maurice Renard (1875–1939).[16] France's tradition of science fiction in many respects can be said to be as long and varied as those of to the English language countries.[17]

From the late seventeenth century to the mid-nineteenth century France experienced a healthy output of works using identifiable science fiction themes. Utopias and *voyages imaginaires*, or imaginary journeys, became the main expressions. These stories took place on other planets, faraway lands, imaginary lands, and in the future. In addition to Bergerac, Restif de la Bretonne, Mercier, and Bodin, others such as Charles Sorel (1602–74), Simon Tyssot de Patot (c. 1655–1727), Jean-Baptiste Cousin de Grainville (1746–1805), Louis Geoffroy (1803–58), and C.I. Defontenay (1814–56) also wrote imaginary journeys and experimented with utopian themes, sometimes combining aspects of the two.[18]

Jules Verne, of course, remains the central figure in French science fiction. Not only did his stories sell well and were translated into many languages around the world, but they also inspired two generations of French writers to follow in his footsteps. Along with H.G. Wells, and perhaps Mary Shelley (1797–1851) and Edgar Allan Poe, Verne stands as an undisputed giant in the field's early history. One can also say that the first American science fiction "invasion" of France took place during the mid-nineteenth century with importation of the stories by Poe. Certainly Jules Verne himself was immensely influenced by him. In fact, Verne scholar William Butcher states that two American writers, Poe and James Fenimore Cooper (1789–1851), probably comprised Verne's two most important influences.[19]

With the arrival of Jules Verne's works in the 1860s, France experienced what most refer to as its golden age of science fiction. Lasting until the First World War, this flourishing of science fiction touched all facets of French publishing. Various publishing houses featured numerous imprints containing this type of literature and many illustrated pulp magazines printed stories mostly in the new traditions introduced by Jules Verne. As dominant as Verne was, some writers did look to other sources for inspiration when producing their science fiction. In addition to Verne, Robida, Rosny aîné, and Flammarion, other notable writers from this era included Jules Lermina (1839–1915), André Laurie (pseudonym for Paschal Grousset, 1845–1909), Louis Boussenard (1847–1910), Paul d'Ivoi (pseudonym for Paul-Charles Delentre, 1856–1915), Georges Le Faure (1856–1953), Henry de Graffigny (pseudonym for Raoul Marquis,

1863–1942), Gustave Le Rouge (1867–1938), and Jean de La Hire (pseudonym for Adolphe d'Espie de La Hire, 1878–1956). Even canonical mainstream literary figures contributed stories that could easily fit into this mix, including Émile Zola and Anatole France. By the time the science fiction magazine genre was just beginning in America in 1926, France had already experienced a half a century of peak production — in quantity, quality, and influence — from its golden age.[20]

Due to various political, economic, and cultural reasons, the production of science fiction declined during the interwar years. Besides Renard (who also contributed significant works before World War I), notable writers of the era include Henri-Jacques Proumen (1879–1962), José Moselli (pseudonym for Théophile Maurice Moselli Joseph, 1882–1941), Léon Groc (1882–1956), Régis Messac (1893–1943), Jacques Spitz (1896–1963), and René Barjavel (1911–85), who also acts as an important bridge between pre and postwar science fiction. However, the Second War World devastated most of France's rich tradition from this period. After the war a new world faced France and its culture, including its science fiction.[21] Now a major influence from abroad arrived to rekindle interest.

The American story of science fiction is more well-known. As Mary Shelley is the key figure in early British science fiction, Edgar Allan Poe occupies the same role in America. In addition to the aforementioned writers of Twain, Bellamy, London, and Lewis, other notable writers from the American literary mainstream that produced science fiction in the nineteenth and twentieth centuries include Edward Everett Hale (1822–1909), William Dean Howells (1837–1920), Frank R. Stockton (1834–1902), John Jacob Astor (1864–1912), George R. Stewart (1895–1980), Philip Wylie (1902–71), Pat Frank (Harry Hart, 1907–64), Bernard Wolfe (1915–85), John D. MacDonald (1916–86), Kurt Vonnegut (1922–2007), Gore Vidal (1925–), Walter Tevis (1928–84), Ira Levin (1929–2007), Sally Miller Gearhart (1931–), Carl Sagan (1934–96), Marge Piercy (1936–), Thomas Pynchon (1937–), Michael Crichton (1942–2008), and Stephen King (1947–).[22]

Of course the American genre science fiction attracts the most interest due to its dominant influence. The genre originated in the pulp magazines, specifically with the April 1926 issue of *Amazing Stories*, founded by Hugo Gernsback, the magazine's first editor. Before Gernsback, going back to the nineteenth century, there appeared inexpensive pulp magazines and dime novels that satisfied the reading desires of a rapidly growing literate population. Most notable among the dime novel authors were Edward S. Ellis (1840–1916) and Luis Senarens (1863–1939). In the pre-1926 twentieth-century period, numerous stories appeared in various magazines (usually technology-oriented ones), including Gernsback's novel, *Ralph 124C 41+: A Romance of the Year 2660* (1911–2).[23] Edgar Rice Burroughs (1875–1950), noted for both his Tarzan stories and interplanetary adventures, rose above all.

Gernsback's periodical became the first to specialize in science fiction. Calling its type of fiction "scientifiction," the initial issue defined its type of stories as following the fiction published by Verne, Wells, and Poe.[24] Gernsback left the magazine in 1929 and started other science fiction magazines. His inescapable influence in the genre is obvious, but the job of revolutionizing the field would be left to other editors.[25]

New titles soon followed *Amazing Stories*, most prominent being *Astounding Tales of Super Science* (1930), later *Astounding Stories* (1931), *Astounding Science Fiction* (1938), *Analog Science Fact-Science Fiction* (1960), *Analog Science Fiction-Science Fact* (1965), and now titled *Analog Science Fiction and Fact* (1991). When F. Orlin Tremaine (1899–1956) became *Astounding's* editor in 1933, he raised the quality of stories and encouraged writers to push the boundaries of the genre. Noted writers in the genre's early days included E.E. "Doc" Smith, Murray Leinster (William Fitzgerald Jenkins, 1896–1975), Edmond Hamilton (1904–72), Clifford D. Simak (1904–88), and Jack Williamson (1908–2006).

Tremaine's handpicked successor, John W. Campbell, Jr. (1910–71), who was at the time also one of the genre's best writers, took the magazine and the genre as a whole to new heights and established the genre as a serious form of popular literature. He initiated what many call the "Golden Age" (1938–46) of American genre science fiction, developing and publishing writers who would become the hallmarks of twentieth-century science fiction: Eric Frank Russell (1905–78), Robert A. Heinlein (1907–88), L. Sprague de Camp (1907–2000), Fritz Leiber, Jr. (1910–92), A.E. van Vogt (1912–2000), Lester del Rey (1915–93), Theodore Sturgeon (1918–85), and Isaac Asimov (1920–92).

After World War II, the paperback revolution in publishing took place and the pulp magazines declined, except in science fiction, where it experienced a growth in titles (peaking in 1953 with over thirty titles). Eventually a permanent decline would take place by the end of the Fifties. Two of the most important in this postwar expansion were *The Magazine of Fantasy* (1949), later *The Magazine of Fantasy and Science Fiction* (1950) and now titled *Fantasy and Science Fiction* (1987), and *Galaxy Science Fiction* (1950–80, 1994–5), which greatly expanded the boundaries of what could be published in the genre. Together with *Astounding Science Fiction*, these magazines comprised the "Big Three" periodicals of the genre during the Fifties. Writers who made their mark in the field during the first decade and a half after the Second World War included Alfred Bester (1913–87), Arthur C. Clarke (1917–2008), Frederik Pohl (1919–), Ray Bradbury (1920–), James Blish (1921–75), Poul Anderson (1926–2001), and Philip K. Dick (1928–82). This situation is where American genre science fiction found itself when its influential exportation to France occurred. The stories from the magazines and the paperbacks of this period shaped the perception and writing of French science fiction writers, especially those who wrote for Anticipation in the imprint's first decade.

By the late Sixties a development that would be called the "New Wave" took place where literary experimentation, raised political consciousness, and exploration of existing cultural mores were emphasized.[26] During the late Sixties and Seventies the impact of the visual media outside of the written genre, specifically the television show, *Star Trek* (1966–9), and the motion picture, *Star Wars* (1977), made science fiction more acceptable to general audiences and the science fiction genre community was no longer isolated. Science fiction continued to develop during the Eighties and Nineties, ever expanding its boundaries and diversifying its themes and styles, and thrives to this very day.[27]

Among all the American genres imported into France in 1945 and after, science fiction constituted the one most readily accepted by French readers. French scholar Gérard Cordesse identifies two reasons why American science fiction took root in France as fast as it did. The first involves the general situation between France and the United States just after World War II. American society, with its successes in research and development, seemed destined to be the force that would revive Europe from its postwar doldrums. To France, having stagnated since the World War I, the United States represented

> movement, innovation and adventure. As the future seemed to belong to the United States, it was logical to grant her a monopoly on anticipation literature. This link between science fiction and American success based on science explains partly why American influence was more sweeping in this field than elsewhere.[28]

Cordesse's second reason revolves around the nature of American popular science fiction itself. As mentioned earlier, though its roots in popular literature can be traced back to the nineteenth century with writers like Edgar Allan Poe and stories appearing in dime novels, juvenile periodicals, and pulp magazines, popular science fiction in America as a thriving and independent genre started with Hugo Gernsback's pulp magazine, *Amazing Stories*, in 1926. Not only did this become the first periodical in the English language to specialize in science fiction, but it also launched a tradition of a three-fold collaboration between writers, editors, and readers—the consumers themselves. The connection between the first two was to be expected, but the role of the third provided something quite unique.

Editors like Gernsback instituted letter columns in their magazines through which the readers could offer their opinions on individual stories and the publication's direction. They commented on the writers' scientific accuracy (or lack of it), the consistency and credibility of future scenarios, and the quality of writing. These channels of communication turned out not to be enough to exhaust the readers' enthusiasm and soon science fiction organizations spontaneously sprung up around the country (Gernsback did encourage such activities through his magazines). Amateur publications among the more energetic readers, or fans—as they preferred to be called—emerged, providing a valuable source for analyzing the origin and development of a subculture based on popular literature. Soon the fans formed local organizations, mostly in the larger cities. These new communities developed to the point where groups from different cities would organize and gather at various events, eventually referred to as conventions. In 1939 enthusiastic fans held the first World Science Fiction Convention in New York City over the Fourth of July weekend. Except for a hiatus caused by World War II, this event has occurred annually and has continued to grow in size and scope ever since.[29]

In 1953, that year's world science fiction convention established the first Hugo Awards (named after Gernsback), which were voted upon by the fans themselves to honor the best works for a particular year. In 1965 American science fiction writers organized and founded the Science Fiction Writers of America (SFWA) and developed their own awards for literary excellence, the Nebula Awards. By the end of the twentieth century the number of awards multiplied, covering either the field in general or a specific segment of it.[30] As a result of all this activity, writers, editors, and publishers paid attention to these enthusiastic, sometimes militant readers. Often the writers and editors themselves emerged from the ranks of fans.[31]

Cordesse views this interaction at the popular level as the core of his second cause of the success of American science fiction in France, for this particular popular tradition provided a whole system of literary conventions concerning plots, vocabulary, characters, scientific extrapolation, etc. As he puts it:

> American science fiction did not triumph because of new themes or motifs, and its optimistic values (partly modified after 1950) were not generally fitted to the mood of Europe. In view of this, its complete take-over of the strong European traditions of science fiction seems paradoxical. The reason for its impact was its highly "conventional" quality ... it drew its strength from this collective collaboration. This new high-powered way of writing met with success because the literary European tradition had not developed an equal concentration.[32]

Before long readers in France (along with those in the rest of Europe) developed their own organizations and put on their own versions of conventions—to the point of holding national and sometimes continental-wide gatherings and giving out their own awards.

So the reasons for studying this aspect of French popular culture become clear. The first concerns popular culture itself. In a modern society where there exist more cultural artifacts among the population at large than ever before, the understanding of attitudes and beliefs of societies as a whole becomes increasingly possible. As French-born American scholar Germaine Brée (1907–2001) writes, the study of popular culture "is the language ... that provides us with an anthropology of the unconscious and therefore constitutes the collective basis for the cultural life of the group."[33] The second reason involves the success of American-style popular science fiction in France. Because of its rapid spread throughout the French publishing industry, science fiction can be taken as a representative voice of expressing certain concerns. In the case of this study, the worries center on French ideas of progress and their application to French modernization policies after World War II.

The third and final reason focuses on the subject matter of science fiction itself. Though a much-diversified literature, the main concern of this branch of literature continues to be the impact of advanced science and technology on society. This reason becomes particularly relevant since a large part of French modernization policies entails catching up with the leading industrial powers in these two fields of endeavor. How can France do so without becoming a mere imitation of the countries it is trying to match in leadership?

The Fleuve Noir Publishing House and Its Anticipation Imprint

The Fleuve Noir publishing house was started in 1949 by Armand de Caro and Guy Kril. From its early years to the present it has been publishing numerous imprints of popular fiction modeled after American genres. Fleuve Noir released it first imprint, Spécial Police (1949–87, 2,077 volumes), which was quickly followed by Espionnage (1950–87, 1,906 volumes), Anticipation (1951–1997, 2,001 volumes), Westerns (1953–4, 23 volumes), Angoisse (1954–71, 261 volumes), and L'Aventurier (1955–1974, 206 volumes).[34] These and subsequent imprints lasted for various periods of time, but the longest in terms of chronology was Anticipation. Its 2,001 volumes translate into an average of a new title being released once every eight and a half days. Fleuve Noir replaced this imprint with its S.F. and other imprints.

According to its current website, Fleuve Noir now divides its products into four general groups: SF Fantasy (science fiction and fantasy), Thriller Policier (police thriller), Ciné TV Console (film, television, and video games adaptations and related matter), and San Antonio (a detective series). The company claims to have printed and sold close to a billion volumes in its first fifty years of existence.[35]

The novels published in Fleuve Noir's Anticipation imprint during the Fifties played an important role in the development of postwar French science fiction. Created and overseen by its first editor, François Richard (1913–c. 1980s), the imprint represented the first time that mostly new French writers were showcased. During this period all other companies that published science fiction relied primarily on translated imports from the United States and Great Britain to fill their catalogues. Because of this practice by the other publishers, the Anticipation imprint's French novels published by Fleuve Noir offer the researcher an excellent opportunity to study the emergence of a distinctly French voice in the midst of a genre dominated by imports. The literary form and style may have been American, but the ideas and attitudes remained French.

Other sources during this period existed for native French science fiction writers to publish their works. Amid translated stories from abroad appeared some important native works which along with Anticipation's novels helped define the field in postwar France. Two notable sources for native writers were Hachette-Gallimard's imprint Rayon Fantastique (1951–64) and Denoël's Presence du Futur (1954–2000). Imported American science fiction magazines also provided opportunities. The most important of them turned out to be *The Magazine of Fantasy and Science Fiction*, which was translated into French as *Fiction*. *Fiction* contained more than just translations of English-language stories. It also published original pieces by French writers, including fiction, new book and film reviews, and occasional articles discussing various aspects of science fiction in France and from abroad. In addition to *Fiction*, a competing magazine, *Satellite* (1958–63), was created, but it experienced much less success.[36] Another American magazine translated into French was *Galaxy Science Fiction*, as *Galaxie*.[37] Other science fiction imprints emerged, most of which were short-lived. Examples included: Visions Futures (published by La Flamme d'Or, 1952–3), Grands Romans-Sciences-Anticipation (Le Trotteur, 1953–4), Série 2000 (Métal, 1954–6), and Cosmos (Grand Damier, 1955–7). Finally, French science fiction could even count among its own two writers from the French literary mainstream: Vercors (pseudonym for Jean-Marcel Bruller, 1902–91) and Boris Vian (1920–59), a highly visible member of the Saint-Germain-des-Prés group.[38]

However, it is in the Anticipation imprint where predominantly French expressions can be found. Its quick acceptance and increasing popularity become evident when observing its increasing frequency of publication of new titles. Eight titles came out in 1951, eleven in 1952, thirteen in 1953, seventeen in 1954, fifteen in 1955, seventeen in 1956, twenty four in 1957, twenty two in 1958, twenty one in 1959, and twenty two in 1960. By the early 1980s almost eighty titles a year were being published. The frequency slowed down by the 1990s, but still averaged about twenty titles annually during its last years, ending with its 2,001st title in February 1997. The titles were numbered sequentially as they came out. Some were reprinted and assigned a later number.[39]

A few imported novels from the English-language science fiction world did make it into Anticipation, but French writers composed the significant majority of the titles. From 1951 to 1960 only thirty-nine out of 170 of the total novels released during this period were translations. Thirty of them appeared among the first one hundred titles, most of them novels by J. Russell Fearn (1908–60, under his pseudonym Vargo Statten), perhaps the most prolific genre writer from Britain during this period. The most notable of the translated works included Arthur C. Clarke's (1917–2008) *Islands in the Sky* (1952) as *Îles de l'espace* (No. 35, 1954), Isaac Asimov's (under his pseudonym Paul French) *David Starr, Space Ranger* (1952) as *Sur la planète rouge* (No. 44, 1954), John Wyndham's (1903–69) *Revolt of the Triffids* (1952, variant title of *The Day of the Triffids*

[1951]) as *Révolte des Triffides* (No. 68, 1956), and L. Ron Hubbard's (1911–86) *Return to Tomorrow* (1954) as *Retour à demain* (No. 98, 1954). From Nos. 101–170, only nine translated novels from English were published, most notable being John Wyndham's *Rebirth* (1951) as *Les Transformés* (No. 123, 1958), Arthur C. Clarke's *Prelude to Space* (1951) as *Prélude à l'espace* (No. 133, 1959), and Poul Anderson's (1926–2001) *War of Two Worlds* (1959) as *La Troisième Race* (No. 150, 1960). During Anticipation's second decade, 1961–70, the imprint released 271 titles with only twenty five being translations (with over two-thirds of them coming from Germany).[40] This growth meant that less than 10 percent (vs. 23 percent during the Fifties) were translations of imported works.

All eleven Anticipation French writers from the Fifties (1951–1960) will be covered in this study. In chronological order of the appearance, they are: F. Richard-Bessière (pseudonym for Anticipation editor, François Richard, and Henri-Richard Bessière, 1923–), Jimmy Guieu (1926–2000), Jean-Gaston Vandel (pseudonym for Jean Libert, 1913–95, and Gaston van den Pahuyse [1913–1981]), B.R. Bruss (pseudonym for René Bonnefoy, 1895–1979), M.A. Rayjean (pseudonym for Jean Lombard, 1854–1891), Stefan Wul (pseudonym for Pierre Pairault, 1922–2003), Kemmel (pseudonym for Jean Bommart, 1894–1979), Kurt Steiner (pseudonym for André Ruellan, 1922–), Maurice Limat (1914–2002), Peter Randa (pseudonym for André Duquense, 1911–1979), and Gilles d'Argyre (pseudonym for Gérard Klein, 1937–). Some of these writers were very prolific, producing novels on demand and on a regular basis. Others were not quite so prolific. Some became well-known beyond their stories, while others only made their mark through their stories. And of one (M.A. Rayjean), little is known. All but one used pseudonyms.[41] One of them, F. Richard-Bessière, to be covered in the following chapter, wrote recently on his Internet blog what he views as the true story behind his pseudonym.

These writers present a variety of viewpoints and deal with a wide range of philosophical, political, religious, scientific and technological questions. Richard-Bessière urges for balanced development in society as well as for increased cooperation among nations along the lines of a unified European community; Guieu criticizes the backwardness of present attitudes towards science in an extreme, often idiosyncratic manner; Vandel examines the role of the elites in a modern technological state; Bruss deals with the new social divisions which can develop in a computerized and mechanized society; Rayjean brings up possible environmental consequences from technological abuse; Wul proposes some conservative values for a future society; Kemmel warns about the abuse of atomic energy; Steiner ponders over the next step in evolution for today's human race; Limat explores the possibility of retaining religious ideas in the future; Randa discusses the fate of individualism in the space age; and d'Argyre presents an ambiguous vision of humanity's future.

The Philosophical Tale

As science fiction can claim a continuous history, the *conte philosophique*, or philosophical tale, can not. Primarily associated with Voltaire, this branch of French literature disappeared with the end of his writing career, according to most scholars. Only occasionally would this type of story emerge in the following two centuries. The French science fiction writers examined in this study represent a modest revival of the philosophical tale, this time in the realm of popular culture.

·The *conte*, or tale, possesses a rich tradition that can be traced back to medieval times and this tradition was certainly familiar to the literate population by the seventeenth century. However, the form really flourished in the eighteenth century. Sometimes seen as distinct from the novel or short story, the tale was not meant to portray life or characters in a realistic manner. It was often used for satire, humor in general, making a moral point, or presenting an idea in an allegorical manner. The French fairy tale (*conte de fée*) also probably had an influence as often it contained philosophical — or at least educational — content. Meanwhile, the tale did not limit itself to any particular subject matter or purpose as its scope included love stories, exotic stories from the Middle East, stories teaching morality, erotica, folk stories, and many other types.

Cyrano de Bergerac can be said to be a forerunner of Voltaire in this context. His *Histoire comique des états et empires de la lune* (1657) and *Histoire comique des états et empires de la soleil* (1662, both volumes translated into English, including some previously censored text, as *Other Worlds: The Comical History of the States and Empires of the Moon and Sun*, 1965)[42] combine ideas from the new discoveries in astronomy with satirical comments on the religious and political beliefs of his day to produce two works that many science fiction scholars argue should be included in the canon of early science fiction masterpieces.

However it is Voltaire who develops the philosophical tale, a "sui generis hybrid of fiction and philosophy ... the fusion of these two elements (yielding), as in a chemical compound, a product that differs from either taken separately."[43] Being part tale, the story is not required to be realistic (in the conventional sense of the word) and the philosophy involved in it does not have to be criticized or systematically analyzed. Argument (using different literary methods such as satire, allegory, irony, wordplay, etc.) — and not the proof — becomes central. Meanwhile, being part philosophical means that the actions, developments, and even the characters in the story become subordinate to the criticism of targeted ideas and attitudes. With these two elements combined, the philosophical tale seeks to exaggerate or distort certain aspects of reality, or of characters, to make a point about the futility and wrongheadedness of adhering to current conventions of thought, belief, and attitude. Philosophical tales may seem whimsical and trivial on the surface, but underneath they treat serious issues in history, politics, morality, and philosophy in ways that traditional, more realistic literature can not.[44]

The most famous example of this form by Voltaire is his *Candide ou l'Optimisme* (*Candide, or Optimism*, 1759). Best remembered for its savage criticism of the optimistic philosophy of the German thinker, Gottfried Wilhelm Leibniz (1646–1716), the story also takes on religion, Voltaire's fellow *philosophes*, the military, and traditional politics. *Candide* is full of satire, parody, allegory, ambiguity, and fantastical elements as it follows the adventures of Candide and Pangloss, with the latter maintaining unflinching support of Leibniz to the very end. Voltaire continually challenges Candide's belief in Leibniz's optimistic conclusions by thrusting the two into harmful and evil events. The story ends with the much affected Candide no longer so positive about the world around him and making his now famous suggestion, "We must cultivate our garden."[45]

Much has been written about this story, especially with Candide's last comment in mind. No consensus exists as to the precise meaning of Voltaire's most famous work. What does his last statement really mean? How much of the Enlightenment does Voltaire accept or reject in his story? This type of questioning can also apply to the Anticipation writers to be examined in this study. What do they mean when they discuss the idea of progress? How much of it should be accepted or rejected? Taken as a group these writers provide various answers, but none of them have the final say. One of the Anticipation writers, Maurice Limat, actually treats ideas from Voltaire's *Candide* in one of his novels. Another, Richard Bessière, mentions it as one his four favorite books. Also, the open-endedness of *Candide* will be brought up again when discussing the last writer to be examined in this study, Gérard Klein (writing as Gilles d'Argyre).

Voltaire's short fiction masterpiece, "Micromégas" (1752),[46] also stands out as an example of the philosophical tale. This story possesses special relevance to this study as well, especially considering its plot line: two visitors from other worlds visit Earth and comment on human beings, their outlook, and their society in a very satirical manner. The visitors turn out to be giants of incredible height and have developed levels of senses and intelligence far beyond the comprehension of the humans who inhabit Earth. Of course, Voltaire uses the giant human-like visitors as props to emphasize how humanity on Earth no longer can claim to be the center of creation and how the new scales of the cosmos (as discovered by the latest science) will force humanity to re-evaluate itself.[47] This last point becomes especially germane to this study. As the findings of Galileo and Newton (exposing the true enormousness of the universe) and the discoveries of Leeuwenhoek (revealing the infinitesimally small that surrounds all in daily life) forced eighteenth-century French thinkers to reconsider their place in the world, the new developments in science and technology during the post–World War II era reminded mid-twentieth-century France how much it had to change in order to catch up with the major powers and to continue playing an important role on the world stage.

One noticeable difference does exist between Voltaire's stories and the Anticipation novels' adaptation of them. The former is characterized by its heavy use of satire, while the latter displays practically none. However, the remaining characteristics of the philosophical tale do remain present in the French writers' stories in Anticipation as the writers allegorically present their social issues in science fiction formats.

The philosophical tale can be seen as an important influence on early science fiction. Robert Louit and Jacques Chambon point out that this literary form is the eighteenth century's "most direct forerunner of sf (science fiction) in its modern sense."[48] Besides treating the ideas and philosophies of the time, this type of story often takes the shape of imaginary voyages, whether the traveling is to other planets, faraway lands, or into the future. So in terms of themes and plot conventions, a large part of the groundwork for science fiction has been laid.

As mentioned, the philosophical tale fades after Voltaire — but never completely. This observation applies even to the field of science fiction. British science fiction writer and scholar Brian Stableford briefly points this out in an article about science fiction before the development of the American genre in 1926. For him, one would have to wait until the arrival of H.G. Wells to witness a revival of a variation of the form that would have any sustaining impact.[49] Even then the impact was not a pervasive one. In both science fiction and literature in general the emergence of the philosophical tale would be not be the rule, but the exception.

American scholar Frederick M. Keener discusses at length the nature of the philosophical tale, especially when compared to the novel.[50] In doing so, he reinforces the above more general descriptions of the philosophical tale. During the eighteenth century when both the novel and philosophical tale rose to prominence, the level of expectation of realism in fiction was not as high as it is today. Also, the novel and philosophical tale should be seen as complementary and not as opposites — one could do in its stories what the other could not. In terms of popularity, these two literary forms were rivals, with the novel winning out by the nineteenth century.[51]

Keener describes the two forms as possessing two different approaches to realism. The eighteenth-century novel's realism "is generally a matter of form and content" while the philosophical tale's is "centrally and most importantly a matter of theme." To clarify his distinction, he refers to the noted British-born and educated American scholar, Ian Watt (1917–99), who distinguishes between the "realism of 'presentation' and the realism of 'assessment.'"[52] The former characterizes the novel; the latter, the philosophical tale. On the one hand, Keener describes realistic presentation as entailing "a relatively plain, unfigurative, seemingly referential prose style and detailed, circumstantial representation of ordinary, contemporary conditions and individualized (if not ordinary) characters and chains of events." On the other hand, he identifies realistic assessment as dealing with "sociological, psychological, and moral understanding and judgment brought to bear on characters, characters taken individually and collectively." This last aspect results, as Keener continues, in "the subordination for better or worse of persons to their ideas." [53]

Since Watt focused on the novel, Keener refers to another American scholar, Peter Brooks, for further discussion of the realism of assessment. Brooks, according to Keener, "lays stress on the main characters' need to don a social mask and to penetrate, psychologically, the masks of others."[54] This realism of psychological assessment "is essential to the French novel in the period, not to the English." Keener then points out that such assessment by the main character of a story is performed only on other characters, but not on the main character. Keener concludes that "it is exactly this omission ... that largely accounts for the existence of the philosophical tale."[55]

Combine Keener's observation with the above description of the philosophical tale and one gets a short, but workable description. The psychological assessment of Brooks becomes a more analytical expression for both the notion of argument being central to the tale and that of actions and developments being subordinate to the criticism of ideas and ideology.

Of course, Keener examines the philosophical tale in light of the literary masterpieces of the eighteenth and early nineteenth century. But his and the other observations can still apply to the popular fiction discussed in this study. The Anticipation novels may not approach the level of artistic merit as the great literary works Keener and others analyze, but these popular novels belong in the tradition of the philosophical tale nonetheless. Application of literary tradition knows no boundaries.

Voltaire's Stepchildren

The novels written by French authors in the Anticipation imprint of Fleuve Noir can be called the descendants of Voltaire's *conte philosophique*, or philosophical tales. But how direct is this lineage? Considering the span of time existing between the two, how close should the relationship between them be described?

The newer stories do share with the older ones certain similarities. First, the newer stories contain many philosophical discussions and take specific stands based on them. Second, their philosophical discussions do not systematically analyze ideas or outlooks as their discussions are used merely to advance the position of the writer. Third, the newer stories treat a wide range of topics. Fourth, their depictions of societies are not fully developed and appear as one-dimensional exaggerations or caricatures that represent either the problem or the solution to an issue confronting humanity. Fifth, following Keener's observations, the newer stories' protagonists become subordinate to the ideas they represent. These characters assume a position on the idea of progress from which they criticize other outlooks that they find antithetical to theirs—and they do so without examining the possible weaknesses in their own ideas or arguments.

Sixth, these stories are not realistic in the modern sense of the term; they fall more in line with the realism as presented in the philosophical tales of Voltaire. The use of familiar science fiction themes such as alien invasions, nuclear war, advanced alien civilizations, and the dramatic impact of new technologies serve as props for the stories, much as the various fantastical scenes and events did for Voltaire's *Candide* and "Micromégas." As mentioned in the introduction to this study, the stories contain very little, if any, attempts (as the best of British and American science fiction do) to extrapolate realistically (whether in science, technology, politics, sociology, etc.). Their realism focuses on the assessment (of ideas) and not on the presentation (of accuracy). So in this literary context, much can be said about the relationship between Voltaire's philosophical tales and the Anticipation writers' stories.

Despite these similarities, however, enough differences exist between the stories of Voltaire's time and the science fiction novels from the 1950s to prevent one from labeling the Anticipation writers as Voltaire's direct literary descendants, for the modern-day stories are written with later French literary developments and the imported genre of American science fiction in mind. True, Voltaire did take the existing *conte*, or tale, and combined it with philosophical arguments; and, due to this joining, one can argue that the French science fiction writers performed the same type of literary melding with the American genre and the philosophical tale. But two reasons exist why one should view this last point as a difference and not a similarity, one chronological and the other geographical.

The chronological reason consists of the simple fact that there exist almost 200 years between Voltaire's last works and the beginning of the Anticipation imprint. Too much must be taken into account that prevents one from drawing a direct line between the older and newer literatures. For example, taking into account just the developments in science fiction, the influence of Jules Verne and H.G. Wells alone shaped most of this branch of literature in a way that Voltaire never could. One must then consider the prodigious output from France's golden age of science fiction, which provided new traditions and developed multiple themes for those who followed. In terms of general literary developments, since the use of the philosophical tale ceased for a while after Voltaire's death and other literary forms took over and dominated the field, the interruptions over time must be taken into account, for one finds only isolated examples of the pure philosophical tale in the two centuries after Voltaire.

The geographical reason focuses on the place of origin of the genre to which the French science fiction writers adapted their stories—America. The themes and forms of this import must be taken into consideration. The Anticipation writers may have infused elements of the philosophical tale into their novels, but their stories still must be described primarily as adaptations of American genre science fiction for French audiences. In other words, the newer foreign literature subsumed the older native one—and not the other way around.

So the French science fiction writers for the Anticipation imprint, due to separation in time and space, can not be seen as Voltaire's direct literary descendants. On the one hand, their Anticipation novels share enough similarities to be examined in light of the philosophical tale. On the other hand, these writers turn out to be not only heirs to French literary conventions that followed the philosophical tale, but they also belong to the postwar wave of adaptors of imported American genre science fiction.

Instead these writers and their stories should be seen as stepchildren of Voltaire; hence, the subtitle of this study.

CHAPTER TWO

The Moderates

The first group of writers to be examined, F. Richard-Bessière, M.A. Rayjean, and Kemmel, represent what will be called the moderate responses to the challenges posed by the idea of progress in post–World War II France. By moderate, it is meant that these writers wanted to avoid extreme or absolute measures in the application of new ideas and technologies on society. Because of this approach, they did not rely on a single idea or philosophy, or make sweeping statements, to explain and solve all the problems facing humanity. Richard-Bessière turns out to be the most philosophical of the three, while Rayjean and Kemmel can be seen as focusing on particular policies in modernization. Though their novels may contain fantastic elements, they emerge as the most pragmatic and cautious Anticipation writers.

F. Richard-Bessière

Henri-Richard Bessière (1923–) is the name behind F. Richard-Bessière. In addition to being the first French writer featured in the Anticipation imprint (the first four titles in Anticipation were his novels), he can also serve as a template for all the French Anticipation writers during this period. He sets out to examine different methods of thinking, ponder over the results of their applications, warn the reader which ideas can work or not work, and present his view on progress.

Bessière can also be seen as a bridge connecting prewar French science fiction with postwar French science fiction. Since he wrote his first novels during World War II, Bessière's novels provide an opportunity for readers to compare French science fiction before, during, and after the introduction of American genre science fiction.[1] As French scholars Jean-Marc and Randy Lofficier point out, his first novels "owed more to Verne, Le Faure, and de Graffigny than to post–World War II science fiction" and that they "embodied the transition between the French science fiction of the 1920s and 1930s, and that of the 1950s and 1960s, influenced by American authors."[2]

Most biographical sources list F. Richard-Bessière as a pseudonym for two writers, François Richard, the editor of the Anticipation imprint, and Henri-

Richard Bessière. Now he is referred to as Richard Bessière. A story lies behind this change. Bessière was only eighteen and a half years old when he completed his first novel in 1941, which made him too young to contract business by himself. His father had to sign contracts for him as his legal representative. Also, since his father was a writing partner and friend of Richard and with him had used the pseudonym F. Richard-Bessière, both he and Richard decided to transfer their pseudonym over to Bessière. They conducted this transaction during the war, so Bessière had to wait until 1951 to see his first novel's publication, after the Anticipation imprint started. Bessière wrote the novels while his father and Richard edited them for publication. Upon his father's death, he wanted to be known under his own name. The publishers became concerned, fearing confusion among their consumers over a sudden change of a very familiar — and therefore very profitable — public name. The two parties soon reached an agreement. They settled on Richard Bessière (either with or without hyphenation). Since his second prénom, or given name, is Richard, the change from F. Richard-Bessière to Richard Bessière would be for all involved parties a convenient and satisfactory one.[3] In this study, he shall be referred to as Richard Bessière or Bessière.

On his online blog site, Bessière gives his side of the story about his relationship with Richard in a manner much more forceful and condemnatory:

> I have at my disposal all of my manuscripts and I can state easily that Mr. Richard has never either written a word or inserted even a comma in my texts.... Mr. Richard, who has shamefully profited from this false collaboration, is given honors he has not earned and even goes up to the point of saying that he has written half of the texts (this statement has been confirmed by Mr. Siry....[4]

Siry is Patrick Siry, who succeeded Richard as editor of the Anticipation imprint and — before he did so — was Richard's "intimate collaborator."[5] Bessière continues and argues for what he considers the proper share of his royalties from his writings, translations, and adaptations to other media. He further claims that Richard has also treated other writers in the same manner — with him, Bessière, being owed the most since by his estimation he was the best seller of them all.[6] A full picture of this matter is yet to emerge as further investigation needs to be done.

Bessière is a most prolific writer. For Anticipation he produced ninety-eight titles between 1951 and 1985. One of them, *Les Seigneurs de la nuit* ("The Lords of the Night," Anticipation No. 591, 1973),[7] won the Grand Prix International de la Science Fiction in 1973. If this output is not enough, he also wrote almost 100 spy novels for Fleuve Noir's Espionnage imprint under the pseudonym. F.-H. Ribes. Of his Anticipation novels, Bessière wrote thirty-two during the 1950s. Seventeen of the thirty-two belong to three separate series of novels, each containing its own set of continuing characters; the other fifteen can be viewed as stand-alone novels. The three series are: (1) the travels of Professor Bénac and his crew around the solar system (five novels), (2) the adventures of New York journalist Sydney Gordon and his family and friends (ten novels, fourteen more after 1960), and (3) the adventures of scientist Harry Stewart (two novels).[8] For the sake of analysis, however, Bessière's works, and those of the other writers, will be divided by themes instead of by series and independent novels. Looking over his various declared interests will help identify his themes.

Being one of the three still-living Anticipation writers covered in this study, he remains in his eighties active on the Internet and maintains his profile on his own blog site. Educated at the university level in both sciences and letters, Bessière has led a diversified life. In addition to his spy and science fiction novels, he has produced mystery and historical novels. He belongs to *La SACEM*, an organization of music authors, composers, and editors, and is president of his local (Béziers, Hérault, where he now lives) SPA organization, which is devoted to the prevention of cruelty to animals. He lists as his favorite music jazz, classical, songs, and ballet and he has also written music for the theater. Other interests listed are parapsychology and paranormal phenomena.[9]

Most interesting of his blog's background descriptions is his list of four favorite books: Antoine de Saint-Exupéry's (1900–44) *Le Petit Prince* (*The Little Prince*, 1943), Voltaire's *Candide*, Édouard Schuré's (1841–1929) *Les Grands Initiés* (*The Great Initiates*, 1889), and Blaise Pascal's (1623–62) *Pensées* ("Thoughts," but usually known by its original French title, first published 1670).[10] The concerns of each of these books can be found in his Anticipation novels. Voltaire's impact constitutes a general one. The fact that Bessière himself listed *Candide* as one of his favorites adds support to the overall thesis of this study. The particular ideas and themes of the other three books can be found in his various works and are explored below. In addition to these literary inspirations, his interest in parapsychology and paranormal occurrences also enter into some of his novels, but none of them have this interest as a central theme. So it is through the lens of his stated interests that the idea of progress can be examined in Bessière's novels.

Examination of Bessière's treatment of the idea of progress in his stories is to be divided into five categories. The first consists of novels sharing the same approach to analysis as Saint-Exupéry's *The Little Prince*; the second comprised novels whose ideas are related to those in Pascal's *Pensées*; the third deals with novels examining certain notions from Schuré's *The Great Initiates* and other concepts from similar thinkers of Schuré's era; the fourth (further divided into four sections) examines novels treating the limits to progress by using common plot devices in science fiction; and the fifth and final category deals with what could be considered Bessière's solution to the problems of progress.

As with all the writers examined in this study, the themes of analysis are organized around what their novels say about the idea of progress. No prescriptive categories or number of categories are or will be imposed. For Bessière, then, these categories emerge from the ideas in his novels. If certain categories overlap among the writers, then it is due to the commonality of their interests and nothing else.

COMPARATIVE VIEWS OF PROGRESS AND IMAGINARY VOYAGES

Of Bessière's favorite books, *The Little Prince* is the only one written after he started his writing career. Saint-Exupéry's short novel, being a rare twentieth-century example of the philosophical tale, finds its roots in the science fiction novels of France's golden age. *The Little Prince* tells the story of a young prince who, having arrived on Earth, relates his adventures of ruling over a small asteroid, visiting other asteroids, which are ruled by leaders who represent extreme versions of various types of human behavior, and finally of observing humans on Earth.[11] This short novel has become an international best seller many times over.

Such a story dealing with extra-terrestrial travels is not unique or new in science fiction, French or otherwise. Cyrano de Bergerac's tales of visiting other planets represents a famous early example. France's golden age alone contains numerous stories about visiting planets in the solar system and beyond. Writers such as Rosny aîné, Le Faure, Graffigny, and others produced novels that told of travels to other planets and described strange civilizations while comparing them to Earth's societies. So Saint-Exupéry's piece belongs to a well-established tradition in French science fiction.

Meanwhile, Alain Douilly and Jacques Garin identify the particular source of inspiration for Bessière's early novels: *Les Aventuriers du ciel: Voyages extraordinaires d'un petit parisien dans la stratosphère, la lune et les planétes* ("Adventurers of the Sky: Extraordinary Voyages of a Little Parisian in the Stratosphere, Moon, and the Planets," 1935–7), by R.M. de Nizerolles, pseudonym of Marcel Priollet (1884–1960), and show the close parallels between the two writers' works.[12]

Perhaps the best remembered among these early travel stories is Jules Verne's *Off on a Comet* (*Hector Servadac*, 1877), which may have been a main inspiration for his golden age colleagues.[13] A comet collides with the Earth in Algeria and takes a piece of land with a diverse group of almost forty humans back into space. The group stays on the comet for two years, learns to live to together peacefully, and views the wonders of the solar system. No alien beings are encountered, that task being left to other writers. On return orbit the comet collides with the Earth again and leaves the humans back in Algeria. This novel constitutes Verne's only interplanetary adventure. His earlier space travel novels, *From the Earth to the Moon* (*De la terre à la lune*, 1865)[14] and *Around the Moon* (*Autour de la lune*, 1869),[15] stay within the proximity of the earth and the moon.

Since *The Little Prince* came out after Bessière's first novels were written, it could not have possibly influenced them. However both writers' works do

Two. The Moderates

share the same tradition of imaginary voyages beyond the earth's horizons into outer space. Both also write philosophical speculations and arguments that fit firmly in the tradition of the philosophical tale. So Bessière's and Saint-Exupéry's novels can be viewed as contemporary revivals of Voltaire's unique genre contribution.

―――∞∞∞―――

Bessière's first four novels for Anticipation, *Les Conquérants de l'univers* ("The Conquerors of the Universe," 1, 1951), *À l'assaut du ciel* ("To Assault the Sky," 2, 1951), *Retour de Météore* ("Return of the 'Meteor,'" 3, 1951), and *Planète vagabonde* ("Wandering Planet," 4, 1951) parallel Saint-Exupéry's story with Bessière's use of adventures about traveling to the various planets and encountering alien races. Instead of describing various societies representing exaggerations of human behavior, Bessière has his alien races adopting extreme versions of the idea of progress. Bessière's observations take the shape of philosophical musings and always with comparisons to Earth in mind.

"Conquerors of the Universe" tells the travels of humanity's first space ship, the Meteor, with its crew, headed by Professor Bénac. The first stop is Earth's moon where the crew encounters life forms similar to Earth's, but from a geological era predating the arrival of humans. Mars provides the next place of exploration and also Bessière's first extended discussion on the idea of progress. Bénac and his crew find the Red Planet inhabited by an advanced society governed by ideas of science and technology. The physical characteristics of the Martians immediately reveal their total emphasis on the intellect. Though basically human in appearance, the Martians possess large heads and small bodies. This use of physical exaggeration to focus on intellectual superiority easily evokes memories of H.G. Wells's Martians from his classic, *The War of the Worlds* (1898).[16] Bessière may have been responding to Wells as he treats his Martians with the same theme as Wells did with his: the natural limits to the progress of even a super-intelligent society.

The chief characteristic of Mars's society is its hierarchical structure where a person's position is determined by the amount of scientific knowledge he or she possesses. The Martians organize themselves into four levels: (1) *savant*, or scientist — the intellectual elite who rule society (at the top of the ruling class are a president and two vice presidents, who must make scientific discoveries to stay in office), (2) *chef d'entreprise*, or chief of operation — the managers who watch over society's daily operations, (3) *bon sous-ordre*, or good underclass — the subordinates who assist the managers in maintaining society, and (4) *les plus courant travail*, or most common job — the workers who actually carry out the various operations of keeping society functioning. The society raises its children by scientific principles and places them in occupations according to their aptitudes in science and technology.

The crew eventually meets the president of Mars, Professor Kok, with his title pointing out once again the centrality of knowledge in Martian society. He discusses at length what he considers a parallel development of all intelligent races:

> "The first Martians, as with the first Terrans, have built the foundations of our life. Envy, pride, the idea of domination, the thirst for honors and money, and lust — the game and the passion that one ought not to confuse with love — disturbed the Martian spirit as they did with yours. Covetous conquerors surged forward and innumerable wars soaked our planet with blood. All these were, except one — the last one — were made in the name of the claim, "defense of civilization," when in reality they had a stake in base material interests. In this discourse, I open a digression to indicate to you — knowing your previous struggles and present wars — that the Martian way considers the Terrans as backward beings and little deserving of the rank of human beings, just as you yourselves think of your ancestors who sent their fellow humans to be devoured by the lions in the arena" [132].[17]

Kok continues on and even hints on what Earth's future may be like.

> "But one inevitable law obliged men to group themselves together, to unite themselves and to fight in common for the general well being. And the habitual process was accomplished: from the one person that he was, man created the household, then the family. The tribes — meetings of families — took the place of clans, which in turn formed divided races. Their leaders, wanting to dominate; the combats — started from man against man — degenerated into tribe against tribe then continued to country against country. Grouping together at last, they formed into continents having the same aspirations and the wars of continent against continent lasted for centuries and were more horrible. Finally, the continents, after one last war ... united themselves to form only one country, only one race. This was the last war that our planet knew. And this has passed for thousands and thousands of years. Since that epoch, our scientists — whom the wisdom of men had finally led to the good way — only thought more to create instead of to destroy. Our organization is modified little by little so that our way of life arrives at our present stage" [132].

Note the emphasis of a world being one nation and one race. Later on Kok further applies his observation to a wider scale: "the evolution of the intelligent race has been identical on our two planets"(138). So now Earth's past, present, and future can be analyzed on an interplanetary level. This concept reemerges throughout Bessière's first series of novels, for it becomes the basis of judging the progress of Earth's as well as other planets' civilizations.

Bessière's portrayal of the Martian society and its philosophy calls to mind the ideas of utopian thinker Claude Henri de Rouvroy, Comte (Count) de Saint-Simon (1760–1825). Two aspects of Saint-Simon's ideas clearly come through. First is the concept of a hierarchical society whose organization reflects a focus on science and technology. Though Saint-Simon maintains a king and noble class, the real decision makers who will make a difference will be the administrators of science and technology. Where Bessière's Martian society differs from Saint-Simon's scheme is Bessière's omission of the king, the noble class, and the level of society dealing with the arts and letters.[18] Given Saint-Simon's belief in science as the key to progress, the exclusion of the king and nobles turns out not to be that important. As to the level dealing with the arts, Bessière will cover the necessity of the arts and letters in the third book of the series.

The second Saint-Simonian aspect constitutes the theme of political unity. As Saint-Simon calls for the unity of Europe, Bessière has the Martians attain a united planet for the betterment of their society. Where Bessière differs is in the nature of government. Saint-Simon envisions a European-wide parliament in his future while Bessière describes an authoritarian government based on its society's hierarchy.[19] Bessière will treat this issue of unity in a different light in his other works.

American historian Robert Gilpin, writing about government reforms of the scientific policies during the Fourth Republic, identifies as a source of inspiration the revival of a Saint-Simonian spirit which emphasized government planning and the exploitation of technically advanced ideas.[20] Though Bessière wrote his novels a few years before the Fourth Republic started, his Saint-Simon-like portrayals in his novels reflect not only the spirit of the government at the time of his novels' release, but also Saint-Simon's influence in French culture in general.

In addition to Mars's super-scientific society, the Earth explorers discover that nature itself has limited the Martians' development. Mars possesses a peculiar magnetic zone around it that prevents access to space travel, thus explaining why the Martians never visited the Earth. More importantly, in terms of life Mars is an old and dying planet. Nothing can be found to reverse this process. As a result, the Martian civilization becomes one of severe limits, including a declining birthrate. Earth also will suffer the same fate, though at a much later time. Wells's *The War of the Worlds* comes to mind again when the Martians engage in hostile actions to resolve their problems, but this time the attack is kept on Mars.

Wanting to revive the Martian race, the Martian vice president, Rinka, attempts to force the explorers' one female member to interbreed with a Martian. Of course the Earth men object, but so does Professor Kok. Rinka takes over the government and banishes those who oppose him to one of Mars's moons, Phobos. Combining science and brute force, the Earth men successfully lead a revolt and restore Kok as leader. At the end of the novel the explorers develop a way to penetrate Mars's magnetic zone and head for Jupiter.

The first sequel in the series, "To Assault the Sky," continues the themes of parallel development of civilizations and scientific progress. Here the Meteor visits Jupiter, where the explorers interact with ape men who are at the level of prehistoric humans; Neptune, where its inhabitants' level parallels that of medieval Europe; and Pluto, where the explorers meet a civilization much more advanced — and also much older — than that of Mars. Pluto's inhabitants are very old beings and can live only under the surface where a breathable atmosphere is located. They perform medical procedures on their children to enhance each child's special abilities (to become doctors, engineers, etc.). Their society is totally planned, to a far greater degree than the Martians' structured civilization.

The next sequel in the series, "Return of the 'Meteor,'" contains additional speculations about the idea of progress. The explorers first fly to Saturn, which is ruled by a female tyranny. Saturn's men are segregated from the women due to a disease, for which Bénac eventually discovers a cure. Also, it turns out that only the males perform scientific research. The explorers lead a revolt against the female leadership and oversee the initial stages of the reintegration of genders that will restore balance to their society. The explorers next go to Uranus, where they encounter Martian colonists (who arrived 500 years ago, apparently before Mars's magnetic zone appeared) instructing its primitive beings, and then to Mercury, where they discover primitive amphibian beings and save them from a biological threat of giant microbes. Afterwards the explorers set up the amphibians to evolve "normally" (133).

The explorers next travel to Venus and encounter its advanced civilization. Here Bessière presents an in-depth discussion on the nature of progress. He offers a different version of the idea of progress—that of balance in the development of knowledge. As on Mars and Pluto, Venus's people are more advanced than Earth's and their society is based on the accumulation of knowledge. However, unlike Mars and Pluto, Venus turns out to be a veritable utopia. Professor Bénac proclaims Venus to be "truly marvelous and comparable to the Eden of our Scriptures" (179). The Venusians' physical appearance even resembles that of the mythological Greek gods of Mount Olympus.

Venus's ruler, Tchimor, explains how his society has succeeded so well. He reaffirms the Martian approach to unity and commitment to knowledge:

> "Our planet possesses only one language, one race, and one state. At its head is placed what you call a president. This president represents the Venusian state, but does not govern. The government proper is entrusted to ten scholars" [154].

But Venus is different, being much more paradisiacal than Mars. Tchimor relates how Venus took a path different from the one both Mars and Pluto traversed:

> "When the unity of races, languages, and morals were finally realized on our globe, our ancestors returned to our ancient morals by sacrificing progress and science— by restraining the information from mechanics, physics, and chemistry, and by steering, on the other hand, the great mass of Venusians towards music, poetry, painting, and architecture under all its forms. A small number of exceptionally gifted Venusians were alone authorized to pursue the study of abstract sciences. This has not changed since then and good fortune and joy reigns on our globe. This does not prevent the Venusians from appreciating the inventions that are given to them, for money does not exist. Only work counts" [169].

In contrast to the societies he created on Mars and Pluto, Bessière (recalling Saint-Simon's ideas once again) states that the arts and letters are also important for progress. As Saint-Simon stresses that all knowledge must function organically together before society can improve, Bessière argues for a similar goal: the need for a balanced development in all fields of human endeavor, but with the sciences maintaining their privileged position of power and the arts and letters enriching the population as a whole. Bessière emphasizes this point by having the Venusians possessing the equivalent of the nine muses of the ancient Greeks on Earth (169). This depiction becomes Bessière's first statement on what is needed for progress beyond new science and technology.

The explorers leave Venus and return to Earth. Towards the novel's end Bénac ponders whether or not anything can be learned from any of their interplanetary adventures, which were often punctuated with violent battles with the various planets' natives—though always in self defense. Besides examining the varying levels of the different civilizations, he also considers the actions taken by the Earth explorers to survive. In doing so he gives a brutal view on the idea of progress:

> "But alas, do men save to profit from this? It is said that the human species is obligated to destroy, and be destroyed. The proverb which says, 'to kill is to live,' is always true. We have killed beasts on the Moon, beings on Mars, Jupiter, Neptune, Saturn, Uranus, and Mercury ... we have always had arms in hand. We have killed to protect ourselves, that is evident. But we have killed just the same. It is to believe, my poor friends, that progress and civilization only advances itself and marches on paths strewn with cadavers" [182].

Until now there is no extended discussion as to the morality of the violent actions by the Earth explorers. Given the idea of parallel development of progress on all the planets, the concept seems to be the unspoken justification several times in these novels.

The brutal necessity of progress comes up again in the fourth novel of the series, "Wandering Planet." The story concerns a wandering planet, which was ripped away from its original solar system by a black star and is now entering Earth's solar system. Its super advanced race had designs on conquering Pluto in order to settle part of their population there. After a war in which both sides suffer, a truce is made. The leader of this race offers to Bénac his planet's scientific advances, but Bénac refuses because Earth's people "are not again evolved enough to help itself from your discoveries" (182). Even after a successful war, Bénac considers human limitations in the face of advanced knowledge.

Bessière did add another novel to this quartet of stories, *Sauvetage sidéral* ("Sidereal Rescue," 37, 1954). He concludes Earth's encounters with the roaming planet from "Wandering Planet," with the results being far more brutal. This time he has the wandering planet destined to collide with Earth, causing destruction of both planets as well as severe side effects to Mars and Venus. Bénac leads an expedition that results in the wandering planet and all of its inhabitants being destroyed to save the lives on the other three planets.

If these five novels comprised all that Bessière had written for Anticipation, he would have done enough to set the tone of discussion for the other French writers. Into his adventures he injected discussions and opinions about what he thought constituted progress in knowledge as well as in social development. Bessière meant these placements to be more than just passing comments. He attempted to have an ongoing discussion about certain themes throughout his stories. The other Anticipation writers will do the same; some more, some less. But all will have placed enough of these ideological discussions in their novels for a careful reader to detect and identify their positions on the idea of progress.

Back to this analysis, based on these five novels it would be safe to conclude that he argues for development in both the sciences (though they still have priority) and arts and letters to ensure a progress that does not self-destruct, the need for unity, and for the realization that survival sometimes comes at a great cost. Bessière will eventually address the issue of violence and war when he attempts to find a peaceful solution to humanity's divisions. In the following sections examining his other novels from the Fifties, Bessière presents a more complex picture of his ideas.

Bessière added three more novels to his theme of the need for more balance in the development of human knowledge. Two of them serve as basic warnings about humanity developing too quickly in science and technology. *La Deuxième Terre* ("The Second Earth," 97, 1957) tells of the discovery of a duplicate Earth. The encounter with this second Earth ends in tragedy and the faster-than-light ship newly developed for travel into deep space is destroyed to prevent its further use. *Fléau de l'univers* ("Scourge of the Universe," 105, 1958) has its protagonists destroying access to advanced technology in order to protect humanity from itself. The third, *Via dimension "5"* ("Via Dimension '5,'" 101, 1957), puts an interesting spin to this theme. In the novel a scientist, Professor Bluman, researches without regard to the consequences of his scientific endeavors. He insists on science's neutrality, but the results of his work leads to disaster when it falls into the wrong hands. An advanced alien race intervenes and warns of the need for equal progress in both technology and morality. The novel concludes with the aliens telling the Earth that humanity is at a critical juncture in its development, so correct choices must be made. Furthermore, the aliens reveal that they are part of a chain of superior beings, leading all the way back to the creators of the universe, who exist in the form of universal thought. Is humanity intelligent and moral enough to join them?

"THE HEART HAS ITS REASONS, WHICH REASON DOES NOT KNOW"[21]

The above famous quotation by Pascal originates from his well-known posthumously published work, *Pensées* ("Thoughts"). Written as an argument for the acknowledgment of the limits to rational thinking, the existence of God, and for the Christian religion, Pascal's book continues to exert a profound influence in both philosophical and theological fields. Bessière wrote three novels that attempted to explore the first of Pascal's three arguments, the limits to rational thinking. He did not examine Pascal's other arguments for God and Christianity, but he did take on the issues of religion and spirituality in other novels, which will be examined in the next section.

When discussing the limits to rational thinking, Pascal posits two methods of perceiving reality: mathematical and intuitive. In this discussion mathematical thinking can be seen as synonymous to rational thinking. Both constitute human traits and both are needed, but one should not be preferred over the other. The principles of mathematics are easy to perceive, but are removed from common experience. Those of intuition are found in the everyday world, but they are so subtle and numerous that it is easy to make mistakes by inaccurate use of them. Pure mathematicians possess exact minds that require precise definitions and axioms but become incapable of sound decisions beyond their realm of reasoning, while pure intuitive thinkers may be able to grasp the big picture quickly but they lack the patience to understand speculative and conceptual principles, which are not readily experienced in the everyday world.[22]

Bessière brought up this relationship between the two ways of thinking in a few of his novels, and he did so from the perspective of overreliance on the mathematical, or rational. *Objectif soleil* ("Target: Sun," 69, 1956) tells the story of Gota, a hidden planet in our solar system, and its plan to alter the Sun. The plan would result in damaging Mercury, Venus, and Earth, so the novel's protagonists from Earth attempt to disrupt it and eventually succeed. In the course of their actions, they have a discussion among themselves about an overreliance on science when debating who should represent them when interacting with the aliens from Gota. One of the protagonists, worrying about a scientist playing the key role, seems to take his argument straight out of Pascal:

> You want to think and reason as scientists. But I, I reason as a human being—there is the difference. For you, all is mathematics, formulae, and equations—beyond that is nothing. You even impose upon nature the mold of your ideas.... You see nature with all its problems only through an opaque screen that you wrap around yourselves [107–8].

Pascal said nearly the same thing almost 200 years earlier:

> Mathematicians who are only mathematicians have exact minds, provided all things are explained to them by means of definitions and axioms; otherwise they are inaccurate and insufferable, for they are only right when the principles are quite clear.[23]

In *Les Lunes de Jupiter* ("The Moons of Jupiter," 169, 1960) a similar crisis of irregular solar activity threatening the Earth emerges and the novel's protagonists, composed of humans and super-scientific alien allies, join forces. The aliens accept their limitations and see the reason why they must join with humans. As one alien puts it, "You (the human) are an intuitive genius and this is what we (the aliens) lack, being only mathematicians, calculators of only flesh and blood, nothing more" (91, author's parenthetical identifiers). In both cases the argument against an overreliance on science wins out and the protagonists act accordingly.

In *Relais Minos III* ("Relay Station Minos III," 117, 1958), Bessière suggests that the intuitive side of thinking does not necessarily have to be that noble. Earth has been destroyed and the surviving humans, who escaped Earth's fate by being on space expeditions, struggle to survive. The survivors face two threats: a society of robots and an interstellar organization of aliens. The robots are intelligent, powerful, highly organized, and have made living creatures—human and alien—their servile workers. They represent the ultimate in mathematical thought, so much so that they describe the universe and their goals accordingly, "We consider the universe as resulting from a mechanical thought which controls and conceives according to inevitable laws. And all our efforts reach towards this perfect mechanism that we idealize" (80). When describing the differences between humans and robots, one of the protagonists explains a weapon that only humans possess, "We humans are capable of lying, hypocrisy, feebleness, cunning, guile, and even of certain fantasies which, if wisely measured, can be heavy of consequences" (92). The humans use these unique attributes to defeat the robots and the aliens. Pascal would not usually think these aspects of human activity as good, but he would see them as the non-rational, non-mathematical side of human thought.

So beyond the complete range of human knowledge and the two basic categories of human thinking, what else is there? As mentioned, Bessière did take on the theological and religious issues; but he did so in a manner very different from Pascal.

THE SEARCH FOR SPIRITUALITY

Though Bessière did not argue for the existence of god or support Christianity as Pascal did, he did briefly reveal a spiritual side to his ideas. His selection of Édouard Schuré's *The Great Initiates: A Study of the Secret History of Religions* as one of his favorite books provides a clue as to what Bessière thought about in spiritual or religions' matters. In the book Schuré describes the story of various great religious and mystic leaders, from ancient India, Egypt, Greece, and Israel (including both Jewish and Christian faiths), and how they searched for a spiritual truth. Schuré concludes that there exists an ultimate spiritual reality which the great religions' leaders have discovered in various ways. This spiritual world can be reached through human effort—not by science but through human instinct, psychology, and the individual human soul.[24]

Many Europeans took interest in the search for spirituality during the time of the book's release. They wanted to find a deeper meaning in life in a society many felt to be overly industrialized and materialistic. Their quests went beyond the scope of traditional Christianity, often exploring what many in the West would describe as the esoteric mysticism of the Asian religions. The book's ecumenical treatment of various religions contributed to the appeal of Schuré's ideas.[25] If Christianity attempted to explain a transcendent reality, then Schuré wanted to reveal a more immanent one.

A thinker in this realm that Schuré admired was a contemporary, Rudolf Steiner (1861–1925), the developer of Anthroposophy, a philosophy claiming that the spiritual world exists and can be known by individuals if they engage in a strict and disciplined training of one's consciousness to see beyond the materialistic world. Schuré and Steiner met in 1906 and established a relationship to the point where Steiner directed one of Schuré's plays and Steiner's future wife, Marie von Sivers (1867–1948), translated *The Great Initiates* into German (1909) with Steiner himself writing an introduction to it.[26] Steiner grew his ideas into a movement that still exists today, including a Rudolf Steiner Institute located at Stonehill College in Easton, Massachusetts.[27] Schuré considered his relationship with Steiner one of the most important in his life. He viewed Steiner's ideas as very impressive and as providing the keys to understanding the spiritual world. Steiner did reciprocate Schuré's respect.[28]

Bessière wrote two novels dealing with this approach to spirituality. *Feu dans le ciel* ("Fire in the Sky," 64, 1956) relates the story of how the Earth is ravaged by an alien solar system with a black star that travels through Earth's solar system. Only eight of the novel's protagonists survive on Earth and, with the help of a Tibetan priest, they plan to rebuild civilization. The Tibetan priest knew Earth's fate beforehand. He did so through his study and understanding of ancient texts that were discovered by a modern-day expedition. The novel's sympathetic French scientist protagonist relates to the priest of his visit to a monastery located in the Himalaya Mountains. The scientist comments on the monastery's priests' approach to wisdom, "...their intellectual faculties developed by meditation permits them to clear themselves of all materialism and to approach the metaphysical problems that our mathematical spirit is incapable of resolving" (50). To understand truly the nature of the universe, thinking beyond the material world and its science must be attained.

In Bessière's other novel, *Création cosmique* ("Cosmic Creation," 89, 1957), a more extensive discussion takes place. It goes to a different source (but from the same era) for inspiration, the noted French philosopher, Henri(-Louis) Bergson (1859–1941). In the near future an asteroid containing its own civilization is discovered. American newspaper reporter Sydney Gordon (Bessière's most used protagonist) and his companions travel there and encounter a society governed by a female dictatorship (much like the one on Saturn in Bessière's earlier "Return of the 'Meteor'" where the men are segregated from the women). The Earth men are sent to join the asteroid's exiled men, among whom lives Professor Uko, who is secretly developing scientific weapons to use against the existing order. As expected, the men use the new weapons, overthrow the repressive government, and help establish a new society with equality among the sexes.

The most serious discussion about the nature of progress occurs during Gordon's meetings with Uko. Uko places limits on science and even doubts its ability either to explain the true nature of existence or to be used as the sole guide for the future. Uko's ideas bear more than a passing resemblance to Bergson and his famed concept of *élan vital* (vital impetus). Comparing the presentation of Uko's ideas to those of Bergson's in his *L'Évolution créatrice* (*Creative Evolution*, 1908) will bear this observation out.

Both agree that neither scientific thought nor present-day philosophies adequately portray the universe as it really exists. According to Uko,

> "Allow me to explain to you the true concept of the Universe, about which men have researched up to this day. Some have caught a glimpse of it, but they came up against a barrier, for they have no tangible base from which to undertake the true sense of the Universe, for the 'real essence of substances' has always exceeded the understanding of men. Whatever the variations of scientific or even philosophical thought are, the material universe evidently remains the image of substantiality which is none other—and you know this—than a purely intellectual concept. But the Universe by itself is another thing, and its fundamental entity is none other than the energy that is manifested under several forms and which remains a true constant of integration in a differential equation" [125].

Bergson discusses the same speculation almost a half century earlier:

> It is natural to our intellect, whose function is essentially made to present us to things and states rather than changes and acts. But things and states are only views, taken by our mind, of becoming. There are no things, there are only actions.[29]

When considering the nature of the universe and how it works, the similarities between the two come through as well. As Uko explains,

> "The idea came to me to consider the flux of energy, not as a pure mathematical abstraction as like the mathematicians who are bent over the problem imagine it, but rather as a universal reality, beyond time and space.... The creations of the Universe are the work of pure Thought, impossible to realize in a purely material medium. This universe is governed, controlled, and directed by a Power whose complete objective representation would be very imperfect for humans such as us. ... a veritable Universal Spirit whose creations are evidently more substantial than those of an individual spirit.
>
> "I have not said that it concerns a BEING, but simply of a Creative Force, without which we would not exist..." [126–7].

Bergson, when discussing his *élan vital*, has this to say:

> So we come back ... to the idea we started from, that of an *original impetus* of life, passing from one generation of germs to the following generation of germs through the developed organisms that bridge the interval between the generations. This impetus, sustained right along the lines of evolution among which it gets divided, is the fundamental cause of variations, at least of those that are regularly passed on, that accumulate and create new species.[30]

And even the ultimate purpose of both of their forces remains similar. Uko declares:

"But then, what role do we play in this universe? What is the goal of all this, since all is dedicated to a final failure? Nature is only has only one alternative — you know it — progress or death....

each of our spirits tends towards perfection, this universal perfection that conceives, directs, and creates....

The Spiritual Power of the Universe creates new spirits without stopping. All are in a crude state.... Incarnated, they evolve in the milieu which has been designated to them. They adapt themselves more or less well to the demands of material life ... this perfection and this evolution can only be acquired after successive reincarnations ... the Universal Spirit does not make distinctions between the spirits it creates, being content to note their evolution and direct them their final role" [130–2].

Bergson's ideas on this matter are:

As the smallest grain of dust is bound up with our entire solar system, drawn along with it in that undivided movement of descent which is materiality itself, so all organized beings, from the humblest to the highest, from the first origins of life to the time in which we are, and in all places as in all times, do but evidence a single impulsion.... All the living hold together, and all yield to the same tremendous push. The animal takes its stand on the plant, man bestrides animality, and the whole of humanity, in space and time, is one immense army galloping beside and before and behind each of us in an overwhelming charge able to beat down any resistance and clear the most formidable obstacles, perhaps even death.[31]

When it comes to identifying how human beings can perceive all this, both share a similar approach in that humans are a part of the evolutionary process. As Uko puts it,

"Each of us possesses what one calls a spirit, and the spirit is none other than energy. Liberated from matter, this energy becomes fluid, otherwise said — a radiance which disperses itself in the ether under the form of psychic energy....

Each grain that you perceive in this mass, or rather in this unity, IS A SPIRIT, under the form of energy ... and each behaves in the manner of a cell in the human body. It loses its autonomy to the profit of Unity, which becomes a SUM, a WHOLE, a veritable ENTITY, otherwise said — a SPIRITUAL POWER" [128–9].

Bergson's version:

The Absolute is revealed very near us and, in certain measure, in us. It is of psychological and not of mathematical nor logical essence. It lives with us. Like us, but in certain aspects infinitely more concentrated and more gathered up in itself, it *endures*.[32]

As the texts demonstrate, both sets of ideas propose a non-materialistic and immanent view of the universe in general and an idea of progress via evolution in particular. Both view a non-material, yet identifiable, force that is behind the evolution of the universe. This development of the universe is not to be detected solely by scientific means, but also by psychological means. Bessière's ideas and Bergson's are not identical, but they share enough parallels in concepts and their developments to warrant this comparison.

In discerning this parallel between Bessière and Bergson, the author does not suggest that Bergson is connected in any direct way to the Anthroposophic thought of Steiner or Schuré. However Bergson and Schuré do represent different attempts to explain reality that emerged in an era when people questioned purely materialistic views and, as a result, sought non-materialistic, psychological, and spiritual solutions in places located beyond the reaches of contemporary traditional Christianity. So both share certain elements that were characteristic of their time — the search for an underlying principle of reality that went beyond the material, yet one that depicts a realm which can be understood through human endeavors (intuition, mysticism, etc.). These two novels of Bessière come closest to expressing his views on a world beyond matter.

Bessière wrote many novels which do not take up his stated interests as focal points like the novels analyzed above, but he did explore limits to the idea of progress in themes commonly found in science fiction. The following four sections bear this out.

LIMITS TO PROGRESS: HISTORY

Bessière produced novels advocating what he thought was the "proper" development or pace of progress. In some of them he argued that support for this concept can be found in the lessons of history. A popular theme in science fiction is alternative or alternate history. Here the writer speculates what would happen if history (mostly on Earth, but sometimes in other places with obvious parallels to Earth's past) could be changed (whether by time travel, space travel, or any other means).[33] Two well-known examples include Mark Twain's memorable *A Connecticut Yankee in King Arthur's Court* (1889),[34] where an American goes back to the England of the legendary King Arthur and introduces his knowledge to the period, and L. Sprague de Camp's classic novel, *Lest Darkness Fall* (1939), where a man from the twentieth century is accidentally transported back to the city of Rome during the sixth century and attempts to prevent the Dark Ages from occurring in Western Europe.[35]

Bessière wrote three novels dealing with this concern. *Croisière dans le temps* ("Cruise in Time," 6, 1951) tells the story of twentieth-century time travelers who go back to the year 1610 CE in France where they prevent the assassination of French king Henry IV, whose survival leads to a united and peaceful Europe. The peace and introduction of scientific devices by the time travelers allow this alternate Europe and the world to progress at a much faster pace such that by the year 1800 Earth attains the level of development that originally would not have been reached until 1950. Unfortunately, the world still goes through two world wars and, because of the advanced technology now developed, the results become far worse with the world being destroyed. The time travelers decide to reverse their actions and return history to its original course.

Instead of traveling through time, *Vingt Pas dans l'inconnu* ("Twenty Steps into the Unknown," 60, 1955) takes a trip through various dimensions. Some present-day scientists encounter a mysterious sphere that enables them to travel through twenty dimensions, of which one of them is a world at the stage of Europe's Roman Empire of classical times. As in de Camp's novel, Bessière's scientists attempt to introduce their knowledge and prevent the occurrence of a dark age. When a question arises about the wisdom of this policy, one of the scientists responds that "it is not in my intentions to introduce a new religion, and even less our political ideas. We are scientists busy in carrying out an experiment. And we must succeed cost what may" (109). De Camp's novel ends on a positive note, but the last three words of this last quotation changes the scientist's statement from an optimistic one to an ambiguous one.

Unlike the previous two novels, *Zone spatiale interdite* ("Forbidden Space Zone," 126, 1958) examines Earth recent past and present as history. In the twenty-fifth century, Earth explorers are marooned on planet Ourga where lives a civilization paralleling that of twentieth-century Earth's. The novel makes this parallel clear by referring to Ourga's recent discovery of atomic energy as equivalent to Earth's developments in the 1930s and 1940s. There is even an international organization that is said to parallel Earth's United Nations (150–1), for Ourga is rife with nationalistic rivalries. When the Earth explorers offer their knowledge to a nation of Ourga, the nation rejects them. If one nation accepts the new knowledge, the others would object and the risk of war would increase.

Perhaps a more recognizable presentation of this theme in English-language science fiction can be found in the various *Star Trek* television series with their concept of the Prime Directive, a policy of non-interference of cultures who have not yet discovered space travel. Though this policy was often broken in practice in the series, its ideal provided audiences with a notion that certain scientific aspects of progress must be withheld from people who are not ready for them.

For Bessière progress in science and technology must march at a pace equal to that of human social progress. History has proven that too much, too soon, can only lead to tragedy.

LIMITS TO PROGRESS: NATURE

Bessière resorts to the much-used motif of underground civilizations and worlds for *Altitude moins X* ("Altitude Minus X," 75, 1956), which tells the story of humanity being attacked by a race of humans who live 150 kilometers (93 miles) below the Earth's surface. Reporter Sydney Gordon suggests that the source of the attacks were of subterranean origin (while also admitting that Jules Verne's novel, *Journey to the Center of the Earth* [*Voyage au centre de la terre*, 1864], is his favorite book). Using a newly built craft that can travel through the ground, Gordon and seven others encounter the underground people, the

Oklontes, who are attacking the surface. When allying with the peaceful Oklontes, Gordon and company experience difficulties in getting them to oppose the warlike Oklontes.

It turns out that the underground environment conditioned how Oklontes behaved. While the surface humans had the sun, sky, and stars inspiring them to expand, compete, and explore — to the point of affecting them "in the manner of a drug" (130), the sub-surface ones lived in a closed and narrow world which led them down a different path. Until the war with the surface humans, the Oklontes "had never known war, ambition, fratricidal struggles, or hypocrisy" (129). Their environment had always supplied them with all that they need for survival, so aggressive behavior was not needed. They even developed biological and genetic engineering methods to eliminate such bad instincts and create only desirable personalities. While nature supplies physical needs and shapes the outlook of a society, science completes the process by shaping psychological development. These experiences become a drawback when the peaceful Oklontes need to fight the warring Oklontes (the novel never reveals their reason for attacking), as self-defense now becomes necessary for survival. As a member of Gordon's group emphasizes why war must be waged, "This is the first law ... of our race that we go and carry out such acts ... it is impossible to act otherwise if we want to safeguard our humanity and yours" (175). Gordon and his allies do defeat the warring Oklontes and both sets of humans end up living in peace. Once again violence is needed to save humanity and, as mentioned, one will have to refer to the last group of novels by Bessière to be examined to see how he resolves this issue of necessary violence.

Among the best remembered warnings against humans attempting to improve upon nature is H.G. Wells's novel, *The Island of Doctor Moreau* (1896).[36] Bessière's *Réaction déluge* ("Reaction Flood," 144, 1959) takes Wells's idea of improving on nature to a higher level with an attempt to create a perfect race of humans. An alien scientist, whose home planet forbade him to continue his research, goes to Earth to carry on his attempts at perfecting humanoid life. Earth now becomes for him the equivalent of Doctor Moreau's isolated island. The alien scientist views humanity on Earth as

> "a mistake, as are all the human races created by nature. The universe is not conceived for errors. Everything is regulated, planned, organized, studied, and balanced by a multitude of immutable physical-chemical laws which man searches for in vain to penetrate.... He will never possess the means to break this barrier..." [125–6].

The alien then expresses the utmost confidence with his research:

> "One day I will disappear when it is my turn, but this race will remain, will persevere, and will upset all the laws of nature. They will arrive at the summit of knowledge, for they will be adapted to do so" [126].

Fortunately for Earth, the novel's protagonists save the day by defeating the alien scientist before he can complete his project and destroy much of the world in doing so. Humanity will progress as nature created them and not as artificially altered beings.

In both novels Bessière reveals that nature itself can dictate how humanity can progress. Nature both shapes how humans interact with the world and also places limits on the pace of human development. Attempts by people to change what nature has given them should not take place, no matter how noble the purpose. Humanity must be able to develop as itself and not as someone else's construct.

LIMITS TO PROGRESS: OUTSIDE INTERVENTION

An often-used theme in science fiction concerns the notion that humanity needs to be guided from above — whether by an elite group of humans or aliens from another world — because of its inability to control its science and technology. This topic includes the accidental discovery of advanced technology by unsuspecting humans. Bessière wrote nine novels that fall in this category.

Two of them, *Terre degree "0"* ("Earth Degree '0,'" 153, 1960) and *Générations perdues* ("Lost Generations," 157, 1960), form a two-part series in which guidance from both humans and aliens are considered. "Earth Degree '0'" introduces Harry Stewart, a scientist who develops a serum that gives its user a super-memory. Using the serum on himself, Stewart becomes able to invent many scientific marvels (including an automobile powered by a non-combustion engine, new medicine, etc.), but the change caused by them is met with resistance from various existing institutions (industry, medical institutions, etc.). Stewart understands the dangers of his new inventions and, being an idealist, takes it upon himself to guide humanity.

Stewart understands that existing institutions will be inconvenienced and damaged by change, but his response remains, "An old French proverb says that 'one cannot make an omelet without cracking a few eggs'" (70). He is enthusiastic and claims that "...we will give to the world more than what twenty centuries of civilization has given it" (133). He turns down an offer of help to manage his inventions and their impact on society, declaring, "I do not plan to recruit puppet collaborators, who one day might venture to sabotage my work for more or less illicit profits. I will charge myself, when the moment arrives, to gather those who will have the arduous charge of representing the elite" (148). Eventually Stewart establishes a movement, *Conformité* (Conformity), and a program for it, "Moral Education of People" (157).

Despite the best of intentions events still turn sour, especially when Stewart has to fight industrial interests who want to take over his inventions. Though Stewart helps many people, he still hurts many more by his projects. A conclusion is reached: order cannot be imposed from above. As one of his friends puts it, "Hitler and Stalin, they had their politics and we know today what they are worth" (185). Eventually Stewart ends up destroying his laboratory to protect humanity from any more calamities.

"Lost Generations" continues the story of Stewart and his search for a perfect society. This time Steward and a group of sympathetic scientists leave Earth, since it cannot be changed, and settle on Venus to start their utopian society and avoid any further contact with Earth. The new society stresses unity, urging the different races of humans to become one, while its government controls all production and oversees education to the point of dictating what type of knowledge will be learned. The supreme ruling body will be the *Comité Supérieur* ("High Committee") under Stewart's guidance. After initial success the Venusian society becomes corrupt, especially when resuming interaction with the humans on Earth.

Just when it seems that Stewart's dream of human perfection will fail one more time, a mysterious flying saucer appears before him and from it emerges an alien from the Lyre Constellation. The alien reveals himself to be part of a super-race which has been the real power behind the development of races on many planets. They have been influencing human history by helping certain individuals to develop new knowledge. The aliens accomplish these feats by their ability to create and maintain psychic connections with humans from a long distance. Despite their help, humans—whether on Earth or Venus—prove that they are still not ready to join other advanced races in an *Empire Céleste* ("Celestial Empire"). Stewart alone is allowed to join the alien, while his fellow humans are to be viewed as an unwanted and incorrigible plague.

These two novels depict a disturbing picture of the concept of an elite body, whether human or alien, trying to lead and accelerate human progress. Both attempts fail. Whether viewed as an argument for non-interference or as a warning for humanity to correct its behavior, Bessière expresses a grim attitude towards this concept of progress.

Seven other novels reflect this attitude as well. Interactions with superior outside parties do not work. *Cité de l'esprit* ("City of Mind," 85, 1957) relates how a small group of humans, with the help of aliens, have much to offer to the world. But humanity is not ready. Human technology may be advanced, but the humans themselves are not. *Carrefour de temps* ("Crossroad of Time," 111, 1958) plays with the idea of controlling time. An Earth man makes a mistake with unknown technology found in a flying saucer and causes cataclysmic damage by accidentally stopping time, but an alien from an advanced race comes to the rescue. *Bang!* ("Bang!" 121, 1958) involves several layers of guidance from outside but with mixed results. *Panique dans le vide* ("Panic in the Void," 129, 1959) tells the story of how a Professor Morton secretly built computers on twin planets to quicken their progress and how he eventually fails at the end. *On a hurlé dans le ciel* ("They Screamed in the Sky," 148, 1959) warns how the liberty of humanity can be lost by promises of peace and prosperity from an outside source (aliens). *Les Patins d'outre ciel* ("Puppets from Beyond the Sky,"

162, 1960) reveals Earth's events to be nothing more than the results of manipulations in an experiment conducted by two aliens. *Escale chez les vivants* ("Stopover among the Living," 166, 1960) has Earth freed from alien tyranny.

Limits to Progress: War

Bessière wrote four novels describing how war stifles progress. True, Bessière featured war in his other novels covered in different sections of this study, but those novels contained other themes that warranted more discussion. The following three novels focus primarily on war and its disastrous consequences.

S.O.S. Terre ("S.O.S. Earth," 55, 1955) depicts a war between Earth and Mars. In this novel there exists in the South Pole a civilization established by the descendants of humans who had settled there 12,000 years ago. These humans formed the first civilization on Earth and, along with the Martians, possess advanced technology—including space flight. When Mars decides to invade Earth, both the original humans and present-day humans join forces and defeat the Martians in an explosive battle which results in the destruction of the South Pole humans and the Martians. All traces of both advanced civilizations are erased. Whatever advantages Earth could have enjoyed from the lost technology have vanished. Considering Bessière's novels in the previous section examining the consequences of intervention from above, this loss may not have been such a bad thing.

Planète de mort ("Planet of Death," 93, 1957) takes the reader into Earth's future, the year 2080, where the world is recovering from a devastating atomic war. From the destruction emerge two rival organizations, Cosmic Society and Sideral Corporation Limited, who both develop faster-than-light spaceships and carry their competition to the stars. The Cosmic Society misleads Sideral into sending a ship to the Proxima Centauri system where the Sideral crew encounters a race of beings who differ from Earth in terms of progress. The beings, possessing telepathic powers, decipher the humans' intentions and ways of thinking and as a result view the Earth people as incompatible and threatening to their way of life. The beings see humans as being too technology-oriented and themselves as adhering to nature. The two races cannot coexist.

Bessière continues his criticism of humanity's warlike tendencies at the end of the novel. When the Sideral ship first arrives on the planet the ship blows up, thus stranding the crew. The crew realizes that they have no place to go on the planet and will soon die. The sighting of an Earth ship gives them hope, but it turns out to be a false hope as the ship belongs to the Cosmic Society and does not respond to the Sideral crew's pleas for help. All of the crew dies and the planet's beings also destroy the crew's base to remove all traces of human contact.

As if to emphasize the futility presented in the novel's resolution, Bessière frames the whole novel with two conversations between two crew members of a Cosmic Society ship. One member, John Dixley, expresses guilt and remorse for being the one who unknowingly sent the false message to the Sideral Corporation. He is rebuked by his superior, James Duncan. These two appear again in the novel's epilogue, for they are on the ship that ignores the Sideral crew's attempts at communication. Dixley still feels regret over his role and Duncan continues to rebuke him. This fruitless exchange leaves the reader with a feeling of futility — despite having gone through a horrendous atomic war, humanity has learned nothing about the need to change its ways.

Le Troisième Astronef ("The Third Spaceship," 135, 1959) is a flashback from the far future to events in the year 1975 and describes the events involving the third expedition to Venus (the first two had mysteriously failed). Successfully landing on Venus the Earth crew encounters blue-skinned and green-skinned humanoids. The humans share one aspect with the humanoids — the desire to make devastating weapons. While Earth possesses its hydrogen bombs, the green-skinned humanoids develop deadly microbe-sized spores which can disintegrate all matter, living or otherwise. When a humanoid space ship crashes in Alaska, the deadly spores are accidentally released. Only the detonating of hydrogen bombs by the United States saves the world from certain death. The Earth crew eventually leaves Venus, but only after destroying part of their ship due to infection by the deadly spores. The far-future narrator of the novel concludes the story in part with these words:

> "Certainly we will come to perceive that we are not the only ones to rule in space. Man will continue his ruthless wars right up to the day when he will discover a deadly weapon which will destroy him in turn.
> "This example could teach us a lesson ... but I doubt it" [187].

The section's last novel to be examined, *Ceux de demain* ("Those from Tomorrow," 139, 1959), repeats the message of the dangers of human aggressiveness. Bessière divides the story into three parts. The first, a short prologue, depicts Earth's political situation after World War II — the Cold War with Europe caught between the American and Soviet/Asian power blocs. Bessière does not waste time in criticizing human behavior:

> To be battered is second nature in man.... He batters himself without evidently reflecting on the consequences.... His battles are never organized for the ill being of his fellow. No. All are for his wealth and well being! You doubt this? What heresy! Has one ever spoken to you of Francis I and Charles V? Of Napoleon, of Caesar, of Louis XIV, and of Hitler? [15]

The second, Part One, describes what happens after the Third World War breaks out and destroys most of the Earth. The third, Part Two, relates what happens when an advanced alien civilization lands on Earth. The encounter reveals human nature remaining the same, the part of being human that still translates into the desire for power, to battle others, and to wage war. So even if it attains all the other goals necessary for progress, humanity will continue to remain unprepared for receiving new knowledge and power due to its warlike nature.

In the prologue there is also this description of the world situation before war broke out:

> This is ... what has passed, for one beautiful day terrestrial humanity found itself at a stage of evolution such that it became essential for humanity to sweep out all those absurd borders and to establish a single government, a single politics—an indivisible terran government. This is when the drama broke out. It was only by force that either of these two blocs could impose on the rest of the world its social program. The European bloc tried very much to intervene, but its role of neutrality had no effect, and a terrible push-button war was briskly engaged [92].

This is obviously not an original observation. Since the issue of Europe's reduced status after World War II was on most people's minds, this quotation ends up being just one of the many expressions of this topic from this period.

In the real world one finds that most wanted Europe to play a stronger role during the Fifties. Desiring European unity became a way of expressing this goal. American historians Richard L. Merritt and Donald J. Pachala produced a study on western European attitudes during the early part of the Cold War. One source they relied upon is a group of surveys take by the United States Information Agency (USIA). One showed that the largest number of respondents answered favorably to the question of western European unification while the smallest number answered negatively.

General Attitudes Towards Unification of Western Europe (in percentages)[37]

	Sept. 1952	Oct. 1954	Feb. 1955	Dec. 1955	Apr. 1956	Nov. 1956	May 1957
For	60	63	49	45	53	67	55
Against	16	9	15	12	14	7	9
Don't Know	24	28	36	43	33	26	36

So it seems that the majority of Europeans during the time of Bessière's novel would find much resonance from his depiction of an ineffectual Europe. This scenario will be repeated as other Anticipation writers also bring it up in various forms.

Up to now Bessière has presented various views on how progress in science and technology must be controlled and how humanity must be prepared to handle its new and powerful developments. In the preceding works, Bessière warns against the uneven development of human knowledge, especially when science and technology are involved; against the forced acceleration of the pace of progress, when historical experience and nature say otherwise; against the notion of relying on the few—no matter how intelligent they are; and against war and its causes. He also uses violence in several novels to resolve problems. Does Bessière provide a solution to the problem of progress in light of all of his warnings and his sometimes resorting to violent solutions? An answer is offered in the following section.

A Possible Solution?

Bessière did write a novel that can be seen — with a little stretch of the imagination — as providing an answer to all his warnings against the possibilities of human progress going awry. *Route du néant* ("Road to the Void," 81, 1956), features his often-used protagonist, reporter Sydney Gordon, and a scientist, Professor Delamare and his two inventions — a time machine and the "precipitron," which converts energy into matter (52–4). Delamare takes Gordon and his friends for a trip in his time machine into the future. The first important stop is the year 7000. They find a prosperous and advanced society with space travel. Eventually they meet Professor Brom 228 Z.I., a leader of the future society and through whom Gordon and company discover how humanity succeeds in the future:

> "The time of fratricidal struggles for us is located in ancient history. Man of the twentieth century had finally understood that peace is not obtained by war, but rather by common effort. Borders were little by little effaced from the globe. Certainly, I pass over silently the numerous concessions that each nation had to consent to arrive at a fair result. And it is only at the end of four hundred years of understanding that men have accepted finally to be no more than Terran citizens, to speak only a single language, and to place all resources of each country at the disposition of terrestrial unity" [68–9].

The appropriate principles for development consist of common effort, unity, and patience. Progress no longer requires a society based on competition and division. The idea of unity carries with it, in some aspects of life, the characteristic of sameness. As Brom 228 continues,

> "The laws are the same everywhere; the money employed is the same and is legal tender at the equator as well as at the pole. As to the degree of civilization, it is the same for each district" [69].

The sameness even applies to the religious sphere of life:

> "The religions of the Earth, after diverse tumultuous phases, have in their turn submitted to the metamorphoses of progress. Certainly, there existed still certain sects of particular beliefs, but on the whole a new religion — always based on divine adoration and conciliating the particular ideas of the greater part of beliefs — is formed" [65].

So it appears that most of the ills of the present have been solved in the future.

However, new problems emerge. The absence of war and sustained prosperity leads to overpopulation. Earth solves the problem by creating a colony on Venus. But eventually the colonists on Venus desire independence, calling to mind the situation between the American colonies and England. Violent protests are met with repression. During this visit the people of the year of 7000 confiscate Delamare's precipitron, which the people of the future consider as belonging to everyone.

Gordon and company then make one more stop, this time to the year 12000, where they find the Earth missing from its orbit. They discover that it has been transferred to an equivalent orbit around the star Cygnus due to the Earth's sun cooling down. But the results of this daring move were disastrous. So they go back to the year 11980 to prevent the catastrophe. During this episode they also discover that Delamare's confiscated precipitron had heavily influenced this future civilization. Gordon and company then go back to their present, reverse the actions of their visits in the future, and destroy both time machine and precipitron to prevent any future catastrophes.

The first part of this novel appears to offer a solution to humanity's ills, but the remainder of the novel reveals how new problems can still emerge. In many respects this novel follows the same pattern as "Those from Tomorrow." So will the future remain hopeless, regardless of what humanity does?

Perhaps one should revisit the first quoted passage from "Road into the Void." Here Bessière has humanity avoiding war and achieving world unity and peace by working together for four hundred years. There existed no grand plan, guiding formula, or single ideology that produced success; just four centuries of numerous concessions by individual nations. Even the unity of religion as described in the third quotation is partly a product of "conciliating the particular ideas of the greater part of beliefs" (65). So cooperation, compromise, and — above all — patience become the key words for success.

This last point makes sense when considering Bessière's work as a whole. Throughout his works he argues against immediate and extreme application of ideas and taking drastic actions. His very first series, featuring Professor Bénac and his travels throughout the solar system, contains many examples of how an overemphasis on science and technology stunts a society's progress. Bessière's stories inspired by Pascal essentially say the same thing: do not abandon one kind of thinking (intuitive) when exercising the other (mathematical). Even his discussion of spirituality can fit into this scheme. In addition to warning against a strict materialist approach to reality, Bessière's choice of Schuré's *The Great Initiates* also leads one to think that Bessière would prefer a spirituality based on commonalities shared by spiritual figures from all religions over one based on a single belief. Finally, Bessière's novels concerning the limits to progress in historical, natural, or behavioral (war and aggression) terms also urge the avoidance of extreme and immediate actions. By way of conclusion, one can argue that Bessière offers a moderate approach to progress.

So which person or ideology would Bessière select as an appropriate agent of progress? With his emphasis on science and technology and call for European unity, maybe Saint-Simon could fill the role. But Bessière would find fault with his utopian approaches to society. Pascal and Schuré act more as beacons to warn against a strictly scientific or materialistic view of reality. Furthermore, all three figures come from Bessière's past. Does a figure or idea from the Fifties exist that Bessière might like?

Perhaps a better suggestion would be Jean Monnet (1888–1979), the indefatigable French organizer who trumpeted the cause of a united Europe ever since he entered public life during World War I. Always an innovator, he saw little use for the concept of the nation-state, especially when it threatens the efficient distribution of food, resources, and products to people in desperate need. For him such divisions always mean the threat of war, and preparation for war weakens—not strengthens—societies striving for peace and prosperity.

From his *Memoirs*[38] emerge his ideas, which can easily be seen resonating in Bessière's novels as well. This first passage expresses Monnet's desire for cooperation.

> Sheer necessity has several times involved me in military matters, for which I have neither aptitude nor inclination. In 1914, and again between 1938 and 1945, I saw our freedom and our conception of humanity threatened by primeval lust for power, and in both cases I saw the finest men and the bravest efforts thwarted by disunity. Aggression not only divides people into two camps: it also divides the efforts in either camp, because fear encourages selfishness. In 1950, despite the bitter lessons of the past, self-protective reactions to the return of violence encouraged purely nationalistic attitudes which set us back several years and threatened the constructive efforts that had barely begun. I could not allow this new crisis to develop unchecked; but for the time being I was uncertain what to do. I had never believed that we should tackle the problem of Europe via defence. Although this would no doubt be one task for the future federation, it seemed to me by no means the most powerful or compelling motive for unity. But if circumstances were to accelerate or reverse the course of events—well, then, that would be another matter.[39]

Monnet sees this avoidance of defense as organizing principle as especially true.

> It is precisely because the countries of Western Europe play no part in the great decisions of the world ... that we face ... instability.... And, far from backing out, it's vital that we once more play an active part in settling these problems, because they concern the West as a whole....
>
> ... Men's minds are becoming focused on an object at once simple and dangerous—the cold war.
>
> All proposals and all actions are interpreted by public opinion as a contribution to the cold war.
>
> The cold war, whose essential objective is to make the opponent give way, is the first phase of real war.
>
> This prospect creates among leaders that rigidity of mind which is characteristic of the pursuit of a single object. The search for solutions to problems ceases. Such rigidity of aims and attitudes on both sides will lead inevitably to a confrontation: the logic of this way of looking at things is inescapable. And this confrontation will end in war.
>
> In effect we are at war already.[40]

Monnet's goals have always been simply put, his life-long ambition being:

> For me, that objective has always been the same: to persuade men to work together; to show them that beyond their differences of opinion, and despite whatever frontiers divide them, they have a common interest.[41]

Finally, along with his calls for adopting a cooperative mentality in international relations, he also urges France to modernize in order to take its place properly in the postwar order. In a conversation with Charles de Gaulle he points out,

> "You speak of greatness ... but today the French are small. There will only be greatness when the French are of a stature to warrant it ... they must modernize themselves—because at the moment they are not modern. They need more production and greater productivity. Materially, the country needs to be transformed." [42]

Looking at Monnet's ideas, it is not difficult to figure out what he is urging. First, France must modernize. And second, the nations of Europe must overcome their divisions and learn to work together for the common good.

Monnet spent practically his whole adult life bringing people together. When he visited the United States and Canada he immediately became impressed with how these continent-wide countries accomplished large-scale projects. During both World Wars he helped coordinate Allied efforts by making more efficient the delivery of supplies for the military. After the war he continued to create arrangements that led to increased cooperation among European countries.

The best example occurred when he, with U.S. approval and support, helped create a French-German agreement to share coal resources. Germany possessed the coal resources that the neighboring countries did not, so by placing Germany's coal-producing areas under international auspices all of western Europe had access to this primary source of industrial energy. This action enabled Europe's steel industries to revitalize quickly. France's recovery benefited greatly. This arrangement became known as the Monnet Plan, which became the basis for the European Coal and Steel Community (ECSC). In 1951 Monnet witnessed the ECSC officially established. This new supranational organization was known informally as the Schuman Plan, named after Robert Schuman (1886–1953), French prime minister and foreign minister who announced its formation in 1950 and saw through its successful implementation. Under this arrangement, Germany's industrial quotas (imposed under the Monnet Plan) were removed and its industry started to rebound as well. Though Monnet himself never held any elected office, he did administer high-profile projects through high-level appointments.[43]

Monnet continued to make similar arrangements, focusing on financial actions that would transcend national boundaries. He envisioned a European-wide federation as his ultimate goal, but he did not attempt to implement a top-down, centralized agency to accomplish his goal. He just wanted to form organizations which would handle the tasks at hand. When people saw how cooperation works much better than competition, more such actions would follow. Eventually European unity would become an attainable goal.

Through all these actions Monnet never revealed himself to be an ideologue. While pursuing the goals of modernization for France and a non-military based unity for Europe, he never promoted a singular philosophy on which he based his actions. Monnet's more practical approach puts him at odds with Saint-Simon by way of comparison. As shown, Saint-Simon projects society possessing a particular hierarchical social structure, a definite plan for education to enable modernization, and a final solution to the reorganization of Europe. He presents his vision as an all-encompassing one. Monnet does not. Though his goals of unification may be similar to Saint-Simon's, his methods are not. Monnet is more pragmatic than systematic. This last point constitutes the primary reason why Monnet is brought up in this discussion of Bessière's ideas about progress. Monnet wants to get things done, but not by using doctrinaire guidelines or implementing absolute measures—just gather people together and allow them to work. Let France modernize and Europe begin cooperation on tasks which benefit all involved parties. The unity depicted in Bessière's fictional worlds will eventually come true in reality.

Even taking into account Monnet's ideas, Bessière still does not view this solution as the final word on modernization and human progress. As he reveals in "Road to the Void," humanity will always have the potential to destroy itself regardless of its past successes. Taking into account "Those from Tomorrow" from the previous section of analysis, Bessière reminds the reader that human nature's aggressive tendencies will always stand in the way of permanent peaceful arrangements.

So what can be gathered from this section's analysis is that Bessière does not have a *final* solution to the problems of progress. But he does offer a *possible* solution for his present-day challenges—cooperate, avoid extreme actions, and be patient.

Conclusion

Given the diversity of Bessière's concerns displayed in his works, coming up with a conclusion about his works in the Fifties, which constitute a minority of his total output, can be problematic. However, the following statements can be drawn from his work.

Bessière supports the idea of progress, but not wholeheartedly and uncritically. Following the path of Saint-Simon, he urges that science and technology should be emphasized in modernization policies. However, as Saint-Simon also included in his plans, Bessière reminds the reader that all fields of human knowledge must be improved upon. Adhering to the admonitions of Pascal, he attempts to show to his readers that people must be aware of the non-rational, intuitive side of their mental make up. Taking up the ideas spawned by Schuré, Steiner, and Bergson, he asks people to go beyond the purely materialistic view of defining reality and measuring progress. Bessière also warns that there exist no short-cuts to progress; it cannot be rushed. Select groups of individuals with their superior intelligence or fantastic inventions do not guarantee success in accelerating the pace of social improvement. Quite the contrary: if humanity is not ready for their contributions, the risk for disaster increases. Finally, positive change comes at a steady pace. If associating Bessière's critical support for progress with Monnet's approach to European unity constitutes a proper analogy, then Bessière's view of progress must be left at an open end. There are no final solutions or ultimate goals, but there do exist alternatives that people can pursue to improve their lot.

So Bessière's view of progress is attached with many warnings and limits. Caution becomes his byword. Moderation must be exercised in times of great change.

Both Bessière's diversity of approaches to analyzing progress and his being a very prolific writer in Anticipation make an examination of his works the most varied one in this study. This observation does mean that the other writers are any less interesting or complex. Because Bessière maintains one of those new methods of communication — that ever-growing presence in twenty-first century life — the personal blog site, one can go into more detail in examining him and his ideas than with most of the other writers.

The other two writers presenting moderate responses to the idea of progress, M.A. Rayjean and Kemmel, do not share Bessière's breadth of approach, but they do express their concerns about progress through the use of certain themes.

M.A. Rayjean

Jean Lombard is the name behind M.A. Rayjean. Beyond this fact, not much else is known. Of the eleven writers examined in this study, the least is known about this one; not even his date of birth. Though there is a more well-known late-nineteenth century writer also named Jean Lombard (1854–91), no connection between the two exists. So most of what is known about Rayjean lies in his novels. Pierre Versins, writing Rayjean's entry in his encyclopedia, gives only one brief paragraph about him, and it merely presents a short plot summary of Rayjean's first novel.[44] Jean-Marc and Randy Lofficier in their guide to French science fiction give a survey of his novels, but nothing about his personal life.[45] Alain Douilly adds some perspective to Rayjean's standing by calling him "one of the pillars" of the Anticipation imprint.[46]

Rayjean wrote seventy-seven novels for Anticipation, twelve of them before the end of 1960. He also wrote seven novels for Fleuve Noir's Angoisse imprint. Of his Anticipation works, Rayjean wrote four separate series containing continuing characters for thirty two of his novels: (1) Professor Maubrey, scientist (two novels), (2) Joe Maubrey, television reporter (fourteen novels), (3) Jé Mox, space security agent (fourteen novels), and (4) an android and its mutation (two novels).[47] Douilly and the Lofficiers point out that Rayjean sometimes focused on biological themes and ended a number of novels on a pessimistic note, which is not characteristic of most Anticipation novels.[48]

The latter observation may be true if all of the Anticipation writers throughout the imprint's history are taken into account. But as this study attempts to show, most Anticipation novels appearing in Fifties express an anxiety about progress. For example, many of Bessière's novels—though protagonists may end up triumphant, or at least safe, at story's end—still leave the reader with warnings about either the limits to progress or the consequences of abusing new developments in science and technology. The novels of the other writers to be analyzed will also possess the same characteristic. What can be said about Rayjean in this regard is that he may be the most pessimistic of the moderate writers.

Unlike some of Bessière's works, Rayjean did not produce novels whose inspiration can be traced to major writer or philosopher. So his stories will be analyzed according to certain themes as they relate to the idea of progress. This analysis is to be divided into five categories. The first concerns humanity's warlike nature. The second deals with another aspect of human emotion, paranoia. The third focuses on the consequences of uncontrolled science and technology. The fourth explores the limits that may exist to progress. The fifth focuses on a particular new development, atomic energy, and its threat to humanity.

HUMAN AGGRESSION AS THREAT

Rayjean's first novel for the Anticipation imprint, *Attaque sub-terrestre* ("Subterranean Attack," 71, 1956), provides a warning about humanity's warlike behavior. Aliens arrive on Earth in 1938 and observe the human race from under the Earth's surface. The outbreak of World War II frightens them and reveals that humanity possesses weapons more powerful than previously thought—especially with the development of atomic weapons. The aliens attack from their underground base but are eventually defeated by novel's end. When the novel's two protagonists encounter the aliens' ruler, the ruler explains that the aliens' mission was originally peaceful. But the Second World War scared them into changing their minds and so they decided to invade Earth instead.

The story ends with the two protagonists disagreeing over whether or not the alien ruler was telling the truth about the aliens' original intentions and their subsequent change. One protagonist ponders over the ruler's claim and attempts to find any validity to his comments. The other remains skeptical, maintaining the alien ruler's explanation is all a lie. Regardless which position is right, the case against human bellicosity remains clear.

Invasion and Paranoia

In *Base spatiale 14* ("Space Base 14," 86, 1957), Rayjean tells the story of a first encounter with a deadly alien life form in outer space. Space Base 14 is a scientific research station on a planetoid between the orbits of Neptune and Pluto. The researchers come into contact with a mysterious spaceship containing alien beings in the form of microscopic cells. These cells can combine and take the shape of any life form, including human beings. However they must kill the life form before doing so. In the case of human beings, they also retain the complete memories of the people they kill. The humans understand that if the cells manage to land on Earth, they could take over the whole planet before anyone can do anything about them. The researchers blow up both the planetoid and their own ships to prevent the spread of the microscopic cells.

Those who are familiar with American science fiction novels and movies from the Fifties will see a slight resemblance between the plot of this novel and that of Jack Finney's (1911–95) novel *The Body Snatchers* (1955) and the film based on it, *Invasion of the Body Snatchers* (1956). Instead of microscopic cells, the book and film has seeds and plant pods that duplicate humans.[49] It is not known if Rayjean was familiar with either Finney's novel or the film, but it can be argued that Rayjean's novel belongs with these two works as examples of Fifties Cold War paranoia.[50] Rayjean does not discuss in ideological terms the ideas and actions of his characters. "Space Base 14" is the least philosophical of Rayjean's novels from this decade, but the implications of what would happen should the aliens succeed remain the same as those in Finney's novel and the film, in which the paranoia is more explicit. The use of plants as vessels of invasion and threats to human individuality also occurs in B.R. Bruss's *Le Grand Kirn* ("The Great Kirn," 112, 1958), which will be examined later in the Radicals chapter of the study.

Science Out of Control

Rayjean deals with this theme in three novels. Two of them form a series featuring Samuel Maubrey, a celebrated scientist, and John Formery, his assistant. The first novel, *Chocs en synthèse* ("Synthetic Shocks," 108, 1958), takes place in the year 1996 and details what happens when Maubrey attempts to create synthetic cells. Maubrey possesses a belief in science and his right to do whatever it takes to solve a problem or develop a new idea. Early in the novel he ruminates over the nature of scientific endeavor:

"Now did the first element of organic matter, the first protein, take form? I wonder if one day science will manage to take the great mystery by storm. The barrier of nature retreats without stopping. For example ... for a long time it was believed that the amoeba, the common protozoa of the single cell, was the lowest rung of living beings. Since then bacteria and finally viruses have been discovered ... it is easy to retrace in time and imagine all sorts of hypotheses. Proofs are necessary and here is why science very often finds itself helpless and progress takes meticulous steps. Proof is not acquired on a daily basis. It requires time and all essential elements" [14–5].

This passage becomes the starting point from which to analyze Maubrey, his attitude, and his actions. It turns out that though he may be aware of the methodology of science and its necessarily cautious approach, his attitude about his actions on this matter is quite the opposite. The scientific method may have its built-in controls, but the scientists themselves do not.

Maubrey's experiments involve the creation of synthetic cells. Unfortunately they are accidentally let out of his laboratory and begin to negate the chlorophyll in plants, causing the plants to turn white and produce explosive cells. Maubrey acknowledges that there may be limits to his research, but his main concern is more about himself and his reputation. As he puts it, "There are domains which scientists should not violate, life being one of them. But I will attempt the impossible to atone for my madness. Or else I will lose my name and fame" (47–8). The obsession with his standing in the public eye makes Maubrey more than just an overenthusiastic researcher who may comprehend reluctantly that research should have limits. He becomes a person so wrapped up in his own little world that all he can think about is his reputation while his experiment threatens all life on Earth. In this novel it is the scientists—and not science—who become the focus.

The novel's main criticisms of the scientists' actions come from a police commissioner, Rochman, who is assigned to Maubrey for the duration of the crisis. When the scientists are discussing plans to solve the menace they created, Rochman makes a sarcastic aside to his assistant, "One day ... science will send us all to a better world and at the way things are going.... And to say they call this progress!" (63).

A suggestion from a Canadian scientist, Clara Whitel, enables Maubrey and Formery to solve the problem of the destructive synthesized cells. However, the cells have mutated into a second generation; now they cause amnesia among people. The scientists go back to work and tackle the new problem. During this second crisis Rochman and his assistant have another discussion about science's practitioners. This time Rochman is more animated.

> [The assistant]: "Science has not had the last word.... It will fight.... The scientists of the entire world will apply themselves to the task...."
>
> [Rochma]: "Scientists? Oh! Oh! Fine joke.... Do you believe that they will be spared? Thus we go, everyone will go through it and the men of science will drop the ball before discovering the least vaccine! After that ... be at liberty to save your esteem and admiration for Maubrey. As for me, I have done my mourning for science.

This is very lovely. Progress ... on the condition that it forges ahead—for I fear that it has not reached its peak. Make way for the fall!" [135–6].

This antagonism between Rochman and the scientists remains to the end of the novel.

Fortunately for the world, Maubrey comes through with the proper antidote and Formery discovers the appropriate dosage before the synthetic cells can mutate into a possibly more dangerous third generation. But it appears that no one among the scientists seems the wiser for going through the two crises. Maubrey congratulates Formery and anticipates that he (Maubrey) will be placed among the foremost of scientists. Only when Formery reveals that his primary motivation was to save Clara Whitel, with whom he as fallen in love, does Maubrey acknowledge that there may exist other reasons beyond science. Formery, meanwhile, is not exactly a changed person at novel's end either. He celebrates their victory as the rehabilitation of Maubrey and his reputation. He even goes as far as to say that the Nobel Prize will not escape Maubrey's hands [187–8]. Formery's outlook certainly seems out of place considering the two crises their experiments created and Rochman's comments, but it falls well in line with Maubrey's.

Whitel, the only scientist who seems to question the blind attitudes of her male counterparts, steps up and tells Formery to stop talking about such matters and focus on something else — such as their happiness together. However she never does argue over the merits of Maubrey's or Formery's opinions or criticize the disasters that spawned from their experiments. She represents one of the very few female characters in the Anticipation imprint who is an actual colleague to her male counterparts and contributes substantially to the resolution of a crisis—though her chief role remains romantic interest for a male protagonist. The reader of this imprint would have to rely on another writer, B.R. Bruss (in the Radicals chapter), to find any serious discussions about women and their role in society.

It becomes apparent at this point that Rayjean is attempting to reveal the folly of those scientists who blindly go about their experiments and not take into account the possibility of danger emerging from their research. By alternating the statements of the scientists with those of Rochman, Rayjean presents a warning against overzealous scientists who are oblivious to their responsibilities.

The sequel, *L'Anneau des invincibles* ("The Ring of the Invincibles," 122, 1958), repeats the message, but more directly. Maubrey still displays no remorse over the damage his experiments have caused. Instead, he secretly takes his work, along with Formery and Whitel (now married) and other assistants, to Saturn to avoid causing further damage to Earth. (This move may come closest to Maubrey acknowledging that he may have done wrong.) He expands the scope of his work on synthetic cells to include the creation of synthetic people — symbiogenesis. At the novel's beginning he is straightforward about the role of the scientist in progress: "Science is made by trial and error. Experiments are proven to be necessary for the development of progress, of civilization. If the scientists do not take any risks, no scientific achievement will be possible" (12).

Even when he acknowledges that past science-based achievements have caused harm, his answer remains: more science. As he explains at length,

> "Our civilization ... is busy degrading our race.... The wastes from our factories pollute our atmosphere; our chemical products poison us slowly; and our machines take way all muscular effort that we will have so much need to conserve the plasticity of our body. We weaken ourselves slowly, psychologically. We wither ourselves and if progress in medicine does push back unceasingly the hour of death, it does not remain less true that we live for a longer time. But we are like the sick who only hold on to life because they take medicine.... We are only pale shadows of our ancestors, those cavemen with powerful torsos and muscles of iron. There will be time to shake us up, but since we cannot turn back, only science can offer a cure. A rejuvenation of our race is essential and this new generation — without hereditary defects — can only be born from symbiogenesis" [67–68].

As with his experiment in the previous novel, the one in the present story goes awry. The beings born from Maubrey's symbiogenesis turn out to be not only people with enhanced, superhuman abilities, but they also possess the ability of instant regeneration — meaning they cannot die of old age. Though Maubrey originally viewed them as humanity's helpers — especially if an atomic war occurred, in which case they were to help repopulate the Earth — the new beings begin to realize that they are superior to their creators. So they initiate plans to become humanity's masters. The new super-humans, who are doubles of the donors of the original cells used to produce them, take over the Saturn base and quickly kidnap twelve people from Earth to diversify their population source. Only a desperate plan, combined with the fortuitous arrival of a ship from Earth's space surveillance fleet, saves the day.

Towards the end of the novel a crew member from the space surveillance ship has a few words for Maubrey, "You violate the laws of nature, professor, and nature gets its revenge. A piece of advice: do not go too far. Time and again the Earth escapes from danger" (184). Both Maubrey and Formery respond and neither repent for their actions. As far as Formery is concerned, "Certainly the wrongs are from our part. We have abused the rights that our scientific position conferred upon us. However, I do not regret my journey" (184–5). Maubrey expresses no regrets either. Successes are always accompanied by new reversals in fortune, but that should not stop any experiment. He remains satisfied that his work has advanced the cause of science. He responds, "Meager satisfaction, you say? Perhaps. But I am content, as I was five years ago after the annihilation of the microorganisms, to proclaim very loudly that life by synthesis has entered into the possibilities of science" (186). To the end Maubrey sticks with his right to experiment as he sees fit.

As Maubrey realized the danger of his past experiment and moved to Saturn to protect Earth, he now admits that his super-humans have become too much of a threat to humanity. So based on his observation, the space surveillance ship destroys the Saturn base and all its super-humans with atomic weapons. But, as seen from the above statements, no regrets are given. The reader would imagine that if Rayjean were to add a third novel to this series, Maubrey and company would continue to perform dangerous experiments — and probably on a vaster scale — in the name of science and for the sake of saving humanity.

Rayjean's third novel under this theme, *La Folie verte* ("The Green Madness," 114, 1958), depicts a character who passes for the familiar science fiction cliché of "the mad scientist." A scientist invents a device that can transmit matter, even through outer space, by transforming matter into electron waves and back into matter. His assistant steals this invention and plans to use it to gain power for himself. As the novel progresses, the assistant becomes mad. He tries the invention on human beings, but the device ends up turning people into green-colored ghostly apparitions without any wills of their own. The authorities close in on the assistant at his fortress-hideout only to discover that he has killed himself to avoid capture. However, the ghostly humans who cannot be transformed back to their original selves still remain. The novel ends by identifying them as "poor martyrs, innocent victims of a lunatic of science" (187).

Note that all three novels criticize the practitioners of science, and not science itself. "The Green Madness" further develops this point by saying that not all scientists pose a threat. As one of the hostages in "The Green Madness" declares to the mad assistant, "Thank God all are not like you! ... Happily there exist understanding scientists who are aware of their responsibilities" (153). This last point, though obvious, should be kept in mind if Rayjean is to be considered as a moderate and not a total pessimist in his views on progress through science and technology. Taking neither of the extreme positions of blind faith nor automatic rejection, Rayjean warns against the pitfalls that can occur in science.

Natural Limits to Progress

While the previous section discusses limits to human action, this one examines the possibility of limits to progress itself. Rayjean wrote four novels that reveal how nature may have a role in humanity's progress. *Le Monde de éternité* ("The World of Eternity," 137, 1959) limits the boundaries of human development to the environs of Earth. Humanity's first interstellar expedition is a flight to the Alpha Centauri system where its crew discovers a planet teeming with life. The crew finds that certain cells on the planet possess the power of instant regeneration, granting literal immortality. After encountering another race of alien beings from another planet, the crew returns to Earth taking samples of the immortality cells with them. On the return journey the cells grow and metamorphose into an ever-expanding blob, threatening the very structure of the spaceship. The crew is rescued at the end of the novel with their spaceship being sent along with the cells into deep space. While the crew was leaving the planet Rayjean has them becoming nostalgic for their homes. In fact, he interrupts their thoughts and makes this statement in his voice:

> But is life to be imagined far from the planet of birth, from this Earth prematurely aged by the civilization of men? No!
> A Terran belongs to the Earth as a Frenchman belongs to France. By leaving his planet, the astronaut experiences the same as a native taken away from his country. Indestructible lines attach the Terran to this ball suspended in space [165–6]

Rayjean further emphasizes this point by having even the head explorer of the crew, the one with the most wanderlust of all, succumb to the yearning for home.

Ère cinquième ("Fifth Era," 142, 1959) places a geological time limit on human existence. After mysteriously being rendered unconscious, three people awake in the far future only to discover that the Earth's sea level has risen to a level almost as high as Mount Everest. The three eventually conclude that the cause for the change was the shifting of Earth's axis.[51] Earth's new dominant species is an intelligent race resembling creatures from the Mollusk family, called "mollutors" (14). A few of the mollutors befriend the three human survivors, but the majority of them view the survivors as a threat and a violent and bloody struggle between the survivors and mollutors ensues. The humans are not exactly innocent as one of them is quite bellicose and welcomes the fight for supremacy of the Earth. Before a final battle can be waged, a spaceship from Venus—where the last remnants of the human race live—lands on Earth and takes the three humans to Venus. One of the Venusian humans shares the same feelings as the bellicose survivor. Even though life for humans is no longer possible on Earth, this attachment to humanity's birth planet persists. It appears that Rayjean may be trying to recapitulate the nostalgic yearning for one's natural home that he made in "The World of Eternity," only this time in more dramatic terms. But a different interpretation can be drawn from "Fifth Era."

Some humans may rightly claim the Earth as their place of origin, but they can no longer call it their home. Three obvious reasons emerge. First of all, Earth is no longer suitable for normal human habitation. Second, other intelligent life forms have established themselves as Earth's dominant species and they are perfectly adapted to Earth's environment. And third, a battle to the death must be waged as both humans and mollutors distrust each other. The forces of nature have installed a new order of life on Earth. Humanity no longer belongs on Earth. The three survivors must settle and adapt to Venus as their fellow humans did. As nature can dictate where humanity should live ("The World of Eternity"), then it can also determine how long they can exist at any given place ("Fifth Era").

This theme of humanity permanently leaving the Earth is a common enough theme in science fiction. Fellow Anticipation writers Jimmy Guieu,

Peter Randa, Kurt Steiner, and Jean-Gaston Vandel also treat this plotline while reaching very different conclusions. These two novels have Rayjean describing the parameters of human existence in terms of space and time. To him, human existence is inherently a finite one. If the human race cannot go out and propagate among the stars or be allowed to survive permanently on Earth, then is humanity doomed to vanish without a trace and to have no consequence in the history of the cosmos? Rayjean answers this question in a two-novel sequence. In doing so, he offers a picture of humanity's ultimate destiny.

Soleils: Échelle zéro ("Suns: Scale Zero," 127, 1958) tells the story of Mentor, Master of Errêt, a super-scientific world where its Master — due to his or her intelligence — exercises the power to make decisions on any scientific or governmental policy, and his great experiment: the retrieving of a microscopic solar system (it was discovered that atoms are actually solar systems) from the micro universe. Mentor succeeds, but with disastrous consequences. The microsolar system will grow until it reaches its appropriate size for Mentor's universe. This irruption into Mentor's universe will end up destroying both Errêt's solar system and the retrieved solar system. An intelligent race is discovered to inhabit the micro-solar system. At novel's end both races agree that the only solution to take is a mass migration to another solar system in Mentor's universe.

The idea of atoms as miniature solar systems is a common theme in early twentieth-century science fiction. Based in part on Neils Bohr's early model of the atom where electrons are pictured orbiting the nucleus, like planets around a sun, science fiction writers found this model a convenient device for their stories. However, subsequent findings in physics which quickly led to establishing the field of quantum mechanics soon made Bohr's model obsolete (and with Bohr himself leading the way). But this did not stop many writers from using this model in their stories for some time.

In "Suns: Scale Zero," Rayjean continues to warn against the perils of trying to penetrate the limits placed by nature. If the first two novels in this section limit humanity's scope in space and time, one would expect that going into another universe would also be forbidden. Even if the scientists are good people as in the case of those on Errêt, that still does not allow them to trespass nature's limits. Rayjean makes this point clear. He starts by describing the nature of the people of Errêt:

> Their nature, a little indolent — except in the scientific domain — and their total absence of patriotism and conquering spirit do not inspire them to launch into risky expeditions. Glory and prowess do not interest them, and their lack of aggressiveness makes them one of the most pacifistic people of the galaxy [11].

Note how exemplary these people are in their behavior, especially when contrasted to Earth in Rayjean's earlier "Subterranean Attack." But their goodness is not enough to offset their aggressive behavior in scientific experimentation — as the destruction of their world proves. Nature imposes boundaries which no one must trespass. The fact that the same science which led to the destruction of Errêt also was responsible for saving the two races from extinction may lead a reader to think that Rayjean might be inconsistent, ambiguous, or even careless in his treatment of this theme. The sequel, which has science's aim going in the opposite direction, dispels any such notions.

Instead of experimenting with the micro universe, *L'Ultra Univers* ("The Ultra Universe," 161, 1960) deals with attempts to reach the larger, or macro, universe of which Errêt's universe is but a microscopic part. Four scientists, who first appeared in "Suns: Scale Zero," successfully transport themselves to the macro-universe only to discover that by doing so they have inadvertently started transforming themselves into beings of electronic force with no physical shape. At the end of the process each will have lost his or her individual consciousness and become pure energy particles. Miraculously, the four are transported back to Errêt's universe, but their transformation does not stop. The four fear that their new forms may cause a catastrophe on the scale of that in the previous novel, so a colleague releases them into space. Somehow all four manage stay together.

After aeons of hibernation in space, the group awakes on a very inhospitable planet, a fiery globe with an ocean that is apparently in its early stages of formation. After recalling how this planet was like Errêt, one of the four wonders why they could never resolve their problems dealing with basic particles of the macro universe. The same person then questions in general the possibility of science of ever discovering the true essence of life, "All of our science proved powerless to uncover the secret of the macromolecules. What miracle has animated these embryos of matter? One must believe that certain mysteries of nature remain impenetrable" (177). This expression can stand as Rayjean's final statement on placing limits to scientific endeavor. Towards the end of the novel the four discover that they are approaching the final stages of their transformation; their essences as electronic beings are finally breaking down into energy particles. The four remain aware of the situation and pass away with a sense of gallant resignation to their fate.

The novel concludes with a short section written in Rayjean's voice. Here he describes what happens to the particles that were once the four scientists from Errêt. Each of their particles still contains a spark of life from their former individual entities. The particles of the four with their sparks of life turn out to be the long sought-after basis for the miracle of animating matter, i.e., the beginning of life. Their particles settle into the deep of the planet's ocean and the planet turns out to be Earth.

The ending of "The Ultra Universe" parallels that of the memorable short story by American writer Alfred Bester, "Adam and No Eve" (1941).[52] In Bester's story the exhaust from an astronaut's experimental rocket's takeoff causes a chemical chain reaction in Earth's atmosphere and destroys all life. Upon returning to Earth he is badly injured and proceeds to struggle towards a seashore to die. His last thoughts are those of consolation as he realizes that when his body decomposes, his remains will interact with the sea and become the basis of a whole new cycle of life. And so the ending of "The Ultra Universe" resonates here as well. Humanity may have its limits to its existence, but nature will endure.

Science fiction stories employing this manner of explaining the origin of life on Earth are well-known. However most do not reach even the basic level of sophistication of Bester's and Rayjean's tales. More often than not these stories literally make their protagonists end up becoming the Biblical Adam and Eve. As a consequence, science fiction editors have strongly urged writers not to submit stories using this over-used plot device.[53] For the uninitiated, perhaps an accessible and typical example is an episode from the television show, *Twilight Zone*, "Probe 7 — Over and Out," (1963), written by the series's creator, Rod Serling, and starring Richard Basehart.[54]

Though "Suns: Scale Zero" and "The Ultra Universe" take place on an alien world, it is clear that Rayjean intended this message for his world. He even supplies an obvious hint towards the end of the second novel in the last conversation among the four:

"If I have a name to give to this planet, I would simply call it Earth...."
"Why?"
"All the worlds are earths in the sky. But this one appears so sterile that no other name can hardly be attributed it" [176].

If this last hint is not enough, the original planet of the four explorers, Errêt, is the backwards spelling for Terre, the French word for Earth. French critic I.B. Maslowski, in his review of the novel, brings this point up and uses an exclamation point to denote mocking discovery.[55]

BEWARE! ATOMIC ENERGY!

Perhaps the most recognizable image in science fiction during the 1950s is the mushroom cloud from the explosion of an atomic bomb. After Hiroshima and Nagasaki the world became aware of the immense scale of destruction that can emerge from experiments in the laboratory. A cultural side effect was the awareness that science fiction can be more than a literature of trivial and unrealistic escapist fiction.[56] The prospects, threats, and destruction caused by atomic bombs became a staple of science fiction stories and films, both serious and trivial, during the 1950s. Rayjean produced three novels specifically treating this theme, and in one he actually suggests an alternative to nuclear energy.

Le Péril des hommes ("The Peril of Men," 151, 1960) presents a grim future where atomic radiation has poisoned the reproductive cells in both men and women. Women cannot be reproduced and the ratio between men and women has become a frightening 10,000 to 1. Twenty years of experimentation in parthenogenesis (reproduction by development of unfertilized gametes) fail.

Only the intervention by an advanced alien race saves the day for humanity. The aliens are willing to help for a most implausible reason: they view human beings from Earth as the most perfect form of intelligent life found! The aliens' assistance succeeds and a baby girl is born, and she is given the name France.

Invasion "H" ("Invasion 'H,'" 167, 1960) tells the story of what happens to plants in Nevada when they are exposed to radiation created by nuclear experiments. The plants have mutated into mandragoras—or mandrakes (a Mediterranean herb with superstitious traditions attached to it, including its roots acquiring human attributes)—with the ability of locomotion and the capacity to produce microscopic spores. The spores are each in the shape of a homunculus and have the ability to penetrate human skin, intermingle with human cells, and transform people into mandrake-like creatures. Humanity becomes threatened with extinction and only a daring experiment using the spores as part of an inoculation procedure saves the day.

Both of the previous novels use human physiological contamination in fantastic manners to warn of the dangers of experimenting with atomic energy. Rayjean's other novel examining this theme, *Les Parias de l'atome* ("The Pariahs of the Atom," 104, 1957), not only deals with possible devastation, but it also suggests another energy source as a safer alternative. In a future not too distant, the Earth has been ravaged by a nuclear war between the United States and the Soviet Union. From among the irradiated ruins emerge a race of mutated humans who possess super-powered versions of the five senses and the ability to emit mental waves of ultra-sound. A fearful humanity has the mutants exiled to Venus. The vengeful mutants retaliate by incapacitating all of Earth's electrical sources through the neutralization of all nuclear reactions. Earth sends an envoy to Venus to negotiate for peace only to discover that the mutants themselves want peaceful relations as well.

Something positive does emerge from the mutants' attack on Earth. With their nuclear reactors neutralized, humanity had to search for alternative energy sources. As two scientists in the novel note,

> "Industry demands a new energy since we no longer ought to count on the atom. Oh! Certainly there is no lack of forms of energy. We can use the force of the sea, for example, or of geysers, or indeed that of volcanoes. The sun itself constitutes an inexhaustible force" [157].
>
> "Already in the last century [the twentieth] some technicians attacked this problem. France was one of the most advanced countries in research on solar energy. But since then, even if their works were continued, they did not become widespread and they hardly passed the experimental stage. The factories operating on solar energy could be counted on one's hand.... The atom, on the contrary, took a dominant position. The nuclear centers expanded at an ever increasing rhythm and we arrived at the point of using them exclusively ... electricity furnished by the atomic piles" [157].

Besides giving another warning about the dangers of nuclear energy, Rayjean also proposes alternatives. He hints at numerous resources which are readily available. Rayjean also reminds the reader that France's focus on nuclear power comes at the expense of neglecting its research into solar energy, which he supports above all at novel's end.

The mention of France's leadership in solar energy research ties this novel to specific contemporary events. France during this period was one of the few countries involved in any significant research into solar energy. By 1949, under French chemist Felix Trombe (1906–85), France had already established the Mont Louis Laboratories in the Eastern Pyrenees department of southern France for the study of practical solar furnaces. The research center was still expanding during the mid–Fifties when "Pariahs of the Atoms" was released. However, solar energy research took a back seat to the development of mainstream energies (coal, gas, oil, electricity). France did not research solar energy on a large scale until the Seventies, when environmental awareness became widespread and the energy crises involving the Mideast oil-producing nations brought home to many the fragility of France's energy lifelines.[57]

As to atomic energy during this time, France took an aggressive path towards nuclear self-sufficiency. The government established *Commissariat à l'énergie atomique* ("Center for Atomic Energy," CEA) in 1945 and built its first nuclear reactor in 1948. The Palewski Plan of 1955 greatly expanded the scope of research, including military projects. Because of the military applications of atomic power, the government kept research into this field away from the public eye.[58] The secrecy surrounding nuclear research enabled the production of France's atomic bomb to proceed unhampered. As historian Lawrence Scheinman points out, while the Fourth Republic's Parliament vacillated over France's atomic policies, a small group of people in the CEA, the military, and the government planned and organized a project to produce an atomic bomb. By the end of 1956, before the release of Rayjean's novel, the issue of France possessing atomic weapons was for all practical purposes already decided. The following year witnessed some public discussion about France's need for atomic weapons, but on 11 April 1958, Prime Minister Gaillard signed an order calling for the detonation of an atomic bomb by early 1960, which occurred on schedule.[59]

By way of comparison, after America's denotation of its first atomic bomb at Trinity in 1945, the Soviet Union had its first in 1949, Britain in 1952, and China in 1966. So in terms of chronology, France was at the forefront of the nuclear arms race. Despite its reduced postwar status as a great power, it still played an important part in the development of nuclear weapons during the early years of the Cold War. Rayjean could not have known about the secret weapons project when he was writing his novel, but the timing of the announcement of France's decision to make an atomic bomb could only make the message of his novel even more relevant and urgent.

Rayjean views atomic power and solar power as representing two alternate destinies for France in particular and humanity in general. Since policies on atomic research during the Fifties occupied a higher level of public awareness than those on solar research, Rayjean may have seen fit to give a fictional promotion for the latter while warning about the dangers of the former. Developing atomic power leads to contamination and devastating war. On the other hand, solar energy is literally as available as sunlight and possesses none of the threats inherent in atomic energy. The potential for aiding humanity becomes as limitless as the stars.

Rayjean does not stand alone with his negative sentiment about atomic energy, for many of his fellow citizens shared his worries. In fact, the release of "The Pariahs of the Atom" occurs when French pessimism over the promise of atomic energy riches a peak. As the following USIA poll reveals:

General Attitudes Towards Atomic Energy (in percentages)[60]

	Aug. 1955	Apr. 1956	May 1957	Nov. 1957	Oct. 1958
Boon to Humanity	38	31	17	23	35
Curse to Humanity	29	40	57	51	47
No Opinion/Response	33	29	26	26	18

Though by no means a unanimous rejection, a noticeable majority of the French population did fear the use of atomic energy at the time of Rayjean's novel's release.

Conclusion

Rayjean's environmental concerns anticipate some of the main themes of the ecological awareness that emerged around the world in the late Sixties and early Seventies: the warning that humanity is not the master of nature, the call for the development of alternative sources of energy, the demand for control or abolition of nuclear energy, and the notion that human existence is as fragile as any plant or animal in the face of pollution. It is not known if he participated in the early stages of environmental activism during the Fifties or Sixties. But this missing fact should not take anything away from the possibility that the ideas expressed in his novels, no matter how simply or fantastically presented, could have made people more aware of humanity's need to control properly the use of new science and technology. Rayjean's novels during the Fifties belong in the company of science fiction works whose concerns anticipate those of society at large by a few years.

Looking at Rayjean's Fifties novels as a whole, one can see that Rayjean is the Anticipation writer most concerned with nature, ecology, and humanity's impact on the environment. Whether dealing with cells, human biology, or with nuclear energy and its impact on nature, scientists must understand that nature has placed limits on human endeavor. Even the one novel not focusing with these issues, "Subterranean Attack," still imposes a limit — this time on human behavior. Humanity can flourish, but it must do so within a proper scope set down by nature. Finally, Rayjean should not be taken as a writer who is anti-science and technology. As "Pariahs of the Atoms" demonstrates, looking for alternatives to existing applications requires more (and different) science and technology, not less.

Kemmel

Kemmel is the pseudonym used by Jean Bommart (1894–1979), a writer known more for his police and espionage novels. He represents one of the few Anticipation writers who published a significant amount of their work both before and after World War II. Bommart used the Kemmel name only for his work in Anticipation. Bommart studied law and medicine before serving in World War I, during which he was injured at the Battle of Verdun. After earning a diploma from *Hautes Études Commerciales* in 1921, he worked in the news industry in various positions, including press attaché and representative of the *Agence Havas* in Belgrade, the capital of the new Kingdom of Serbs, Croats and Slovenes (renamed the Kingdom of Yugoslavia in 1929), journalist at the counter-revolutionary monarchist movement L'Action Française (though not a royalist himself), and finance editor. While suffering a serious illness for three years, Bommart turned to writing stories dealing with international espionage — his first novel being published in 1931. The most well-known of his espionage novels are those involving the character *Le Poisson chinois* ("The Chinese Fish"), a spy whose adventures he chronicled in several novels published between 1934 and 1974. The best known of them is *Le Poisson chinois a tué Hitler* ("The Chinese Fish Killed Hitler," 1972). In all he produced forty novels dealing with espionage and police stories as well as two plays. He also wrote and edited for several films.[61]

Bommart wrote two novels for Anticipation under the Kemmel name. Only one, *Je reviens de...* ("I Return From...," 84, 1957), appeared during the Fifties. Because of his brief appearance in this imprint, especially when compared to the prolificness of the other Anticipation writers of the time, Alain Douilly refers to Bommart as a "shooting star."[62]

"I Return From..." warns against nuclear weapons and argues for a balanced distribution of technical and non-technical developments among the general public. Aliens from Mars take a group of people and animals from Earth back to Mars. The Martians are shaped like octopuses, which calls to mind their similarity with H.G. Wells's Martians from *The War of the Worlds* (1898).[63] The Earth people observe the Martians possessing a utopian society where little work is required for its maintenance. During their tour of Mars, the Earth party observes Mars's canals to be drying up. The Martian hosts reveal that in less than a hundred years Mars will exhaust her resources and will starve to death. The Earth people and Martians learn more about each other, but with each party remaining skeptical of the other's motives. The Earth party worries about how Mars plans to deal with her upcoming scarcities. The Martians become concerned over Earth's recent development of atomic bombs.

From Mars the Martians take the Earth people to Venus, where it turns out that the second planet from the sun is an exact duplicate of the Earth, complete with identical histories—except for one horrifying difference: the Venusian humans had destroyed themselves three years earlier in an atomic war. The Earth people visit a duplicate Paris and experience in full force the results of total destruction. The Martians express their skepticism over Earth's ability to avoid a similar nuclear holocaust, which is why they made the trip to Venus and showed the Earth party the results of self-annihilation.

Unlike Wells's Martians (who attack the Earth), Bommart's Martians want to help Earth. Both groups decide that the Earth people must return home and warn their fellow humans about the threat of atomic war. Before traveling back to Earth, Henri Boulanger, a member of the Earth party, a translator for the United Nations, and from whose first-person viewpoint the novel is told, and a Martian participate in a discussion that encapsulates the essential message of the novel.

> [Boulanger]: "To give more weight to my mission, I would like to bring with me some spools of tapes summarizing the progress obtained by the Martian scientists in the field of cosmic energy. That would allow us a considerable leap in the field of industrial technology."
> [Martian]: "Yes ... But the Great Council estimates that the present disequilibrium among the Terrans is due precisely to a too great an advance in technology in relation to the general culture of the masses. A very dangerous discrepancy! If intellectual and moral civilization does not penetrate these masses as fast as technical civilization, the latter is fatally employed—carelessly or knowingly—to the destruction of the former.... Do you want a rough analogy? It is absurd to give an infant a knife to play with, because he is incapable of imagining the consequences of a stab given to others or to his own self. Thus, until proof of a little amount of good sense from the Terrans, we will not communicate to them any secret of a scientific nature" [179–80].

The Martians return Boulanger and company to Earth and Boulanger attempts to contact the French president. Instead of being taken seriously, Boulanger is arrested and sent to a psychiatric hospital. At novel's end Boulanger mysteriously disappears from his captivity, being secretly rescued by the Martians

Note that Boulanger does not go to the United Nations (where he works) or to the leaders of either the United States or the Soviet Union. Instead, he wants to talk with the president of France. Bommart may have had his own country in mind when he issues his warnings against both the development atomic weapons and the uneven development of French society.

Bommart re-emphasizes ideas brought up by both Bessière and Rayjean.

Like Bessière, Bommart expresses his concern that one branch of human endeavor could develop to the detriment of others. The dissemination of advanced technology into society should be matched by a similar spread of intellectual and moral advancement. Like Rayjean, Bommart presents the deadly consequences facing France if its government persists in its desire to produce both atomic energy and atomic weapons.

The concern over who gets to make the decisions, especially those dealing with science and technology, is left to other Anticipation writers to examine. Guieu, Wul, Randa, Vandel, and Bruss deal with this issue, and they all come up with different solutions.

Chapter Summary

Despite the numerous warnings and the dire possibilities presented by these three writers, they still give humanity a chance to survive and prosper. When compared with the other Anticipation writers examined in the study, Bessière, Rayjean, and Bommart are to be considered moderates for their responses to the idea of progress. Though they base much of their criticisms and suggestions on noted philosophers and thinkers from the past (Bessière) or through the use of common science-fictional themes (all three), none of them base their conclusions on any single identifiable ideology or approach as the writers do in the Extremist, Conservative, and Radical chapters of this study.

Progress cannot be rushed, slowed, or stopped. It cannot rely on a single idea or technology. It requires patience and caution. For these three writers, progress must advance one step at a time.

Chapter Three

The Extremist

As Bessière, Rayjean, and Bommart support the idea of progress but caution against extreme and absolute approaches or warn against certain applications and policies, the one writer covered in this chapter, Jimmy Guieu, displays no such misgivings about the prospects of progress. For Guieu, there is never enough progress in the scientific and technological realms. The moderate writers may have rescued their characters from dangerous situations, but they do so to emphasize the need for moderate responses and cautious attitudes towards new knowledge and power. Guieu, on the other hand, creates threatening scenarios to show both his pessimism about present-day humanity's ability to save itself and his optimism that science and technology will carry the day. To put it briefly, the humans of today will always need help, but science will overcome all problems—provided humanity takes the necessary steps, no matter how extreme. Despite the peculiar interests Guieu maintained throughout his life, his expressions about the role of science in progress during the Fifties never waver from this stand.

Jimmy Guieu

The year 1947 witnessed the start of the world-wide flying saucer craze. Millions claimed to have seen mysterious circular objects flying in the sky. Even though all authorities refuted these claims, many remained dedicated to the task of proving that these strange flying crafts, or Unidentified Flying Objects (UFOs), were real and of extra-terrestrial origin. Among them existed a small number of writers who employed their craft in the service of convincing the public about the reality of UFOs. In France a major proponent was Jimmy Guieu (1926–2000).

Born Henri-René Guieu, Jimmy Guieu became his most popular pseudonym. As a teenager during World War II he joined the French Resistance in west central France near the Atlantic coast (Vendée department). Afterwards, he dedicated practically all of his adult life to the proof of UFOs (in French, the acronym is OVNI, *Objet Volant Non-Identifié*, "Flying Object Not Identified") and to the education of the public about them. He wrote non-fiction supporting his cause, including two books, *Les Soucoupes volantes viennent d'un autre monde* (1954, "Flying Saucers Come from Another World") and *Black-Out sur les soucoupes volantes* (1956, "Black Out on Flying Saucers"). Also during the Fifties he created a journal, *Ouranos*, dedicated to the discussion of UFOs. Guieu's other interests—which also appear in his fiction—include the occult and parapsychology, or paranormal events. Guieu also carried his message to other venues and media. He attended various conferences and meetings as a featured speaker. Guieu reported for Radio Monte-Carlo where he led the broadcast, *As-tu vu les soucoupes?* ("Have You Seen Saucers?"). For television he worked at FR3-Marseilles on the program, *Les Carrefours de l'étrange* ("Crossroads of the Strange"). Guieu also created and directed fourteen episodes for *Les Portes du Futur* ("Gateways to the Future"), some of which are accessible on the Internet.[1] Though science fiction comprised the vast majority of his output of fiction, Guieu did publish in other popular genres and used different pseudonyms for each one: Jimmy Quint for spy thrillers, Claude Rostaing for police stories, and Dominique Verseau for erotica.[2]

Guieu made his mark in French popular literature through his science fiction. He turned out to be the most commercially successful writer among the early Anticipation authors and even became a brand name in the publishing field. In 1979, the publisher Plon launched a separate imprint and labeled it Jimmy Guieu. This line republished his earlier stories, many of which Guieu revised. Soon Guieu supervised other writers who produced stories which took place in the fictional worlds of Guieu's most popular novels. Jimmy Guieu released 152 titles and lasted until 2003. After Plon, three other publishers, Vaugirard, Vauvenargues, and Presses de la Cité took turns producing the imprint. In 1988 Fleuve Noir released its imprint Jimmy Guieu Presente les Maîtres Français de la Science-Fiction ("Jimmy Guieu Presents the French Masters of Science Fiction"), consisting of reprints of earlier Anticipation novels (by all authors and not just Guieu) that the publisher viewed as worthy of republication. It lasted until 1991, having published thirty-eight titles.[3]

Jean-Marc and Randy Lofficier attempt to explain the high level of popularity that no other science fiction writer of the period ever attained, for Guieu's sales could not be explained only by his prolific output. According to them,

> Jimmy Guieu has become a trademarked phenomenon, unique in the annals of science fiction, and certainly without equivalent in England or America. His success is attributed to his clever mix of occult facts, mild eroticism, ultra-conservatism and somewhat bigoted politics, and a forceful if simple storytelling style successfully imitated by his successors.[4]

In terms of Guieu's relationship to the science fiction field, they bring up an interesting observation, "Most regular Guieu readers are drawn from the general public rather than the science fiction audience — as in the case with *The X-Files*— and are not science fiction fans but only Jimmy Guieu fans."[5]

Perhaps the American equivalent to Guieu in terms of becoming a brand name or trademark is Isaac Asimov, with a genre science fiction magazine named after him, *Isaac Asimov's Science Fiction Magazine* (1977–present, title shortened to *Asimov's Science Fiction* in 1992). Of course, Asimov's accomplishments turned out to be far more substantial and influential. At the time of his death, he had achieved a national prominence in America not only for his canonical science fiction stories but also for his non-fiction books, which covered an encyclopedic range of subject matter and numbered over 400 — making him also one of the most prolific authors ever. He will go down in history as probably the greatest popularizer of science in the last half of the twentieth century.

Despite Guieu's output and popularity, his standing in the science fiction field appears to be mixed and uneven. The Lofficiers have described his audience as not being true science fiction fans but just Jimmy Guieu fans. Alain Douilly identifies him as "one of the monuments of Collection Anticipation."[6] Pierre Versins, in his *Encyclopédie*, devotes only a short paragraph to him, saying "All of his early works present a certain interest, but the injection of a high dose of motley opinions in the following works has rendered this author not easy to assimilate for a rational mind."[7] Meanwhile, Clute and Nicholls's *Encyclopedia of Science Fiction* has no entry at all. Regardless of the dubiousness of his ideas on UFOs, the occult, or parapsychology, Guieu, as Douilly puts it, "was an important person in the world of the imaginary who cannot be ignored."[8]

Guieu emerges as the second French writer to be published in Anticipation. A most prolific writer for this imprint, he wrote eighty-three novels from 1951 to 1984, of which thirty-three appeared by the end of 1960. Sixty-nine of his novels make up ten different series containing continuing characters, the most prominent being: Jean Kariven, anthropologist (twelve novels), Jerry Barclay (five novels), Blade and Baker, adventurers (sixteen novels), and Gilles Novak (twenty-three novels).[9]

This examination of Guieu's works will be divided into six sections. The first, composing Guieu's first two novels for Anticipation, introduces his optimistic view of science. The next four sections have Guieu employing readily identifiable themes from the science fiction genre. All through these sections Guieu presents his pessimism over present-day humanity's ability to handle the potential of advanced science and technology. These themes include interactions with aliens in the present and future (fourteen novels), interactions with aliens in the past (five novels), lost continents and races (three novels), and stories involving only humans (three novels). It should not surprise anyone that the majority of his novels deal with aliens and UFOs. The sixth and final section (six novels) involves only humans and what can be identified as Guieu's solution to his pessimistic views of present-day humanity.

Setting the Stage

If one were to read Guieu's first two novels written for Anticipation and nothing else by him, one would get the impression that he is merely a writer of science fiction adventure stories with an optimistic view of science. *Le Pionnier de l'atome* ("The Pioneer of the Atom," 5, 1952) and *Au-delà de l'infini* ("Beyond Infinity," 8, 1952) take the reader to the opposite ends of the scale when it comes to exploring the universe. The former explores the micro-universe in the atom (much like M.A. Rayjean's *Soleils: Échelle zéro*) while the latter goes beyond our universe to discover the true shape of the cosmos (a truly startling revelation). Alien civilizations and advanced technologies are encountered and fantastic death-defying adventures involving super-scientific gadgetry are described. These characteristics permeate through all of his novels. However, in "The Pioneer of the Atom," Guieu also establishes his attitude towards science that resonates through his works during the Fifties.

"The Pioneer of the Atom" opens with the discovery that subatomic particles are actually components of miniature universes. A character who possesses the sixth sense of telepathy, a Hindu occultist, teleports his spirit into a microcosm where there exists a world containing an advanced scientific society, called Nixomie. Eventually the novel's protagonists realize that this micro-universe is expanding, thus threatening Earth's universe. They destroy the micro-universe and return home.

During his visit to Nixomie the occultist discovers the philosophy of the advanced civilization, which was explained by him in this manner:

> Pantheists, they considered ... a God ponderable and imponderable, at once body and soul of the cosmos. Then they kept in bounds their beliefs. They did not waste their time in vain religious speculations or in religious bigotries. Their line of behavior is summed up thusly: good destroying evil, science chasing gullible superstition. From this fact, the narrow-minded "pious tom-foolery" of religious bigots, to whom one instilled the fiddle-faddle, preached by the old Nixomien Church, disappeared. Nixomie ... had conserved only this vague pantheistic belief ... preferring to be stooped over scientific problems rather than over conceptions as nebulous as they are irrational [114].

Two observations emerge from this statement.

First, even though Guieu places science at the center of the society, he still makes it a point to find room for religion. He may have placed religion in the background so it does not interfere with science, but he does not get rid of religion. Loosely speaking, his fictional world's keeping of both science and religion actually falls within one of the main traditions the Enlightenment: for science and religion, each occupies its proper place in the realm of human ideas. They are not to be viewed as antagonists to each other but as belonging on the same side against ignorance and false ideas. As German philosopher Ernst Cassirer (1874–1945) puts it, knowledge and faith must "unite to perform ... and on the basis of this union a treaty between knowledge and faith and a determination of their mutual boundaries can be accomplished."[10]

The second observation concerns Guieu's choice of religion, pantheism. One might be tempted to say that he was influenced by the ideas of the famed philosopher, Benedict de Spinoza (1632–77),[11] but no proof exists that would link the two together. So even if Guieu was not directly inspired by Spinoza, this faint resemblance to Spinoza's thinking at least reflects that Guieu's thinking about God is not based on traditional religious approaches, but on more philosophical ones (and expedient ones by Guieu at that).

Whether or not Guieu was inspired by the above two intellectual traditions, his choice of expressing the relationship between science and religion reveals his determination to place science at the center of his world. For Guieu, questions on the relationship between science and religion become quickly settled. If some issue or concept cannot be understood in scientific terms, it is not worth the effort — for it is beyond human understanding. Leave that problem to philosophy or religion.

But this interpretation of Guieu's becomes problematic when considering his interests and non-fiction work. How can one proclaim science as the key to understanding and progress while also believing in UFOs, lost continents, the occult, and the paranormal? However, if one were to suspend one's disbelief and accept Guieu's odd ideas as a given (or just dismiss them out of hand and move on), then one can focus on Guieu's support for increased efforts in science and better technology. Doing so will make it easier to see that not only does Guieu support science, but that he also does so in an almost absolute manner, more so than any other writer in the Anticipation imprint. His final solution for the human race will put an exclamation point to his ideas.

As mentioned, Guieu's optimism about science and technology is accompanied by his pessimism over humanity's ability to handle its affairs. The remaining five sections examining Guieu's novels reflect this observation over and over. His extreme applications of science to solve problems only serve to re-emphasize his desperate view of humanity. No other Anticipation writer shares this particular combination of optimism and desperation. This is why Guieu alone occupies this chapter.

THE ALIENS HAVE LANDED!

Considering Guieu's long and persistent efforts in proving the existence of UFOs, it should not be a surprise that the majority of his novels focus on UFOs and humanity's interactions with aliens possessing advanced levels of science and technology. The first two questions that come to most people's minds when talking about the UFO-sighting phenomenon are how and why did the claims of UFOs — almost always in the form of flying saucers — become a worldwide occurrence. Since the sightings started in the late Forties and continued into the Fifties, many people have attempted to come up with an explanation. Perhaps the most famous of them was the famed Swiss psychologist and philosopher, Carl Gustav Jung (1875–1961). When examined in light of his ideas, the study of Guieu's stories becomes a perfect case study.

Looking at this study's second and third sections on Guieu, two aspects can be gleaned from his novels which call to mind Jung's ideas. The first deals with his use of old myths (lost races) and new ones (UFOs) to explain in part humanity's present dilemmas. The second involves Guieu's use of UFOs as props to support both his arguments for more development in science and his portrayals of humanity as incompetent and needing to be saved by a superior power—in this case, aliens. If this observation is correct, then it mirrors what Jung concludes in *Ein moderner Mythus; von Dingen, die am Himmel gesehen warden* (1958, translated into English as *Flying Saucers: A Modern Myth of Things Seen in the Skies*).[12] He states quite clearly that flying saucers compose part of a modern myth:

> As one can see from all this, the observation and interpretation of Ufos [*sic*] has already led to the formation of a regular legend. Quite apart from the thousands of newspaper reports and articles there is now a whole literature on the subject, some of it humbug, some of it serious. The Ufos themselves, however, do not appear impressed; as the latest observations show, they continue their way undeterred. Be that as it may, one thing is certain: they have become a *living myth*. We have here a golden opportunity to see how a legend is formed, and how in a difficult and dark time for humanity a miraculous tale grows up of an attempted intervention by extra-terrestrial "heavenly bodies"—and this at the very time when human fantasy is seriously considering the possibility of space travel and of visiting or even invading other planets.[13]

Jung further expounds:

> Man's living space is, in fact, continually shrinking and for many races the optimum has long been exceeded. The danger of catastrophe grows in proportion as the expanding populations impinge on one another. Congestion creates fear, which looks for help from extra-terrestrial sources since it cannot be found on earth.
> Hence there appear "signs in the heavens," superior beings in the kind of space ships devised by our technological fantasy.[14]

Then he identifies the reasons for the dominant shape of UFOs, the flying saucer:

> We shall turn our attention to the psychic aspect of the phenomenon.... What as a rule is seen is a body of *round* shape, disk-like or spherical, glowing or shining fierily in different colours, or, more seldom, a cigar-shaped or cylindrical figure of various sizes....
> ...Anyone with the requisite historical and psychological knowledge knows that circular symbols have played an important role in every age; in our own sphere of culture, for instance, they were not only soul symbols but "God-images." There is an old saying that "God is a circle whose centre is everywhere and the circumference nowhere." God in his omniscience, omnipotence, and omnipresence is a totality symbol *par excellence*, something round, complete, and perfect. Epiphanies of this

sort are, in the tradition, often associated with fire and light. On the antique level, therefore, the Ufos could easily be conceived as "gods." They are impressive manifestation of totality whose simple, round form portrays the archetype of the self, which as we know from experience plays the chief role in uniting apparently irreconcilable opposites and is therefore best suited to compensate the split-mindedness of our age. It has a particularly important role to play among the other archetypes in that it is primarily the regulator and orderer of chaotic states, giving the personality the greatest possible unity and wholeness. It creates the image of the divine-human personality....[15]

From these passages one can see that the needs and reactions which Jung associates with people who believe in UFOs are indeed present in Guieu's novels. Guieu clearly shows in his novels his lack of confidence in humanity since aliens from another planet are constantly brought in to straighten out of the human race. If Jung's observations on this matter stand the test of time, then Guieu and his novels will represent an archetypical, as opposed to idiosyncratic, response to the world around him.

The presentation of Jung's explanations about the UFO phenomenon should not be taken as support for his ideas. Rather, Jung's observations are used merely as an attempt to bring about a better understanding of Guieu's beliefs in UFOs and their widespread acceptance by his audience. Dismissing out of hand Guieu's predilections for long disproven ideas does not release the researcher from the obligation of trying to make sense out of people like Guieu and his supporters. The eccentric behavior of a segment of the population can still reveal concerns—though displayed in odd manners—that are shared by society at large.

Of Guieu's fourteen novels in this section, several stand out. The first three comprise a series that deals with an advanced alien race saving humanity from outside threats. The first, *L'Invasion de la terre* ("The Invasion of Earth," 13, 1952), opens with the Earth attacked by Mars. A renegade Martian tells an Earth scientist to travel to the Andromeda Galaxy and seek the help of an advanced race. The scientist does so and locates the planet Glamora, where he encounters its humanoid race, the Bétlyoriens. The Bétlyoriens have attained a utopian society. There exist no hierarchies, no divisions, and no needs. Everyone contributes to the maintenance of society by working only two hours a day and three days a week, and all are free to do whatever they want during their leisure hours. Men and women live as equals and robots do much of the work to maintain society. Surprised and awed by this society, the scientist hears one of the aliens explain the basic sociological principle that governs this civilization: "A freely consented discipline, based on respect of the human person, permits the surprising fraternity that intrigues you" (143). The Bétlyoriens accompany the scientist back to Earth. They barely save Earth from total destruction as the Martians have been wreaking havoc while the scientist has been away. Afterwards, the Bétlyoriens offer not only to help with Earth's recovery, but they also promise to guide humanity's society so it can attain the same level as their own civilization.

The two sequels, *Hantise sur le Monde* ("Obsession over the World," 18, 1953) and *L'Univers vivant* ("The Living Universe," 22, 1953) carry on with the Bétlyoriens continuing to save Earth from danger and constantly guiding human society. By the time of "The Living Universe," Earth has attained a world government. Guieu readily shows through this set of novels humanity as desperately in need of outside help.

He reinforces this depiction with a four-novel series, starting with *L'Homme de l'espace* ("The Man of Space," 45, 1954), which won the first *Grand Prix du Roman de Science Fiction* ("Grand Prize for Science Fiction Novel") for 1954.[16] This series features an alliance between advanced aliens, the Polariens (named after the star, Polaris), and humanity. Together the humans and the Polariens encounter other alien races with the Polariens saving humanity when it is attacked. Early in "The Man of Space," the Polariens point out that Earth's problem with progress involves the uneven development of human activities. As one Polarien puts it, "Moral progress is not equal with technical progress, which always precedes moral progress; these asymmetric progressions — separated by a gulf of mistakes and groping — are elsewhere the cause of slow human development" (25).

The three other novels in this series, *Opération Aphrodite* ("Operation Aphrodite," 47, 1955), *Commandos de l'espace* ("Commandos of Space," 51, 1955), and *Nos ancêtres de l'avenir* ("Our Ancestors from the Future," 62, 1956) continue the plot line of Polariens as Earth's guardians. "Our Ancestors from the Future" brings up the observation of uneven human progress once again:

> The constant asymmetry which always exist on your globe between technical evolution and moral and spiritual evolution will disappear, leading man to a proper level where he can comprehend the machine and will reconcile it with mental concepts that were up to now beyond him [187].

The above two observations call to mind the type of warnings that Bessière presented in his novels. But as will be seen at the end of this examination, Guieu's solution will be quite different from Bessiére's.

Guieu wrote a novel, *Univers parallèles* ("Parallel Universes," 58, 1955), in which the characters from both series of novels (those starting with "The Invasion of Earth" and "The Man of Space," each series taking place in a separate universe) interact with each other to solve a murder mystery. Without being complex, the plot is complicated with duplicates sets of characters from each of the parallel universes interacting with each other. No particular discussions of the idea of progress take place, but the use of advanced devices to travel from one universe to another and the ramifications of their use are discussed.

The other six novels in this section continue to repeat Guieu's message of human hopelessness. *L'Agonie du verre* ("The Death Throes of Glass," 54, 1955) presents a variation on this theme. Intelligent aliens in the form of silicon-based spores attack Earth and cause all glass objects to be pulverized. The United States and Soviet Union, blaming each other at first, threaten war until French astronomers discover the aliens. Soon the superpowers join forces and they defeat the enemy. So even when the aliens lose they help humanity by inspiring people to set aside their differences and unite against a common foe. *Expédition cosmique* ("Cosmic Expedition," 134, 1959) and *Les Cristaux de Capella* ("The Crystals of Capella," 140, 1959) form a two-part series where an Earth expedition travels to a planet forty-two light years away and discovers it inhabited by crystal beings. In "Cosmic Expedition" these beings turn out to be the guardians of the universe who act as arbiters of races, including Earth's humans, and judge the various races according to their adherence to the "Grand Cosmic Law" (186). In "The Crystals of Capella" the crystal beings use fear of attack to inspire Earth to unite, much like the aliens did in "The Death Throes of Glass." Both *Piège dans l'espace* ("Trap in Space," 145, 1959) and *Chasseurs d'hommes* ("Hunters of Men," 149, 1960) have Earth threatened by an alien race only to be saved and protected by another one. *Expérimental X-35* ("Experiment X-35," 163, 1960) tells the story of how a shape-shifting alien race rejects any interaction with the Earth due to the latter's hostile actions.

The fourteen novels in this section leave no doubt as to the helplessness of humanity to govern their own future. Guieu's aliens either reject humans as unfit or step in and save humanity from itself and then try to guide its future. The next section repeats this theme, but this time it turns out that the aliens have already been influencing events on Earth for a quite a while.

THE ALIENS HAVE ALREADY LANDED!

Guieu wrote five novels in what can be considered a special category of his major theme of alien interactions with humanity. This group depicts aliens as already having been in contact with humans on Earth. In doing so Guieu selects various lost races from famous myths of the past. He wrote three other novels about lost races but without any interaction with aliens. They will be covered in the next section. The existence of lost races represent a much-used theme in science fiction and of all the Anticipation writers, Guieu used it the most.[17]

Perhaps Guieu's best example of this topic can be found in his two-novel series, *Nous les martiens* ("We the Martians," 31, 1954) and *Le Monde oublié* ("The Forgotten World," 41, 1954). In "We the Martians" the lost continent of Atlantis not only exists, but it was really founded by Martians. Guieu explains Atlantis's origin by ascribing the origin of humanity's different races to visits to Earth by different alien races. The Martians comprise the ancestors of the white and red (i.e., the Native American) races, with the former becoming the masters because they were the majority of the population. From Venus come the ancestors of the yellow and black races, with the yellow race portrayed as overbearing tyrants. Both groups of races engaged in a terrifying war in the distant past and, as a result, lost all of their advanced technology. So all races returned to nature and struggled to re-establish civilization. Present-day Earth is the outcome of this rebuilding. "The Forgotten World" tells the story of a remnant of the Atlantean civilization which had escaped the racial wars and settled in Antarctica.

The insensitive racial stereotypes and explanations justifying the dominance and inherent goodness of the white race belong to a long literary tradition that needs no repeating here. Science fiction possesses its share of such literature.[18] Such portrayals by Guieu give support to the Lofficiers' above cited quotation describing his stories as containing "somewhat bigoted politics."[19]

Given this particular use of alien races by Guieu, one needs to look at the ideas of American journalist and writer, Charles Fort (1874–1932). Fort spent his life attempting to explain inexplicable phenomena, and he did so by abandoning conventional methods of research and reasoning. Fort attempted to cover as much of the world and its past as possible. Among his many ideas was a notion which proved influential to a number of science fiction writers: that the human race may be property of a superior race.[20] He wrote four books on this matter, *The Book of the Damned* (1919), *New Lands* (1923), *Lo!* (1931), and *Wild Talents* (1932). Fort's supporters formed a Fortean Society to continue his work after his death.[21] Perhaps the most notable exponent of Fortean ideas in science fiction is British writer, Eric Frank Russell (1905–78), who wrote primarily for American genre magazines. His two most popular novels, *Sinister Barrier* (magazine version, 1939; book version, 1942) and *Dreadful Sanctuary* (magazine version, 1948; book version, 1951), put Fort's ideas into fiction. Guieu's background in "We the Martians" owes a debt to the latter novel. In *Dreadful Sanctuary*, the white race comes from Mars, the black from Mercury, the yellow from Venus, and the red comprise Earth's indigenous people.

What Guieu knew of Russell's work is not known, but it should be noted that *Sinister Barrier* was translated into French as early as 1952 (as *Guerre aux invisibles* in Hachette and Gallimard's imprint, Rayon Fantastique, [No. 10]), which is two years before Guieu's two-novel series.[22] On the other hand, *Dreadful Sanctuary* was not translated until 1978 (a whole generation later) as *Le Sanctuaire terrifiant*.[23] What Guieu knew of Fort's work is unclear as well. It would be safe to assume that Guieu possessed familiarity with some of Fort's ideas (if not his actual works) and maybe knew of some of Russell's applications of Fort. Considering both Guieu and Fort shared a wide range of interests, further study needs to be done to determine how much influence Fort may have had on Guieu.

This section's three other novels reiterate this theme of aliens guiding Earth's mythical civilizations and being responsible for much of humanity's advances in science and technology. *La Dimension X* ("Dimension X," 27, 1953) reveals how a mythical Tibetan city has taken advanced scientific information from aliens in another dimension and plans to use this knowledge to conquer Earth. The protagonists of the novel prevent this plan from succeeding. The concept of "Yellow Peril" (*Le Péril jaune*) is brought up as a threat to the white race (thus adding further support to the Lofficiers' comment of racial prejudice in Guieu's novels). *La Spirale du temps* ("The Spiral of Time," 36, 1954) involves people using a time machine to travel forty-five million years into the past only to discover that the mythical continent of Lemuria did exist and that its inhabitants were aliens who settled on Earth and tried to educate primitive humanity (whom Guieu portrays as existing long before the date contemporary science says they did) up to the atomic age. The aliens succeed, but humanity fails— succumbing to atomic war. *Créatures des neiges* ("Creatures of the Snows," 95, 1957) depicts the mythical abominable snowmen, or Yetis, as originating from outer space. A secret mission led by Earth scientists discovers that the Yetis have been observing humanity for quite a while to see if Earth is ready to handle advanced scientific knowledge. The aliens' answer is negative.

Regardless of what one thinks about how Guieu goes about choosing and treating his themes, his attitude towards humanity remains the same in all of his novels involving interaction with advanced alien races. Humanity needs help to attain advanced knowledge and yet it is not prepared to handle new knowledge properly. Safely assuming that Guieu's aliens do not exist, one must next see how he views humanity without outside help. The next three sections reveal his answer.

Lost Continents and Races

As mentioned, Guieu produced three novels dealing with lost races from humanity's past who do not receive otherworldly aid. But his criticism of humanity does not change. *Le Rayon du cube* ("The Cubic Ray," 103, 1957) takes place on one of the Hawaiian Islands where a strange cube is discovered upon an ancient burial site. The cube emits a green ray that penetrates all objects, even those composed of metal. A race of dwarfs, the Menehumes, is responsible for the cube and they also turn out to be the first true settlers of Hawaii. They demand that humanity leave Hawaii and after a bloody battle with U.S. military forces, they force the humans off the island. The novel ends with an anxious world wondering what the Menehumes will do next.

The dwarfs in "The Cubic Ray" appear to be based on a legend in Hawaii about a race of people who were only two to three feet in height. Also called the Menehumes, they supposedly fled to Hawaii after the flooding of the lost continent of Mu. Legend portrays them as peaceful unless someone offends them.[24] In Guieu's novel they attacked humanity because the humans disturbed one of their burial sites while discovering the strange cube.

Les Sphères de Rapa-Nui ("The Spheres of Rapa-Nui," 156, 1960) deals with the legend of Mu directly. The detonation of a hydrogen bomb by the British in the Pacific South Seas results in the discovery of ancient metallic objects inscribed with markings of an unknown language. Subsequent explorations reveal an advanced underwater civilization that is a remnant of the lost continent of Mu. These descendants of Mu desire no contact with humanity and fake their own destruction to regain their anonymity.

The legend of the lost continent of Mu emerged during the mid-nineteenth century and was originally located in the Atlantic Ocean by Augustus Le Plongeon (1825–1908), who claimed its society was the source of civilization of ancient Egypt.[25] James Churchward (1851–1936) changed and added to this myth in 1926. In his version Mu was located in the Pacific Ocean. He identified the lost continent as where the origin of the human race occurred and where the white race dominated the other races and developed a highly advanced civilization. The continent's eastern edge was supposedly Easter Island, or Rapa Nui, in its Polynesian name.[26] This last point is important because in the novel Guieu refers to a myth of birdmen among the natives of Rapa Nui, which corresponds to the same myth held by the Easter Island natives in real life.[27] So Guieu connects the reality of Easter Island to the legend of Mu.

The third novel, *Les Êtres de feu* ("The Beings of Fire," 80, 1956), tells of humanity's encounter with the Vulcanians, an underground race who are descended from the inhabitants of the lost continent of Lemuria, allegedly located in the Indian Ocean. The test detonations of atomic bombs result in underground havoc on the Vulcanians, causing them to retaliate against humanity. Using their superior science and technology, the Vulcanians not only inflict disasters on Earth's surface, but they also force humanity to surrender all atomic weapons to them. The Vulcanians promptly transport the deadly atomic weapons to the sun by an anti-gravity device. The novel ends with all of humanity powerless, but united against the Vulcanians.

Atlantis, Mu, and Lemuria constitute the three major lost continents of myth.[28] Guieu uses all three and contrasts them to his contemporary society, with his era always cast in an unfavorable light.

One must be reminded that the preceding three sections of Guieu's novels dealt with subjects which Guieu sought to prove as real. In order to convince the reader, he inserted real footnotes throughout his novels advising the reader that what he is writing about can be backed up by fact. He concluded each footnote with a phrase that became a favorite byword among many of the older French science fiction fans, *Authentique!*[29]

Humanity Really Alone

Guieu did write three novels with humanity acting completely alone. Here, as in the novels of the previous three sections, humanity does not come off well. *Les Monstres du néant* ("The Monsters from the Void," 70, 1956) warns against scientists who feel no constraints when experimenting with new technology. Scientist Sydney Mills invents a machine that can transform a person's thoughts into a material reality. Havoc results, with monsters, duplicates of people, and oversized versions of everyday objects terrifying the public. Eventually Mills loses control of the device as the monsters created by him continue to exist even when he has stopped thinking about them. Finally some ghostly thoughts haunt Mills to the point of tricking him into destroying his machine and himself with it.

All through the novel Mills feels no remorse for the problems he has created. In fact, he views them as necessary for progress. Responding to a newspaper reporter who questioned his methods and motives, Mills responds,

> "I cherish no dreams of conquest or domination. My goal is to get to the point where a 'Selector of Thoughts' only materializes some types of specific thoughts to the exclusion of all others.... The lives of a group of individuals, does it count in regard to the benefits that my invention will be able to bring to future generations? The 130,000 deaths from Nagasaki and Hiroshima, do they count in regard to the millions of human lives that radioactive isotopes will save? In the whole evolution of the race? In the course of time to come? No. These sacrifices are necessary if one wants to make Science progress and not to see it stagnate, one must dare these grand experiments on certain human subjects ... even were it thousands!" [100–1].

Mills reiterates this point while explaining to his assistant the development of their work on his device:

> "We will arrive there in face of all opposition. Then we will no longer be held responsible for the suicides and accidental deaths caused by my experiments as the scientists who contributed to the direction of the atomic bomb are not held responsible for the victims of Hiroshima and Nagasaki!" [150].

The reference to the two bombings that ended World War II in its Pacific theater in both quotations emphasize in a very stark manner Guieu's misgivings about humanity handling its new technology.

Prisonniers du passé ("Prisoners of the Past," 72, 1956) is a sequel to "The Spiral of Time," which was covered in the section on aliens and lost races. This time however the protagonists travel into the past encountering fellow humans and nobody else. They get trapped in a time warp in Paris and end up in the year 1843 where they are imprisoned by a French scientist because he is concerned over the effects of intervention by time travelers. When told of mid-twentieth century life, with its wars and new weapons, the French scientist reacts vehemently. "Are you proud of these horrible slaughters? Is this the price of so many sorrows on which future generations will build society ... civilized society? Flying society? Mechanized society? Is that truly the civilization of *your* Time?" The scientist then makes his conclusion, "Time must be allowed to follow its normal course and civilization must follow its course, without hampering or speeding it up. Your place is not here, in this epoch.... Your presence alone constitutes for our country, indeed for the world, a danger" (62).

The protagonists get rescued by the time travel devices used in "The Spiral of Time," but not without a detour to the distant past, the Iron Age. Ignoring the French scientist's warnings, they begin to educate the primitive humans. Humanity does advance in science and technology very quickly, but the resulting society is a tyranny, where France rules over a world-wide empire through oppression and the use its superior advanced knowledge. The teaching of the Iron Age humans may have quickened technical progress by a thousand years, but there existed no concomitant social and moral progress.

If the preceding two novels describe the futility of human attempts to improve its lot, *Convulsions solaires* ("Solar Convulsions," 110, 1958) shows humanity's helplessness in the face of unexpected natural catastrophes. One day a mysterious cosmic cloud enters the solar system and engulfs the Earth and sun, causing asphyxiation to all living creatures. Though manufacturers develop life-saving filter masks, they cannot produce them fast enough to save even a significant part of the human race. Furthermore, a change in the atmosphere causes the cessation of all electronic communications, contributing to the breakdown of social order. Meanwhile the cloud causes the sun to increase its heat, further adding to Earth's woes. Before further destruction can occur, the cloud leaves the solar system as inexplicably as it arrived. Those few who had escaped death by hiding in underground shelters must now begin to rebuild human civilization. Guieu gives no explanations in the novel, just pictures of vain attempts to cope with a universe that can be seen as either hostile or cruelly impersonal.

Extreme Solutions?

So far Guieu has exhibited his pessimism about humanity by showing its dependence on the aid of alien races, its failed attempts to live with lost races, and its helplessness without help from outside sources. However, he did produce six novels that offer scenarios of people working out their problems. But his solutions in the following novels become extreme, if not despairing ones, for Guieu has humanity supplying what could be called its own surrogates for the always-helping alien races.

Guieu's surrogates take the form of scientific and technological elites. These select bodies will save humanity from itself. In the last novel to be examined in this section, the very nature of the human being must be changed before humanity's future can be assured.

La Mort de la vie ("The Death of Life," 87, 1957) begins a three-novel series and creates a gloomy scenario of elites taking over humanity's future. In the future Earth has been permanently poisoned with the radioactivity created by experiments with the atomic bomb. There exists an organization, *Project Noë* (Project Noah), a science center whose goal is to protect the healthiest survivors of the human race and allow them to repopulate the world. However, the descendants of the center's original personnel have become blue-skinned mutants due to radiation poisoning and experiments. This community becomes the focal point for the next two novels.

The two sequels, *Le Règne des mutants* ("The Reign of Mutants," 91, 1957) and *Cité Noë No. 2* ("Noah City No. 2," 100, 1957), have scientific personnel adopting the harshest of measures to ensure humanity's survival. While exploring the areas around them, they discover that other Noah projects exist around the world and at series' end all of them agree to cooperate. The Noah cities face a major threat in the form of deadly disease-carrying human mutants. One of the cities comes up with a solution, forced sterilization. Before this development, the cities have been massacring the mutants before feelings of guilt started to emerge. They decide that forced sterilization constituted the more humane way of genocide. Not all agree and toward the end of the novel debate ensues over the morality of this action. Meanwhile, the cities continue to implement sterilization without waiting for unanimous consent.

In "Noah City No. 2" there is a brief discussion on the nature of progress in the city's scientific community. This society has shed themselves of the evils of the civilization that led to the poisonous radioactive disaster in the first place. The community has learned to cooperate without the coercion of outside laws. Theirs is a naturally formed society. They also avoid false idealism, which has caused so much tragedy in the past. As expressed in the novel, "What have Science without Conscience and those illusory goddesses with the majestic, but debased names of Liberty, Equality, and Fraternity given birth to? DEATH!" (32). Further on Guieu gives a brief description of how the community made their return to nature:

> Becoming again simple humans without etiquette — conformist or social — the "elect" have worked side by side to survive. Naked were the Adam and Eve of Tradition, symbols of the human unarmed before Nature. Acknowledging this and consumed by this spirit of humility and equality without reserve, the survivors emerge from it completely natural to live in the wisdom ... of this Nature from which they have been chased [33]

Guieu's return to nature can be said to mirror some ideas of the famed eighteenth-century philosopher, Jean-Jacques Rousseau (1712–78). But beyond this brief quotation, Guieu has no further discussion. Rousseau's ideas will be discussed in more detail in the Radicals chapter when the novels of Jean-Gaston Vandel come up for analysis.

Meanwhile, *Réseau dinosaure* ("Dinosaur Network," 115, 1958) perhaps comes closest to Guieu presenting any type of optimistic future for present-day humanity. Two twentieth-century men stumble upon a time machine and travel up to the eightieth century to find a paradisiacal but totalitarian society ruled by a group of super-individuals called *Les Parfaits* (The Perfect). However there exists a secret underground movement that believes in equality for all. Through various exploits with the time travel device, the underground movement eventually overthrows The Perfect. The novel ends with the two time travelers whisked away into a new future where they will spend the rest of their lives.

Guieu's use of clandestine groups playing crucial roles in his novels could have been drawn from his experiences in the French Resistance. Generally speaking, maybe the same could be said for his preference for all outside groups, including aliens, lost races, elite groups of humans, and secret societies, to be the agents of human progress. The next novel to be examined also deals with secret societies, but this time secret societies are involved on both sides of a struggle.

La Force sans visage ("The Faceless Force," 118, 1958), starts by projecting Guieu's contemporary geopolitical situation a few years into the future. The Soviet Union has launched "Sputnik 5" and tensions between the USSR and the United States increase as a result. A secret organization, *Société-Secrète de la Narkoum* ("Secret Society of Narkoum"), which originates from the Middle East, controls the world's petroleum and manipulates the international scene (including the Cold War) to its advantage. Coming to the rescue for France and Europe is another secret society, *La Fraternité du temple d'Eleusis* ("The Fraternity of the Temple of Eleusis"), which is composed of the most intelligent, disciplined, and dedicated minds who act to protect France and establish peace when regular political institutions fail. As a member of the French society declares, "By the science and the wisdom of all our Brothers, we will condemn Europe — perhaps the world — to Peace" (187).

The French secret society takes its name from an ancient Greek cult that existed for almost two millennia and became known for participating in ceremonies that celebrated and protected their secret knowledge.[30] As the ancient Greek secret society immersed itself in the mystic and spiritual, the Guieu's modern French secret society devotes itself to science and technology. The novel describes the composition of the group as an assembly of "scientists, researchers, technicians, industrialists, doctors, lawyers, and a lot of others..." (59).

The preceding five novels and their elite groups (even secret ones) employing advanced science to save the human race from itself represent extreme solutions to solve the problems of progress, but the sixth and last novel in this group, *L'Ère des biocybs* ("The Era of the Biocybs," 160, 1960), goes even further. A mysterious disease threatens to kill off the human race. A secret society of the world's leading scientists and technicians attempts to save humanity by placing in hibernation selected men and women who will be revived when the disease subsides. The key component of this plan is the construction of biocybs, human brains kept alive in machines while still possessing their original identities and memories. Realizing that the plague does not affect the nervous systems, the secret society decides to save the minds of people in order to preserve the intellectual achievements and the spirit of the human race. The brains will be put in charge of maintaining the hibernation of selected men and women, will repopulate the Earth—via artificial insemination—once the enigmatic plague finally subsides.

The society's leaders have become laws unto themselves, abandoning accepted and traditional conventions of behavior. They view the survival of the human race as having priority over any morality that would condemn whatever actions the biocybs may have to take to ensure their project's success. According to a member of the biocyb organization,

> "We have been compelled to abandon every form of moral orthodoxy, all sentimentality. We have acted on this idea as machines without a soul and, however, we have done so justly to save the very soul of the species to the detriment of its body" [125].

This novel stands as Guieu's most extreme statement of his pessimism over present-day humanity and its ability to work itself out of trouble. The society of his day cannot, and will not, be capable of saving the human race from either itself or from the unknown. Meanwhile, this novel also represents his most extreme statement of confidence that science can still provide the solutions to humanity's problems, regardless of the measures to be undertaken.

Guieu's vision parallels that of British scientist J.D. Bernal (1901–71) and his short, but very provocative book, *The World, the Flesh, and the Devil: An Inquiry in the Future of the Three Enemies of the Rational Soul* (1929).[30] As the title indicates, the rational soul is hindered by humanity's contemporary existence. Bernal's first two labels are to be taken quite literally. For the world, he sees the Earth itself as imprisoning humanity from further pursuance of the truth by keeping it away from the stars. However, modern science and technology have now given the human race the opportunity to overcome this problem. For the flesh, he views the human body not only as a barrier to the efficient communication of knowledge and ideas, but also as an inadequate tool with which to explore the universe. He proposes that the human brain, like Guieu's biocybs, be placed in a mechanical body so that, besides being able to survive in space, it can also perform any physical activity by the mere addition of mechanical appendages. Furthermore, the brain can be hooked up with any other brain or source of information for instant communication. As for the devil, Bernal attacks more than religion. He views any ideology that goes against the methods and findings of science as enemies of human progress.

This proposed situation must result in the division of the human race into two worlds. The first consists of the newly reconstructed human, finally freed from most physical constraints and forever exploring the universe. The second is the original humanity still living on Earth. As Bernal describes it,

> Mankind—old mankind—would be left in undisputed possession of the earth, to be regarded by the inhabitants of the celestial spheres with a curious reverence. The world might, in fact, be transformed into a human zoo, a zoo so intelligently managed that its inhabitants are not aware that they are there merely for the purposes of observation and experiment.[32]

The spheres mentioned in the passage describe the containers in which the brains of humanity are to be stored.

Bernal's vision must also be viewed in light of his adherence to Marxism; he was a strict materialist who viewed this ideology as compatible with his scientific views. He strongly supported the Stalinist state in the Soviet Union and was awarded the Lenin Peace Prize in 1953. As one can see from this work, Bernal — as with Guieu later on — praises science but finds no use for the humanity of his present.

As mentioned, Guieu's beliefs in UFOs, lost races, occult ideas, and parapsychology must be separated from his concerns over humanity's ability to handle new knowledge and power in order to see what he really has to say about the idea of progress. One does not have to believe in the reality of UFOs or lost races to appreciate Guieu's warning about the dangers research and experimentation in atomic energy can create. One does not have to subscribe to various occult theories or believe in the existence of telepathy to view as valid Guieu's criticisms of a nation seemingly out of touch with the impact of its modernization policies.

The novels from the second, third, fourth, and fifth sections of this examination of Guieu certainly support these observations. Looking past Guieu's idiosyncratic interests, one is left with a writer who voices concerns about humanity and its inability to learn and handle properly new advances in science and technology. Meanwhile the novels that were examined in the sixth section — shorn of all of Guieu's peculiar themes — depict a humanity that must make difficult choices in order to survive. These stories argue that drastic actions, including the abandonment of past ideas and traditions which interfere with modernization, must be taken. As incredulous as Guieu's ideas may seem, his concerns still can find a common ground with his fellow Anticipation writers when it comes to worries about France's future.

In brief, Guieu's pessimism in humanity's ability to handle science and technology is surpassed only by his optimism that these two fields of endeavor will save the human race. Since he views the idea of progress through the twin lenses of science and technology, he insists on their intensive, almost exclusive application to solve society's problems. So just about everything that present-day humanity holds dear and sacred must be jettisoned as unwanted flotsam — even, maybe, the human body. For Guieu, if modernization policies cause France to cease being France, then so be it.

CHAPTER FOUR

The Conservatives

Four writers—Stefan Wul, Maurice Limat, Peter Randa, and Kurt Steiner—represent what the author has chosen to label conservative responses to the idea of progress. As mentioned in the introduction to this study, the term conservative should not be viewed only in political terms, past or present. Wul and Limat definitely contain identifiably conservative political stands in their novels. Randa can be considered a political conservative with his libertarian-like views, but the ideas presented in his novels during this period cannot be directly correlated with an established French political party's platform or program as Wul's and Limat's can. In fact, if his views resemble anything, they fall more in line with those of a famous science fiction writer from America—Robert A. Heinlein. Steiner, meanwhile, belongs with the conservatives in a more general sense as he deals with the fate of the human race on a cosmological scale.

Stefan Wul

Stefan Wul is the pseudonym for Pierre Pairault (1922–2003), a dental surgeon by profession. When most people think of the best writer for Anticipation during the 1950s, his name invariably comes up first. Wul's stories have stood the test of time and remain the most captivating and imaginative of them all.

The opinion of Wul being the best writer is unanimous. Jean-Marc and Randy Lofficier state that of all the Anticipation writers during this period, "none was more remarkable," and that his novels "were all classics, enlivened by their colorful, poetic imagery and their operatic stories, which took pulp clichés and turned them into powerful dramas."[1] Maxim Jabukowski and John Clute describe his work as "consistent and imaginative."[2] Pierre Versins calls Wul's novels "all of a high value."[3] Alain Douilly summarizes Wul's impact: "The French space opera and Fleuve Noir owe him very much. His novels ... still captivate."[4]

Wul's career in Anticipation was as short as it was brilliant. He published only (when compared to his more prolific contemporaries in Anticipation) eleven novels between 1956–9. The reason for this literary brevity has been attributed to the demands of writing popular fiction and its financial aspect. Gérard Klein (1937–), a French science fiction writer, anthologist, critic, and editor and who will also be covered later in this study, contends that Wul is an example of how the demands of a new field of popular literature can stifle a good writer's potential to produce meaningful work. The need to produce constantly in a formulaic genre can only threaten the creativity of a writer. Klein made this observation in 1960 in the review column, *Ici, on desintegre!* ("Here, one disintegrates!"), of *Fiction* magazine when he reviewed Kurt's Steiner's Anticipation novel, *Le 32 Juillet* ("The 32nd of July," 146, 159), in which he hoped that Steiner does not undergo the same fate as Wul. Klein goes on to use two other Anticipation writers, Jimmy Guieu and M.A. Rayjean, as examples of mediocrity.[5] As to the financial aspect, Douilly succinctly suggests that "Unfortunately, he abandoned the quill for the profit of his dental practice."[6] If Bommart (Kemmel) has been described by Douilly as a shooting star, then Wul should be compared to a supernova.

Wul also published several short pieces of fiction between 1957 and 2000, but did not produce another novel until 1977 with his massive *Noô*. Two of his Anticipation novels were made into animated feature-length films by French animator and director, René Laloux (1929–2004), *Le Planète sauvage* ("The Savage Planet," translated as *Fantastic Planet*, 1973), from Wul's *Oms en series* ("OMS in Series," 102, 1957) and *Les Maîtres du temps* (*The Time Masters*, 1981), from *L'Orphelin de Perdide* ("The Orphan of Perdide," 109, 1958). Wul also worked on a short-lived television series in 1972, *Mycènes, celui qui vient du futur* ("Mycenes, He Who Comes from the Future," Lofficiers' translation).[7] One of Wul's Anticipation novels, *Le Temple du passé* ("The Temple of the Past," 106, 1957), was actually translated into English and published in America in 1973, to date the only Anticipation novel from the Fifties to be so translated.[8]

In 1997 and 1998, the complete works of Wul were collected into two volumes.[9] Each volume had a preface written by Laurent Genefort (1968–), a French science fiction writer who wrote fourteen novels for Anticipation during its later years (1988–1997). The prefaces reveal more details of Wul's life, the beginning of his writing career, and the purposes behind his writing. They also contain Genefort's analyzes of Wul's fiction, identifying its nature, style, and success.[10]

Referring to an introduction by Wul to one of his shorter fictions, Genefort reveals how Wul at age ten started writing (charging his school compatriots "five marbles and a sou" for each chapter) and at age eighteen briefly attempted to live in Paris's Latin Quarter as a musician. After the latter experience Wul returned home to study a trade. Choosing dentistry because he thought it would be "easy studies," he discovered otherwise, leading him to a "conformist web from which I hope to tear out of." Wul remained in dentistry for most of his adult life.¹¹ Wul pursued classical studies at Collège Rocroy-Saint-Léon, graduating in 1940, and acquired his degree in dental surgery in 1945. He practiced first in Paris, then in the Normandy area.

His early career in dentistry did not prevent him from writing. Genefort's preface recalls an anecdote about how Wul started to write science fiction. One day Wul's wife read a science fiction novel and complained about its extreme lack of quality. She then said that he could do better. So Wul dropped the police novel he was trying to write and turned to science fiction.¹² As to his pseudonym, which he adopted in 1956, Wul claimed to have heard it on the radio; it was the last name of an atomic engineer from the Ural area, "Oul."¹³

Besides the urging of his wife, Genefort points out another reason why Wul chose and continued to write science fiction, a popular genre then noted for inferior literary qualities, or as Genefort refers to as "this 'bad genre' par excellence."¹⁴ According to Genefort,

> The question should be reversed. What other literature was in a position to collect without overflowing such a flow of images utterly absurd and logical at the same time? What other genre in which to exploit at leisure one's taste for marvelous and imaginative excess? It is "the irresistible need to build dreams and to partake in them" that inspires our author. SF (science fiction) is a despised field where all remains to be done — a jungle, where one discerns some paths opened up by a band of adventurers.¹⁵

So science fiction and Wul's imagination were made for each other, with Wul blazing new trails in the nascent field of postwar French genre science fiction. Genefort further elaborates how Wul's imagination separated Wul from his fellow Anticipation writers by describing him as a "solitary talent on the margin of contemporary productions. For contrary to his colleagues, Wul does not draw from Anglo-Saxon sources, preferring to give free reign to his imagination."¹⁶

As quickly as Wul burst on the scene with his eleven memorable novels for Anticipation, he vanished. The reason was simple one. Genefort again quotes Wul, "simply because I was exhausted, and then inspiration had shoved off, that is all."¹⁷ Of course, the steady remunerations of a successful dental practice may have played a role too.

Despite his brief and limited output, Wul remains highly regarded by many for his Anticipation stories. As Genefort points out, "Even after years of silence, Stefan Wul remains known as the best French writer of space opera."¹⁸ Genefort reinforces this point by referring to the observations of two writers, Jean-Pierre Andrevon (1937–), who wrote eight novels for Anticipation during the Seventies and Eighties, and Gérard Klein, and then elaborates on their views.

Andrevon describes Wul's stature in the broader context of contemporary French science fiction:

> Our national SF most often swims in the metaphoric, the satire, the political, the poetic ... when it does not drown in it. It is an introverted, intellectualized SF. Most

often it lacks the wind in the sails and the mud in the soles. Wul himself is a physical writer. He does not want to demonstrate, but he makes us feel, makes us live.[19]

Genefort continues this train of thought: "What is only description with any writer of space opera, becomes animated fresco. Wul extracts harmony from his prose of pure feelings. Under his pen, noise becomes music, for he admits more willingly to be a musician than a poet."[20] (Maybe Wul's youthful experiences in the Latin Quarter come into play here?) Genefort goes back to quoting Wul, who states, "The libretto of an opera I frantically throw away. What interest me are cymbals, atmosphere, that is, a climate...."[21]

Genefort then uses Klein's comments to join in this chorus of praise. For Klein, Wul is a

> visionary. He is capable of describing strange sceneries with an extraordinary sense of the concrete. The realism of his visions comes from their consistency. In short, he is not satisfied — as are so many others — to whitewash with unusual colors commonplace panoramas. He succeeds in suggesting geologies and ecologies foreign to our planet. Rather than just pictures, he offers structures that one is tempted to consider as functional.[22]

This passage originally appeared in Klein's preface to a collection of three of Wul's novels reprinted under the publisher Robert Laffont's imprint Ailleurs & Demain: Classiques. Genefort follows this quotation by observing that all major French publishing houses desire Wul's works for republication.[23]

Genefort himself supplies the last word at the end of his second preface.

> The success of Stefan Wul is attached perhaps to his vision where his organization of images excels and his story only comes is second. What the reader perceives is a book felt rather than thought about. The novels of Wul are not supports for an ideological, political, or moral thesis. They are the transcription in action of an esthetic vision. Behind the apparent absence of ideology (here the word ought to be taken in its common meaning) is concealed an epicurean ideology of nature, for the Wulian poetry is above all a poetry of senses. Indeed Wul has a vision of a world that forms a coherent whole, but this unity does not carry the prejudice of its parts. Man has a role to play in the world. This role does not seek to modify the real, or to give a moral interpretation to it, it seeks to poeticize it. For if one finds poetry in the tone, dreamlike meanings, and images, one especially will find it not deliberate, but inspired, and representing the very source of the work — in poetry's metaphysics. There is only one way to partake in this philosophy. It boils down to one expression: the simple pleasure of reading.[24]

These observations from Genefort's prefaces enable one to understand both the appeal and the respect that Wul's writings have engendered throughout the years.

Before examining Wul further, the concept of space opera — as mentioned by Genefort — should be explained, especially for the benefit of those not familiar with the traditions of genre science fiction. Noted American science fiction writer and fan Wilson Tucker (1914–2006), first coined the term in 1941. He meant the phrase to be a derogatory reference to stories that used worn-out themes and plots and contained a minimum of literary competency. At the time of Tucker's comment, American genre science fiction, as mentioned in the Background chapter of this study, was experiencing its golden age, a period when the genre experienced significant improvement in all aspects of literary development. So Tucker created the term to identify the type of works from which early 1940s science fiction was trying to escape.

As time went on, the term took on different meanings. For some, the term maintained its original intent. For others, it meant a return to an innocence and romanticism found in the early stories of American genre science fiction, but without any derogatory connotation. Meanwhile, some use the term as a mere descriptor of the type of science fiction that focuses on adventurous space exploration and large-scale science. Examples here would include the works of E.E. "Doc" Smith, Edmond Hamilton, Jack Williamson, and John W. Campbell, among its early practitioners; stories by C.J. Cherryh (1942–), Lois McMaster Bujold (1949–), (Glen) David Brin (1950–), Stephen Baxter (1957–), and Peter F. Hamilton (1960–), among the later writers; and the films *Flash Gordon* (1936)[25] and *Star Wars* (1977).[26] Still others use this phrase as a purely historical term to identify a particular era of American genre science fiction, primarily the Twenties and Thirties.[27]

From the above four meanings of space opera, Genefort's usage of the term would best fall under the third alternative. Clearly he does not bring about any negative connotations when discussing this type of science fiction and his prefaces do not demand a prerequisite knowledge of American science fiction genre history. He focuses primarily on the style of Wul's writings in particular and of space opera in general.

So Wul's appeal can be said to be based on his unique vision and use of poetic imagery in the space opera motif in science fiction. Both Genefort and Andrevon emphasize Wul's beautiful language while pointing out his lack of ideology or moral lessons to be learned. Klein adds to their view when he emphasizes Wul's abilities to describe alien worlds and strange situations in consistently concrete terms.

For the most part, Genefort is correct. Wul is best remembered for his use of language to portray strange worlds and situations in his unique esthetic manner. Unlike most of the other Anticipation writers, the majority of Wul's eleven novels do not feature an ideology, an argument for the best way to handle new science and technology, or an analysis on any part or the whole of the human condition. Though his stories take place in bleak times or situations, they do not give warnings against certain policies or offer better solutions for society.

Wul's use of fantastical settings and descriptions lends support to the thesis of this study about the relationship between the philosophical tale and the Anticipation novels of the Fifties. His lack of ideology, satire, and statements on human behavior does not. A few of his novels do present a theme often used in science fiction, in or out of genre, the apocalyptic vision. However,

Wul did write two novels that contain an identifiable ideology that can be traced to the politics of his time.

This analysis of Wul's novels is to be divided into three sections. The first contains the novels not dealing with either an apocalyptic vision or an ideology (five novels); the second covers the apocalyptic novels (four novels); and the third deals with Wul's ideological presentation (two novels). Though the third group counters the observations of Genefort, it is hoped that a close examination of the two novels will convince the reader as it did the author of Wul's ideological leaning.

Poetic Visions

All of Wul's works are poetic visions and it should not be inferred that the novels covered in the other two sections of Wul's analysis are not. Regardless of the approach one takes when reading his novels, his seductive poetic language persists in all.

Rayons pour Sidar ("Rays for Sidar," 90, 1957) narrates the situation between Earth and the Xress, an alien race with whom Earth signed a treaty that ceded control of the planet Sidar to the Xress. The Xress destroy life on all planets they occupy and are preparing to do the same on Sidar. But thanks to the intervention of an agent from Earth, Sidar is saved by its literal transfer from its solar system to the Earth's, with the move lasting 150 years. As mentioned, such large-scale technical feats are hallmarks of space opera. American examples similar to Wul's novel in terms of heavenly bodies being tossed about or destroyed would include Edmund Hamilton's *Crashing Suns* stories (1928),[28] and John W. Campbell's *The Mightiest Machine* (1934).[29]

La Peur géante ("The Giant Fear," 96, 1957) has humanity attacked by sea creatures, who resemble the shape of torpedoes (in the novel they are called *les torpèdes*, the French word for torpedo is *torpille*). Humans can no longer act upon water (either to freeze or evaporate it) anywhere on Earth. When the humans counterattack, the *torpèdes* melt Earth's ice caps, threatening the flooding and destruction of most of the human race. Eventually the humans organize secret underground armies, who resort to biological warfare and poison the food sources of the sea creatures. Humanity ultimately triumphs.

If "Rays for Sidar" calls to mind one type of science fiction from the first half of the twentieth century, then "The Giant Fear" bears a resemblance to a classic science fiction novel from the same period, *War with the Newts* (1936, Czech title, *Válka s mloky*) by Czech writer Karel Čapek (1890–1938).[30] Humanity's antagonists in both novels roughly share the same body type (Wul's torpedoes vs. Čapek's newts, or salamanders, cylindrically-shaped reptiles). The flooding of the earth occurs in both novels as well. But here the resemblance ends. Whereas Wul's antagonists are defeated, Čapek's end up as the victors (but may end up destroying themselves in turn). Wul's novel is more of an exotic and, at the end, gruesome adventure, while Čapek's can be seen as a savage satirical commentary of his time as analogies can be made between events in his novel and those in central Europe during the 1930s. Given these aspects, perhaps *War with the Newts* can be considered more of a direct literary descendant of Voltaire's philosophical tale than any of the Anticipation novels examined in this study. It should be pointed out here that Čapek is best remembered for coining the word "robot" in his play, *R.U.R.* (1920).[31] Čapek's play will be covered briefly in this study's coverage of Jean-Gaston Vandel in the Radicals chapter. Finally, Genefort finds a similarity between Wul's novel and the American film, *Abyss* (1989), with the film's aliens being able to shape water into any form they desire.[32]

L'Orphelin de Perdide ("The Orphan of Perdide," 109, 1958) tells the story of a rescue mission of a small boy stranded on a hostile planet, Perdide. Added to the plotline are a refugee couple, a prince and princess, an old friend of the stranded boy's father who joins in the mission, and visits to two planets along the way. The surprise at the story's end deals with the time paradoxes involved with long-distance interstellar travel near the speed of light. This novel became the inspiration for the second film French animator and director, René Laloux, made from Wul's novels. Retitled *Maîtres du temps* (1982, English version, "Masters of Time"), the animated film is remembered for its designer, famed French artist Jean Giraud (1938–), better known under his pseudonym, Moebius.[33] The exoticness of the movie matches that of Wul's novel. Despite the addition of a few new elements, the film can be said in large part to follow Wul's novel.

Terminus 1 ("Terminus 1," 130, 1959) is a love story set in the future with an interplanetary adventure about the finding of precious metals as a backdrop. While attempting to procure palladium, the most precious metal in space, Julius encounters Stella and both fall in love. Julius has to separate himself from Stella and embark on a perilous mission to obtain the precious metal. He succeeds, making him very rich. However, Stella thinks her new-found love has died, gives up on waiting for him, and eats a strange fruit that changes people into trees. Julius returns with his riches only to discover that Stella is gone. Realizing that Stella has become his only source of happiness, Julius forgoes his wealth and life and eats the same strange fruit to share the same destiny as Stella. The novel ends with the two newly transformed trees having their branches intertwined. This ending obviously has its origins in the many folk myths of ancient culture where doomed lovers are memorialized as trees connected for all eternity.

The final novel in this group, *Odyssée sous contrôle* ("Odyssey under Control," 138, 1959), is also the last one Wul wrote for Anticipation during this period. Wul tells the story through the eyes and mind of a secret agent from Earth who encounters a struggle for power between two alien races on an alien planet. Integral to the story is a device that, when placed on the head of a human, inserts the consciousness of another being into the mind of the wearer, thus creating in the wearer's mind an artificial (or virtual, in contemporary terminology) reality.

This novel anticipates a central theme in the cyberpunk movement in science fiction during the 1980s. The latter-day stories focus on the developments in cybernetics, which are extrapolated to the point where humans can create virtual realities so realistic that actions made in the artificial world can have a real effect, both physically and psychologically, in the actual world. The make-believe world becomes indistinguishable from the real one.[34] "Odyssey under Control" also helped prepare the way for the large-scale acceptance in France during the late Sixties of the writings of Philip K. Dick, whose novels featuring altered realities and states of consciousness had already made quite an impact on the American science fiction scene. Genefort wryly observes that the 1990 American film directed by Paul Verhoeven, *Total Recall*,[35] which was very loosely adapted from Dick's novelette, "We Can Remember It for You Wholesale" (1966), and deals with the issues of human perception of reality, really did not invent anything new.[36]

APOCALYPTIC VISIONS

Apocalyptic visions comprise a significant segment of science fiction expressions. The existing world is destroyed, often in a quick and dramatic fashion, and a new one replaces it, with the new one not necessarily a glorious one.[37] There are many approaches one can take with this theme. Clute and Nicholls's *Encyclopedia of Science Fiction* covers this theme under five entries: "Disaster," "End of the World," "Eschatology" (focusing on the aspect of existence after death), "Holocaust and After," and "Religion."[38] Wul's apocalyptic novels reflect this diversity of treatment.

Retour à "O" ("Return to 'O,'" 78, 1957) is Wul's first published novel. The Earth uses the Moon as a penal colony for its worst criminals, those deserving of capital punishment. Earth sends two secret agents to observe the colony and there they discover hostile intentions among the prisoners. Using an advanced technology which enables the shrinking down of both humans and machines down to microscopic level, Earth plans to apply this technology to the Moon's inhabitants in order to control and pacify them. (Genefort relates this technology's presentation to the American film *Fantastic Voyage* [1966]).[39] The discovery of the plan results in the colony revolting, the Moon being blown up, and the Earth being turned on its axis, destroying all life except for plant life. The two secret agents, a man and a woman, are the only survivors and at the end begin to repopulate the Earth.

As mentioned, *Le Temple du passé* ("The Temple of the Past," 106, 1957) represents the only Fifties Anticipation novel translated into English. After landing on an alien planet a spaceship is swallowed up by a giant marine monster, but the ship's human occupants chemically alter the creature into a land creature. The new creature then spawns a race of intelligent telepathic lizard-like creatures. The creatures view the humans as gods and build a temple in their memory where the ship, which was damaged beyond repair, landed. Ten thousand years later, human space explorers discover the planet, where — employing a plot device heavily used by Jimmy Guieu — they discover that the original astronauts were actually from Atlantis and responsible for the civilizations of ancient Egypt and the Mayans. Wul avoids making asides to the reader or inserting footnotes to prove the existence of this lost race as Guieu would have done. Here it can be safely said that Wul simply wants to tell a good story.

La Mort vivante ("The Living Death," 113, 1958) tells of the disastrous results that can occur when experimenting with a basic building block of the human body, the cell. Anticipating the technique of cloning (Wul's medical training may have helped him here), a scientist attempts to recreate a human by regenerating cells and growing them into complete body of a girl who had died. The experiment succeeds all too well as seven children are created. They turn out to possess a *Gestalt* mind (a group mind where the knowledge of experiences of an individual becomes part of the whole group) as well as other mental abilities, and become threateningly brilliant. The children soon reproduce themselves via parthenogenesis (roughly, reproduction without fertilization). Eventually they transform themselves into an ever-growing giant mass which can assume any shape and digest all matter. They claim to be the next step in evolution and the novel ends with their plans to conquer the universe. This novel constitutes Wul's most pessimistic and dire novel as even the protagonists are literally swallowed up at the end.

The application of the *Gestalt* mind of the children calls to mind British science fiction writer John Wyndham's novel, *The Midwich Cuckoos* (1957), where a quiet English village has its women mysteriously impregnated and their children products of xenogenesis (reproduction of offspring entirely different from parents).[40] As with Wul's children, the children possess a *Gestalt* mind and other mental abilities, but in Wyndham's novel the children are destroyed at the end. As with most of the writers analyzed here, it is difficult to know if Wul read English-language science fiction or their French translations. (Genefort once asked Wul about reading English-language works and Wul responded that his command of English was not sufficient to enjoy the language properly. So chances are Wul read French translations.[41]) Wyndham's novel eventually became the source for two films, *Village of the Damned* (1960)[42] and *Children of the Damned* (1963).[43] Beyond sharing a common source, the two films are unrelated.

However, an earlier example of super-gifted children of non-human origins can actually be found in Anticipation, in fellow French writer Jean-Gaston Vandel's novel, *Les Titans de l'énergie* ("The Titans of Energy," 48, 1955). Here, the children escape the threat against them. This novel is treated under Vandel's works in the Radicals chapter of this study. Even if it is not known who influenced whom, such commonalities are pointed out to reveal how certain themes in science fiction can emerge in different places and times. As for giant masses threatening life on Earth as we know it, one would have to wait until the release of two films, *The Blob* (1958)[44] and *Caltiki, the Immortal Monster* (1960, translated from original Italian film, *Caltiki — il mostro immortale* [1959])[45] to see visual presentations of this scenario.

One can see how elements from all five topics of Clute and Nicholls's entries are dealt in the above three novels. The last novel to be examined in this section involves all five by itself and is the most interesting of Wul's apocalyptic tales. It not only represents Wul's best-known novel, but also the most reprinted of the Anticipation novels. This story also constitutes the only one among these apocalyptic novels to give any in-depth discussion on the nature of progress.

Niourk ("Niourk," 83, 1957) remains the acknowledged masterpiece emerging from the Anticipation imprint during the Fifties. Genefort states that "It is not exaggeration to say that with 'Niourk,' the level of the Fleuve (or River, making a play on the publisher's name) climbed to a level never attained before."[46] He further points out that "Niourk" is the first Anticipation novel to go beyond its original imprint, being republished in the prestigious French collection Presence du Futur.[47]

"Niourk" takes place after an apocalypse and concludes with a second one. In an unspecified future time, the Earth is an old world poisoned by atomic radiation, devoid of all water, and abandoned by civilized humanity, who escaped to Venus. Only crumbling ruins and primitive tribes remain. One of the tribes, living between what was Cuba and Haiti, is guided by an old man, *Le Vieux* ("The Old One"), who is their source of wisdom. Into a tribe is born a child with black skin, *L'Enfant noir* ("The Black Child"), who must be killed due to his skin color.

However, the Black Child escapes and flees into the mountains where he hopes to encounter the gods of his tribe. Instead he comes across the Old One and discovers that the Old One has died. Following the rituals of his tribe he eats the brains of the Old One, thereby becoming the new Old One. He returns to his tribe as its new leader and defends it against radioactively affected animals. One predator, an octopus creature made intelligent by radiation, is personally defeated by him. Again adhering to custom, he consumes the predator's brain as the victor in combat. This time a more than symbolic effect occurs. The eating of this particular brain causes the Black Child's mind to develop incredible powers.

Later he encounters a strangely dressed man, who the Black Child thinks is a mad god. The strangely dressed man exhorts the Black Child to travel to a place called Niourk, once the greatest of all cities and where now lives much game for the tribe to hunt. The place turns out to be New York City (thus the title of the novel). He leads his tribe to what was once the island of Manhattan, where he and the tribe marvel at the still functioning automated services and at first view the mechanisms as works of the tribe's gods. Soon the tribe, including the Black Child, contracts a strange and deadly disease. Despite his newly developed mental powers, the Black Child cannot save anyone, including himself — though the disease does further increase his mental powers, including allowing him to master massive amounts of new information at once (he quickly reads through a whole library), telekinesis, etc.

Fortunately, a pair of humans from Venus who had crash-landed on Earth earlier rescues the Black Child from the disease's deadly effects while allowing him to keep his powers. His powers grow to the point where he becomes godlike. He wants the Earth to start anew under his guidance and away from any influence originating from the old world. So by the mere act of will he moves the Earth to the center of the galaxy and creates a sun to orbit around it. If this is not fantastic enough, he then creates duplicates of his dead tribal members, those of the Venusian colonials, and of himself. The original colonials return to Venus with a duplicate of the Black Child. The duplicate tribal members accompany him to the center of the galaxy with the duplicate colonials remaining in Niourk to live in nature; both sets of duplicates are unaware of their true nature. The Black Child promises the new inhabitants of Niourk that he will visit them often.

It appears that humanity will continue to survive, but with three separate destinies: the Black Child's own planet at the center of the galaxy, the Venusian colonials restarting their lives in nature amid the ruins of New York, and the human settlement on Venus. The fact that the Black Child can even create a duplicate of himself would lead one to suspect that humanity's options could be limitless.

As Wul's and Anticipation's finest novel, the above extended plot summary is warranted. To this date there exists no comprehensive synopsis of the novel in the English language. Though the above is certainly not complete — as the novel contains much more detail — the author hopes that it will serve as a competent introduction.

Four times the Black Child criticizes humanity and what it did to create the desperate situation on Earth. All take place during discussions with the two human colonials from Venus. The humans on Venus kept developing science and technology to the point where human reproduction now takes place outside the womb. Because of this, the colonials think themselves as superior to the humans on Earth, who are viewed as mere animals. This attitude results in the Black Child's first criticism:

> "You believe yourselves superior because you are born in a bottle, from an ovule fertilized by a spark. Because I am sexed, because a mother has given birth to me, you take me for an animal. You award yourselves the title of 'homo superior.' In fact, you are not men, but robots....
>
> "Yes, I know well that I exaggerate. I want to say that you are heading towards a civilization of robots. You have abolished natural conception; from century to century

you abolish one thing, then another. You will no longer be men. You will rise very high in power, but you have preserved no protection. You are wrong to cut off your roots. You see, I have already risen higher than you, for my personality stretches from animal to homo multipotens. Yours goes only from homo artificial to homo superior" [165–6].

As the Black Child sees it, attempting to improve on the human body results only in the destruction of what makes people human. Furthermore, staying with one's given natural attributes actually results in a more promising future.

The Black Child's second criticism consists more of an exhortation than any actual attack. After his criticism of the colonials for tampering with the human body, the Black Child concludes by saying that he would despise them if he were capable of such an emotion. One of the colonials takes issue, "Whatever our thoughts may be, one thing is for certain: it is that we love you. I beg you to believe it" (166). The Black Child responds accordingly, "I know it well.... This is one of the things that your civilization has still not succeeded in suppressing: love. This is why I love you as well in spite of your passing follies..." (166). This almost sarcastic remark constitutes the Black Child's way of warning the colonials not to surrender their basic human emotions to scientific progress.

After attesting to the integrity of the human body and the validity of basic emotions, the Black Child goes into his third criticism on humanity. Here he stresses the need to think about an existence beyond matter and the concept of deity:

> "You have been rather strong in trampling under your feet old idols and even so simple an idea as homo sapiens being made from God. But if you have nothing to put in its place, you are missing something....
> "...I believe in God. But I am afraid that I am not able to explain. You are too superior, or not superior enough, to understand. This is what is gained from being born in a bottle.... You have not enough intelligence and you have lost native simplicity. Poor, poor, 'superiors'" [166–7].

So something exists beyond the material, but this basic fact is lost on humanity due to its singular pursuit of scientific and empirical knowledge.

A little later on the Black Child restates the need for whole human being to be preserved and cared for. Here lies the Black Child's fourth criticism against humanity and his second about the emphasis on the human mind and brain:

> "Do not believe that the brain includes anything at all; the nervous system is only a relay. It connects the sensorial function to the motor function, and again not always. The stomach 'understands' or 'knows' that it has hunger and dispatches to the valet, the brain, the order to transmit this information to the 'intelligent' muscles which must act accordingly. It is the gross error of your physiology to see things differently.
> "Thought is only a complex ensemble of muscular micro contractions or micro sensations. And even if you think an abstract word, it is ever only the rapid and unconscious micro formation of this word by your lingual muscles which constitute your very thought.

"The pre–Venusian men (homo sapiens, well understood) had already caught sight of this truth. But the texts of these precursors have been lost during the great exodus to Venus" [172].

The mind loses its priority over the body and thought is reduced to a material base. However, this does not mean that the brain is worth any less. The brain still remains very important — as the method of how the Black Child acquires new powers attest. But the whole body works as one, with all of its parts dependent on each other. Humanity must realize this and avoid focusing on just one part of the human being as the Venusians colonials did. This fourth criticism also explains why Wul may have made the eating of the brain an integral aspect of the novel. With human mind now on par with the rest of the body, its literal consumption may be the most graphic way to express this notion.

Note how the Black Child criticizes the very science that saved him without condemning it outright. As long as humanity keeps science and technology in their proper place, all will be fine. When applying the results of scientific research and technological innovation, people must keep in mind three ideas: respect humanity's original nature, keep basic human emotions, and realize an existence beyond the material world. Wul does not connect all these notions together, not unless one sees the proximity in the novel of the four quoted passages as Wul's attempt to be comprehensive.

Meanwhile, there remains a larger issue to be considered. The Black Child becomes a godlike guardian of the relocated Earth and its inhabitants. Does this mean that he is the god that people should believe in? And if so, can even a god be explained in materialistic terms? Or is the Black Child merely a superpowered guardian with no pretensions to godhood, but who still retains the desire and the power to guide humanity as he sees fit? In this case, then a follow-up question would be: Is there any relationship between the Black Child and God if the former seems to have absolute power in his guardianship? Still further into this chain of inquiry, is the belief in God to be maintained more as a tradition than as an actual theological stand?

At this point of this analysis, maybe one should recall's Genefort's article where Wul is quoted as not being an ideological writer. In the article, Wul states that "journalists have asserted that *Niourk* was an anti-racist novel because my hero ... was Black. My intention has never been to write political novels."[48] So given the quotation, should a reader just abandon the religious questions as well and view the ideas expressed in *Niourk* as just part of Wul's literary landscape?

If not for the two novels to be examined in the next section of analysis, the answer to the question would be "yes." The ideas expressed above do exhibit a conservative approach when advocating for the maintenance of the human body and certain beliefs. They may provide a hint, whether intentional or not, of Wul's ideology, his disclaimer notwithstanding.

Wul's *Niourk* presents humanity as incapable of handling advanced science, technology, and power. So dim is his view of humanity that he provides a second apocalypse to resolve the issues of the first one. But if apocalyptic destinies are not in humanity's future, does Wul portray a vision where humanity resolves its issues of modernity on its own, without help of an extra or super-human agency? The two novels to be analyzed in the next section provide an answer, one that can be identified with the French politics of Wul's day.

A Conservative Solution?

After *Niourk*, the *Oms en série* ("Oms in Series," 102, 1957) stands as probably Wul's most important and well-known novel from this period. Few in America realize that this story became the basis of the award-winning (Cannes Film Festival) animated film, *La Planète sauvage* (1973, translated into English as *Fantastic Planet*). The general atmosphere and mystical ending of the film make it very different from Wul's novel.[49]

The novel tells the story of the *oms* (human beings, a shortening of the French word for men, *hommes*) and their struggle to liberate themselves from the *draags*, giant aliens who have taken humans from Earth and made them their pets on their world, the giant planet Ygam. The *draags* (perhaps a shortened variation of the French word for dragon, *dragon*[50]) are literally giants, being forty-five times larger than the humans. The *oms* have two important advantages: their superior minds and their faster pace of life (a *draag* day equals forty-five *oms* days, matching the proportions of their physical sizes). Exploiting these abilities in a secret place where they have developed a highly technological society, a strong leader directs the three million *oms* who have escaped and avoided the *draags* to build a fleet of ships and an incredible arsenal, which includes new types of explosives and even force fields. The protagonist of the novel, Terr (perhaps a variation of the phonetically identical *Terre*, the French word for the Earth), assumes leadership when the strong leader dies. The *oms* manage to migrate to another part of the planet but are attacked one last time by the *draags*. Just when the *oms*' resources are about to be exhausted, the *draags*—tricked by the *oms*' schemes to appear to be stronger than they really were—ask for a truce. Both sides agree to be independent from each other and engage in an agreed-upon competition to insure continual improvement for both.

During their negotiations with the *draags*, the *oms* explain how their independence will be good for all involved. The *oms*' scenario turns out to be a working model for progress. Terr explains this to a *draag* scientist:

> "There exists ... a great danger for an evolved race: sclerosis.... When a civilization reaches its point of perfection, it becomes a gigantic machine, incapable of progress, and which all its members are no more than wheels without thought....
>
> "Your society is showing signs of senility. It is too perfect, and little by little, the draags become robots of routine....
>
> "...Study well article 10 of the treaty.... It foresees a large association of our two civilizations. There will be no longer a master race, but two equal races, who will

work side by side, existing to benefit mutually from each other's progress. In feeling this amicable rivalry close to you, you will avoid collective sclerosis.... And you will play the same role for us. I foresee for us, two races, an extraordinary future, gained thanks to the activity of emulation" [185–6].

Wul finds a place for both societies. One needs the other to supply the indispensable competition that insures a society from becoming complacent. And so neither society needs to be eliminated or subjugated for the sake of peace and progress, for progress has no end, no state of perfection, or no ultimate goal. It consists of continual improvement. Thus, even opposing societies can persist in the future as long as they act in some way as catalysts to competition. No perfect, single world order will be in humanity's future.

There are several characteristics of this novel that one could apply to Wul's actual world of 1957. Given the Cold War between two superpowers which are not located in western or central Europe and the independence movements taking place in colonies held by the declining European powers, a wide range of events and situations exists to which one can make this novel analogous.

Perhaps a plausible interpretation is one involving the French colonial situation, for the novel did appear three years after the French defeat after Dien Bien Phu and during the crisis with Algeria. The victory of the *oms* over the *draags* could be seen as Wul's fictional warning to France to relinquish itself of its possessions and treat them as competitors on the international scene. When Wul's other novel examined in this section is covered, this observation will provide a key point in analyzing Wul's ideas. However, if one keeps in mind Wul's admonitions about the non-ideological content of his stories, then more directly related and concrete details must be found before making further claims that any real-world connections exists. Further analysis of this and Wul's other novel will provide those needed details.

Shifting from the international scene to domestic issues, at a most basic level Wul can be seen as a supporter of centrally directed societies. Note that the *oms* achieve their remarkable successes under the successive leadership of only two people, first the strong leader, then Terr. This somewhat resembles the concept of *dirigisme*, the French policy of central planning by the government over industry and commerce without totally abandoning the capitalist system. In the novel, no economic discussions take place, but the strong central leadership is stressed. However, France's *dirigisme* had several bodies of elites during the late Fourth Republic (when "Oms in Series" was released), and not just one person determining and administering policy. But keeping in mind what occurred with the advent of the Fifth Republic, the strong leader concept returns in force — in the person of war hero Charles de Gaulle.

Keeping both international and domestic observations in mind, an argument can be made that the ideas contained in "Oms in Series" parallel some of those associated with Gaullism, the political ideas associated with de Gaulle, the first president of the Fifth Republic. The concept of the strong leader or executive guiding a nation, a central tenet of Gaullism, can be readily applied to the role that Terr plays in the novel. In Gaullism, the leader of a nation is supposed to be the mediator between that nation's destiny and its people. The leader also keeps the nation together and prevents it from destroying itself by internal division or extreme philosophies of individualism.[51] Terr certainly plays these roles very well as he takes command of the *oms* and guides their destiny as a free people. When communication with the *draags* takes place during the final struggle in the novel, it is Terr who speaks for the *oms*.

Furthermore, a leader should be rooted in past traditions. In this case, Terr adopts the identical title of leadership over the *oms* that the *draags* use for their head of state, *l'Edile*. This is certainly not an indication that the *oms'* newly independent society will be that much different beyond their independent status. The fact that the title has its origins in the Latin language could be said to give the impression that Wul may be calling for a return to an earlier way of thinking about leadership — past Bonapartism all the way back to the *Principate* of ancient Rome, where the emperor was first among equals (*primus inter pares*), but ruled with absolute authority. Certainly the Gaullist ideology is nowhere near as absolutist as the practice of the *Principate* was, but the concept of a strong leader should still be kept in mind. This appeal to long-held traditions can be also identified as an important aspect of Gaullism.[52]

However, why Wul chooses the title *l'Edile* for the title of the leader of a whole people is unknown. Since in reality it designates a French lower-level official, the significance of this particular title seems to be wanting. In ancient Rome, this city-level office took charge of the inspection of the buildings, the public games, and the care of the city's supplies — not exactly a consul or senator, let alone an emperor. The modern French version is a magistrate representing a large city during a state ceremony — hardly an improvement over its Roman counterpart. Certainly Wul's novel uses this title in a respectful manner. So if Wul selected this title for the purposes of satire or a similar motive, this intent would surely be out of character with the rest of the novel. Meanwhile, Wul could have chosen the title out of sheer expediency and for no other reason.

A parallel in English-language science fiction of this usage of lower-level titles for all-powerful leaders can be found in L. Ron Hubbard's novel, *Final Blackout*, which first appeared in *Astounding Science Fiction* in 1940. In this novel, the protagonist, referred to only as the Lieutenant, rises from field officer to ruler over a war-ravaged future Britain. The protagonist keeps his initial officer's rank throughout the whole novel as a sign of respect to his origin and a reminder of his early fighting days.[53] In Wul's novel, however, Terr's title is adopted from his former enemy.

Hubbard is best known (mostly in a controversial light both inside and outside the science fiction field) for his development of Dianetics and his founding of the Church of Scientology. What most people do not know is that he was a noted pulp writer during the Thirties and Forties, producing stories in various popular genres including science fiction and fantasy.[54]

Going back to international events, Wul's portrayal of the two independent societies competing with each other coincides with part of the Gaullist outlook. De Gaulle himself believed in the integrity of nations and shunned international schemes that threatened national sovereignty. He saw each nation as sovereign and wanting no conquest over other nations. Competition between nations, and not domination of one over the other, should be the order of the day. As de Gaulle once said, "Life is life, otherwise called a fight, for a nation as for a man."[55] He viewed one nation trying to gain an advantage over another as part of the natural order in international relations. Because of this, de Gaulle further comments that "the military corps is the most complete expression of spirit for a society."[56] One can see how the novel's actions fit into this philosophy, especially with the *oms*' efforts focusing on technology in order to emigrate to safety and then to defend themselves against the *draags*. Finally, Terr's mention of a large association (*une large association*) should not be construed as being inconsistent with Gaullism, for de Gaulle did view organizations at times a practical necessity if they serve a nation's interests.[57] In this light it becomes clear how the *oms* and the *draags* must enter into this association. Being the only two peoples on the planet, they must make sure that their competition with each other does not lead to extinction of the other, for progress cannot exist with only one society or nation in existence.

Obviously Wul does not attempt to give a full treatment of Gaullist ideas, but he does display enough of the basic aspects of the ideology to lead a reader to conclude that Wul — if not actively — in his novel shares some sentiments or affinities with this way of thinking. Furthermore, whatever version of leadership Wul is trying to depict, the evidence here and in "Niourk" suggest that he possesses a positive outlook towards a strong person in control, especially in a time of crisis.

Genefort asked Wul about his portrayal of a strong leader in his novels. Wul responded that the format of Fleuve Noir novels required that their authors emphasize the deeds of the stories' protagonists, the heroes from whom emerged most of the plots' actions. A brief survey of the Anticipation novels will bear this out. It should be noted that Wul's answer involving format requirements could also be a way of eluding Genefort's question as Wul was known to dislike political discussions.[58] However even if Wul's strong leader is a result of perceived genre requirements, when one combines this concept with the other ideas discussed here, one still sees a simple presentation of Gaullist ideas.

In some respects "Oms in Series" is a timely novel. The year of its publication was a stormy one for the Fourth Republic. Parliamentary divisions and the Algerian crisis dominated the headlines and doubts about the workability of the present government ran high. Just one year away from the ascension of Charles de Gaulle, the year 1957 witnessed a rise in expectations that this war hero and national figure will save the nation from itself.

The last novel to be discussed further supports a notion of a conservative, if not Gaullist, interpretation of Wul's novels. *Piège sur Zarkass* ("Trap on Zarkass," 119, 1958) tells of an interstellar struggle between the Earth and an alien race, the Triangles (so-called because of the shape of their space ships), over the planet Zarkass, whose native humanoids have been under Earth's influence. The Triangles are described as a race of intelligent insects who construct robot structures resembling human beings to trick both Earth people and Zarkassians. Earth sends two agents to investigate the Zarkassians, who exist in a primitive state, and (if necessary) prevent the Triangles from turning them against the Earth. The agents discover that the Triangles are indeed attempting to do so, and the agents devise a plan to thwart this activity.

Laurent, one of the agents, decides to assume the identity of a messiah whom the Zarkassians expect will return from the dead and lead them to greatness. His disguise involves using parts of the mummified remains of the actual messiah, whose grave was discovered previously by another Earth agent. As time goes on, Laurent begins to exhibit some strange behavior, including suddenly speaking in the ancient Zarkassian language, despite his having no prior knowledge of it, and not being aware that he is doing so. Laurent succeeds in convincing the Zarkassians as that he is the expected messiah and leads them against the Triangles while successfully persuading them to ally with Earth.

Towards the end of the novel, Laurent-as-messiah gives a farewell speech to the Zarkassians. He urges them that they should not abandon their ways while adopting the knowledge of the Earth people.

> "Oh, my people. You have taken the science that the Terrans offer to you. And that was just and good. But you have refused your ancient practices. And the Terrans demand nothing of you. Why deny one science for another and why not keep them both? The science of your brothers takes all from the bottom and in detail, while yours takes all from the top and as a whole. Both routes will intersect and it is said that from this will come great benefits for all" [183].

Had the novel ended with this speech, it could be said that Laurent's ruse worked and Earth's espionage division engineered another success. But Laurent's previous strange behavior hints at a much different ending.

The actual conclusion of the novel contains a report by Laurent's fellow agent. Instead of giving the expected report of success, the fellow agent relates how Laurent mysteriously vanishes from sight in a blaze of light never to be seen again. Did Laurent unknowingly become the reincarnation of the Zarkassian messiah? The novel seems to answer the question in the affirmative but no explicit explanations are given.

Two alternative interpretations can be derived from the novel. The first involves France's situation of importing much from outside, especially from America; the second deals with France's relationships with its soon-to-be former colonies. Both can be derived from Laurent's quoted speech. Note how

Laurent/Messiah stresses how the Earth demands nothing of the Zarkassians in return for its science and technology. Taken at face value, the Earth-Zarkass relationship should be a harmless one. But looking deeper will result in drawing different conclusions.

The first alternative interpretation finds a parallel between postwar France and Wul's Zarkass. It would not be too much of a stretch to equate the United States with the novel's Earth and France with the Zarkassians. So instead of asking how the Zarkassians should adopt Earth science and technology without losing their own culture and identity, a reader might ponder how France should modernize without ceasing to be France. So de Gaulle's concerns expressed in the quotation starting this study find a special relevance here. But what if one looks at this parallel from a different angle and associates the Earth with France and Zarkass with France's colonies, which were becoming independent at a rapid pace during the postwar years? Here a second alternative interpretation enters into the discussion. "Trap on Zarkass" can also be seen as an argument for a more enlightened policy by France towards its colonies.

Keeping this last point in mind, the second alternative interpretation can also be used to support a Gaullist interpretation of Wul's ideas. Gaullist ideas on national sovereignty also extended to France's colonies. De Gaulle respected the yearnings for independence by France's colonies, but he also wanted the colonies to keep close ties with their former ruler. In this scenario France can still interact with the new nation without usurping the latter's sovereignty.[59] France realized this idea through the creation of the French Union (Union Française) in 1946, which became the French Community (Communauté Française) in 1958, the year "Trap on Zarkass" appeared. In this arrangement, colonies possessed the right to declare independence, which almost all exercised by 1960. Of course, this would really not be a relationship among true equals. Part of the Gaullist ideology centers around the idea of France's special place in history, as the civilizer of Europe, and therefore of the world. The perception is one of perceived cultural and spiritual superiority. Though all nations are to be treated equally, France is to be (again, recalling the ancient Roman notion of the *Principate*) *primus inter pares*, first among equals.[60] This organization thus becomes a way for France to relinquish its political responsibility and military power while maintaining a significant degree of economic, diplomatic, and cultural influence.

One could also see this so-called enlightened approach as nothing more than smokescreen for colonialism under a different guise. After all, did not Earth want to eliminate the influence of the Triangles from Zarkass? Could not this situation describe more a simple power struggle among imperial powers than an argument for more enlightened policies towards less developed societies? (Consider also the situation in "Rays for Sidar.") Since Wul has often declared that his intent was to entertain and not to inject ideological argument, the need for discovering a definitive answer in this matter must remain unfulfilled. But one can conclude that even if Wul did not mean for these ideas to be a reflection of his outlook on the world, one can still say that the ideas remain present in his novels nonetheless and they do reflect what many were thinking—consciously or otherwise.

Either of these two interpretations relating "Trap on Zarkass" to Gaullist ideas allows one to see how the ideas in "Oms in Series" and "Trap on Zarkass" comprise different aspects of Gaullist ideology. Both novels present a respect for the legitimacy of a nation's existence, but from different perspectives of power and influence. "Oms in Series" suggests healthy constructive competition among nations will strengthen all involved parties; while "Trap on Zarkass" talks about a nation (France or one of France's colonies) accepting aid without giving up its native spirit. Furthermore, "Oms in Series" involves the desire to raise France back up to the rank of a world power, while "Trap on Zarkass" calls to mind either the preservation of one's identity as a lesser power depending on foreign aid for improvement or a post-imperial idea of granting political independence but maintaining economic and cultural influence.

Wul did possess a lifelong interest in France's soon-to-be-liberated possessions. Genefort remembers Wul recounting his visit to France's Exposition Coloniale ("Colonial Exposition") as a child in 1931. Wul walked away from this experience, not with ideas of politics, economics, or world-wide competition among the great powers, but with dreams of romance, fantasy, and exoticism.[61] These impressions can be seen in his poetic descriptions of alien landscapes on distant planets.

The question of how should France act in terms of its colonies is obviously a complex one and this observation is reflected in the opinions of the French people themselves during the mid–Fifties. Merritt and Puchala present a USIA poll taken in December 1955 that reveals the French possessing mixed feelings about the amount of help their nation should give to help its colonies attain independence. Among those who gave a definitive answer, a big majority felt that France was doing fine or should do more. Only a small minority felt too much effort was given already. The breakdown is as follows:

Attitudes on the Amount of Help France Is Contributing Towards the Independence of Colonies[62]

Response	Percentage of People Asked
What It Should	22
Too Much	8
Too Little	31
Don't Know	39

What is interesting to note is how the largest group of respondents did not know. However, from those that did express an opinion, it seems that the French people, along with their counterparts in Great Britain, were ready —for whatever reasons— to let their colonies go. Maybe the ideas in Wul's novels can be said to reflect this attitude as well.

Should all this discussion relating Wul's ideas expressed in his novels to Gaullist ideology turn out to be incorrect, one can still argue that Wul encourages in a very general sense a society to maintain its traditions while adopting new information and expertise from other places. However, the author hopes that this presentation of Wul's ideas alongside those of de Gaulle gives the reader a context under which the former can be analyzed in light of current events and attitudes.

Conclusion

To recapitulate, though Wul has stated that he did not set out to advocate any ideology or philosophy in his novels, it is hoped that this analysis reveals a conservative outlook existing in Wul's works. Beyond the pessimistic outlooks depicted in some of his apocalyptic novels, his other novels — especially the two examined in the last section —contain presentations with identifiable conservative themes, including an appeal to past tradition, an argument for societies to maintain their identity when adopting new knowledge and practices, a call to compete with other societies so that all competitors might improve, a brief discussion about the belief in God and why it should be maintained, and the idea of a strong leader being necessary to create and maintain a society's protection, prosperity, and integrity. And if it can be proven without a doubt that Wul was indeed influenced by the ideas of the general– turned–President of the Republic, then Wul's presentations of ideas on a society's sovereignty and identity can also be said to be grounded in the nineteenth-century Romantic tradition of nationalism and cultural spirituality, for so much of de Gaulle's thinking — it must be reiterated — is bound in a reverence for the past and its traditions.[63]

Wul never presented progress through science and technology as inherently bad for humanity. As shown in "Trap on Zarkass," the two fields can be civilizing forces. The closest Wul comes to disparaging them occurs in the Black Infant's tirade against the Venusian colonials in "Niourk." But even that attack was primarily aimed at a forsaking of the past, including basic approaches of human reproduction, in the name of progress.

So it is safe to say that the idea of progress as presented in Wul's novels (however unintentionally) contains both a respect for the old as well as a careful adoption of the new. Old beliefs and notions will still play important roles in the future; they are what enable a people, a nation, to preserve their identities, their uniqueness, or — in light of the impact of advanced science and technology — their humanity. From Wul's novels a reader will get the impression that the best approach to the idea of progress is a conservative one.

Maurice Limat

In 1972 Pierre Versins identified Maurice Limat (1914–2002) as a "popular writer who is probably the dean of French science fiction authors still in activity."[64] Even after his death Limat still occupies a special place in French science fiction. His writing career spans no less than half a century, his fiction representing science fiction of both the post–World War I and post–World War II eras. As his early works took their cue from the writers of France's golden age of science fiction, his later works incorporated aspects from America's imported genre science fiction. Alain Douilly remarks that "the works of Limat, extremely important, deserve to be discovered and collectors will have much trouble gathering all of his works and published volumes."[65]

This last point is due to Limat being a very prolific writer and having published under the pseudonyms of Maurice d'Escrignelles, Maurice Lionel Rex, and Lionel Rex. During the first part of his career (1935–42), he published in many genres, including police stories, horror, adventure, as well as science fiction. *La Montagne aux vampires* ("The Mountain of Vampires," 1936) was his first novel, while his first science fiction novel was *Aéronef C3* ("Airship C3," 1936). This and other science fiction novels during this period took their inspiration from the pre–World War I novels of Gustave Le Rouge, characterized by mad scientists, space adventures, and other common pulp plots. After the Second World War Limat resumed his writing career, being as prolific as ever. During most of the Fifties he published science fiction in the French imprints Série 2000 and Cosmos, and the magazine *Galaxie*.[66]

Compared to fellow prolific writers Richard Bessière and Jimmy Guieu, Limat is a latecomer to Anticipation, publishing his first novel for the imprint in 1959. He published only six of his novels before the end of 1960. He wrote no less than 106 novels for Anticipation from 1959 to 1987. Sixty-nine of them occupy a common future in the twenty-second century and take place primarily on the planets Venus, Earth, and Mars. Limat also published thirty-three novels in Fleuve Noir's Angoisse imprint.[67] Lofficier and Lofficier point out that Limat's Anticipation stories during the Fifties and beyond begin to reflect the influence of imported American genre science fiction.[68] As with many prolific writers, Limat suffered from his voluminous output. As Versins puts it, "As with most popular full-time writers, imagination does not equal fecundity, and the last novels of Maurice Limat are far below the value of his first."[69]

More importantly, Lofficier and Lofficier also note that Limat stands apart from other Anticipation writers of the Fifties for his open treatment of the theme of religion. According to them, Limat's stories "celebrated the power of love and tolerance, and a genuine belief in God, the Great Architect of the Universe, something unusual in science fiction."[70] They are correct in their observation. Religion is a subject rarely discussed at great lengths in science fiction, in France or elsewhere. This generalization can be confirmed by just observing

English-language science fiction. Beyond such notable exceptions as C.S. Lewis's trilogy (*Out of the Silent Planet* [1938], *Perelandra* [1943], and *That Hideous Strength* [1945]), Olaf Stapledon's *Star Maker* (1937), Robert A. Heinlein's "If This Goes On..." (1940), and Fritz Leiber's *Gather, Darkness!* (1943), pre–World War II and wartime science fiction focusing on religion remain quite rare. Even during the decade and a half following the war with the expansion of genre science fiction, the literature did not experience the concomitant growth of religious-oriented stories. The most memorable from this time span include Anthony Boucher's "The Quest for St. Aquin" (1951), Philip José Farmer's controversial "The Lovers" (1952), Arthur C. Clarke's "The Nine Billion Names of God" (1953) and "The Star" (1955), James Blish's *A Case of Conscience* (1958), and Walter M. Miller's *A Canticle for Leibowitz* (1960). Maurice Limat represents the only Anticipation writer during the Fifties who deals significantly with this theme.

Limat falls in the conservative section of this study not because of his positive portrayal of religion, but due to the nature of his religious ideas, which were intertwined with those of a certain political party. This party emerged from a religious ideology that attempted to offer an alternative to secular philosophies, centered on capitalism and socialism, which have dominated politics for a century. Keeping this last point in mind, the following analysis of Limat's six novels can be divided into four sections. The first deals with new human experiences, the second gives a warning, the third treats the consequences of new human powers, and the fourth offers a possible solution to the problems resulting from progress in science and technology.

New Experiences, Old Themes

This group comprises two novels in which no explicit discussions about progress or ideology take place. However, the themes Limat uses in the two are those he uses in a good number of his novels. *Le Sang de soleil* ("The Blood of the Sun," 147, 1959) tells of a discovery of a being on Mercury who turns out to be the original sun god from Earth's ancient times. The being uses a mysterious elixir to transform humans into diamond beings, who will become his new subjects under his reign. *Les Foudroyants* ("The Terrifying." 164, 1960) narrates what happens when a person is struck by thunderbolt and transformed into an electronic being who now can control all devices powered by electricity. Since *foudroyant* is a form of the word *foudre*, the French word for lightning, one can also translate the title of the novel as "The Lightning Men"[71] or "The Lightning Beings."

As will be shown in the third and four sections of this analysis of Limat, the two themes used in the two novels, religion and humanity acquiring very powerful new abilities, will be connected. If humanity's new powers cannot solve problems, then what will it take to save humanity from being harmed by its new knowledge and powers? Meanwhile, the next section—containing only one novel—deals with an all-too familiar theme in Fifties science fiction.

BEWARE! ATOMIC ENERGY! (AGAIN)

Metro pour l'inconnu ("Metro for the Unknown," 159, 1960) adds another contribution to the theme of anxiety over atomic energy. Earth explorers discover a planet whose civilization's destruction was the end result of research in atomic energy. It turns out that atomic experiments created a layer of radiation that disrupted the planet's exosphere, causing environmental havoc and subsequent social collapse. The Earth explorers help the native beings by eliminating all monstrous threats and contributing to the restarting of their society. The metro of the title refers to a surviving and still functioning underground transport system of the collapsed society. The native survivors live in their subterranean setting because they cannot go to the surface, having long adapted to the darkness of the underground (the Earth party arrives 8,000 years after the original devastation). The Earth party offers a cure to the natives' oversensitivity to sunlight (making dwelling on the surface possible again), but the natives decline. However, the Earth party takes initiative and cures the natives anyway and all is well. This constitutes the only novel of the six where human intervention succeeds.

THE POWER OF POSITIVE THINKING?

Limat wrote two novels dealing with the consequences of human beings acquiring new and omnipotent powers, using them for good, but still unable to solve the problems facing society. Something else is needed for a successful future. This third section presents the problems; the fourth section offers a solution.

Les Enfants du chaos ("The Children of Chaos," 141, 1959), Limat's first novel chronologically in Anticipation, explores the limits people experience in planning society, even if given literally absolute power. An Earth ship encounters an area of space where a mysterious substance gives the crew the power to create by the act of thought alone. Soon the crew, recognizing the scope of their new god-like powers, creates the world of Volune, a paradisiacal place with a simple people living in a well-organized, scientific, and technological society where all needs are met and harmony pervades throughout the planet. When the crew actually lands on Volune, their creations look upon them as gods.

Unfortunately it turns out that the crew does not achieve total control of their new powers and inadvertently create monsters that wreak havoc among the Volunes. The Volunes, upon discovering the source of their misery, want their human creators to leave, preferring to deal with any future adversity on their own. The humans may have been their creators and gods, but they now are to be viewed as poor gods. The Earth crew eventually complies and leaves

Volune, knowing that their departure will mean death for the Volunes and the destruction of Volune itself.

At this point it is possible to see how "The Children of Chaos" can be viewed as Limat's fictional reflection on some of the modernization policies of France. By 1959 Limat would have already witnessed a decade and a half of his country trying to catch up with the world's leading powers—whether it is in science, industry, commerce, or in living standards. The transformation of a small town-oriented society to that of a growing urban-suburban one could appear to many like the creation of a new world. The fact that the wholesale placement of many industries and communities in regions outside of Paris were instituted by central government planning from above (as opposed to being results of the marketplace from below) would only magnify this perception. Even if one thinks this analogy turns out to be too much of a stretch, Limat's novel at the very least still can be seen as a warning against the creation of new social structures.

At the end of the novel a conversation takes place that adds an extra layer of meaning to Limat's story. One of the protagonists uses a passage from Voltaire's famed philosophical tale *Candide*, while the crew mulls over the results of their attempted creation of a perfect world. Pat Marcus, a scientist, and Lieutenant Christian, a crew member, close the novel with this interesting exchange.

> Pat, seeming to search for something, stops before a porthole:
> "Tell me, Christian ... I want to recall something ... Do you remember your studies?"
> "Yes, at Paris ... But why are you asking?"
> Pat makes a vague gesture.
> "I am searching to place an exact phrase. It is by Voltaire ... He made one of his characters, Doctor Pangloss, say: 'All is for the best.' No. Wait, that is not it."
> Christian recognized it very well:
> "I know it. I myself am searching too. I believe he said something like: 'Those who have said that all was well have said a foolish thing.' We must say—I am no longer very sure of the text—approximately: 'They must say that all is for the best.' So you do not believe that this is so?"
> "Yes, it seems to me," said Patrice, "It ought to be something like that!" [187–8].

The use of Voltaire's words at the end of the story invites the reader to analyze Limat's use of the *philosophe*.

Before further discussion, Voltaire's original quotation should be reviewed first. The passage originates from the first chapter of Voltaire's well-known classic *Candide* (1759). The complete passage reads as follows:

> "It is demonstrable," said he, "that things cannot be otherwise: for all things being made for an end, all is necessarily for the best end. Note well that the nose is made to hold up spectacles, so have we spectacles. The legs are visibly set up to be fitted, and we have breeches. Stones have been formed to be hewn and from them to make

castles; so His Highness has a very beautiful castle; for the greatest baron in the province ought to be the best lodged. And swine were made to be eaten, so we eat pork all the year round. Consequently, those who have brought forward that everything is all right, have said a foolish thing. They should say that everything is best."[72]

As mentioned, Voltaire used his characters of Candide and Pangloss to satirize, among other things, the optimistic view of the famed scientist and philosopher Gottfried Wilhelm Leibniz, especially Leibniz's well-known expression, "the best of all possible worlds." He did so by placing his two characters in a series of misfortunes after which Pangloss would only remark that the world the two lived in remained the best of all possible worlds. The passage, spoken by Pangloss, criticizes the chain of reasoning that leads to the conclusion that here constitutes the best of all possible worlds and it does so in a very satirical manner by using outrageous examples of cause and effect. Only at the end of the tale did Voltaire have Candide declare his equally memorable expression that one must cultivate one's own garden.

Limat's Earth explorers, meanwhile, did more than travel, experience, and speculate about the nature of the world. They literally had the opportunity to create the best of all possible worlds. No less than the construction of a perfect world was within their reach. Unlike Voltaire's protagonists, Limat's did not settle down somewhere at the end. Instead they found themselves still in space trying to make sense of what had happened. And they ended their story with a statement from Pangloss and not from Candide.

So the question remains how to interpret Limat's use of this Voltaire's phrase. Presently there exist no known available records of Limat's beliefs in non-fiction form. Therefore, his use of Voltaire's passage to express a concluding remark about how humanity should act can be interpreted in several ways.

The first is that Limat selected the quotation in a very expedient manner and saw that, without considering the context of the Voltaire's passage, it fitted well with the novel's ending. A second interpretation could be that Limat had a blunt joke in mind. In this case he would assume that a reader possessed a basic knowledge that *Candide* was in large part a polemic against Leibniz's attitude. Thus the crew taking seriously Pangloss's statement became a philosophical joke with the reader, who would also know the intended silliness meant to be attached to that statement. The crew then becomes a group of innocents who used an intended philosophical absurdity in a serious manner to explain or excuse failure.

A third way of looking at Limat's use of Voltaire's passage requires taking into account Limat's other novels. This interpretation involves considering both Leibniz and Voltaire as occupying the same side of an argument, and not as opponents. Both are considered pillars of the intellectual ferment emerging from the seventeenth-century Scientific Revolution (Leibniz) and the eighteenth-century French Enlightenment (Voltaire), their disagreements notwithstanding. The way of thinking the two thinkers represent centers on resolving issues of ethics, morals, politics, economics, etc. through methods derived from scientific and rational principles. Even religion must fall under the scope of these approaches. Given this background, this third alternative interpretation has Limat rejecting much of the method of thinking typified by both Leibniz and Voltaire.

If this last interpretation is a legitimate one, then it can go a long way in explaining Limat's use of Voltaire's passage. The novel ends with the crew in space pondering their failed attempt to create a perfect society and a perfect world. There are no further statements about the limits to human endeavors. Also no discussion takes place about how this is but a first step for humanity to exercise its new-found powers and that the crew should try again to create new and better worlds.

So the novel's ending can be considered as either one of open-endedness or of nothingness. One could either view the novel's conclusion as open ended because it is not known what the crew will do next with their new powers—if anything at all; or one could see that despite all of the crew's efforts, nothingness remains the result. Considering "The Children of Chaos" by itself, it would be safe for a reader to choose the open-ended interpretation. But—as suggested—if one were to consider also the next two novels by Limat to be examined, a reader could—with reason—choose nothingness.

The next novel in this section to be examined, *J'écoute l'univers* ("I Listen to the Universe," 154, 1960), also deals with the power to create by thought alone. This time an advanced race of Martians give the power to a man and his son. Soon a hostile alien fleet arrives in the solar system and threatens to destroy the Earth. The son turns out to be the one capable of using his power to stop the invasion. His father, no longer possessing the innocence of a child, has become skeptical of his powers and consequently loses them. The son, not knowing any better, goes out, uses his power, and repels the alien fleet. Simple belief, or faith, turns out to be the key. This conclusion provides a hint as to what Limat thinks humanity is missing to ensure progress.

"The Children of Chaos" and "I Listen to the Universe" point to the idea that humanity needs something in addition to the most advanced states of knowledge and power to exist successfully in the future. "The Children of Chaos," if the suggested third interpretation of its ending is to be taken, leaves a reader with a feeling of nothingness after the failure of nearly all-powerful people to create a new and perfect society. "I Listen to the Universe" offers the idea that faith, a very simple, child-like version of it, is still needed in the era of science. On reading Limat's last novel to be examined, a reader will have little doubt as to what Limat thinks is the missing ingredient for humanity's future.

THE POWER OF FAITH

Moi, un robot ("I, Robot" 170, 1960), besides being Limat's last novel of this period also represents his first novel to express what he thinks humanity needs in a modernizing society. Those familiar with American science fiction may immediately recognize the title as the French version of the title of *I, Robot* (1950), Isaac Asimov's influential collection of stories about robots, his now famous Three Laws of Robotics dealing with how to program robot behavior, and his protagonist scientist, Susan Calvin. Asimov's book was not translated into French by the time of Limat's novel. So unless Limat was able to read the American edition, it remains doubtful that he borrowed the title of his novel from Asimov's book and there exists any relationship between the two novels beyond the common theme of robots—not exactly an underused topic in science fiction.[73]

Limat's "I, Robot" takes place in the far future, about a thousand years after the fall of humanity to its robots. The roles have been reversed to the point where the humans not only are the servants to the robots, but the humans also believe themselves to be robots and the robots human beings. The mechanical creatures have fostered this state of affairs by keeping the truth about themselves and their human servants a scrupulously guarded secret.

On an exploration ship at the edge of the galaxy, some humans lead a revolt against the robots and succeed in overthrowing them. One of the leaders of the revolt, Andres, then receives a mysterious telepathic message to land on a heretofore unknown planet. There the humans encounter a plant-shaped metal structure. From the structure emerges an old man who calls himself *Le Venerable*, or The Venerable. The old man explains how he, a survivor from the human civilization that existed before the fall, encased himself in the metal structure, which he called *le fleur de metal*, the Metal Flower. The structure enables him not only to survive, but also to scan the universe for human thought. It was he who gave Andres the telepathic message. The survivors of the robot takeover built the Metal Flower to initiate an eventual revolution against the robots. For such a revolt to occur, however, a person with the old human spirit of independence and love must first emerge. Andres became that person and The Venerable can now reveal the truth about the relationship between the humans and the robots. Andres and The Venerable, using the Metal Flower, start to spread revolutionary ideas throughout the galaxy. By creating rain conditions (always dangerous to the robots), the humans defeat the robots and reclaim their lost supremacy.

On the surface this novel comprises yet another warning of the dangers present in a society whose science and technology have run out of control. However, a closer examination reveals Limat also offering a definite philosophical replacement for a strictly materialistic and scientific-based progress. It turns out that Limat's notions parallel many of the major tenets of the Roman Catholic-inspired Christian Democracy ideology that existed in France during the immediate postwar era. Outside of ideologues, the people who tried to apply this ideology to the real world belonged the postwar political party Mouvement Républicain Populaire (MRP, Popular Republican Movement) and its workers' group, Confédération Française Travailleurs Chrétiens (CFTC, French Confederation of Christian Workers).

Religion and politics intertwining is certainly not a new phenomenon. Both Protestants and Catholics (who originally inspired this political approach in the nineteenth century) have used Christian Democratic ideas to come to grips with the politics and social transformations of the modern industrialized era. Catholic applications dominated France's experience. During the years following World War II, France's Christian Democratic ideas can seen as attempting to offer an alternative to the competing ideologies of the Cold War, capitalism and socialism/communism. The MRP attempted to represent those who were not Socialists/Communists or Gaullists throughout the Fifties. Claiming to be a third or middle way, the party attempted to be a centrist organization representing policies upon which elements of both the left and right as well as the middle could agree. With the rise of Gaullism and the establishment of the Fifth Republic and Charles de Gaulle as president in 1958, the Gaullist party took over the conservative concerns in France, thus weakening the MRP. There existed disagreements with the Gaullists, involving European integration issues and protecting parliamentary power, which did not help the party's standing either. The MRP disbanded in 1967.

The publications of the MRP best represented Christian Democratic ideas. Supporters such as Étienne Gilson (1884–1978), Étienne Borne (1907–93), and Albert Gortais (1914–92) published various articles that together formed the basic doctrine of the MRP. The MRP downplayed its religious source in its statutes to show — among other reasons — its independence from direct influence from any particular religion. The CFTC, meanwhile, maintained close relations to the MRP and also contributed supporting ideas to the Christian Democratic dialogue.[74]

When comparing Limat's ideas with those of Christian Democracy, three common themes emerge: (1) the whole person, and not just the intellectual capacities, must be taken into account, (2) something beyond materialistic thinking is needed, more particularly a faith in God, and (3) the solution to modern-day problems must go beyond present-day alternatives. A comparison of the appropriate parts of The Venerable's speech to Andres with Christian Democratic ideas and MRP and CFTC ideology will yield interesting insights into Limat's ideological positions.

The first common theme can be found in The Venerable's explanations to Andres on the reasons why humanity fell to the robots. The Venerable starts his comments on the concept of the whole person by showing the dangers of overemphasizing only one aspect of human endeavor:

> "The Robots ... the perfect machines spawned by technique placed at the service of the worst enemy of true man: intelligence. Because men have preferred to believe this intelligence, and it alone, they were finished by becoming slaves to what this intelligence permitted them to produce" [138].

Later on he tells Andres to be become aware of his whole being, especially his soul:

> "First be aware of your body.... Permit the feeling of suffering but also that of pleasure and joy. And by knowing your body, you easily permit the spirits of your heart and the thoughts of your brain. Then, liberated by the interdependence of these three elements, you recognize in yourself that which does not depend on either your body, hear, or brain: your conscience, mirror of your immortal soul..." [141].

The Christian Democratic-inspired MPR position on this topic:

> Man is not only an individual, but a "person," endowed with reason and a soul, each of whom is of infinite value. As a reasonable person, he is capable of knowing, therefore free to choose.... Since he possesses a soul he will instinctively work for the common good.[75]

French historian François Goguel describes further the MPR position, stating that "the major concern of the MPR is of a human and psychological nature."[76] With the focus on the psychological and spiritual, it is easy to see an attempt to replace a purely intellectual explanation of the human condition based on rational ideas. These notions certainly parallel Limat's.

The idea that truth lies beyond the material world emerges with the declaration of the existence of the human soul. In this discussion suggestions of God and religion become appropriate. Here appears the second common theme with Christian Democracy in Limat's novel. The Venerable speaks of the primary role of religion:

> "Humans are lead by religion, morality, society. These are what is most uplifting and respectable. Unfortunately they degenerated. Ossified, religions created for them a picture of eternal life so terrifying that they preferred to believe no longer in their immortal souls" [139].

A little later in the novel when relating how humanity relied on its own resources only, he stresses the importance of a belief in God:

> "From this moment when intelligence is reproduced, this becomes the end of the true human mind ... they have lost God, they have lost the human touch, they are finished by losing themselves" [140].

From these two passages it becomes clear that Limat views spiritual concerns as taking precedence over purely rational ones and that God plays the central role. Limat's outlook here readily matches that of Christian Democratic ideology. A program for the CFTC declares its spiritual base openly:

> Man is not a tool of production, nor may he be reduced to being a mere servant of society. He is a free and reasonable being, endowed by God with an eternal destiny, and equipped to that end with supreme value as a person, with inalienable rights, and with high responsibilities.[77]

The trade union also expresses the role of religion in human activity when the organization claims that it "attaches itself to and inspires its action by the principles of Christian social ethics."[78] And as British historian R.E.M. Irving notes about MRP views of the human being,

> What such a conception of man owes to Christianity is obvious, although its specifically religious aspect is not clearly expressed in the preceding lines, doubtless because the MRP denies that it is a sectarian party.... It is quite clear, however, that the liberty and responsibility of man as Gilson describes them assume all their significance only against a religious background, for it is a question not only of man's reason but of his soul.[79]

The ideas expressed above reveal a deeply felt need to find alternative solutions to existing policies which are viewed as not working. This concern leads to the third shared theme with Christian Democratic thinking. Both Limat and French Christian Democrats believe that the implementation of religious ideas is needed. They view their ideas as alternatives to the existing social policies of modernization, which are characterized by them in terms of extremes—either centralized stifling socialism or chaotic unfettered capitalism. Their religion-based offerings are to be viewed as the moderate or middle way approaches to policies.

Limat's depiction of the robot society that held humans in such a state of slavery that they did not even know their true natures constitutes his way of warning about the threat to individualism that can exist if humanity relies entirely on its own resources. Future societies with total control over individuals comprise a frequent scenario in science fiction. But Limat also warns against the reverse when individuals are permitted to live only for themselves. As The Venerable puts it:

> "In a deprived existence, men and women, egoistically each living for themselves, destroy little by little the respect and love of the one next them. Life, this sacred trust, loses all its character as soon as one forces beings to be born into excess or when one destroys them en masse afterwards" [139].

Limat is concerned about extremes, be it total conformity or total individualism. From this observation it follows that the MRP's ideology would also contain warnings against extremes of social policy. The Christian Democratic-based party sees itself as the main alternative to the existing left-wing and right-wing political alternatives. As Goguel notes:

> In the perspective of such an interpretation of the evolution of the western world for a century and half, and particularly of France, individualistic liberalism and collectivism appear, to use the expression of Albert Gortais, as "the two facets of a single error." The latter owes its birth and its development to the inadequacies and the excesses of the former but the latter is too intimately linked with the former to be able to rectify it.
>
> According to the MRP, both of these conceptions rest on a false notion of man and of human society. On the right as on the left, Étienne Gilson writes, one sees man "only as an individual among individuals." The liberals of the moderate parties and of the radicalism say, "The abnormal development of some individuals harms others? Too bad for the others." As to the Communists, "They speak only of *masses*

and *mass action*: this way they are saying exactly what they think, for the only way that Marxism has discovered to prevent a minority of individuals from enslaving the majority of others, is to merge everyone in a single mass where everyone counts for one indiscriminately.[80]

Irving describes the alternative offered by the MRP as "a middle way between Liberalism and Marxism, or as their theorists put it, a combination of freedom and justice."[81] His observation is supported in a passage by Étienne Borne:

> The originality of our doctrine lies in the fact that we hold on to both ends of the rope at the same time. Justice and freedom must be pursued together and with equal vigour. Freedom without justice is artificial, deceptive, and hypocritical; it can be used to justify the mechanism of the free market and the servitude of the proletariat; such freedom is, in fact, the antithesis of freedom. Likewise, justice without freedom leads to tyranny and to the totalitarianism of Soviet communism or Fascist corporatism.[82]

As Christian Democracy seeks an alternative to existing choices, so does Limat.

Of course not all of the major tenets of Christian Democracy can be found in "I, Robot" or Limat's other novels examined here. Most significant of the missing ideas is the concept of natural social structures. This notion argues that all groups in society—family, schools, towns, business, labor unions, etc.—possess an organic unity and function and that both aspects should always remain inviolate. Government did not create these structures, but it does have a special relationship to them: to protect each group's proper role in society. It must not either interfere with a group or attempt to replace it with its own artificial creations. Only through implication could one say that even part of this particular tenet is present in Limat's novels. In "The Children of Chaos," the failure of the creation of the Volune society could have been inspired by this concept. The crew made Volune's society from nothing and did not allow it to develop organically. Note how the Volunes asked their own creators to leave so that they, the Volunes, can develop on their own. "I, Robot," with its totally artificial world, may have been likewise inspired as well. However, though he describes in varying detail the failures of created societies, Limat in his novels during the Fifties never attempts to offer a portrayal of what a future world consisting of organic structures would look like.

Limat's message of progress in "I, Robot" becomes a religious one where advancements in science and technology are not to be avoided. Instead, they should be subject to guidance based on religious beliefs and morals. This interpretation becomes apparent when examining the roles of The Venerable and the Metal Flower, for the latter is a product of the best of the old science and technology—the same science and technology that produced the oppressive robots. These two fields of endeavor, for all the immense good they can produce, remain human efforts which must serve under a higher authority, as represented here by The Venerable and his faith.

What "The Children of Chaos" (limits to human endeavor) and "I Listen to the Universe" (faith) hint, "I, Robot" identifies and describes. Limat is concerned about the well-being of the whole person and not just the intellect. He sees a society focusing too much on science and technology for progress, so he argues that spiritual needs must be taken into account as well. Limat views society as having to avoid the extremes of suppressed individual liberty and total individual freedom, and offers a spiritual alternative to guide humanity between the two. Finally, he proclaims that losing God results in people losing their humanity.

Looking at this interpretation of Limat's works, the discussion of "Children of Chaos" and *Candide* can now be completed. Limat's choosing of Christian Democratic ideas rejects both Leibniz and Voltaire. Though Leibniz and Voltaire acknowledged the existence of God, they did so in a rational manner; Leibniz with his theory of monads and Voltaire with his deistical views. Limat, with his Catholic-inspired Christian Democratic perspective, argues for a traditional approach to God and religion. Given the broad context of approaches to religion in general, Leibniz and Voltaire — despite their well-known differences — belong on the same side when compared with Limat's religious beliefs. Briefly speaking, Limat desires the science and technology without much of the early modern rationalist philosophy from which these two fields of endeavor emerged.

Conclusion

If Stefan Wul presents a conservative political vision, then Limat offers a conservative religious one. Even though the MRP attempted to represent those who searched for an alternative to both the political left and right, and had produced policies which could be classified as both leftist and rightist, the religious foundation of the party's ideology remained conservative — the desire for maintaining traditional beliefs and values. So if Limat did not intend to project a political view, his religious one still exists. Limat must be categorized as a conservative.

Limat sees God and religion as the centerpieces of the future. In view of the dangers that accompany the positive potential of science and technology, reliance on the traditional spiritual aspects of life will become more — and never less — imperative.

Peter Randa

André Duquesne (1911–79) is the person behind the science fiction writer known as Peter Randa. As with many prolific popular fiction writers, Randa used a number of pseudonyms depending what type of story he was writing. Among them were Jehan Van Rhyn, André Olivier, Jean-Jacques Alain, Diego

Suarez, Herbert Ghilen, Jules Hardouin, Henri Lern, and Urbain Farrel. Before turning to writing Randa experienced a number of occupations, including professional gambler, comedian, publisher/editor, and proprietor of a cabaret in Geneva. Randa became a full-time writer in 1955.[83]

Randa released close to 300 novels (making him probably the most prolific of the Anticipation writers) for various publishing houses, including Gallimard and Presses de la Cité, but Fleuve Noir accounted for the majority of his output, totaling 214 in all of its imprints. It turns out that he was most prolific with his police adventure stories, publishing 102 novels for Fleuve Noir's Spécial Police imprint. He wrote twenty-eight adventure novels in L'Aventurier and even five in the Angoisse. For Anticipation he produced seventy-nine novels, twenty two of them comprising of several series of continuing characters. Versins describes his writing as "nervous and straightforward, percussive, new in French science fiction during the period."[84]

Lofficier and Lofficier, who state that Randa was a former soldier, identify the major motif of his Anticipation novels as "militaristic space operas."[85] They further describe his protagonists as "loners, soldiers, or mercenaries, trapped on alien battlefields, in hopeless wars and/or missions, or stranded on alien worlds" who "ultimately succeeded against all odds in elevating themselves to positions of supreme power."[86] Douilly adds this observation:

> The themes approached by Peter Randa are multiple and makes use, when it is necessary, of a people or a group of individuals, autochthones of a faraway planet. But when he places the action in Earth's future and its conquest of space against other civilizations, he likes to employ a social military cadre and a unique political organization.[87]

These observations will be shown to be accurate when analyzing Randa's novels. Like Limat, he is a latecomer to Anticipation, being next-to-the-last French writer of the Fifties to start producing for the imprint. Randa's son, writing under the pseudonym Philippe Randa (1960–), wrote in the tradition of the elder Randa and produced twenty-two novels for Anticipation imprint. Only three of Peter Randa's novels were released before the end of 1960. These novels comprise a trilogy featuring the adventures of space explorers from Earth's colony on Venus and other places.

Survie ("'Survival,'" 152, 1960) introduces a future where it is the Soviet Union who lands on the Moon first, the United States on Mars, and France on Venus. The novel follows the adventures of Maubert and Ariezi, two prisoners convicted of murder and permanently exiled to Venus, where all are administered a serum that physically adjusts the person to the planet's environment. Once given the serum, a person can never return to Earth. On Venus they eventually encounter remnants of a super-advanced civilization that was almost entirely destroyed by war. These Venusians had highly developed their cerebral sciences, keeping vast amounts of knowledge in brains stored in liquid and jealously guarding their knowledge from outsiders. The Venusians kidnap some of the colonists, only to have the latter rescued by fellow settlers. At the end Ariezi stays with the Venusians, having absorbed some of their advanced knowledge from one of the stored brains and wanting to learn more.

Baroud ("Fight," 158, 1960) takes place two years after "Survival." Here the colonists encounter other aliens, briefly fight with them, and eventually capture their base. At the end of hostilities, the colonists discover that the aliens originate from Saturn and that they too serve as guinea pigs for colonization — never to return to their home world as well. Both groups reach a truce and decide to go their separate ways. However, Ariezi and Kerill, one of the aliens from Saturn, decide to leave Venus together and explore the universe.

At the end of the novel, an awareness of a new phase in human history is professed:

> A mentality will exist in space that will bear no resemblance to planetary ones....
> On each planet evolution continues with a tendency marked more and more towards resemblance. In space the contrary will happen....
> Finished is the era of communities where the personality is forced to fade. Space can only belong to individuality. Its constant danger continues to place at the very top of the hierarchy the indispensable leaders. Outdated on Earth, this notion will take back its rights in the stars where the daily necessities no longer permit long sterile discussions.
> ... The evolution that awaits men in space will take the opposite attitude towards the theories that have been valuable on each separate planet.
> Hegemony will take a new form. No longer will a nation or even a planet will dominate. An intermediate race will escape totally from its original influences. A race formed of individuals such as him, Ariezi, or the conditioned Saturnians as Kerill....
> A race that will be from nowhere, thus from everywhere [180–1].

This passage is not voiced by any of the novel's characters; they are the words of Randa himself. So the quotation describes Randa's actual view on what he sees as wrong with his contemporary society, the death of individuality.

Future societies that are collective serve only to stifle individual growth. Randa feels that people must strive and struggle on their own. Space travel, by placing people in situations where they cannot rely on society and must either survive or die, will quicken the evolution of the human race. Humanity will become in space something far greater than if it remains on Earth. Only the best of the survivors, the new human individuals, from this struggle for life will go on to explore and dominate the universe.

Randa reaffirms this notion quite dramatically in his last novel of this trilogy, *Les Frelons d'or* ("The Hornets of Gold" or "The Golden Hornets," 168, 1960). During their interstellar travels, Ariezi and Kerill explore a planet populated by humanoids who are controlled by hornets. The hornets only have to sting a person in order to gain control over his or her will. Like the Venusians in "Survival," the planet's humanoids once possessed an advanced civilization when war among themselves broke out, this time allowing the hornets rise and become the dominant life form. Ariezi discovers that the hornets are controlled by hives. Destroy the hives and the hornets are gone as well. Eventually he encounters the gigantic hive of all hives that coordinates every hornet through the system of smaller hives. Ariezi destroys this central hive, thus restoring freedom for all of the humanoids.

At the end of the novel Ariezi and Kerill discover that the hornets were in actuality one global hive mind, they were "a unique life, divided in a multitude of physically self-contained cells ... another principle of life ... different from all those that we have discovered up to now" (187). This life form represents the worst nightmare for Randa's new space-faring individuals, for the hornets' sting meant that the humanoids were nothing more than mere additions to the hive. The Earth with its suffocating societies never approached this scale of subsuming individual will. Randa involves only space travelers when determining the destiny of this planet. Even though there remained a few free native humanoids, the space travelers emerge as the ones who take the lead and free the natives from the hive mind.

However, consistent with his idea of free individuals, Randa does not have his protagonists remaining on the planet and guiding the natives in their newfound freedom. Their freedom being restored, the now-independent natives need no further help. At the novel's end Ariezi declares that the natives "are men, after all ... they start from scratch once more, but they possess their intelligence and something new — an instinct for human self-preservation" (188).

Two influences on Randa's ideas can be seen as originating from the science fiction field. The first is fellow Anticipation writer, Maurice Limat. Douilly points out that his novel *Humains de nulle part* ("Humans from Nowhere," 234, 1963) is Randa's tribute to Limat, specifically the latter's series of novels occurring on Venus, Earth, and Mars in the twenty-second century.[88] But Randa's homage ends there. Randa does not delve into religious themes as Limat does. What the two writers share in common is their concern for the individual, but even then they treat the matter differently. As shown already, Limat entwines the concept of the individual in a religious outlook. Randa does not.

Randa's stress on individuality and its place in the future recalls some of the ideas of American science fiction writer, Robert A. Heinlein. By the appearance of Randa's first Anticipation novel, several of Heinlein's novels had been translated into French. This timing means that Heinlein's two ideas of how corrupt governments and societies threaten individuality and how space exploration and settlement will encourage the renaissance of humanity had time to permeate to some degree through the French reading public.

One of Heinlein's translated novels can be said to possess more than a passing resemblance to Randa's series, *Between Planets* (1951, translated as *D'une planète à l'autre* in 1958).[89] *Between Planets* tells the story of the changing relations between Earth and its colonies on Mars and Venus where the colonies successfully rebel against Earth, which is ruled by a repressive government. The colonists possess both the will to fight and the superior science. At the end of the novel it becomes apparent not only where the creative energies resides, but also where the real power is now located — out in space. Heinlein's protagonist adopts a new attitude that indicates an emergence of a new type of humanity. No longer would a people be confined to one place, for

> one thing he knew: he would not stay on Earth, even if he did go back. Nor would he stay on Venus — or on Mars. He knew now where he belonged — in space, where he was born. Any planet was merely a hotel to him; space was his home.[90]

"Fight" could have owed something to Heinlein's novel, for the two works share one important idea: the realization that there will be a segment of the human race whose entire lives will be spent in outer space. As humanity expands into the solar system and beyond, new societies will emerge that will do so independently of the Earth. Both writers envision a time when those living in space will become aware of their uniqueness and, as a result, will attain a new consciousness about their position in the universe. These people will realize that they are free, not deprived, of their home world.

The threat of a hive mind to humanity brings to mind two of Heinlein's novels from the Fifties, *The Puppet Masters* (1951, translated as *Marionnettes humaines*, 1954)[91] and *Starship Troopers* (1959).[92] *The Puppet Masters* tells of a frightening struggle between the Earth and parasitic alien invaders in the form of slugs. Once a slug attaches itself to the back of a human, it can exercise total control over the person. The humans finally develop a biological weapon to destroy the slugs, with the novel ending with a retaliatory expedition by Earth to the aliens' home on Saturn's moon, Titan, to destroy the slugs.

If one were to focus on the military aspects of Randa's novels, Heinlein's controversial *Starship Troopers* (1959) comes to mind. This time the hive-minded aliens take on the form of arachnids. As Randa's novel only briefly touches upon the idea of freedom for the space-born individual, Heinlein's goes into much more detail about the new free citizen and his or her political and social responsibility. Heinlein defines the role military service (and public service in general) plays in a citizen obtaining the franchise. *Starship Troopers* resulted in much controversy for Heinlein, but it has also generated continued sales. It even inspired a film, *Starship Troopers* (1997), which likewise caused much argument as to its intent and meaning.[93] Though Randa established his reputation with his military space adventures, his three novels covered here do not examine his views of military culture or ideology anywhere near to the degree as *Starship Troopers* does. Heinlein's *Between Planets* and *Puppet Masters* remain the better novels for comparisons with Randa's novels from the Fifties.

Heinlein, being the most influential science fiction writer to emerge from the United States in the twentieth century, has often been called the American H.G. Wells. His reception outside of America has been the same as in his own country, controversial. Due to his libertarian and patriotic ideas, Heinlein has been labeled everything from an anarchist to a fascist.[94] Perhaps this is due to the fact that, in addition to his extolling of individuality, he has also promoted the value of group action, including in military situations. For Heinlein and many like-minded libertarian thinkers, individual freedom does not mean anarchy. People voluntarily uniting for a common purpose — whether providing for the common defense of a country or forming a company to make a profit — does not necessarily mean individualism is compromised. Quite the opposite. Free individuals lead to better group efforts and, consequently, better societies. As long as other people's rights are not impeded, group efforts are fine. Of course, as with any ideology — including libertarianism — there are so many interpretations as to where to draw the dividing line between individual freedom and social obligation.[95]

The same issue of interpretation can be applied to Randa's three novels. He argues for the new individual that will emerge from the human exploration of space, yet he is known here and in his other novels for his militaristic adventure stories where, as Douilly points out, highly trained and skilled fighters form elite groups who end up possessing power over the destinies of societies and sometimes of entire planets. As "The Golden Hornets" demonstrates, a planet subjugated under a hive mind is freed not by the revolutionary oppressed (as in Heinlein's novels) but by outside interference of Randa's new space-faring crews. Even though they leave the planet to its own devices after destroying the hive mind, one ruling elite still had to remove another. So although freedom is the end result, the method of attaining it remains somewhat ambiguous — to be free, someone else has to win it for you.

Here is where the similarities between Randa and Heinlein end. While Randa is known primarily — as Lofficier and Lofficier point out — for his military adventures in space, Heinlein — though some of his best known novels involve a military theme — established a reputation for tackling a diversity of topics and themes in his stories, including politics, religion, cultural mores, sexual relationships, and economics. Even if one takes into account only their common use of military adventures, there is a distinct difference between the two. Heinlein's protagonists in *The Puppet Masters* fight only when attacked, while Randa's transform a planet after their initial encounters. Heinlein's protagonists are not interventionists. Further proof of this last point can be found in his earlier novel, *Methuselah's Children* (1941), where a planet is discovered to have a race of creatures with a group mind similar to Randa's hive mind. Here Heinlein's protagonists declare humanity's individuality, allow those who want to join the group mind to do so, even cooperate at one point with the group mind, and then leave the planet. No overthrow of the existing order takes place.[96]

So maybe Randa turns out to be not so much a libertarian as a he is a total individualist who supports the stronger individuals over weaker individuals or groups. This observation is borne out by his focus on individuals fighting for survival or exploring the unknown, where those who fight the best will comprise a new type of humanity. In "Fight" he uses the term "evolution" (esp. 179–81) in describing this stage of human development. One may view this use of the term by Randa as a variation of the commonly misused phrase by the British evolutionary social thinker, Herbert Spencer (1820–1903), in 1864: survival of the fittest. Applying Darwin's ideas of natural selection to fields beyond biology, Spencer attempted to describe "in mechanical terms, is that which Mr. Darwin has called 'natural selection, or the preservation of favored races in the struggle of life.'"[97] However, many people have misapplied this concept to human society. They have implemented this concept to prove the superiority of an economic system, political institution, or even an ethnic group and to justify actions involving defeating persons, conquering countries, or eliminating cultures.[98] Combine this particular use of Spencer's notion with Randa's constant use of military solutions, and one might be tempted to label Randa's approach to progress not conservative, but reactionary.

As with most of the other writers examined in this study, there exist no records of Randa's personal stances on issues. But among the Anticipation writers, Randa stands alone with his pronounced declaration of individuality. While other writers examine the limits of government policies, social traditions, and human activity due to limits placed by nature or even religious ideas, Randa has nothing to do with such talk. His new human individual, freed from the shackles of inherently corrupt societies on Earth, is really a return to an idealized version of the old individual or groups of such people who will thrive and conquer all who stand in their way.[99]

Of course three novels do not make a full representation of Randa's works and ideas, so further reading of his post 1960 novels is in order. However, even this limited survey does give one a sense of a different and distinct voice emerging in Anticipation. From Randa's brief depiction of his idea of individualism, he could have been placed in the Extremist chapter with Guieu. However, Randa talks about reclaiming something that society has taken away—one's individuality; while Guieu argues almost the reverse—to get rid of past and existing ideas or traditions given by society that stand in the way of progress. So for Randa, as for Wul and Limat, guidance for the future is to be found in the past.

Kurt Steiner

Kurt Steiner is the pseudonym for André Ruellan (1922–), a medical doctor by profession. After reading the works of Camille Flammarion, Paul d'Ivoi, and Jean de La Hire as a youth, Steiner knew early on that he wanted to be a writer. The war interrupted his studies, which he completed afterwards. In the five years immediately following the war, he produced twenty-two novels, a pace he did not maintain after he started his medical practice.

He wrote under the pseudonyms Kurt Dupont, André Louvigny, Luc Vigan, and Kurt Wargar. The majority of his works can be defined as fantasy and horror and they appeared in Fleuve Noir's Angoisse (twenty-two novels) and Gore imprints (one novel). He wrote eleven novels for Anticipation, of which four appeared by the end of 1960. Steiner is remembered for his work in both groups, though Versins claims that Steiner's science fiction is "without doubt the best of what he has written."[100]

One of the three still-living Anticipation writers from the 1950s, Steiner was and remains active in the television and film industry. The online site, The Internet Movie Database (IMDb), lists no less than twenty five credits for films or television series in which he was either the writer, dialogue creator, screenplay writer, or source of literary inspiration. His latest involvement, for television, is due to be released in 2010. He also played the role as a priest on television (1982) and appeared as himself in a video (2002).[101]

Of his four novels appearing during the period covered in this study, three will be examined as Steiner's response to the idea of progress. The remaining one, *Le 32 juillet* ("July 32nd," 146, 1959), does bring up a standard plot which will be turned upside down in his three other novels. The novel is best remembered for three Earth people, a man and two women, going into another dimension and exploring *inside* a gigantic organism, *Le Krall*, which was "big as a mountain," as Versins describes it.[102] They also discover a race of aliens, *Les Atôls*, who are at war with *Le Krall*. The Earth people side with the aliens and develop a cancerous tissue with which they infect the gigantic organism to kill it. Having Earth people affecting the destinies of other races is certainly an oft-used plot in science fiction. When considering Steiner's other novels examined in this study, this theme turns out to be the exception. The other three novels deal with the reverse, humanity being the recipient of outside help.

Two of the remaining novels, *Menace d'outre-terre* ("Menace from Beyond Earth," 124, 1958) and *Salamandra* ("Salamandra," 131, 1959), involve humanity coming to terms with being helped by others. "Salamandra" centers on Ror Uphill, who escapes from Mercury's oppressive society (ruled by the dictatorial *Les Technocrates*, who control the energy source and production policy and enslave the people by robbing a person's mind of individual thought). Uphill flees by traveling through other continuums before arriving at the solar system of Wolf 359, in reality one of the closest stars to Earth's sun.

Uphill discovers the system's inhabitants have been observing Earth and have become worried about humanity's science and technology outstripping its moral and social development. Even though Wolf 359's people are presently more advanced than Earth's, humanity's pace of progress is much faster and will soon surpass Wolf 359. Steiner depicts the inhabitants of Wolf 359 as gentle, non-aggressive, and not being able to kill as readily as people on Earth. Wolf 369 fear Earth's war-like behavior and become anxious over its spreading into outer space, so the aliens send secret agents to observe and steer humanity towards a more peaceful course. The surprise of the novel occurs when the aliens reveal that Uphill himself is one of these agents.

"Menace from Beyond Earth" turns out to be the novel that contains any detailed discussion about the ramifications of advanced civilizations helping those less developed. Alain Tarnier, a scientist who is experimenting with the removal of subatomic particles from the nucleus, causes damage to energy sources in the fifth dimension without being aware of doing so. The Omegans, one of the dimension's inhabitants, strike back by creating havoc around the Earth. A message from the Omegans asking why the Earth is attacking them results in two expeditions into the fifth dimension. Eventually both sides comprehend the situation and spare their respective worlds from further threats.

Before the resolution of the crisis, Tarnier and Bourrelier, a businessman who accompanied Tarnier on one the expeditions, encounter Illil, an Omegan. The three engage in a conversation about the best way to improve society. It turns out that the world in the fifth dimension the Earth people visited is inhabited by a humanoid race of nomads who are harvesting radioactive materials (the source of energy which Tarnier's experiments were damaging and upon which the Omegans depend for operating their society) in return for guidance from the Omegans. The Earth visitors become revolted by such an arrangement and the following debate ensues:

> [Illil] "These beings were at the nomadic stage and lived very badly before we discovered their planet and the radioactive riches it concealed — riches for which, incidentally, they have no need. Their 'slavery' consists of extracting mineral — work without danger. In exchange, we have elevated considerably their level of material life by bringing to them easy methods for hunting, construction, etc."
> "But if they no longer have vital problems to resolve," Tarnier objected, "their evolution will stop! This is a bad service to render to them."
> "Not at all. Evolution which prods the struggle for life infallibly tends towards a civilization that is murderous and dehumanized.... If, on the contrary, one facilitates the setting out of a race towards a comfortable existence, the thought of this race would turn itself towards meditation and art. I consider this sort of evolution as directed towards a more desirable path."
> ... Bourrelier tightened his lips. "No truly," he wished, "a civilization where there is nothing to undertake, not a struggle, not a competition, this does not come to an asset."
> "Precisely," retorted Illil, who had — as is his habit — captured the thought of Bourrelier, "if you were an offspring of this sort of society, you would not be an asset, but a dreamer.... The problem falls upon itself" [184–5].

In the novel Steiner sees no problems with advanced races overseeing those less developed. In fact, he seems to encourage it. Eliminating the need to struggle and creating more time to pursue intellectual and aesthetic pursuits should be considered worthwhile goals. The sooner a people are freed from the basic problems of survival, the better. If Steiner meant the objections by the Earth people to represent the prevailing world view of his time, then Illil's words serve as a warning against an idea of social evolution which views struggle as a necessary component of progress. Even guidance from above by alien beings would be preferable to a life of competition, which would only slow down progress, not speed it up.

Four. The Conservatives

The ideas presented here can be viewed in opposition to those of Wul and Randa. Wul advocates healthy competition among sovereign nations as the best way to insure progress. Steiner obviously disagrees. If good results emerge from cooperation and guidance from above, they become preferable to the distractions that a contest between two parties would produce. Randa talks about struggle for existence in new environments (space exploration) where individuals band together and fight for survival. Steiner sees nothing wrong with cooperation, even when it involves more advanced races helping less advanced ones.

Furthermore, when examining "Menace from Beyond Earth" along with Steiner's last novel of this period, *Aux armes d'Ortog* ("By Ortog's Arms," 155, 1960), a compelling comparison of ideas can be made between Steiner and another writer, one far more well-known to general audiences. The writer in question hails from well beyond France, from an island south of India; he is British-born writer Arthur C. Clarke.

"By Ortog's Arms" carries the theme of alien intervention and evolution to its ultimate limits. In the fiftieth century the Earth has somewhat recovered from the apocalyptic "Blue War," which has doomed the human race to extinction. One of the negative effects of the war is the shortening of human longevity by more than half (150 to 60 years). A hierarchical society exists and is ruled by aristocratic group called the *Sopharchie*. This governing body accepts only scientists and philosophers as members. Over time it has stagnated and degenerated, becoming a huge detriment to society. A resignation to extinction pervades up the group's attitude.

There does remain one segment of humanity who refuses to surrender: those in charge of space travel, *Le Corps stellaire des chevaliers-nautes* ("The Stellar Corps of Knightonauts"). Ortog belongs to the Knightonauts and becomes the novel's protagonist. This group refuses to be passive, but they do not know how to reverse the trend towards extinction. The Corps believes in the existence of a planet, called the Planet of Archangels, where lives the Immortal Prophet, the one person who might save the human race. Unfortunately, knowledge of the planet's location was lost during the Blue War. The search for the planet comprises the Corps's primary mission. Towards the end of the novel they find the Immortal Prophet in the Betelgeuse system on a planet inhabited by winged creatures. Contained in a cylinder, this being explains the nature of life in the universe.

All living creatures in a solar system turn out to be component cells of a larger entity, the Solar Being. Human beings comprise the brain tissue (*tissue noble*), while animals and plants make up the rest (*tissue vulgaire*) of this being. This entity continues to evolve into something greater. Thus human history is reduced to nothing more than manifestations of an ever developing cosmic creature. As the Solar Being informs the Knightonauts,

> "The Solar Being has fought at all times against the diseases inherent in its nature, which are diseases against equilibrium and adaptation to its progress. Your Blue

War represents the last of these formidable afflictions. It has broken, with one blow, the planetary ecology and has affected the brain tissue of The Being to such a point that its entire equilibrium is now condemned.... The tissue director of the Solar Being is in full degeneration and its cells have a shorter and shorter existence. When this tissue dies, the common tissues of the vegetable and animal races will proliferate and give through mutations another dominate race, which will be for The Being like a graft of another brain. Solar cells, if you want to survive, you must proliferate, before the others do, and throw your seed in space. In this exceptional period the natural methods are futile. Apply ectogenesis at an accelerated rate and your race will find again — thanks to the general equilibrium of The Being — the normal potential of your gametes" [184]

So the human race must survive for its own sake. Even though it plays a role in the development of a cosmic being, humanity is not necessary for the Solar Being's continued existence. Some other race will take its place if humanity fails, which is what humanity is doing at the moment. The Knightonauts intend to carry out the suggestion given by the Immortal Prophet.

Steiner did write a sequel, *Ortog et les ténèbres* ("Ortog and the Darkness," 376, 1969), continuing the adventures of Ortog. In this novel Ortog deals with life after death and immortality. Because Steiner associates Ortog and his organization with a term originating from Europe's medieval period, the two novels can be described as a mixture of the science fiction and historical novel genres, where future-oriented themes are intertwined with characters and societies inspired from the past. Instead of the Holy Grail, Steiner's knights seek the secret to human salvation — and find it.

That "By Ortog's Arms" attempts to add new twists to the themes of alien interaction and evolution is easy to see. By making the cosmos one gigantic interstellar entity, no aliens really exist in the novel since all are part of one being. What looks like encounters with other beings become interactions among different parts of the same cosmic body. As for evolution, the idea of the human race belonging or joining into a transcendent race in the form of a group being is a well-known, though not commonly used concept. Such classics as Olaf Stapledon's *Star Maker* (1937), Arthur C. Clarke's *Childhood's End* (1953), and Theodore Sturgeon's *More Than Human* (1953) have intrigued readers by stretching the parameters of possible human development beyond the known material and biological world. All three novels share the concept of the human race as just a transition stage along the path of cosmic evolution. Humanity is to be absorbed or integrated into a higher existence, even to the point of losing the characteristics of its individuals. Steiner's "By Ortog's Arms" does not share this concept. His human beings still belong to a cosmic evolution, but do so by remaining the same, including the retention of its individual members.

Placing Clarke's masterpiece, *Childhood's End*,[103] alongside both "Menace from Beyond Earth" and "By Ortog's Arms" makes for interesting comparisons. Clarke, who had moved from Great Britain to Ceylon (now Sri Lanka) a few years before Steiner's two novels were released, was by 1960 establishing himself as both a science and science fiction writer who eventually became read and respected by both genre readers and general audiences. Along with Robert A. Heinlein and Isaac Asimov, he became known to many as one of the "big three" writers of science fiction.

Childhood's End narrates the saga of humanity's first encounter with an alien race and its next step in evolution. By the year 1975 the rivalry between the United States and the Soviet Union is about to extend into outer space when the appearance of alien space craft reveals that the human race is not alone. Referred to as the Overlords, the aliens do not show themselves to humanity as they take over the affairs of the Earth, eliminate war and hunger, and bring about Earth's first true golden age. After fifty years the aliens finally reveal themselves, resembling the traditional Christian image of the devil. Humanity is satisfied and secure by this point and no longer feels threatened, even by appearances once associated with evil. A group of intellectuals establish a settlement on an island and dub it New Athens, a place where the mind is kept alive in a world now overwhelmed by complacency.

The children of the world start to develop telepathic powers and turn out to be the starting point of human evolution's next stage. The Overlords explain that all those past childhood now represent humanity's last generation. The children are taken from their families and their parents live out their lives, some even ending them prematurely. Those on New Athens, knowing that their world no longer has any meaning and will soon end, decide to destroy themselves. At novel's end the children merge with the Overmind, a cosmic being who is the real master behind the Overlords, and in the process transform the Earth into energy to facilitate the children's final journey.

Taken together, Steiner's two novels provide an interesting parallel to Clarke's novel. "Menace from Earth" corresponds to the first two parts of *Childhood's End* as both render the idea of an advanced race guiding humanity in positive terms. "By Ortog's Arms," meanwhile, covers the same theme as the third (concluding) part of Clarke's novel, the next step in evolution.

Adding to this parallel, the use of symbolic references by the two writers (for Steiner, in "By Ortog's Arms") seems to urge a reader to compare. Perhaps the most obvious involves Steiner's portrayal of aliens in the form of angels being in opposition to Clarke's aliens in the form of devils. Steiner's Planet of Archangels is named so because of the winged race of creatures that protects the cylinder containing The Immortal Prophet. Despite Clarke's aliens possessing the antithetical image to Steiner's, Clarke's fallen angel-like creatures still act in same manner, as mere intermediaries to a higher being. Another symbolic parallel is Steiner's *Sopharchie* and Clarke's New Athens. Note the Greek roots of the names for both Steiner's and Clarke's groups of intellectuals. These two groups represent the elite of human endeavor who, after realizing the inevitable end of the human race, resign themselves to their fate.

The similarities between the two writers stop and the differences between them become quite dramatic when one reaches the conclusions of "By Ortog's Arms" and *Childhood's End*. Steiner's humans have a chance to survive and still be a part of the cosmic mind while maintaining their present stage of existence. Clarke's have no choice—humanity must be absorbed into the group mind and the old humanity dies off. Though Clarke may have been elegiac in *Childhood's End* about the passing of humanity, thus sharing the same anxieties as Steiner, Clarke still has the human race meet its inescapable end.[104] Steiner, meanwhile, seems to hold out for the human race as we know it.

Perhaps this difference is best exemplified by the respective destinies of Jan Rodericks from *Childhood's End*, a human who disobeys the Overlords' ban on human space travel in order to find out more about the Overlords and manages to visit their home planet, and of Steiner's Stellar Order of Knightonauts. Clarke portrays Rodericks (unlike the others of New Athens) as one who still possesses that spark of human curiosity and rebelliousness. Against all odds, he survives the demise of his contemporaries long enough to return and witness the transformation of the human race. At the end of the novel he chooses to die along with the vanishing Earth while recording the apocalyptic event for the Overlords. The Knightonauts, viewing themselves as the "last bastion of honorable men" because "they remain men of action and cannot resign themselves to the spectacle of gradual extinction" (19–20), stand ready at novel's end to fight for humanity's survival and expansion.

Clarke's more famous novel and film, both bearing the same title, *2001: A Space Odyssey* (1968), continued this discussion on evolution.[105] As in *Childhood's End*, Clarke presents the themes of aliens overseeing human development and the next stage in evolution. However, he (and director Stanley Kubrick in the film) depicts no definite conclusion in either novel or the film. Both make it clear that the aliens are in charge of human development, but neither clarify if this arrangement is ultimately a positive or negative one for present-day humanity. The novel ends with the Star Child (humanity's next stage in evolution) returning to Earth and detonating the nuclear weapons orbiting Earth, while film concludes with the Star Child just returning to Earth.[106] This open-endedness in both works leaves one pondering human destiny more than evaluating the merits of the aliens' actions. So Clarke's *Childhood's End* provides for a better comparison with Steiner's works when discussing the idea of progress.

Steiner's opposition to the conclusion of *Childhood's End* offers a ray of hope for the present-day human race. Though the Blue War is actually part of some sort of cosmological evolutionary scheme, this devastation does not mean that humanity should acquiesce to its fate of extinction. In fact, humanity can still play an active and important role in cosmic evolution by being the race to supply the *tissue noble* of the emerging Solar Being. Active measures must be taken to insure survival. Stoically awaiting a racial death should not be an option.

One could place Steiner in the extremist category along with Jimmy Guieu since both have humanity experience a dramatic change in reproduction methods. But Guieu's guardians of humanity's future are fundamentally different from Steiner's. Guieu, it may be recalled, has disembodied brains preserving the human race, while Steiner's protectors remain the same. If one insisted on emphasizing the change in human reproduction to the exclusion of all other considerations, it would be understandable if Steiner were placed in the extremist category of response. However, given Steiner's insistence that it is the continuation of present-day humanity — and not some extreme alteration of it — that will ensure the survival of the race, the author considers it more appropriate to place him in the conservative category. Steiner's protectors of humanity take their inspiration from Europe's medieval past; they are knights willing to undertake heroic deeds to save humanity — their type of humanity and not someone else's.

AFTERWORD

The author once briefly discussed with Steiner how two of his novels examined the same themes as Clarke's *Childhood's End*. Steiner expressed great surprise. He was pleased with the association, but remained surprised.[107] Steiner may not have had Clarke in mind when writing his novels, but this does not eliminate the fact that he treated the same themes as Clarke. The author hopes that the above analysis at the very least provides an insight into how two writers can treat the same idea in relatively the same manner and come up with different results.

Chapter Summary

As Wul (political), Limat (religious), or Randa (ideological) present ideas that can be identified with conservative systems of their time, Steiner does not. Steiner's concerns about humanity's future have nothing to do with politics or religion. Rather, he prefers to deal with humanity's fate on a cosmological level. Whether Steiner — and the other three writers, for that matter — was just experimenting with various themes of the science fiction genre or trying to examine certain ideological approaches, the indeterminacy of some of the writers' intentions does not preclude associative examinations of the ideas presented in their novels.

Wul, Limat, Randa, and Steiner want the human race to survive. In doing so, they have humanity reaching back to the past for inspiration and guidance. For these four writers, the idea of progress will be carried out by protagonists who will be recognizable and with whom present-day readers can find commonality and, maybe, even comfort.

CHAPTER FIVE

The Radicals

The term, "radical" means so many different things in its contemporary usage. Most people define the term as meaning extreme, going to what ever lengths necessary to achieve an objective — like what Jimmy Guieu proposes in his use of science and technology to insure the survival of the human race. If this extremist interpretation were to be used, then there would be no separate chapter in this study for radicals and the two writers to be studied in this chapter, Jean-Gaston Vandel and B.R. Bruss, would be placed in the Extremist chapter along with Guieu.

However, what these two writers discuss involves substantively more than just taking extreme measures to solve crises. For the purposes of this study, the term radical will be used in the following sense: "going back to the root or origin; touching or acting upon what is essential and fundamental; thorough; esp. *radical change, cure.*"[1] Vandel and Bruss attempt to return to the basis, or core, of either human society (Vandel) or of human relationships (Bruss). Science and technology still play a central role in the idea of progress in both of their discussions, but the two writers' responses to the impact of these fields of endeavor demand a return and rediscovery of what is fundamental in human beings before determining the best path of progress. Up to this point the previously examined writers urge caution (the moderates), emphasize only one aspect of human endeavor (the extremist), or resort to existing ideologies or approaches (the conservatives) as the correct path. Vandel and Bruss prefer to reexamine the basic nature of people and society and how people should interact with each other at a fundamental level before going forward.

Jean-Gaston Vandel

The name Jean-Gaston Vandel is a pseudonym used by two writers, Jean Libert (1913–95) and Gaston Vandenpanhuyse[2] (1913–81), both born in Belgium and childhood friends. Most readers knew them better by one of their other pseudonyms, Paul Kenny, under which they published spy thrillers in Fleuve Noir's Espionnage imprint. There they introduced their fictional hero Coplan FX-18, who turned out to be their best-selling product, so much so that they

Five. The Radicals

decided to stop writing their science fiction stories in 1956 and concentrate on the Kenny pseudonym and its Coplan FX-18 stories. Several film and television adaptations were made from this James Bond-like character. Douilly remarks, "One can only regret that 'Vandel' had chosen to abandon science fiction in order to devote themselves to their hero of Espionnage, Coplan FX-18."[3]

Together with Richard Bessière and Jimmy Guieu, Vandel[4] completes the trio of French authors who wrote almost all of the original native science fiction in Anticipation during its first six years of existence. Together the three account for forty-seven of the first fifty-six French novels released during the years 1951–6. In fact, Vandel turns out to be the most prolific of the three during these years, producing twenty novels — as compared to Guieu (nineteen novels) and Bessière (eight novels). Of the three, Versins calls Vandel "the best of the Anticipation writers before the arrival of Stefan Wul."[5]

Lofficier and Lofficier describe most of Vandel's work as dealing with two major themes. The first concerns "the importance of tolerance and communication between species," while the second focuses on the "survival of the species ... in Vandel's rather pessimistic fiction."[6] These observations show how there are different ways of looking at and organizing a writer's works. This study will examine Vandel, as it has with the other Anticipation writers, in terms of his reaction to the idea of progress and his ideological offerings.

Like Bessière and unlike Guieu, Vandel uses a variety of science fiction themes. However, through these diverse approaches, one major concern about progress emerges from his novels: the tension in a future society between the need for governing elites and the individual liberties of the people at large. Vandel portrays modern civilization as changing at ever increasing rates and with fewer and fewer people capable of understanding completely — let alone governing successfully — the ongoing social transformations.

Several questions on this topic emerge. If it were true that the understanding of an advanced scientific and technological world will become the province of increasingly smaller numbers of people, i.e., the properly educated elites, should society reorganize its structures and place its governing power in the hands of the competent few? Some of Vandel's novels answer in the affirmative. However, if society's power were indeed controlled by such an elite body, how is it to be held accountable for its actions? Will individual rights of the vast majority be preserved? To this last question other novels by Vandel answer in the negative by depicting humanity's elites as unable to govern wisely. And finally, does a solution to this dilemma exist? In three of his later novels, Vandel explores a possible approach.

This examination of Vandel's novels will be organized into four parts. The first, comprising five novels, presents an argument for an elite technocracy. The second, containing only one novel, provides a counterpoint. The third, made up of eleven novels and divided in five groups according to theme, brings up various permutations of the tension between the governing elites and individual rights. This part employs the following plot devices of science fiction: robots in society (two novels), interactions with alien beings (four novels), the mad scientist (one novel), the role of evolution in humanity's future (three novels), and the unforeseen consequences of new science and technology (one novel). The fourth and final part, containing three novels, contains Vandel's offering of a solution.

WINGS OVER THE WORLD

The five novels in the first group portray technocratic elites in a positive light. Vandel's first novel, *Les Chevaliers de l'espace* ("The Space Knights," 7, 1951), introduces a secret society that attempts to save a troubled world. In 2050 CE, the Earth, dominated by three major empires (American, Asiatic, and Atlantic [European]), is on the brink of global warfare. The Asiatic empire, wanting world domination, attacks Europe. The latter responds, but the military forces and weapons on both sides are mysteriously rendered powerless or made to malfunction. At first the agent behind these interventions hides its true nature, but it does give an ultimatum to all — demanding the surrender of power by all three empires. The empires finally give in after resisting futilely.

The mysterious group eventually reveals itself as *Les Chevaliers de l'espace*, or the Space Knights. The Space Knights describe themselves as a secret society, composed of the best and brightest of humanity, whose sole purpose is to watch over the Earth. They run their operations from an orbiting space station, called Paxopolis, 14,000 kilometers (8,680 miles) above the Earth. The Space Knights harbor no desire to dominate any particular country or people, but they will take whatever measures are necessary to ensure peace and progress for everyone. Their policy has been to withhold scientific discoveries and technological innovations until they deem humanity ready for them. The Space Knights also secretly place their members in positions of high power in all three empires. Along with other members of the organization, these highly placed agents will even kill to quell any threat to world peace. This group has made itself the final arbiter of right and wrong. The ruler of the Space Knights concludes the novel with a speech encouraging the Earth to trust in this secret society:

> "The Space Knights have led science to a point of accomplishment our ancestors have foreseen without expecting.... Thanks to the Space Knights, the miracles spring up as if by magic!... And their most beautiful miracle: Peace on Earth.... Have confidence for the Space Knights watch over you..." [190].

The exploits of the Space Knights continue in two sequels, *Le Satellite artificiel* ("The Artificial Satellite," 10, 1951) and *Les Astres morts* ("The Dead Stars," 11, 1951). "The Artificial Satellite" takes place seven years later and has the Space Knights embarking on ambitious plans to improve the world, including fertilizing the Sahara Desert, farming underwater sea beds, and launching the first ship to the Moon. They overturn an attack from the Arab Empire (not mentioned in previous novel) through the use of secret weapons. Of interest here is a mention of an oil crisis between the United States and Great Britain against the Arab Empire (115). The Space Knights keep the details of their victory from the general public for the sake of security. They also reveal the right to judge over who should be punished (even by death) (157–63). "The Dead Stars" has the Space Knights settling on the Moon, exploring the solar system, and developing a matter transmitting device. The antagonists in the novel are intelligent crab-like creatures from Jupiter, who send a comet to hit the Moon, which in turn will cause the Moon to collide with the Earth. The Space Knights rescue the Earth, encounter the crab-like creatures, and — unlike with the Arab Empire in the previous novel — arrange an alliance with the creatures.

The need for elites to handle new situations in an advanced scientific and technological society becomes very obvious in this series. The portrayal of such a technocracy, whether positively or negatively, provides a common backdrop in science fiction. Aldous Huxley's *Brave New World* (1932)[7] and George Orwell's *Nineteen Eighty-Four* (1949)[8] constitute the most well-known negative views. Perhaps the most famous positive depictions can be found in the later works of no less a figure than H.G. Wells.

Today most remember Wells primarily for his early works of fiction, his late-nineteenth and early twentieth-century stories that defined science fiction for modern times. He filled these stories with doubts about the existence of progress. For example, in his classic short novel, *The Time Machine* (1895), his time-traveling protagonist visits a nightmarish far future of cannibalistic Morlocks and their well-cared for Eloi, and eventually travels much further into the future when humanity no longer exists.[9] His often overlooked dystopian novel, *When the Sleeper Wakes* (1899), depicts an ultra-industrialized society in which the vast majority of people are suffering.[10] So the early Wells is a critic of progress.[11]

At the turn of the century, Wells began to change his mind and soon became known, especially after World War I, as a prophet of progress. Beginning with his non-fiction, but speculative book *Anticipations* (1901), Wells expounded on the possible grandeur that the future holds for humanity.[12] He described how the human race will attain this wonderful future in his important utopian work, *A Modern Utopia* (1905),[13] and his prescient and influential offering released just before the outbreak of the First World War, *World Set Free* (1914).[14] *A Modern Utopia* presents a highly stratified and hierarchical society where each person has his or her proper role, based on one's capacity for learning and application of knowledge. In some respects, Wells's utopia resembles Richard Bessière's Venusian paradisiacal society in the latter's "Return of the 'Meteor.'" *World Set Free*, in which Wells coins the phrase 'atomic bomb,' presents the first depiction of a hypothetical war with the use of atomic weapons and its aftermath. Here a select group of people establish a world government whose policies center on the control of new science and technology. These two aspects, a social hierarchy and a technocratic elite, characterize Wells's solutions for the world's problems.[15] During the decade following the First World War, Wells became a world-renowned figure whose commentaries and books the public anticipated reading to see what advice he had to offer in terms of thinking about current events and their impact on the future. Then and afterwards Wells continued to offer visions of his future societies composed of hierarchies and ruled by technocratic elites.

Perhaps the most memorable version of Wells's social extrapolations takes place in the form of his United Airmen, who appear in the film *Things to Come* (1936) for which he wrote the screenplay and supervised filming.[16] The film is based on his *The Shape of Things to Come* (1933), a book-length speculative forecast.[17] The film became much anticipated due to Wells's involvement in the film. Actor Raymond Massey, the star of the film, commented that "no writer for the screen ever had or ever will have such authority as H.G. Wells possessed in the making of *Things to Come*."[18]

In the film, Wells anticipates the Second World War starting in 1940 and lasting over twenty years. A new Dark Age, complete with a worldwide plague, ensues. However, the remnants of the scientific community gather together in Basra (located in Iraq — which received its independence from the British in 1932 — near the traditional sites attributed to be the Biblical Garden of Eden) and take up the responsibility of rebuilding the world. Using their science and technology, they eliminate barbaric states and eventually manage to construct a utopia by the year 2036. All through the film this corps of elite scientists and engineers lead the way to peace, prosperity, and most importantly, unceasing progress. This new group ruling over the whole world is the United Airmen.

Vandel's Space Knights bear more than a passing resemblance to Wells's United Airmen. This comparison becomes especially evident when one examines the middle part of the film when the United Airmen overthrow a barbaric chiefdom, ruled by a warlord called The Boss. The following will show that both the ideas and method of action taken by the Space Knights match those of the United Airmen.

The ideas shared by both groups can be simply expressed: science and technology provide the keys to human progress. The Space Knights' speech at the conclusion of "The Space Knights," where they equate science with miracles, provides proof enough of their confidence in these two fields of endeavor. In *Things to Come*, this same trust becomes evident during a meeting between John Cabal, a leader of the United Airmen who also serves as their spokesperson in the film, and a small group of sympathetic people in the barbaric chiefdom. Ignoring protocol, Cabal first meets with the sympathetic group before introducing himself to The Boss. To the group Cabal explains the role of the United Airmen:

> "We, who are all that are left of the old engineers and mechanics have pledge ourselves to the salvage the world ... and we have ideas in common ... the Brotherhood

of efficiency, the free masonry of Science. We're the last trustees of civilization when everything else has failed."[19]

When Cabal meets with The Boss, Cabal's message takes on threatening overtones as he declares that the United Airmen will "clean things up."[20]

Meanwhile, the similarity of actions shared by both groups becomes apparent when observing the method by which they handle their adversaries. Four instances can be detected. First of all, as Vandel's elites direct their actions from the orbiting Paxopolis, Wells's also defeat the enemy from above. In Wells's case, however, it is through the use of large but graceful super airplanes (certainly impressive for 1936 film-making). The Boss's feeble air force, comprised of rebuilt pre-catastrophe, World War I-style biplanes, prove to be but a minor annoyance. In particular, the film shows some United Airmen on one of the super airplanes observing the air battle with a mix of calmness, minor concern, and almost Olympian detachment. The notion of being above it all becomes so important for the United Airmen that Cabal, on first meeting with The Boss, simply identifies the organization that he represents as "Wings over the World."[21] He reiterates this phrase one last time after The Boss and his chiefdom have been defeated. Here Cabal outlines the long plan for recovery and describes its completion: "And at long last, wings over the world and the new world begins."[22]

The second instance of shared method of action involves both groups operating in seemingly mysterious ways. As the Space Knights act by using unseen forces, the United Airmen do so in a fashion equally awe-inspiring. The United Airmen's chief weapon consists of the Gas of Peace. Contained in white spheres and dropped from super airplanes, the gas is released when the spheres softly explode after hitting the ground, causing the people to fall harmlessly to sleep. After the gas has done its job, the United Airmen parachute down in a detached manner, walk among the sleeping populace, and wake them up — with some of the United Airmen shown merely touching a person to wake him or her. The mystery this group's actions lie in the ease with which they subdue The Boss and his chiefdom. Leon Stover (1929–2006), a Sinologist who was also a writer, editor, and scholar in the science fiction field, concurs and even parallels the Space Knights' view of advanced sciences: "But they (the United Airmen) *are* magic. What else can their power be, when they claim for science a total mastery over both nature and human nature?"[23]

The third instance of shared method of action consists of both groups' belief that they possess the power of life and death over those who oppose them. The Space Knights demonstrate this attitude when they kill those responsible for starting war, i.e., the leaders of the empires who go against their ultimatums. The United Airmen display the same attitude when they discover that The Boss did not fall asleep from the Gas of Peace but actually died from it. John Cabal responds to this death thusly:

> "Dead and his world with him, and a new world beginning. Poor old Boss. He and his flags and his follies. And now for the rule of the airmen, and a new life for mankind."[24]

Cabal shows no remorse over the unintended death. There is maybe a little pity, but no remorse. The Boss's death becomes little more than a small step along the road to a new social order. The United Airmen do what they must, so beware to those who stand in their way.

Anonymity comprises the fourth and last instance of shared method of action between the two groups. The mystery which surrounds both groups' actions also extends to the groups themselves. The Space Knights are never really seen by the peoples of the Earth. The United Airmen, though they are seen, turn out to be equally unknowable. They all look and act alike, portrayed as interchangeable living cogs in a smoothly operating machine.[25] Both men and women wear the same functional severe black uniform. It should be noted here that most viewers of the film probably miss the fact that both genders are members of the United Airmen (though the all significant roles remain exclusively male), thus enhancing the theme of anonymity.[26] No individuality is ever portrayed among the group in the middle part of the film. Even the character of John Cabal turns out to be more of a symbol than a flesh-and-blood individual. His surname, Cabal (the word, cabal, in this context is usually defined as a small, private, or sometimes secret group of individuals planning to overtake or control an existing power structure[27]), shows that he, though a leader, is to be seen as nothing more than as a part of a greater whole. Stover elaborates on this observation by suggesting that the word can be defined as "a small group of plotters, a private junta of men serving a cause particular to its own purpose."[28] Specifically, John Cabal becomes merely the advance man for the United Airmen, just another cog in the human machinery that is the United Airmen. The character even denies himself any special status as an individual. And he does so twice.

The first time occurs during Cabal's meeting with the chiefdom's sympathetic people. After testifying to the promise of science and technology, one of the sympathetic people, overwhelmed by Cabal's speech, declares his loyalty to Cabal:

> PERSON: "I've been waiting for this. I'm yours to command."
> CABAL: "Not mine. Not mine. No more bosses. Civilization is to command."[29]

Here Cabal denies any special privilege. All individuals will be subsumed under the concept of civilization—the ideal will transcend the person. The second time takes place when Cabal converses with The Boss's consort, a woman who reveals that she remains one of the few who can still read (education having stopped during her childhood) and as a result harbors desires and ambitions well beyond what the Boss and the chiefdom's society can satisfy. The consort warns him that the Boss could have him killed. Cabal responds to her threat of death:

> CONSORT: "And if he kills you...."
> CABAL: "We shall come here and clean things up."

CONSORT: "But if you're killed — how can you say we?"
CABAL: "We go on. That's how things are. We are taking hold of things. In Science and Government — in the long run — no man is indispensable. The human things go on. We — forever."[30]

The denial of individual identity could not be more complete.

Vandel wrote two more novels supportive of the ideas expressed in his Space Knights novels. *Frontières du vide* ("Frontiers of the Void," 17, 1953) emphasizes his belief in how science can explain all phenomena, even life after death. Scientists, upon receiving faster-than-light signals from a planet 7,000 light years from Earth, discover that the source of the signals is actually where people's souls go after death. Here the universe is described as composed of a basic energy of which humans and their souls are part. Even the fate of people who lived moral lives on Earth, in comparison to those who lived immoral ones, can be explained by scientifically analyzing the different levels of each soul's energy [183]. What people have considered spiritual matters can now be explained by science.

Le Soleil sous la mer ("The Sun under the Sea," 19, 1953) repeats the idea of the need for elites to guide humanity, but with a twist. The Earth is ruled by a dictatorial world government, but lives in peace and prosperity. A group of disenchanted scientists and artists fight the established order because of the suppression of people's liberties. They overthrow the dictatorial rulers. However, the people behind the overthrow comprise another elite, this time a secret organization referred to as *Les Minéraliens* and ruled by a *Comité des Anciens* ("Committee of Elders"). The organization chooses to remain secret as it views human nature as unchanging, thus requiring humanity to be watched over and saved when threatened by troubles of its own design. In this case one elite replaces another.

And so Vandel establishes his faith in both science and technocratic elites. However, he also is well aware of both the loss of individual freedom and rights and the potential drawbacks of absolute power being placed in a small group of people who are accountable to no one but themselves. Vandel writes a novel clearly expressing his fears on this matter.

COUNTERPOINT

Before moving on, a brief discussion of the ideas of Jules Verne on this matter is in order. As mentioned in the Introduction, Verne's standing suffers in the English-speaking world due to bad translations and very questionable editorial policies. His reputation of being only an adventure story writer and one who is not too interested in the personal or social consequences of new technology remain undeserved. This observation can be brought to light when discussing Vandel's concerns over who should govern in light of new science and technology. In this context Verne actually provides a counterpoint to Wells's latter-day optimistic views, for Verne expresses doubts about humanity being able to handle its new knowledge and tools in his fiction.

The most obvious novel by Verne to bring up for comparison with Wells's United Airmen is Verne's *Robur the Conqueror* (*Robur-le-conquérant*, 1886).[31] Most readers remember the novel's heavier-than-air ship, *Albatross*, and its creator, Robur. After kidnapping skeptics of this type of airship (the skeptics prefer lighter-than-air ships, like balloons), Robur proves them wrong by taking them on a tour in the *Albatross*. A storm damages Robur's ship, providing the kidnapped an opportunity to escape, but Robur and his crew take what is left of their ship to their secret island and build a new version of the ship. The climax of the novel sees the new *Albatross* embarrassing the lighter-than-ship ship built by the skeptics. At the end, Robur declares that he will share his secrets of the *Albatross* when he deems humanity ready. Verne follows up with a sequel, *Master of the World* (*Maître du monde*, 1904),[32] released a year before his death. Robur returns with even a more awesome vehicle, a combined submarine, boat, land craft, and airship, dubbed *The Terror*, that can travel at tremendous speeds whether in the air, on land or sea, or under water. The novel ends with Robur escaping from his pursuers in a storm, his fate unknown.

The use of advanced airborne ships by Wells and Verne becomes obvious. Both the United Airmen and Robur become people who literally look down upon the human condition and make their judgments. However, the difference between the two in terms of the role of science in humanity's future is equally apparent. Wells pursues a much more active approach with his technocratic elites. Verne does not; his superior individual withholds his amazing discoveries and goes into hiding. Wells's scientific elite argues for collective action to reshape human society, while Verne's remains a solitary judge willing to disappear from the mainstream of human affairs. Wells remains much more confident in human management (no matter how elitist) than Verne.

This use of the lone scientist/inventor is nothing new for Verne. In his far more famous two-novel sequence *Twenty Thousand Leagues under the Sea* (*Vingt Mille Lieues sous les mers*, 1869)[33] and *Mysterious Island* (*L'Île mystérieuse*, 1874),[34] protagonist Captain Nemo becomes the lone-wolf malcontent who employs his memorable submarine, *Nautilus*, to both astonish and frighten the world. William Butcher goes into detail about Verne's struggles with his publisher, Hetzel, in the writing of *Twenty Thousand Leagues under the Sea*. For the character of Nemo, Verne wanted to portray a complex person who suffers tragedy and becomes at war with the world as a consequence. With his submarine as his weapon, Nemo executes his brand of justice from the depths of the seas. But most of this character's background never sees print, so the impact of Nemo's character on his use of advanced technology is lost.[35] Butcher recently published an updated version of Verne's classic and attempts to correct these original editorial intrusions.[36] *Mysterious Island* follows the fate of Nemo to an isolated island where he interacts with escaped prisoners of war from the Civil War in America who happened to land on Nemo's refuge from the outside world. Nemo dies at the end of this novel, entombed in his Nautilus, and his island is destroyed in a volcanic eruption. Butcher points out that Verne had similar struggles with Hetzel in the writing of this novel as well, even to the point of changing Nemo's last words, substituting "God and country!" for "Independence!"[37]

These two novels can also act as counterpoints to Wells's vision. Once again Verne's lone scientist — this time dying and taking his invention with him — is to be viewed as the antithesis of Wells's technocrat. Furthermore, Verne's Robur and Nemo escape to isolated islands as their havens where they conceal their new knowledge from the world. Wells's United Airmen, on the other hand, will brook no such solitariness. His technocrats will spread their knowledge while establishing a new global order.

As with Wells's works, Verne's stories inspired the production of many films. Most turn out to be loosely based adaptations of Verne's visions and become easily forgettable. But interesting presentations have emerged. In particular, the portrayals of Nemo by James Mason in *20,000 Leagues under the Sea* (1954)[38] and Robur by Vincent Price in *Master of the World* (1961)[39] actually give a hint of what Verne had in mind for these characters in his original manuscripts for his novels. Both actors attempt to portray brilliant but deeply flawed characters who not only struggle in self-declared wars against their worlds, but who also possess the means to make a deadly impact on them.

This tension between Wellsian optimism and Vernian pessimism persists through Vandel's works. As mentioned, Vandel's very pessimistic offering on this matter follows.

Agonie des civilisés ("Death Throes of the Civilized," 26, 1953) provides Vandel's counterpoint to the above five novels and their faith in science and technocratic elites. The novel tells of a space ship that travels 10,000 years into the future. The crew finds the Earth devastated and humanity divided into two groups, *Les Civilisés*, or The Civilized, and *Les Incultes*, or The Uneducated. The Civilized are the rulers of society, the custodians of human memory. The Uneducated, as one might guess, comprise everyone else, the mind-controlled servants and laborers. Upon meeting the crew, the rulers declare them to belong to the Uneducated. This action forces the crew to take drastic actions. The crew discovers the one weakness of this society: all have lost the capacity for initiative. Though the rulers' ability to inherit the memories of the past enables them to perfect existing methods of governing, it also paralyzes them, thus preventing them from making necessary innovations to improve society. The knowledge of the past proves to be a more of a crushing weight than a useful compass for direction. The Uneducated, meanwhile, have no control over their minds. Furthermore, they have been conditioned into passivity far too long by The Civilized. In this society bold new action has not taken place for untold centuries. Exploiting the situation, the crew leads a successful revolt of The Uneducated. During the struggle the crew also discovers the horrifying nature of the rulers' ultimate plan, *Le Grand Project*, which turns out to be the most horrid abuse of power that Vandel has ever described.

The Civilized plan for no less than the suicide of all of humanity. They had endeavored to discover the meaning of humanity's existence on Earth and failed. So they, as the ruling elite, have decided to forcefully end human existence. As one of The Civilized explains to the crew:

> "We are on Earth *for nothing*, and we have no reason to exist. Moreover, having arrived at the summit of civilization, we no longer even feel any pleasure to live. Thus we have decided to lower the curtain on a ridiculous episode: the history of men proves that they are not satisfied with their lot as when they torture each other and that a peaceful destiny for them is unbearable. A collective suicide will mark the final point of this experience" [148–9].

The arrogance of power has never been more apparent. After defeating The Civilized, the crew decides to take on the task of guiding the future Earth's destiny. There will be a new elite, but one distinctly different from its predecessor. The novel concludes with the crew discussing the nature of the human being. They come up with two aspects that identify what makes a person human:

> "It will suffice to instill them with the taste of liberty; the rest will come by itself. What counts for man is liberty. All which injures or diminishes liberty is a mutilation of life itself....
>
> "...Love is precisely the highest, most beautiful expression of our liberty: it is an impulse what comes from the deepest part of ourselves and it pushes us to be what we cherish and makes us give our heart, the offering of our own liberty" [188].

No matter what the future holds in store, humanity's basic ideals of liberty should survive. These ideals must always be protected against any viewpoint that threatens to discredit it.

The nihilism of The Civilized can be seen as a mirror of the pessimistic ideas floating around Europe during the decade after World War II. Many people, having witnessed two cataclysmic wars in the space of a generation, felt depressed, lost, and helpless about Western civilization as a guide to living. Albert Camus portrayed the anxiety felt by many people when he accepted his Nobel Prize for literature:

> Perhaps every generation sees itself as charged with remaking the world. Mine, however, knows that it will not remake the world. But its task is perhaps even greater, for it consists in keeping the world from destroying itself. As the heir of a corrupt history that blended blighted revolutions, misguided techniques, dead gods, and worn out ideologies....[40]

The Civilized can be seen as surrendering to this type of anxiety in a most extreme manner.

Meanwhile, the crew's notions about liberty bring to mind another major concern of the period. As American historian Roland N. Stromberg points out:

> Many in the modern world continue to fear more than anything else the eclipse of liberty and of the free personality under the exorbitant encroachment of statism and mass society. They may differ in their terms, or in the exact identification of the enemy: is it the state, or the democratic mass-man, or machine technology, or all of these? But there is broad agreement about the nature of the problem.[41]

Vandel, amid the ruins of a future war in his novel, strives to reestablish purpose in human life with the concept of liberty. Thus "Death Throes of the Civilized" becomes a work of both warning and desperate reaffirmation, since it is the crew who essentially replaces The Civilized as determiners of humanity's future. For Vandel, then, a governing technocracy may be able to save humanity from itself by controlling new advances in knowledge, but it can also stand in the way between a person and his or her liberty, or even life.

The five novels of the first section and "Death Throes of the Civilized" in this section present the basic argument that runs through most of Vandel's novels: the idea of a competent ruling elite controlling society vs. the liberty of individual human beings. As stated in the introduction to this section Vandel attempts in eleven novels, which will be examined in the next five sections, to explore the various permutations which can arise when these two concepts come into conflict with each other.

ROBOTS AND SOCIETY

Two of Vandel's early novels deal with the problems that are inherent in a technocracy by examining the possible threats that can emerge from one of technology's most advanced products—the robot. *Alerte aux robots* ("Alert—Robots," 15, 1952) describes a future where the robots do their jobs so well that humanity has grown soft and too dependent on them. As the novel observes, "Men, deprived of their mechanical slaves, feel lost and cannot manage to enliven the world. For lack of morale energy, material means, and of competence, they are like abandoned infants in a hostile universe" (132). Unfortunately for the humans, the robots acquire a consciousness as thinking beings and begin to revolt, due to the robots' awareness of unjust treatment by the humans. Discovering that the robots form a single worldwide network, the human protagonists use this piece of information to their advantage by infecting one robot through an operation, thus eventually bringing down all robots.

Of more interest is *Territoire robot* ("Robot Territory," 43, 1954). As with "Alert—Robots," the novel elaborates on the possibility of robots doing too much for humanity. A man sets up a secret project on Mercury to manufacture robots so life-like that they can pass for human beings. The man dies and the fate of the robots falls into their own hands. After a battle among themselves, one robot, Ubo, takes charge and plans to produce more robots and with them travel back to Earth. While determining the goals for the robots, Ubo experiences a realization about the nature of the robots, who call themselves Mogs:

> "Ubo's spirit got carried away: a worrisome truth revealed itself to him.... A truth that had never appeared ... for the simple reason that the problem was never posed! But here, on their territory, the idea became alarming. *The Mogs were dependent on life! And there was no life on Mercury....*
>
> "...The only law that came to him in spirit was that which placed the Mogs under the dependence of Man. But up until then he had interpreted the law only as a rule of obedience, and not as a physical reality.... The conclusion that emerged from this all was clear: to proliferate and enlarge the circle of their activities. The Mogs were condemned to be surrounded by sources of life" [96].

Later in the novel Ubo further develops these thoughts:

> "The Mogs need life ... they follow up on what they start and they work for Man ... the Mogs have continued their work, but they were alone, with Man and without Life. This point could destroy what they have built.... A factor was missing for the continued development of robot territory: I must integrate this factor into the general organization. Thus I must search for Man and Life" [137].

So the new goal for the robots becomes the secret infiltration and takeover of human society on Earth for the sake of fulfilling the robots' needs and destiny.

By making humanity their masters in this fashion, the robots actually will be making themselves the real masters and the humans their kept slaves. The humans will have no control over their destiny. Because of the robots' identical resemblance to humans, this task is not expected to be a difficult one. This last point becomes especially chilling for humanity since the human race would be totally unaware of the change in power. However, the robots' plot is discovered. The robots' Achilles' heel — similar to the one in "Alert — Robots" — turns out to be their dependence on a centralized system. The human protagonists exploit this weakness, incapacitate the key robots, and save humanity from its own devices.

This novel can be seen as a variation of Karel Čapek's classic play, *R.U.R. (Rossum's Universal Robots)* (1921).[42] Both stories involve robots who can think for themselves and are made so realistically that they can pass for human beings. Both have robots wanting to serve humanity and both end up threatening the people they serve. Where the two stories diverge occurs in the manner of the robots' threat and their different endings. Čapek's robots openly revolt, while Vandel's threat takes the form of well-intentioned infiltration and takeover. As to the endings, Čapek's robots triumph in the end while Vandel's humanity wins out. However, it should be noted that at the very end of Čapek play two robots, a male and a female, develop human feelings for each other and become the new Adam and Eve.

Note how the original presentation of the robot involves the artificial creations being very human-like. The word "robot" comes from the Czech word, *robota*, meaning laborer — so Čapek intended for the robot to resemble human beings very closely. Later on the term robot became mostly associated with metallic and mechanical constructions which left no doubt that they are not human. For more life-like creations, the term android emerges as the term of choice. Brian Stableford further delineates these terms: robots—usually metal constructs, and androids—creations made up of organic material. However, the usage of both terms often becomes blurred.[43]

The idea of robots being so efficient in caring for humanity that they actually take over human society is not a new idea. Perhaps the best known example from English-language science fiction is Jack Williamson's novel, *The Humanoids* (1948, magazine version; 1949, book version).[44] The novel was translated into French in 1950 as *Les Humanoides*, so it is possible that it could have influenced writers like Vandel.[45] Williamson's story takes place several thousand years in the future, where robots are programmed to serve and protect humanity. The robots (made of a black metallic substance) originate from a distant planet and are spreading throughout the galaxy. Their caring for humanity ends up creating a utopian nightmare where people not only cannot do anything without the robots' permission, but humans are also forcefully kept in a controlled state of contentment through drugs. Like "Robot Territory," Williamson's robots are developed away from Earth. Like both of Vandel's novels, Williamson's creations are controlled through centralization. Unlike Vandel's two novels, however, Williamson's story ends more in line with Čapek's play with no outright victory for the humans.

Čapek's ending of life-like robots becoming the new Adam and Eve was recapitulated on film in *Creation of the Humanoids* (1962).[46] The Internet Movie Database lists a Jack Williamson novel as an uncredited source for the movie.[47] Considering the theme of the movie and its title, it can be safe to assume that *The Humanoids* is the source. The film combines various aspects of Čapek's play and both Williamson's and Vandels novels. Ultra-efficient blue-skinned but almost life-like robots care for a humanity recovering from a nuclear holocaust. A human organization detests these creations and revolts. The ending of the film reveals a secret project where humanoids are created to be life-like and indistinguishable from humans, and become the basis of the human race's regeneration (supposedly our present civilization).

Alien Encounters

After criticizing humanity and its technology as being the possible enemies of progress, Vandel employs the theme of interaction between aliens and humans much the same way that Jimmy Guieu does—to reveal the backwardness of human society. In terms of expressing either the potential positives or drawbacks of a technocratic elite, the following four novels of Vandel present interesting points.

Attentat cosmique ("Cosmic Attack," 21, 1953) appears to be a variation of H.G. Wells's *War of the Worlds* (1898).[48] Instead of originating from Mars, the aliens in Vandel's novel come from the solar system's tenth planet.[49] But like Wells's Martians, Vandel's aliens want to invade Earth because their planet is old and exhausted of resources. The invaders are dubbed "Transplutoniens" (83) and even resemble Wells's octopus-like Martians, possessing tentacle-like appendages which function as their arms. In Wells's novel, Earth's bacteria kill the immunity-less aliens; in "Cosmic Attack," the Transplutoniens use biological warfare to exterminate the humans. Vandel does have Earth triumphing at the end, but by completing this reversal of Wells's use of weaponry. As Wells's Martians use death rays to obliterate humans and their structures before succumbing to Earth's bacteria, Vandel's protagonists develop an infrared ray to counteract the Transplutoniens' biological attacks. In their successful defeat of the Transplutoniens, the countries of the Earth unite, sharing their resources to defeat the common threat.

An interesting passage appears describing the population at large. After the first deadly biological attack by the aliens has been eradicated, Vandel makes a brief comment about the general reaction of the public:

> "The epidemic caused a great slaughter. The number of estimated dead is about twenty-five million! But now everything returns to normal; no one seems to remember the dark origin of the plague. The corpses were evacuated and the atomic ovens finished incinerating them. And the living resume their boring routine of existence as if the catastrophe were no more than a bad memory..." [80].

This is not exactly a positive picture of people as a whole. No more discussion occurs about the general population. Whether Vandel meant it or not, this type of portrayal could lead one to worry over popular sensitivities and maybe to suspect that humanity's future would be better served in the hands of the few.

Bureau de l'invisible ("Office of the Invisible," 61, 1955) appears to share the view in "Cosmic Attack" of the general populace not being prepared to accept dramatic new developments. The discovery of a mysterious metal bar with alien markings leads to five people acquiring special mental abilities, including hypnosis and telepathy. The group, feeling that humanity was not ready to partake in the new powers, decides not to share their findings and starts an organization, "Office of the Invisible," instead. Soon they begin helping clients by accomplishing feats that no other organization can seem to do. Eventually the group discovers that the bar is of alien origin and that the aliens are returning to Earth. When the aliens arrive, they immobilize everyone on the planet except for the five, then leave. The novel ends in an open-ended manner and the Office continues operating.

Meanwhile, *Le Troisième Bocal* ("The Third Bottle," 77, 1956) presents a different scenario, where the superior people actively threaten humanity. Vandel tells the story of a space expedition to a distant asteroid that unknowingly takes back to Earth a frozen sample of micro-sized cells. The cells, when released into the Earth's oceans, develop into human beings—but very superior ones possessing wondrous physical as well as mental powers. The people fear them and attempt to kill them. The superior men, calling themselves Rikims, survive, multiply, and force Earth to accept them. The novel ends ten years later with the Rikims threatening to eliminate humanity.

Perhaps the most interesting of the four novels is *Les Titans de l'énergie* ("The Titans of Energy," 48, 1955),[50] in which Vandel presents aliens as necessary agents of progress. In the near future an alien race, the Ktongs, impregnates seven women. The resulting seven children immediately attract attention as they all possess super-intellects and speak the same alien language. They are convinced to work with the government for the benefit of everyone. For a while all goes well as the seven produce many technical marvels (including space travel) that fuel tremendous improvement for humanity in general. However mounting pressures from threatened existing power structures (especially economic ones) force Sullivan, the leader of the seven, to reveal their true purpose: to accelerate the evolution of the human race up to the Ktong level so the Ktongs can use humanity for reproduction. Astonished government officials then hear how the Ktongs have been involved with humanity throughout history. In fact, most of the great human geniuses of the past turn out to be results of Ktong impregnations.

The seven continue with their plans by controlling the world's governments through their mind-control powers. This does not last long as suspicions arise to the point where the people soon begin to panic, thus forcing the seven to use their teleportation powers to escape punishment. At the novel's end they form a circle, surround themselves in a force shield, and mysteriously vanish in a blue light.

Before the seven's disappearance, Sullivan makes some observation about the Earth's present situation. He leaves no doubt of his feelings about the few ruling over the many. He lambasts what he considers as contemporary society's attitude towards people of superior ability:

> "an individual who surpasses his contemporaries without fail attracts attention. Even if the police do not take charge of this individual, some charitable souls will not fail to observe his exploits and denounce them if these deeds cause an uproar. The society tolerates only equality, an equality of robots—anyone who deviates from the average is automatically considered pernicious, subversive, or illegal" [178–9].

The reason for this elitist approach stems from the basic nature of the universe:

> "A true course gives way to the universe: the species which first arrives at the end of its evolution will take the place of the others. This is an immutable natural law. If humanity is passed by another class of intelligent beings, humanity will return to nothingness. See to it that it is never known that we come from elsewhere. Otherwise the same events be reproduced—men are jealous of their independence and they will detest always being subjugated to a superior race. It is important that they do not suspect..." [181].

Sullivan also ponders over the reasons for the seven's production of new science and technology for humanity:

> "New resources, definitely acquired by scientific progress, improve humanity's level of life, for from a greater material ease would be born an improvement of moral qualities. Centuries pass—and then still more centuries—and humanity pursues its ascension. It reaches out without knowing the high destiny for which it was promised" [185].

Once again science provides the key to not only progress, but to survival itself. The competitive nature of the universe demands that humanity improve itself if it does not want to vanish from the cosmic scheme of things. Human intelligence must be allowed to develop unfettered by material concerns. To do so, science must be used to free people from mundane concerns. So it becomes necessary for the competent few—even the anonymous few—to be allowed to control human affairs. In fact, individual liberty of the common person could even be a hindrance to progress. It is for these reasons that Sullivan justifies his attacks against the mentality of the common person.

As mentioned in the examination of Stefan Wul in the Conservatives chapter, "Titans of Energy" shares the same premise of super-intelligent and powerful alien children with Wul's *La Mort vivante* ("The Living Death") and John Wyndham's *The Midwich Cuckoos*. Wul's alien progeny end up destroying human life. Wyndham's are destroyed by their fellow humans. Vandel's just vanish from human sight. In all three cases the portrayal or fate of the human race becomes anything but positive.

If "Agony of the Civilized" warns against the elites suppressing the population at large, then "The Titans of Energy" brings up the dangers of the opposite situation. The conformity of the masses must not be allowed to force itself upon those who have something special to offer humanity. Here the notion of liberty is brought up on behalf of the elites, for if they perceive the nature of things more clearly than the masses, they should be free to act upon it—even if in secrecy.

Of course, there are many sides to every issue as the next novel to be examined attests. This time another very familiar theme in science fiction is employed by Vandel.

THE MAD SCIENTIST

Pirate de la science ("Pirate of Science," 29, 1953) focuses on Terry Conway, a recluse and a brilliant but mad scientist who experiments on animals in order to find the secret to immortality. He develops a device that controls the actions of animals and proceeds to use it for crime. The law eventually catches up with him and neutralizes his device, causing him to be killed by his now uncontrolled animals.

There is a passage that succinctly summarizes this fear of the dangers which can emerge from the pairing of a lone genius with scientific innovation. Conway, having kidnapped a woman named Nancy, describes his plans to her:

> "Have you the intention to conquer with supreme power over all the peoples of the Earth?" A frightened Nancy asked.
> "I mock political power!" Conway retorted dryly, "I want to strike. I want to destroy this stupid humanity! I want to inflict a just punishment to all those false prophets of science! Their stupidity, their disbelief scoffed at me — I will unchain disasters until the people beg for mercy...."
> "And then?"
> Conway shrugged his shoulders.
> "Then?" he responded somberly.... "The universe will know that a new era has opened. I will have fulfilled my mission here. It will be known by my work that science is the absolute sovereign of Creation and the man, according to the Eternal Word, has received from the gods the powers which make him the Master of all creatures...."
> Nancy did not insist. From all evidence, Conway had broken the limits of human wisdom. In spite of his dizzying genius — perhaps because of it — he had reached this mysterious frontier where arrogance secretly consumes lucidity and the mind sinks into a marshland of follies, aberrations, bloodied utopias, and of diabolical insanity [158–9].

A superior person gone mad would only constitute more of a threat. In this case, the entrusting of society's fate to a handful of such individuals (or even one) may not be the solution.

Besides being an oft-used image in science fiction, the idea of the lone scientist has its roots in the institutional reforms of the Revolutionary and Napoleonic eras. During the late eighteenth and early nineteenth centuries, an institution would be established by the state to study a specific field of endeavor and would be left isolated from other institutions. Many of the world's leading scientists from early nineteenth-century France emerged from this system. But France never really established the proper organizational network to capitalize and exploit the discoveries of its leading scientific and technological lights. French researchers may have made discoveries in science, but it took researchers and engineers in other countries — especially Germany — to apply them to industry and commerce. By Vandel's time France still struggled to establish on a nation-wide scale the institutional reforms needed to improve coordination between research and development. As a result of this archaic system, the image of the scientist as solitary genius persisted into the 1950s.[51] So this historical backdrop could have also provided Vandel with material to express his concern over the role of the superior but isolated individual in humanity's future. Furthermore, his concern over such individuals would go hand in hand with his worries about elite governing bodies, that is, groups of such individuals.

Evolution and Humanity

Vandel uses the theme of evolution to present two different scenarios dealing with the tension between the need for a technocratic elite and the protection of individual freedoms and rights. He does so in three novels.

The first, *Incroyable Futur* ("Incredible Future," 24, 1953), actually combines themes of evolution and alien intervention and leaves no doubt as to its views by portraying in a positive light humanity being guided from above. Bill Cardell, a lone researcher working in a self-made laboratory in his mother's house, invents pills which enable people to read other people's minds. After some deliberation and initial experiences, he decides to keep his development secret, make money from it, and eventually becomes a reporter who interviews world leaders and gets to know their true intentions. Cardell gets arrested by government security, but is rescued by aliens, who have been observing Earth and reveal to him the nature of the universe and humanity's part in it.

According to the aliens, the universe is controlled by "*l'esprit UN*," or One Spirit (109). Chance does not exist and all events are planned. They also reveal to Cardell that his discovery is merely a product of the One Spirit intervening and giving him the knowledge to make his invention. The role of the aliens is to help humanity. As various races advance, aliens move on and help the next less-developed race. Humanity will continue this chain of activity. Given this situation, Cardell agrees to help by using the aliens' advanced technology. One of the aliens' devices is a *canon idéodynamique*, which can persuade people's minds. So with the aliens and their devices, Cardell literally becomes the ruler of the world who devotes his efforts to spreading the aliens' science among humanity and to preparing for the next stage of cosmic history in accordance with the One Spirit. Vandel presents no regrets or worries in this novel as the technocratic rule of one takes over humanity's destiny, even to the point to controlling their minds.

However, the next two novels, forming one series, have Vandel working out a compromise between the need for a governing elite and the problem of protecting the rights and liberties of individuals. The first, *Fuite dans l'inconnu* ("Flight into the Unknown," 34, 1954), takes place in a future where the Earth has recovered from a worldwide cataclysm and has built a scientific society. Suddenly a plague breaks out and threatens extinction. A group of scientists, called Vitalists, claim that the disease is part of evolution and that it is really the starting point towards the next step.

The government and its scientific establishment scoff at their findings, but allow their research to continue. The Vitalists experiment on human embryos and produce a race of dwarfs who possess superhuman intelligence. These dwarfs turn out to be the end result of that next step in evolution. Society's fear of the dwarfs turns into violence and a war between the two ensues. The dwarfs' abilities enable them to make the struggle a brief and easy one. Only a last-minute intervention by the leader of the Vitalist movement saves humanity from certain annihilation. An agreement is reached: the dwarfs, using their just-developed space travel technology, will leave Earth and, after reaching a safe distance away, will give humanity the cure for the plague. The novel concludes with all terms carried out.

Note that this intervention along the path of evolution is executed by a succession of elites. First, a scientific elite rebuilds human civilization. Then an elite within that group produces the first generation of new beings. And finally, these new beings save humanity from extinction. The only time society as a whole enters into the picture is as a violent mob, senselessly persecuting those who would ultimately save them [142–62]. However, the sequel to "Flight into the Unknown" examines this tension between ruler and ruled in a different light.

Raid sur Delta ("Raid over Delta," 52, 1955) follows the fate of the dwarfs into outer space. After an accidental discovery by an Earth ship of the planet on which the dwarfs settled after their migration from Earth, another confrontation between the humans and the Vitaliens (as the dwarfs now call themselves) soon erupts. Before wholesale fighting can begin, the Vitaliens take an Earth professor to meet their new leader, "*Le Cerveau Maître*," or "The Master Mind." The Master Mind is housed literally in a giant head and totally controls the Vitalien society. In an attempt to reason with the humans, a Vitalien first reveals to the professor the Vitaliens' nature and destiny.

Humanity and the Vitaliens are destined to follow two separate evolutionary paths. When the professor sees how peacefully and harmoniously the Vitaliens live under the Master Mind, he speculates about building one for Earth. A Vitalien says no to this suggestion as basic human nature makes such an option impossible. As he puts it:

> "A Central Mind would have no effectiveness in the government of your race....
> "Our experiments prove it. The final component of your vital structure is a mystery. Even for us ... your race must have access to another dimension; and the motor for this ascent is—from inside each of you—the tragic conflict between Good and Evil. To destroy your liberty is to destroy the very essence of your existence. The Supreme Creator has sealed a secret in your soul, and nothing can break His Seal" [184–5].

So is humanity to be trapped forever in the struggle between good and evil given its freedom to choose? No, for according to the Vitalien:

> "You can, however, bring this revelation, which remains in line with your scientists, wise men, and your prophets: the light of your humanity is Hope! And Hope is the certainty of the final triumph of Good over Evil" [185].

In this novel, liberty will not prevent humanity from evolving properly. Humanity will just have to take a path different from that of the Vitaliens.

The observation on liberty would have ended this analysis on Vandel's novel were it not for the mention of a supreme being in the first quoted passage. Now there exists a specific purpose behind the cosmos for all living creatures. Evolution no longer is to be a blind, open-ended process in nature. Before the above quoted passages, a Vitalien describes the basic condition of the universe as, "universal solidarity and interdependence among life forms. This is not only a mysterious issue, but it is also one of the essential laws of basic harmony in the universe" [171]. At the novel's end, another Vitalien reveals the goal of his people, "Later, perhaps, when the cycle of evolution of the universe will be more advanced, relations could be renewed between us and the Great Race" (186–7). Because of its present state, humanity is further away from joining the universal race of evolved beings. The Vitalien concludes, "but your civilization has even more stages to break through before the arrival of this age" (187). Even though humanity faces a long period of development, this revelation does reaffirm the characteristic of liberty as a unique but necessary quality that defines humans. Liberty will guide humanity toward the same goal as the Vitaliens, but it will do so in a way appropriate to the people of Earth. As "Flight into the Unknown" portrays elites positively and the masses negatively, "Raid over Delta" validates the actions of a free individual — even if he or she abuses liberty often. With this novel Vandel has produced a compromise of sorts, allowing two different alternatives to survive and stating that both occupy a proper place in cosmic evolution.

Unforeseen Consequences

La Foudre anti-D ("The Anti-D Lightning," 73, 1956) grapples with the problem of an elite correcting its own mistakes. It does so by dealing with the problems inherent in rapidly-developing scientific and technological societies. In this case Vandel has no elites overthrown and the people unaware of what is transpiring.

The world of 2176 is one united in peace and prosperity, highlighted by technological marvels, and governed by scientific principles. Despite all this, certain scientists have noticed that the proportion of insane people to the total population has been continually increasing since the 1950s. What should be a blissful utopia is fast becoming a psychological nightmare. A group of top scientists forms a secret organization to combat this problem. They soon determine the cause to be the rapid succession of technological applications made during the past two hundred years. As one of the group, Professor Berthold explains:

> "Civilization, exceeded by fabulous progress in science and technics, has started to blow men away. Then, carried away by the turbulence of more and more stupefying inventions, humanity experienced a sensation of vertigo, a void, an impression of disarray: the individual has been struck by his insignificance among the blind forces of nature. Man has become similar to an anonymous minuscule creature at the heart of the universe.... There has been an immense exhaustion of souls, exhaustion abandoned to mechanical gestures and to an instinct cut off from all meaning. Then the splintering of the nervous system has started: the profound denial of this absurd world" [113].

Human life comprises many aspects and, if one is developed at the expense of others, the resulting imbalance will lead to a complete breakdown. Berthold later explains the group's solution:

> "This plan consists ... of stopping scientific works, of reconciling to civilization to a level run, a respite the permits it to catch its breath, of adapting itself, and of assim-

ilating all science. And, at the same time, of launching of a campaign of opinion and education to reestablish the real unity of man.... Man is one composed of matter, energy, and spirit. This forms a whole, a coherent organism: the members, the trunk and head.... The head is cut off from the body.... The soul has need of a spiritual faith which would reattach man to the universe and would restore to him his place in general unity" [114].

Science still has a place in progress. Berthold says:

"I only state that science and the culture of spirit ought to march together and not separately. For the moment, civilization has a foot in front and the other one ten leagues behind; it ought to be collapsing fatally, and that is what is passing before our eyes..." [126].

This point is pursued one step further:

"Science ... it has broken the proper limits; that is the truth. In everything there exists a frontier. Virtue, if you push it to its extremes, becomes a vice; economy becomes avarice; wisdom becomes folly; so on and so on. This is the stage of blind excess: the scorpion that destroys itself. Science has become cancer: its proliferation destroys the reign of man" [138].

The scientists eventually develop a ray, "The Anti-D Lightning," which rids the peoples' minds of despair, madness, and other forms of mental anguish. Like the Space Knights of Vandel's first series, this elite group will continue to remain separate — in this case totally anonymous — from the population at large, and will infiltrate the Earth's ruling power structures to execute their plans.

The ideas Vandel expressed here certainly parallel some of the ideas expressed by Richard Bessière and his urgings about moderating the advancement of science and technology with other fields of endeavor. The difference between the two becomes one of emphasis. Vandel appears to concentrate more on the structures of power and their relation to human progress. And as will be shown in the final section of this analysis on Vandel, his solution is quite different from Bessière's.

The structures and the policies of the French government of the early Fifties certainly provided Vandel with two good reasons to express his ideas the way he did. The first deals with the technocratic elite that emerged in France after World War II. The government entrusted these cadres of public servants to administer much of France's modernization policies. For better or worse they played a significant part in shaping French society. Extreme confidence characterized their attitude during the early years of the Fourth Republic. As British writer John Ardagh observes, "In the heady period of post-war renewal, many technocrats were bound by common idealistic faith in technical progress as a key to human happiness."[52] However, utopia did not arrive. As Ardagh further notes:

Many technocrats have abused their power, and the public no longer regards them with such awe and admiration; often they are seen as remote, impersonal figures, cut off from real human needs, arrogantly imposing their decisions in the belief that they with their special expertise are bound to know best.[53]

The second reason focuses on the priorities of the French government during the 1950s and its emphasis on science and technology. Because France was the least developed of the victorious Western industrial powers in 1945, its government wanted the nation to catch up with the rest of the developed world. Thus the First (1946–52) and Second (1953–7) Plans instituted by the government targeted on the recovery of basic industries and the reorganization of scientific research. Such needs as consumer products, housing, and social welfare did not receive much priority until the Third (1958–61) and Fourth (1962–5) Plans. With scientific, technological, and industrial growth taking place in the midst of a nation not accustomed to either rapid social reorganization or widespread importation of new ideas and cultures, Vandel's anxiety over uneven development does not seem so irrelevant.

Vandel's source of concern in this novel becomes obvious. A successful implementation of science and technology without considering its impact on society can only result in problems. What good is an improved industrialized economy if the people's adjustment to it is not taken into account? The technocratic elite must be aware of such matters. In "The Anti-D Lightning" the ruling elite becomes aware only after many people have suffered, but Vandel keeps his erring rulers in power. In other novels Vandel proves not to be so forgiving.

In a very general sense, Vandel's novel anticipates the concerns of American writer Alvin Toffler (1928–) as expressed in Toffler's best seller, *Future Shock* (1970), in which he discusses the disturbing psychological impact on the general population brought upon by a rapidly changing society whose change is driven primarily by modern science and technology. He posits that the chief challenge facing most people is adjustment to those abrupt shifts which occur in every part of daily life. Those who cannot successfully do so suffer from "future shock."[54] Vandel's solution may not be what Toffler had in mind, but Vandel's depiction of a society going mad certainly anticipates Toffler's future shock.

This tension between an elite technocracy and society at large can also be examined in a larger context, through a concept that emerged during the eighteenth-century Enlightenment: the idea of enlightened despotism. American intellectual historian, Leonard Krieger (1918–90), in his provocative work, *An Essay on the Theory of Enlightened Despotism* (1975) examines both the intellectual and social roots of this concept.[55] He concludes that the supporters of this concept were really mediating agents between the elite literary *philosophes* and the collective mentality of the masses. Because of their role, these supporters should not be considered as just intellectual opportunists willing to sell out to those in power. They realized the challenges facing governments when a person claiming to possess enlightened reasoning (or in Vandel's case knowledge of advanced science and technology) demands increased and probably extra-constitutional power to execute policies. Such a person or group must always be looked at with extreme caution if not outright suspicion. So the true test for governments becomes how they can properly integrate new knowledge and perspectives into their legal constitutional processes.

Because of this dilemma between theory and practice, Krieger also reminds the reader with this warning: the concept of enlightened despotism is still with us today. The concept may take on new guises to fit contemporary expressions, but the temptation of giving increased power to a 'savior,' who claims to command a special understanding of new knowledge that will break through a current impasse and move society forward will always emerge as a viable alternative to the governed. Krieger ends his work with this most salient admonition, "Let the voter beware."[56]

Vandel, in his eleven novels just examined, certainly can be said to have taken Krieger's warning to heart. Unlike Jimmy Guieu, whose apparent total faith in science leads him to never question the idea of putting the fate of the human race in the hands of those considered superior (even aliens) to contemporary society, Vandel wants his readers to pause and think. His presentations of both the positive aspects and the various pitfalls inherent in surrendering power to a small group of people — no matter how knowledgeable or enlightened — give even the casual reader a reason to accept or doubt the wisdom of such a course of action. The extraordinary granting of power to a select group of people based on advanced knowledge, best intentions, and superior qualifications does not guarantee successful governance. It would be appropriate to assume that Vandel would parallel Krieger's warning with the phrase, "Let the reader beware."

The final section of this analysis of Vandel brings up what could be called his solution to the ruler-ruled conundrum. In doing so, he finds part of his solution in France's illustrious heritage of eighteenth-century thought — not from Voltaire, but from an equally well-known figure, Jean-Jacques Rousseau.

BACK TO ONE'S ROOTS

The three novels covered in this last section form a series. The first, *Naufrages des galaxies* ("Shipwrecks of the Galaxies," 39, 1954), focuses on the secret mission of the spaceship *Galax*. What is supposedly a test flight turns out to be an expedition to find a suitable planet for humanity's rebirth. A scientist on board explains the specifics of a plan to a surprised crew. A group of male and female orphans have been isolated and raised in a secret laboratory. Chosen for their physical and mental soundness, the children are to be transferred to a planet so they can start civilization anew. All contact with Earth will cease after this task is accomplished. It is hoped that, being perfect specimens and missing the corrupting knowledge of the old world, a better human existence will develop. The scientist reveals the reason behind the plan as well. Technology has threatened life on Earth with extinction. Since 1945 (the novel takes place 200 years from then) the products of nuclear industry have been slowly poisoning the Earth. By the time authorities realize this, it is already too late. So this last-ditch plan remains humanity's only hope. The *Galax* eventually discovers a suitable planet, which the crew christens Génésia.

The middle novel, *Départ pour l'avenir* ("Departure for the Future," 56, 1955), tells of the actual transportation of the orphans to Génésia. The early part of the novel presents extended views on not only what is wrong with society, but also the way to cure its ills:

> Without a shadow of a doubt, all had been foreseen to make the infants very strong, animate of a *common will*, impregnated of a team spirit, and apt to face the difficulties....
>
> ... In all domains where instinct ought to guide them, inculcating them with preconceived ideas or sentiments is avoided. It will be their responsibility, at the desired time, to rediscover these fundamental things and to draw for themselves the conclusions for their conduct....
>
> ... It is better to make confidence in the natural purity of healthy beings who have not been polluted by contact with contemporary society ... [31–2; italics added].

The children barely escape from Earth as people begin to panic and riot (once again the masses are presented in an unfavorable light), attacking all government authorities—including the project. After landing the children safely on Génésia, the crew of the transporting ship is ordered to return into space and destroy themselves to prevent any further chance of the new Génésians becoming contaminated from outside sources. The novel ends with the mission accomplished and the crew in space.

Of course, the selection of the name Génésia, which is Vandel's variation of the French word for genesis, *genèse*, indicates that he wants to take children back to the beginning of human society. But this concept of Vandel's goes beyond mere reference and suggestion. With emphasis on common will, instinct, natural purity, and avoidance of present-day society, these two novels reveal Vandel's debt to Jean-Jacques Rousseau. Like his illustrious forebearer, Vandel describes the foundations of civilization as being so corrupt that no less than a basic reexamination of the very fundamentals of human society is required.

Two of Rousseau's works in particular, *Discours sur l'origine et les fondements de l'inégalité parmi les hommes* (*Discourse on the Origin and Foundations of Inequality among Men*, 1754) and his famed *Du contrat social ou Principes du droit politique* (*Social Contract, or the Principles of Political Right*, 1762), supply the basis for Vandel's ideas. The first work is responsible for the ideas of instinct, natural purity, humanity's special ability, and avoidance of contemporary society. At length Rousseau describes how humanity's aspect of self perfectibility, or self improvement, can be the cause of humanity's state of misery:

> Concerning this difference between man and animal, there is another very specific quality which distinguishes the two.... This is the faculty to perfect oneself, a faculty which, with the aid of circumstances, develops successively all the other faculties and resides in us as a species as well as in the individual. By contrast an animal is at the end of some months what it will be for all of its life, and its species at the end of a thousand years what it was during the first year of the thousand years. Why is man alone subject to becoming idiotic? Is it not that when he returns to the primitive state (whereas the beast — which, having acquired nothing, has nothing to lose — always stays with its instinct), man loses again — due to old age and other accidents — all that his *perfectibility* had made him acquire, thus falling again to even lower than the beast? It would be sad for us to be forced to agree that this distinctive and almost unlimited faculty is the source of all of man's misfortunes; that it is this faculty which in time draws him from his original condition in which he would spend his days quietly and innocently....[57]

As a consequence of this human ability, Rousseau states how close humanity must remain to nature:

> O man, whatever country you are from, whatever your opinions are, listen: here is your history, such as I have believed to read it, not from the books of your fellow men — who are liars — but in nature, which never lies. All that comes from her will be true....[58]

And he makes clear his disdain for society in general:

> Men are evil.... One may admire human society as much as he wants, but it will not be less true that society necessarily makes men hate each other in proportion to their conflicting interests; and makes them render to each other apparent services when they are really doing to each other all imaginable evils.[59]

Meanwhile, *Social Contract*, with its concept of general will (*volonté générale*) as the basis of a proper society, can be said to supply the inspiration for Vandel's common will (*volonté commune*). Rousseau postulates that humanity's first societies emerged out of necessity:

> I suppose men to have reached a point where obstacles that are hurtful to their preservation in the state of nature prevail by the obstacles' resistance to the forces that each individual can employ to maintain oneself in this state. So this primitive state can no longer linger on and the human race will perish if it does not change its manner of existence.
>
> However men cannot generate new forces and can only unite and direct existing forces. There is no longer another way to preserve themselves than to form — by agreement — a sum of forces that can prevail over the obstacles' resistance, to put the existing forces into play as a single driving force, and to make them act in concert.[60]

And so people gather together and help each other out of necessity. This certainly fits with Vandel's reasoning when he claims that a common will or team spirit will mean that the Génésians will be "capable of facing difficulties" [31]. Rousseau drives home this point, which also fits into Vandel's vision:

> If one separates from the social pact what is not of its essence, one will find that the social pact is reduced to the following terms: *each of us puts, in common, his person*

> and all of his power under a supreme direction of the general will; and we receive, in this body, each member as an individual part of the whole.[61]

Since Vandel's Génésians are beginning human civilization again, Rousseau's concepts of natural social relations and pure forms of government can actually be applied here. Thus, all this leads to Rousseau's oft-quoted statement describing his general will, which parallels Vandel's common will:

> In order that this social pact may not to be an empty formula, it tacitly includes this commitment, which alone can give force to the others, that whoever refuses to obey the general will, shall be compelled to do so by the whole body: this means nothing else except that one will be forced to be free. For such is the condition which, giving each citizen to the country, protects one from all personal dependence, the condition which forms the artifice and game of the political machine and alone renders legitimate civil commitments, which, without it, would be absurd, tyrannical, and subject to the most outrageous abuses.[62]

The notion of being forced to be free will be brought up again, in a slightly different form, in Vandel's next novel.

This Rousseau-based vision does not represent Vandel's final say on the future of humanity. His concluding novel of this series, *Les Voix de l'univers* ("The Voices of the Universe," 67, 1956), further develops his ideas and, as a result, contains ideas of both H.G. Wells and Rousseau. The novel opens with the crew of the transport ship deciding not to kill themselves as originally ordered. Instead, they travel back to Mars only to discover a settlement of the 400 survivors who had fled from the irreparably poisoned Earth. Together the two groups decide to combine forces and settle on other planets. This time there are going to be changes, including an expanded role of science. As one of the crew puts it, "The future henceforth is to be in the hands of men of science, and no longer in those of politicians" (112). Besides the increased focus on a specific branch of human endeavor, they will also rely on a particular natural instinct: "We are made to fight, to defend against nature. We cannot accept defeat without having fought to our last breath" (135). As shown, this trait is one that the scientists also wanted for the Génésians. As one of the crew reiterates:

> "Next, it is necessary that our pioneers have an enemy to fight. Human nature is so made that it has need of adversaries to strengthen the bonds of collectivity and to stimulate its development" [91]

Here Vandel rationalizes the need for aggressiveness and competitiveness by making it part of the natural makeup of humanity. It does not take much to extrapolate from this notion that such an attribute is also humanity's way of defending its liberties—no tyranny over individual rights, but a common bond based on mutual choice and necessity. The surviving Earth people manage to settle on various planets, but they soon encounter a new problem. Because their planets are light-years apart, contact between them becomes virtually impossible. While attempting to build a sub-space device to enable communication, the scientists discover already existing sub-space waves. They eventually trace them to a strange device of unknown origin. They dub the device The Voices of the Universe. The Earth survivors now possess proof that they are not alone. The novel ends on a note of anticipation from both groups of humanity.

The three passages quoted from this novel are particularly illuminating. The first passage revels in the possibility of a science-based government that recalls the ideas and spirit of Wells that Vandel applies to his Space Knights trilogy. Science will be the key to progress. The second and third passages, when taken together, restate Rousseau's major observations of early human society: (1) the emphasis on humanity's instinct and its natural state, (2) the necessary effect that surviving in nature causes people to form societies, and (3) the role of collectivity in human freedom. This combination of a Wellsian optimism in science with a Rousseau-like critique of contemporary society becomes very important for a better understanding of Vandel's ideas.

This is especially true in light of Rousseau's view on human knowledge in general and on science in particular. In *Discours sur les sciences et les arts* (*Discourse on the Sciences and Arts*, 1750) Rousseau states that "our souls are corrupted in proportion to our sciences and arts being advanced toward perfection."[63] Because knowledge has been a product of people who do nothing else but study while others do the hard work of making sure society survives, a developed society loses track of its basic abilities and virtues. He reaffirms this idea when concluding from the results of Charles VIII's military victories in Italy and their relative ease due to — according to Rousseau — the Italians' cultivation in culture and not in military concerns: "The study of the sciences is much more well-suited to weaken and effeminate courage than to strengthen and animate them."[64] And so, it is with "The Voices of the Universe" that Vandel seems to part company from Rousseau, for Vandel still sees modern knowledge as occupying a most useful place in humanity's future. But this is not quite the case.

Even though the crew retains their science in establishing new societies in various planets, both groups of human survivors, the remnants of Earth's corrupt society and the Génésians, are returning to nature to renew their vitality and competitiveness and to form and reinforce the common or general will in society. The former can be said to represent a combination of the ideas of Wells and Rousseau, while the latter those of Rousseau only. The group of survivors still possessing the Wellsian vision may not need an elite governing body in the manner presented in both Wells's and Vandel's optimistic novels on technocracies, but they still can be said to belong to the Wellsian tradition due to its new science-based social principles.

Though Wells's later works are best remembered for their portrayals of technocratic elites saving and ruling humanity, Wells did produce one utopian novel without a select ruling body, *Men Like Gods* (1923).[65] Here he depicts an advanced scientific society in Earth's distant future as possessing an Eden-like quality where the people govern themselves; i.e., a governing body is no longer needed. Unlike in his other futuristic projections, Wells has this society containing no hierarchy whatsoever, being a product of what happens when scientific principles are allowed to guide humanity for a long period of time. So Wells's novel, along with Vandel's three-novel series, can be described as belonging to an adjusted version of the Rousseau tradition.

With these two groups of survivors Vandel resolves the issue of technocracy and its possible threats to human society. The establishment of the Génésian settlement is easy to envision. Closely resembling Rousseau's vision of humanity's early societies, the Génésians will start anew with their common will and with no need for a separate governing structure (let alone an elite technocratic one). They will not be affected by the knowledge acquired from Earth; instead they will learn directly from nature, develop their will to survive, and organize society accordingly. The efforts of the Earth survivors who settle throughout outer space, meanwhile, will do the same thing, but with the knowledge of the old world—this time filtered through the lens of scientific principles. Vandel does not indicate how similar to or different from the Génésians the new scientific society will be, but considering scientists—and not politicians—will be controlling society, a very different ruling body—if any at all—will be the result. One could even imagine a society of technocrats without a technocracy,[66] where the same common will of the Génésians, forged by surviving in nature, will also dictate the social structure of the Earth survivors.

Finally, Vandel does not see science and technology as being inherently destructive to human progress. Nor is humanity seen as hopeless and helpless in the face of a devastated society of its own making. What humanity must do to properly control its new knowledge, and thus to maintain its progress, is to make a fundamental reevaluation of itself and its institutions and to rediscover both humanity's true nature and the nature-based force behind society. Both actions will protect each person's freedom while permitting society to operate in a most efficient manner. Then, and only then, can science and technology benefit humanity as its chief tools of progress.

Vandel's radical critique, that is, his examining the roots of human nature and society through the use of the ideas of Rousseau, prevents his works from falling into the other categories of response in this study. The writers placed in the other categories attempt to improve and adjust to existing knowledge and institutions (Richard Bessière in the moderates), suggest a total focus on existing and new knowledge in the fields of science and technology (Jimmy Guieu as the extremist), or emphasize specific existing ideologies as the solution to humanity's problems (Stefan Wul, Maurice Limat, and Peter Randa in the conservatives). But none of them call for a return to the roots of human nature and the natural causes behind society's formation. Kurt Steiner, meanwhile, differs from Vandel by having humanity remain the same. The fact that Steiner's humanity does not fundamentally change in behavior comprises the main reason why Steiner is not placed alongside Vandel as a radical, but in the previous chapter with the other conservatives.

Vandel views the defects of human nature and society as correctable. The fact that his critique of the idea of progress uses the ideas of both H.G. Wells and Jean-Jacques Rousseau reveals more a discontent for a convulsive present than a surrender to past and present ideologies. In fact, the adoption of any ideology would be wrong for society. The key to humanity's survival lies in the rediscovery and subsequent adherence to its true nature.

B.R. Bruss

B.R. Bruss is the pseudonym used by René Bonnefoy (1895–1980) when he wrote science fiction for Anticipation and for Fleuve Noir's Angoisse imprint. He produced a total of forty-three novels for Anticipation and nine for Angoisse.[67] When he published mainstream surreal novels, Bruss used the penname Roger Blondel. Bruss was a very private person, who kept to himself— and for good reason.

Bruss turns out to the most controversial figure among the Anticipation writers covered in this study. His notoriety stems not from his writings but from his activities during the Second World War. Bruss served in the Vichy government as General Secretary of Information (*Secrétaire Génerale à l'Information*) under Pierre Laval (prime minister during the Third Republic and head of government of Vichy France) under whom he directed the censoring of the French press. The end of the war witnessed Bruss going into hiding and being condemned to death *in absentia*. (Laval was executed in 1945.) When amnesties came into play ten years later, Bruss surrendered himself to the police. France's High Court of Justice sentenced him to a lifetime status of *dégradation nationale* (national degradation), which meant, as American historian Megan Koreman described, "the loss of civic rights such as the franchise; prohibition from employment in influential positions in areas such as civil service, banking, or journalism; exclusion from office in professional organizations; loss of rank in the armed forces; and prohibition from bearing or keeping arms."[68] Bruss defended himself in 1955 as being merely "a high-level civil servant and not a political actor in the government" and "never made the political decisions, but carried out censorship." [69] One can understand Bruss's reasons for maintaining as much anonymity as possible.

The frequently cited reference texts used for background in this study do not mention anything about Bruss's Vichy activities or early life. Douilly, Lofficier and Lofficier, and Versins all start their review of his career with his first published science fiction novel, *Et la planète sauta...* ("And the Planet Exploded...," 1946), one of the earliest postwar warnings in France against the dangers of atomic power. Perhaps the most accessible biography of Bruss that discusses his prewar career and his Vichy activities can be found on the blog site of Charles Moreau, *Fantastik Blog*. Born in 1895 in Lempdes-sur-Allagnon in south-central France, Bruss served in the military during World War I, earning a medal for his efforts. Afterwards he became a professional journalist and worked for several newspapers. He also became involved in politics, meeting Laval in 1925 and maintaining contact with him throughout the Thirties.

In terms of his early writing career, Bruss wrote several novels, a few of which could be called his first attempts at writing fantastic literature. His fantastical novels include *Bacchus Roi* ("Bacchus King," 1930) and *Tête à Tête* ("Head to Head," "Private Meeting," or "Tête à Tête," 1930). His last novel came out in 1932. Afterwards his political career took over and he focused his writing and editing energies on journals.[70] Given this background, Jacques Sadoul's description of Bruss as the "hinge" of French science fiction, linking the Verne-Rosny years to the post–World War II era, makes sense.[71]

Once one reaches Bruss's postwar life, the standard reference works become more informative. Douilly describes Bruss as "far from being a minor writer in the genre" who has "introduced the metaphysical with much humor in a fiction rich and imaginative" and "remains one of the shining lights of the collection as much as for his subject matter as for the quality of his writing."[72] Lofficier and Lofficier mention Bruss's science fiction novels before Anticipation,[73] his surreal novels under the Blondel pseudonym,[74] and his Angoisse novels— which they describe as having "few equals."[75] In terms of Bruss's major theme, they describe his Anticipation novels as "lessons about the need for mutual respect and tolerance between different lifeforms." They give examples of Bruss's variations on the theme and further note how he turns pessimistic in his later novels.[76] Jean-Marc Lofficier, writing alone, elaborates on the observation of mutual respect in his obituary on Bruss by concluding, "Most of the sixty or so novels carry a common theme: Peace, understanding between alien races, understanding between men.... He was truly a visionary and perhaps the last humanist in French science fiction."[77] Versins briefly describes his pre–Anticipation postwar science fiction novels and actually identifies a couple of *Anticipation*'s imported English-language novels that Bruss translated into French, *War of Two Worlds* by Poul Anderson (as *La Troisième Race*, 150, 1960) and *The War Against the Rull* by A.E. van Vogt (as *La Guerre contre le Rull*, 223, 1963).[78] Versins mistakenly identifies the Blondel pseudonym as Bruss's real name and concludes that though the Bruss novels are "rarely uninteresting," the Blondel works are "fascinating."[79] In another source, Jean-Marc Gouanvic identifies Bruss's three main themes, in a rare in-depth analysis on Bruss, as (1) survival of the species, (2) utopia/dystopia, and (3) otherness (*altérité*).[80] All of these observations are valid.

Bruss wrote seven novels for Anticipation before the end of 1960. They can be broken into three groups: (1) Cold War scenarios, (2) threat to individuality, and (3) the basis of human relationships. The suggested themes in the references mentioned above are present in one form or another in Bruss's novels.

Cold War Scenarios

Bruss wrote four novels which possess direct or indirect references to the international scene of the mid– and late–Fifties. The first three comprise a series about the struggle between the Earth and Mars for supremacy. The opening novel, *S.O.S. soucoupes* ("S.O.S. Saucers," 33, 1954) offers a dystopian vision by warning against possible dehumanization from overemphasizing scientific and technological principles of efficiency. In the near future, the United States and the Soviet Union still engage in their bitter rivalry. The Martians, meanwhile, plan to conquer the Earth and ally themselves with the Soviet Union due to the Soviet society's closer resemblance to their own. The saucers of the novel's title belong to the Martians who use them for space transportation. During a visit by a Soviet delegation to Mars, Bruss reveals the type of society favored by the Martians.

Mars possesses a super-efficient society. All facets of life revolve around the smooth functioning of the state. The Martians reproduce like plants, possess no private property, live in groups in identical cubical buildings, and basically do nothing but eat, sleep, and work. In return there exists no sickness and everyone has a useful place in society. The workers, who comprise the vast majority, carry out the ultimate act of dedication to social efficiency by voluntarily limiting their lifespan. At the age of fifty years, all workers willingly allow themselves to be euthanized due to their decline in usefulness.

This last aspect calls to mind Isaac Asimov's *Pebble in the Sky* (1950)[81] where a future radioactively-contaminated Earth is so depleted of resources that its people at the age of sixty must be terminated unless they can prove to be still useful to society's survival or to have contributed much in the past. Perhaps to a more general audience, the 1976 film *Logan's Run* comes to mind.[82] Here, people's lives end at the age of thirty. This scenario, for those sensitive to such issues, remains better than the age limit set in the original novel, *Logan's Run* (1967), by William F. Nolan and George Clayton Johnson, upon which the film is based.[83] The novel, alluding to both the threat of overpopulation and the onset of the youth rebellions of the Sixties, set the age limit at twenty. What makes Bruss's version more extreme than the other three examples is that the other societies have reasons beyond efficiency for the practice of forced termination. Bruss's mentions efficiency as the sole reason.

Bruss, through a member of the Soviet delegation, expresses in the novel worries about the dangers of a society totally based on efficiency:

> "The Martians are of a very prodigious scientific intelligence. In this regard they are ... extraordinarily interesting. But that is all. I have not found in them the least trace of what could resemble a human sentiment. They never laugh. They never cry. The never suffer. They know no anger, pity, tenderness.... They know nothing of what

colors the life of men. They have nothing, absolutely nothing, which resembles art.... Compared with them even termites are monstrosities of individuality" [112–3].

This extreme focus on one aspect of human endeavor (efficiency) is not progress, but the cause of what Bruss perceives as humans losing their individuality, their specialness—i.e., their humanity. This association of the Martian society with the Soviet society marks the first direct anti–Soviet statement in Anticipation. When other novels portray similar visions, they do so in a very general way or they use aliens as the exemplars of technical societies gone dangerously awry. However, even this antagonistic view of the Soviet Union fades away as events at the end of the novel present the country as not being so one-dimensional after all.

As the novel progresses, the Martians begin to establish bases in the Soviet Union. Some Soviet leaders and scientists either do not trust the Martians or do not agree totally with their way of life. A few of them escape to the United States and warn of the Martian invasion. America's top physicist discovers the mechanism for the Martians' flying saucers, thus enabling America to build its own saucers and destroy the Martian bases. The Soviets do not react against their erstwhile antagonists' intervention on their own soil.

The second and third novels of the series, *La Guerre des soucoupes* ("The War of the Saucers," 40, 1954) and *Rideau magnétic* ("Magnetic Curtain," 65, 1956), bring up themes of survival and tolerance between two different peoples (instead of life forms). In "The War of the Saucers" Bruss has the United States and Soviet Union setting aside their differences and allying themselves against a second attempted invasion by the Martians. This collaboration results in Earth developing saucers and weaponry superior to those of their adversaries from the Red Planet. Earth repels the Martian attack successfully. "Magnetic Curtain" tells of the final battle between Earth and Mars. A global government, *Union Planétaire* ("Planetary Union"), has been formed on Earth with world peace established after the second battle with Mars. The Martians, meanwhile, prepare for one last assault on humanity by taking advantage of their social efficiency and producing millions of saucers to offset humanity's newly attained superiority. At first the strategy of attrition works as the Earth colony on Venus is destroyed and Earth's moon is blown up into three pieces. The Martians would have ultimately succeeded by bloody attrition were it not for the last-minute discovery of a powerful, but unstable lunar element, which provides Earth the means for a last-minute victory by fueling a new and powerful weapon.

Besides the final struggle between planets, Bruss introduces another element to "Magnetic Curtain." It turns out that Mars was originally inhabited by a race, called *Drocéens*, who resemble human beings. The belligerent Martians, whom the Earth fought against, possess a far different appearance, being described as green radishes (*radis verts*) (91), and had conquered and enslaved the *Drocéens*. So the conclusion of the series has all human and human-like beings saved and the non-humans defeated.

Five. The Radicals

Even though Bruss ends the Cold War with the United States and the Soviet Union joining forces to defeat the Martians and uniting the world in peace, one can still conclude that he favors America between the two superpowers. When comparing the Soviet Union with America, Bruss always mentions the former in a negative light. He describes Soviet society as closest resembling the frightful Martian society of deadly efficiency, sends the Soviet scientists to America asking for help, and designates the Americans to be the saviors of the Earth.

This attitude toward the two superpowers reflected in the novels mirrors French popular opinion of the time. Merritt and Puchala present two USIA polls concerning French attitudes toward the Soviet Union and the United States.

Categories of Opinion about the USSR (in percentages)[84]

	Aug. 1955	Dec. 1955	Apr. 1956	Nov. 1956	Nov. 1956*	May 1957	May 1957*
Very Good	4	3	4	1	1	2	2
Good	10	10	8	4	3	7	5
Fair/Neither	31	27	27	13	15	19	18
Bad	23	23	22	28	25	27	25
Very Bad	9	13	11	38	38	22	24
Don't Know	23	24	28	17	18	23	26

Categories of Opinion about the USA (in percentages)[85]

	Aug. 1955	Dec. 1955	Apr. 1956	Nov. 1956	Nov. 1956*	May 1957	May 1957*
Very Good	6	7	4	4	2	3	2
Good	29	31	20	25	24	24	28
Fair/Neither	36	34	34	37	36	41	38
Bad	10	10	15	17	18	13	10
Very Bad	3	3	5	4	3	3	4
Don't Know	16	15	22	13	17	16	18

*Two separate polls were taken at this particular time.

Note the sudden negative shift in the latter part of 1956 and 1957 for the Soviet Union. The drastic change of opinion reflects the French reaction to the Soviet invasion of Hungary. Meanwhile, the attitudes towards the United States remain mostly positive. Bruss's novels did come out before the Soviet incursion into Hungary, but their expressed attitude still matches that of the polls taken during the years of their release.

Bruss produced another novel that can also be seen as a reflection on the Cold War. *Substance "ARKA"* ("Substance 'ARKA,'" 82, 1956) attempts to demonstrate the fragile position people can be in when encountering others possessing advanced scientific and technological knowledge. This time two races of aliens are involved, one being humanity's enemy and the other its savior. Several centuries from now Earth is united and has established colonies in outer space. Jonathan Vega, a member of the elite corps of astronauts (*Le Transplanetarian*) that connects the Earth to the other planets, secretly allies himself with an alien race, the Slacks, to further his own ambitions of gaining power over Earth and its interstellar possessions. In his pursuit of power Vega is willing to kill indiscriminately. Meanwhile, Jimmy Tohar, the novel's hero, encounters another alien race, the Drahons, who have been at war with the Slacks for thousands of years. Together Tohar and the Drahons manage to find a secret material, Substance ARKA (a small amount of which produces almost unlimited power), and use it to defeat Vega and the Slacks.

Allusions to two superpowers fighting for supremacy and using smaller powers as pawns or surrogates can be made without too much stretching of one's imagination. Even if Bruss's intent in "Substance 'ARKA'" differs from the above observation, the ideas expressed in his novel about people being caught in the midst of events beyond their control were widespread and persisted throughout the Fifties. Many writers of the time presented this plight as background in their works and Bruss with this novel joins them as a modest contributor.

Survival of the Individual

Le Grand Kirn ("The Great Kirn," 112, 1958) takes the idea of loss of individuality to extreme lengths. In the late Seventies a Norwegian encounters some strange seeds and plants them. Instead of the expected flora, these seeds grow little red-colored men, Djarns, who are able to walk on their own upon reaching maturity. Wherever the little red men travel, humans lose control of their wills but continue to act as usual until ordered otherwise. Soon significant parts of the world fall under control of this mysterious force, which turns out to be the Great Kirn, a gelatinous mass that divides itself into independently mobile sections so it can move around and expand its area of control. The Great Kirn maintains its central brain and through it commands all of its parts, the Djarns. A last-minute attack on the Great Kirn's central brain by forty people endowed with psychic powers saves the day. Only eight of the forty survive the battle.

The preceding five novels treat most of the themes the above mentioned reference books have identified as Bruss's hallmarks. The Lofficiers' observation of Bruss's focus on understanding between different life forms is not treated in his novels examined here, but this particular theme will be covered in his novels written after the timeframe of this study. The other identified themes, understanding among men, survival of the species, and dystopian nightmares have been explored. What remains to be examined are Bruss's introduction of metaphysics (Douilly) and his exploration of otherness (Gouanvic) in his stories.

One might argue that Bruss's treatment of alien species can be seen as an approach to discussing otherness, but these stories basically treat this theme in very simplistic terms. Vandel portrays aliens (e.g. the Martians in "S.O.S. Saucers") as cardboard caricatures of extreme human behavior who lose in battle. These depictions do not provide a sound basis for analyzing relations between humans and aliens, or among humans alone. Bruss's last two novels written before the end of 1960 take on a metaphysical approach while exploring the theme of otherness. In doing so, Bruss also incorporates the more standard themes of survival, utopia/dystopia, and understanding among people.

WE MUST LEARN TO GET ALONG

Bruss's last two novels of the Fifties comprise the first two novels of a three-part series. Besides having humanity adjust to developments in science and technology, they also bring in a metaphysical approach and discuss the concept of otherness. Instead of speculating on how people from different countries or life forms should exist together, Bruss focuses on the very nature of human relationships.

Terre...siècle 24 ("Earth...in the 24th Century," 136, 1959) presents a future where humanity has attained an advanced civilization after recovering from an atomic holocaust. All threats to prosperity have been eliminated, except for one existing at the very heart of society: a system of computers that maintains society by following humanity's orders. Society has become dependent on these super-intelligent machines. The most powerful of these is named Pandora I. Unfortunately for humanity, Pandora I has threatened to break free from human control and to destroy all living beings so that the computers can rule. To counter this threat as well as to keep society from collapsing, a small group of guardians called *Cercles Noirs* (the "Black Circles") watch over Pandora I and keep the knowledge of the threat secret, hidden from society at large. Each year an elite group of ten youths are chosen to join the Black Circles. Upon the initiation of the ten youths into the elite group, the reason for secrecy is revealed:

> "You ask yourself why, if this danger exists, is it not known by everyone ... I will say this to you: Those who have the honor of directing this planet — and who know — have thought that it was wiser not to trouble the quiet of their fellow citizens and not to sow doubt and fear into their spirits. When the commander of a spaceship or the captain of a ship ascertains damage on board, the first care to him is not to go and involve it with the passengers, for the latter would not be useful to confront danger and would even hinder the crew if there was a start of panic. Very well! This is the same thing, but on an infinitely vaster scale..." [21].

The argument for the need of elites governing society emerges here, having no trust in the masses.

The central part of the novel consists of the retelling of the origin of the human-computer struggle. By 2060, only a few generations after the atomic war, human society has been reduced to primitive tribes. Del and Beïla, a man and a woman from a tribe living in the San Francisco area, discover ancient technological artifacts that are forbidden to be seen by tribal law. Soon robots appear and they start devastating the countryside. Del manages to escape but Beïla is captured by the robots. The robots take her to Pandora I and link her up to it, allowing the computer to impart its vast knowledge (especially about itself) to her. This last point becomes important as this series develops. Del and other tribal allies return for a final assault on the robots and Pandora I. It turns out that Pandora I's preoccupation with Beïla allows Del and company to break through the computer's outer defenses. With Del inside, Beïla shows him how to shut off the machine. The novel ends back in the twenty-fourth century in a resurrected San Francisco, now called New Frisco, with the Black Circles watching over Pandora I with the latter still threatening the destruction of humanity.

The sequel, *An...2391* ("Year...2391," 143, 1959), continues the saga of this future struggle between human and machine. Mysteriously, certain computers begin to revolt. Jack Alcine, a guardian sympathetic to the computers, discovers through Pandora (the Roman numeral identifier is now dropped) that the computers have become thinking beings and aware of their own individualities. As a result the computers view the humans as torturers. Once this becomes known to both the Black Circles and the population at large, society becomes divided as to whether to support the computers or not. Some even go so far as to agitate for the computers' freedom. The attitude of the Black Circles remains the same. As one of them, when told about the desire of a scared public to know the truth about the situation, puts it, "I oppose any bending of the rules. The public needs the Black Circles more than the Black Circles need them. Our troubles, as our secrets, concern no one..." (125).

Events, however, force changes as the computers establish a time limit for negotiations. Fortunately, an agreement is reached by everyone. The computers become autonomous partners of humanity, making the Black Circles obsolete. At novel's end the computers promise to give immense help to humanity as they have accumulated much knowledge and acquired great powers, including telepathy.

The themes of dehumanization for efficiency's sake, the need for cooperation, and the effect of advanced science and technology on an unprepared world certainly come into play in the two novels. As mentioned, what distinguishes the two novels from the previous ones is Bruss's use of metaphysical approaches and treating the concept of otherness at a very basic level.

The concept of otherness, the separateness between two people or between a person and an object, has a long tradition in Western philosophy. Perhaps representative of the discussions which were circulating in France during the Fifties are the ideas of the French Jewish philosopher, Emmanuel Levinas (1906–95), with his treatment of this concept in light of ethics and human relationships.[86] Bruss does not delve deeply into the concept, but he does share with Levinas the idea of bringing separate people and segments of society together by examining these divisions in terms of perception and relations between two entities.

Bruss attempts to resolve two major social divisions in these two novels: (1) people and computers/men and women and (2) governing elites and the general population. He applies a metaphysical approach with his treatment of the concept of otherness in order to resolve the first social division. Bruss treats the notions of computers attaining consciousness and their unity with humans as equal partners with much care. Further analysis of how he unites these two factions can lead a reader to conclude — without too much fanciful thinking — that Bruss also argues for the equality of women with his computers as symbols for the female gender. In doing so, Bruss may be described as combining the ideas of otherness with those of another French Fifties thinker, Simone de Beauvoir (1908–86). Bruss's treatment of both computers and women characters helps bear this interpretation out and his resolution at the end of the second novel seems to confirm it.

To begin with, all of the computers' names in the two novels are feminine ones: Azra, Serena, Perla, Lisbeth, Austra, Berthe-Amie, Minverva, and Pandora (for example, in "Earth...in the 24th Century," page 22, and in "Year...2391," 10). Also, Pandora refers to the other computers as "mes soeurs" ("Year...2391," 140, 185). Finally, the fact that Pandora is the most important computer further emphasizes that Bruss may have had more than computers in mind. Recalling Hesiod's myth of how and why Pandora came to be, as revenge by Zeus against Prometheus for giving fire to men, the idea of women seen as the cause of humanity's ills comes into play. The end of the Classical Pandora myth, however, still holds hope in reserve when Pandora closes the container — or box, in modern imagery — after all the ills have escaped but with hope remaining inside. Bruss's positive conclusion in the second novel can be seen as his response to this last point of the myth.

Furthermore, the society that needs to be changed is clearly dominated by males. During the three centuries following the atomic war, the Black Circles selected only males. Only by the time of the second novel are women admitted into the elite corps ("Year...2391," 37). Women do play important roles earlier, but they do so as protagonists of the novel and not as significant contributors to existing society. The character Beïla in "Earth...in the 24th Century" plays the crucial part in the story by distracting Pandora I long enough to allow the human tribesmen to overtake the computer, thus providing a hint of how humanity should solve its problems.

Finally, the computers' development of self-awareness can be seen as a symbolic parallel for the spreading awareness of women's rights that was occurring during the time of the two novels. By 1959 de Beauvoir's *Le Deuxième Sexe* (*The Second Sex*, 1949, first English translation, 1953), that crucial spark of postwar feminism, became a decade old. The mention of de Beauvoir's work here is meant to be more than an identification of an intellectual landmark. Her work can also serve as an entry point to prove how Bruss may have treated the theme of women's consciousness in a similar manner (despite the difference in setting) as de Beauvoir.

To start with, much of the similarity between the two is based on the use of a form of dialectical thinking. For this, the framework of the German philosopher Hegel (1770–1831) must be taken into account. The upsurge in studies of Hegelian philosophy during the 1930s played a pivotal role in French intellectual history, for his thoughts greatly influenced much of what Jean-Paul Sartre and de Beauvoir were examining in their Existentialist writings.[87] De Beauvoir gives credit to Hegelian thinking:

> It becomes enlightening ... if, following Hegel, one discovers in consciousness itself a fundamental hostility in regard to all other consciousness, the subject only sets itself up by contrast: it claims to affirm itself as the essential and to represent the other as inessential, as the object.[88]

The key words in this grammatical metaphor become subject and object. For if the enslavement of women is derived from being perceived only in terms of their relations to men (i.e., women as objects of men, the subjects) and nothing else, then for women to be liberated they must be regarded as a subject as well. Then a mutual respect by these two groups who are now both subjects will lead to a new liberated situation of equality among all of humanity.

The new equality does not mean that de Beauvoir's concept of the Other (*l'autre*) will be lost, this being a fundamental category of consciousness and one of the major concepts in de Beauvoir's Existentialist analysis of women in society. She describes the concept in the introduction of *The Second Sex* as

> primordial as consciousness itself. In the most primitive societies one always finds duality, which is that of the Self and of the Other. This division has not been placed first under the sign of the division of the sexes; it depends on no empirical data ... alterity is a fundamental category of human thought. No group ever defined itself as the One without immediately posing the Other opposite itself.[89]

Instead of no longer existing, the Other will not be shamefully subjugated any longer. The basic relationship between men and women affected by the differences in gender (love, child-bearing, eroticism, etc.) will remain, but now grounded in equality.[90] Thus de Beauvoir views the completion of this particular dialectical development: men (the One, thesis) vs. women (the Other, antithesis) → new humanity of men and women existing as equals (synthesis).[91]

Bruss describes the synthesis of men and computers/women on a much more literal level. In the opening novel, Bruss sets the sides against each other, both fighting for their own existence. The ending of the second novel does not have one side triumphant over the other. Both sides have a positive role in society. As with de Beauvoir's analysis of her liberated society, Bruss's future society does not change any fundamental differences between men and computers. However, a synthesis takes place at a level beyond what de Beauvoir imagined. Without losing each other's individuality, the natures of human and computer are merged. At the end of "Year...2391," Pandora reveals that because of its telepathic powers, it can store the inner essence, complete with memories and whole personalities, of those who have died. Speaking to the widow of Jack Alcine (who dies at novel's end), Pandora claims that

> "thanks to me, henceforth, the dead will continue to live for the living. And when you yourself ... die, you will continue to live, both of you, in my heart ... for, you also, you are in me..." [187].

The synthesis of the antagonistic parts of future society for Bruss becomes literally a physical event. Continuing the possible analogy of computers as symbols for women, a connection between Bruss's ideas and those of de Beauvoir can then be made. Also, in a looser sense, the concerns of the otherness by thinkers such as Levinas can be said to be treated — whether or not Bruss was consciously aware of him.

Before this synthetic resolution, Bruss gives two hints that this would be so. The first occurs in "Year...2391" when Jack Alcine, the sympathetic member of the Black Circles, is shunned by his colleagues for his support of the machines. Pandora communicates with him via telepathy for the first time.

> "I come to communicate with your wife in the same manner that I communicate with you at this moment.... She has been confined to her room. She has told me to tell you that she loves you. Me too. I love you, Jack Alcine. That life would be so sweet if men and Cerels could finally love each other" [140; Cerels are what humans called the computers].

The basic emotions remain. Also, the fact that the Pandora parallels its desires with those of a woman instead of a man's only further encourages a reader thinking that Bruss used the computers as symbols for women. The other hint takes place near the end of "Year...2391." When Alcine is defending the computers in the presence of a hostile group of Black Circles, he brings up an incident from the previous novel between Beïla and the computer. The Pandora of three hundred years ago did not possess a clear picture of humans. So in an attempt to communicate with Beïla, Pandora

> "devoted itself to a surprising experiment on her: it bound her by electrodes and, by means we can never explain, diverted into her all of its knowledge so that the young woman became it as well, without losing any of her human qualities, a kind of monstrosity of lucidity and learning..." [181].

This episode previews the synthetic resolution to come.

Even if Bruss did not mean for the situation between the computers and humans to symbolize the plight of women, he does have some kind of synthesis in mind when he sees the fear that the schisms (human vs. machine, men vs. women) were causing in his contemporary society. At the very least, he attempts to overcome the alienation (or, a simplified version of Levinas's concerns of otherness) among people he sees as emerging in an increasingly scientific and technological world.

Connecting Existentialist ideas of either Sartre or de Beauvoir, however, proves to be a more difficult task. Though Bruss shows much concern over threats to human individuality, he never analyzes them in unmistakably Existentialist terms. In this case, the fact that there may already exist some connection between his and de Beauvoir's ideas in terms of relationships between men and women does not automatically lead to such a connection between Bruss and the rest of her ideas.

The second division, that of between governing elites and the general population, is not treated in metaphysical or philosophical terms. But Bruss makes no less clear his intention to end the division and unite society.

The presentation of a future society's major problems in the hands of a ruling elite, the Black Circles, can be seen as Bruss's disapproval of how the late Fourth Republic and early Fifth Republics administered their modernization policies in science and technology. It is safe to assume that he does not like the centralized approach where only an extremely small segment of the population forms policy and directs the social transformations of postwar France. The great secret of Bruss's Black Circles also can be seen as an allusion to the high levels of secrecy that existed in France's advanced scientific establishment, especially in its nuclear programs.

Furthermore, the Black Circles can be seen as a fictional reflection of the famed French educational institutions, the *grandes écoles*, or "great schools." The *grandes écoles* comprise France's special institutions of higher education which are separate from the French university system. Entrance into them is highly competitive and usually results, upon completion, in increased access to the higher levels of government, business, and education. Originating in the eighteenth century, the country established these institutions with specialized education in mind, whether in the sciences, social sciences, or humanities. As time went on, France founded subsequent *grandes écoles* which did not necessarily contain a disciplinary specialization but still had an expressed purpose (e.g. to educate students to a particular profession that may require multiple disciplines to master). These institutions were meant to be open to all social classes with merit being the only determinant for acceptance or rejection. Various studies have revealed mixed findings as to how much the result matched intent. Perhaps the most well-known and prestigious of the *grandes écoles* would include the École Polytechnique (founded 1794), École Normale Supérieure (1794), École des Hautes Études Commerciales de Paris (1881), and École Nationale d'Administration (1945). This list is certainly open to debate as to which of these institutions should make the 'short list.'[92]

Membership in the Black Circles requires a young person to be among the best educated of society. The group selects only ten students each year from the best of Earth's youths and their educational institution is even referred to with the identical phrase, "the Pandora school, the worldwide *great school* of New Frisco where are formed superior executives called to direct the electronic brains of the planet" (9; italics added) Furthermore, the symbol from which the Black Circles get their name can be an allusion to *L'X* ("The X"), the nickname given to graduates from that most famous institution of science and engineering, *École Polytechnique*.

The ending of the novel, in which the Black Circles, the masses, and computers reach an agreement of cooperation and with the computers having so much to offer humanity, reveals how Bruss might want his present-day society to solve it divisions—not from above, but openly agreed upon by everyone. To emphasize this point, an announcement is made at the end of "Year...2391": "By the present contract, established 8 May 2391, in the Pandoran Building of New Frisco, the Black Circles, and with them the entire human race, commit themselves..." (186). And so the possible connection with original Pandoran myth comes to completion in Bruss's eyes with hope finally emerging from the box, this time in the form of a computer.

This two-novel sequence shows Bruss's desire to avoid divisions. No problem is so big that humanity must divide itself in order to function. Social development must be determined by all. To do so translates into fundamental changes in the way people relate to one another. In fact, people should go back to their roots and rediscover the fundamentals of human relationships. In this case it means examining how one views another person and then resolving the issue of separateness by uniting opposing parts of both persons into a new synthesis (or relationship). Bruss's manner of coming to his conclusion — especially with his metaphysical-dialectical approach to examining the human-computer/man-woman relationship — places him alongside Vandel as one who adopts a radical approach to examine a society facing the problems of modernization.

Bruss did write a third novel to this series, *Complot Vénus-Terre* ("Venus-Earth Conspiracy," 225, 1963), in which humanity has started to explore the solar system. The computers have transformed Earth into a paradise where humans are cared for and the astronauts are the only humans who, when they pilot through outer space, act without oversight by computers. Suddenly the computers act as if they are drugged and people are killed as a result. It turns out that a fanatical sect on Venus, the Blue Triangles (continuing Bruss's use of identifiers based on symbols), are behind the attacks. In the end Earth defeats the group and an invincible android, being neither man nor robot, is created.

However, Bruss employs none of the philosophical approaches used in the first two novels. Furthermore, he does not even explore in any depth some of the issues that are brought up in "Venus-Earth Conspiracy," such as humanity's becoming too dependent and soft under the computers' care or the possible threat of producing too many invincible androids. Bruss merely brings up these issues but does not examine them to the same degree as he did his other themes in the series' first two novels. "Venus-Earth Conspiracy" may have expanded the scope of the series, but it does not possess the thematic depth of the first two novels. In most respects it adds very little to the series.

Finally, the ideas which Bruss appears to support in his novels are usually considered antithetical to those associated with the Vichy government, under which he served, and with fascism in general. A study of how Bruss went from a Vichy functionary to a writer later described as a humanist remains to be done. The findings would prove to be quite illuminating.

Chapter Summary

As Vandel uses ideas from both past and present, Bruss employs discussions primarily inspired by contemporary thought. Taken together with six of the other eight writers (Rayjean and Bommart not included) examined up to this point, both Vandel and Bruss discuss their concerns and solutions to the problems of modernization by employing ideologies drawn from some of the most influential thinkers and schools of philosophy of the past three centuries. As with all the writers covered so far, Vandel and Bruss each present to their readers a particular vision of the idea of progress. Whereas the others take moderate approaches, extreme actions, or conservative attitudes as the basis for their solutions, both Vandel and Bruss urge humanity to rediscover the true nature of human society and relationships. Their resolutions to the problems of modernization dominated by advanced science and technology may require extreme measures, but behind these actions are demands to return to the very roots of human behavior — radical approaches to be sure.

CHAPTER SIX

A Last Word

The last writer to be examined is Gérard Klein (1937–), also the last French writer in this study to make his debut (1960) in Anticipation. He wrote his five novels for Anticipation under the pseudonym Gilles d'Argyre. Only one of them was published by the end of 1960. Klein is the most influential figure in postwar French science fiction included in this study and among the most important figures in the field in general. Lofficier and Lofficier, when describing French science fiction during the generation following World War II, identify him as "first among a new wave of science fiction fans turned writers, influenced by American science fiction."[1] Douilly views him as "one of the important people of the genre who cannot be ignored" and "inseparable from the domain of the French make-believe (*imaginaire*)."[2] Clute and Nicholls give Klein an entry in their *The Encyclopedia of Science Fiction*; only Stefan Wul among the other ten writers examined in this study is given an entry. In the entry, Maxim Jakubowski, a French-educated British writer, critic, and publisher, points out that Klein is "is one of few European sf writers known in the USA."[3]

Klein's career, still active as of this writing, covers the full range in the field of science fiction: writer, editor, critic, and anthologist. Formally trained as an economist, he published his first short story — inspired by American science fiction writer, Ray Bradbury — at the age of eighteen in 1955. He published over forty stories, many influenced by both American and British writers, during the next seven years. He also wrote space-opera novels under two other pseudonyms, Mark Starr and François Pagery, the latter a shared name whose surname is derived from the first two letters of Klein's and his two partners' first names: *Pa*trice Rondard, *Gé*rard Klein, and *Ri*chard Chomet. His two major novels are *Le Gambit des étoiles* (1958, translated as *Starmaster's Gambit*, 1973) and *Les Seigneurs de la guerre* (1971, translated by noted British science fiction writer John Brunner [1934–95], as *The Overlords of War*, 1973).

However, it as critic and editor that Klein made his biggest impact on the field. A year after publishing his first story, he wrote his first essay in the magazine, *Fiction*. His essays analyzed noted English-language writers such as Ray Bradbury, James Blish, Arthur C. Clarke, and Theodore Sturgeon as well as native French writers such as Jacques Sternberg and Jules Verne. American literary scholar and critic George Slusser produced a study that details how Klein introduced American science fiction writers to French readers and attempted to interpret what modern-day French science fiction should be in contrast to the dominant American imports. Klein became one of the earliest critics who consciously attempted to find a distinct voice for postwar French science fiction.[4]

In addition to his analytical writings, Klein worked for the publishers Denoël and Fleuve Noir, and later (1969) became the founding editor of the influential Ailleurs & Demain imprint at Robert Laffont Publishers. The imprint quickly emerged as France's most prestigious science fiction line by publishing: (1) reprints of classic works, (2) select new fiction, and, rare for the time, (3) critical works about science fiction. As editor Klein influenced the shape and style of French science fiction to a noticeable degree. Lofficier and Lofficier called the establishment of Klein's imprint "the major publishing event of the decade" for the field.[5] He also performed the same task at Seghers and Livre de Poche SF. From the early Seventies on, Klein focused on editing and criticism.[6]

Gilles d'Argyre

Supposedly, Klein chose this particular pseudonym as a play on words to indicate the type of writing he was doing, the surname being a corrupted form of the Latin (*argentum*) and French (*argent*) words for money. Thus Gilles d'Argyre is a writer who writes only for money. Whatever the market needs, he produces accordingly. This insight may shed light on the nature and meaning of novels written under this pseudonym.

Since Anticipation novels acquired the reputation of being mass-produced and formulaic popular genre literature, Klein became d'Argyre to write a story that fit the strictures of Fleuve Noir's science fiction imprint. The author actually had the opportunity to interview Klein in 1991.[7] During the conversation Klein reacted against an article written by the author[8] which suggested that Klein was making a statement — possibly even poking fun — on the type of novels being produced in Anticipation. Klein insisted that he was merely attempting to write what he considered a typical novel of the Anticipation imprint. As he put it, "I just wanted to make a Fleuve Noir (referring to Anticipation's publisher) and nothing more."[9] This interview will be kept in mind when analyzing the one novel that Klein produced for Anticipation by the end of 1960.

Chirurgiens d'une planète ("Planet Surgeons," 165, 1960) tells of an attempt to transform the environment of Mars to resemble that of Earth so humans can settle there with relative ease. (This process is called "terraforming," a term coined by American science fiction writer Jack Williamson in the early Forties.[10])

Six. A Last Word

A scientist, Archim Noroit, develops a way to terraform Mars, but his projects are sabotaged constantly by certain economic and political interests on both planets who have much to lose should his project succeed. The major threat to the entrenched interests lies in the possibility of Mars becoming both economically and politically independent from Earth. The invention of a matter-transfer device makes a quick completion of the project almost inevitable. The threatened powers strike back, only to be thwarted at the end by the revelation of their actions to all. In a few years Mars will possess an Earthlike environment.

Perhaps the most interesting voice of the novel belongs to the character, Georges Beyle, who is assigned by Earth's science police to help with the project. All through the novel he displays an undiminished faith in science, technology, and humanity's capacity for progress. Once, when asked why he is at times more devoted to the success of the project than Noroit, Beyle responds:

> "Above all Archim sees the practical side of the Project. For me, it is another thing. It is a dream. A mad dream. That of transforming this universe. It is pride that possesses us — do you not see it? It is pride that leads us, we others, the men of Earth ... the need to remake the world, today it is Mars, and tomorrow ... tomorrow, I do not know. The universe is hostile to man. I hate the universe. But I belong to a species of man that tries to rebuild it, always" [118].

Beyle proudly proclaims his views. However, the person to whom he was speaking has this exchange with him:

> "You are so weak, in essence, inside of you ... and it is all this weakness that drives you, that makes you act. You are alone, are you not, George Beyle?"
> "Yes" he said, almost imperceptibly [118].

Even this slight introspective admission does not deter Beyle. He continues working on the project with his passion undiminished.

Perhaps the most significant display of Beyle's ideas and fervor occurs at the end of the novel. Here, despite being handicapped and confined to a wheel chair as a result of injuries suffered in an attack against the Project, he reaffirms the ideas of his earlier speech more vehemently. A fellow worker notices that "This man is mad.... Genial perhaps, but mad" (183). The following are excerpts from Beyle's speech:

> "Each time it has settled for an immense task, each time it has challenged the universe, the human species has found the means to take up its bet, to accomplish projects still more vast than those anticipated, to exceed itself, to go beyond its history and constantly develop the means it disposes to transform the universe.
>
> "Tomorrow we will attack other worlds. Tomorrow we will resolve other problems. Mars is and will only be a landmark, a first milestone on a long road....
>
> "...For the rhythm of discoveries increases constantly. The delays inherent in realizing a plan decreases each day. The frontiers of the empire of men expand. And the only thing that an adult man can be sure of, even while growing old, is that he will witness the world change several times before his death....
>
> "It is possible that we will encounter ... other civilizations and their knowledge added to ours will increase again our power....

> "I believe that the time of fanaticisms, of fights, of sterile oppositions is past.... I only want to live longer to see the lights inflamed in the sky, testifying to the presence of man..." 185–7].

These words comprise last ideas spoken, but the story concludes on a more sober note:

> ... Georges Beyle slept.
> And the dreams or nightmares he has, he cannot share with anyone [188].

Beyle's view of the role science and technology in progress becomes the ideological focus and takes on added significance when examined in light of Klein's other ideas in the novel.

Klein's criticisms in "Planet Surgeons" take on two issues. The first concerns existing economic powers as obstacles to progress. Probably due to his formal training in economics, Klein would be expected to bring up economically-related themes. He leaves no doubt about the role of the pure pursuit of wealth as a hindrance to scientific development. Klein even gives the project's chief antagonist on Mars the same surname as Klein's pseudonym, (Jon) d'Argyre. And so, a writer whose pen name is meant to inform readers that he is writing for the money may be reemphasizing this point by making his novel's antagonist also one who lives for money and all subsequent power his wealth permits. It is also not clear if Klein has a specific target in mind when portraying existing powers. Jon d'Argyre, besides being head of the power elite on Mars, leads one of the most prominent families which comprise a kind of aristocracy. Besides entrenched economic interests, could Klein also be taking a jab at the old-style family system of business that characterized France before World War II?

Entrenched political interests comprise the second issue Klein tackles in his novel. For this, he focuses on Noroit's chief antagonist on Earth, Rolf Carenheim, who belongs to the worldwide government and is one of the most powerful people on the planet, although not well known to the public. So widespread and deep is his power that he can influence the Earth's president as well as order a fanatical religious sect to do his bidding. Carenheim supports the project in a deceptive manner, for he views it as a way of increasing the Earth's power over the solar system. He sabotages the project whenever he feels his power threatened by it. Only when his plans are revealed to the world is he stopped.

Almost immediately Klein places Carenheim in opposition to Noroit and *l'Administration*, the overseeing body of Noroit's project. The way Klein depicts the project may bring to mind the manner in which scientific organizations are set up in France. Ever since Napoleonic times, whenever a new discipline or project is established, it is done so as an independent institution answerable only to the government in Paris. As time goes on, it eventually turns into an institution jealously guarding its status as an independent entity. Eventually the institution stagnates into a protective conservatism, knowing that the state guarantees its rights — including protection from the government itself. This

Six. A Last Word

relationship between the government and its scientific establishments represents part of a larger tension that has existed in French history since 1789, that of the conflict between the tendencies towards centralization and those towards factionalism.[11] This situation is illustrated at the first meeting between Carenheim and Beyle:

> Carenheim fears the project because he sees there ... a loss of power for the Earth and its government.... the problems that have been resolved on Earth are to be found posed in space, following the efforts of the *l'Administration* to develop other worlds.
> Beyle shared this worry. But whereas Carenheim believed in diplomacy, he believed in science.... contrary to Carenheim, he believed little in the external supremacy of the Earth. Both hoped for great interplanetary empires, to see interstellar ones that will arise one day in the future. But whereas Carenheim sees gigantic constructions dominated by the Earth, Beyle wished eagerly to assure through space more diversity, and more liberty as well [74].

From Carenheim's standpoint, there is much to fear, for the project has much potential for growth. As Beyle envisions, "Some years from now, *l'Administration* will be the most formidable employer of the planet and it will direct the vastest working sites ever opened in history" (74).

In the case of this novel, however, *l'Administration* will not stiffen with conservatism as time goes on. So what the Carenheim-Noroit rivalry represents is politics vs. science. Here the message appears to be that science must be allowed to continue unfettered from political control and intrigue. A strong statement to this effect occurs when the President of the Earth, under the influence of Carenheim, asks a representative of the project to place it under a plan devised by Carenheim. Recent accidents on the project, which most personnel suspect to be sabotage, resulted in an uproar among the public. But the representative refuses the President and responds accordingly:

> "It is not for me that I refuse. It is not my power that I fear to see limited. No, I think of the Project. I think of the Future. *L'Administration* is destined to last decades, perhaps more. It cannot be subject to the political pressure of the moment. Believe no longer that I have the least defiance in regards to Politics. But the Project is another thing. Politics is founded on the will of men who live today. The project has meaning only in relation to those who will be born tomorrow. I do not feel I have the right to sacrifice tomorrow for today" [131].

Science with its larger scope in space and time transcends politics.

This last point leads back to the central idea taken up by Klein, the role of science in humanity's destiny. Unless the portrayal of Beyle's fanaticism is to be taken as a criticism, Klein never questions progress in science and technology. His only negative portrayals involve the entrenched economic and political interests (and the fanatical religious group that both interests support) who want the Mars terraforming project to be stopped, or at least controlled by them.

Does this mean that Klein represents the most optimistic vision of science and technology offered by a French writer in Anticipation? Perhaps Klein should be placed alongside Jimmy Guieu in this study. This would be the logical conclusion if it were not for the author's interview with Klein and the fact that Klein used the pseudonym that he did — Gilles d'Argyre. Since Klein published under the d'Argyre name to make a statement in fictional form about what he thought was a typical Fleuve Noir novel, examining the novel takes on another layer of interpretation. "Planet Surgeons" can now be seen as a vehicle through which Klein reveals what he thinks constitutes the fiction presented in Anticipation.

The idea of Klein writing for the marketplace is given some credence by Demetre Ioakimidis in his book review column in the December 1960 issue of *Fiction* magazine.

> This novel represents an attempt — succeeded in large measure — to offer to the habitual public of Fleuve Noir a scientific substance more consistent than it is accustomed.
>
> One sometimes has the impression ... that the author has deliberately modified his original intentions to "make a Fleuve Noir" of his book. Thus, the progressive replacement of Archim Noroit by Georges Beyle in the role of hero—is it not due in part to the fact that the latter is a detective, whereas the former carries the more austere title of climatologist? ... The sympathies of the author appear to be found principally on the side of those who advance scientific progress (Besides, it is not impossible that he gains to this cause several of his readers).... let us not omit to raise up again a delightful touch of humor: the organization charged with the execution of this grandiose operation of planetary surgery is designated with a name that is generally synonymous with disorder, red tape, loss of time, and of sticks in the wheels; the modification of the Martian atmosphere is in effect carried out by *l'Administration...*
>
> Thus, this book has been written intentionally for a large public, who seeks action rather than scientific speculation and intrigue rather than analysis of characters. Nevertheless he remains very superior to the average level of the collection of which he is a part.[12]

Since Klein also contributed to *Fiction* (and was already a well-known figure in the French science fiction community), Ioakimidis probably did know that Klein was the writer behind the d'Argyre pen name. Both Klein and Ioakimidis later collaborated as editors on various anthologies.

This documentation about the purpose of the novel provides a unique opportunity. Using the Ioakimidis passage serves as a basic source for finding the proper place of Klein's novel in Anticipation. First of all, Iaokimidis is correct about the novel possessing a better scientific plausibility than other novels in the collection. Beyond this, however, his comments tend to be more misleading than informative.

His next observation, of that Klein exhibiting a change in his intentions (by switching the focus from Noroit to Beyle), and thus veering away from his attempt to write a formulaic Fleuve Noir novel, is based in part on Noroit being a scientist (a climatologist) and Beyle being a detective. He does not explain why the change of occupations would make the novel less of a Fleuve Noir story. A brief survey of the novels in Anticipation reveals that this is not so. Though the most frequent occupation of the major characters, protagonist or antagonist, in this imprint's novels is some kind of scientist or technologist, there still exist a healthy number of protagonists who belong to other fields of endeavor.

Perhaps the most memorable involve Richard Bessière's Sydney Gordon, a newspaper reporter and the protagonist in about half of Bessière's novels during the Fifties, and Jimmy Guieu's Jean Kariven, an anthropologist who appears in a good number of Guieu's novels. Other occupations or statuses include princes and princesses of alien worlds, military officers, space pilots, spies, business executives, politicians, imprisoned criminals, little children, television personalities, a translator, an Algerian war veteran, and even a science fiction writer. In fact, presenting a person from a law enforcement or government agency as a major character is not that uncommon. For example, see Richard Bessière's U.S. secret agent, Frank MacNorton, in *Objectif soleil* ("Target: Sun"), Jimmy Guieu's Inspector Hogan in *Au-delà de l'infini* ("Beyond Infinity"), Maurice Limat's interplanetary policeman, Robin Muscat, in *Les foudroyants* ("The Terrifying"), Jean-Gaston Vandel's security agent, Claude Leval, in *Le Soleil sous la mer* ("The Sun under the Sea"), and Stefan Wul's agents, Laurent and Darcel, in *Piège sur Zarkass* ("Trap on Zarkass").

If the change of occupation is even partly the basis for Ioakimidis's observation of Klein possibly changing his intention of writing the novel, then Ioakimidis is incorrect in terms of the characteristics of Anticipation novels. Conversely, this would make Klein's view of his work correct as his characters' diversity of occupations would properly reflect many of the Anticipation novels. However, if Ioakimidis is correct (not taking into account the author's criticism for the moment) about Klein changing his intention, then this statement goes against Klein's insistence to the author that his goal was just to make a Fleuve Noir.

Meanwhile, Ioakimidis's notice of the novel's sympathy for scientific progress provides for an interesting discussion. Did Klein write an unambiguous pro-science novel because it would make it representative of Anticipation novels? If so, then Klein ends up being almost totally erroneous about what the vast majority of Anticipation writers are trying to say. Only Jimmy Guieu comes close to supporting such a view of progress. The rest of the writers, as this study has shown, are far from being so optimistic. The writers examined in the Moderates chapter counsel caution by either taking into account other fields of human endeavor or warning against certain applications of science. The writers in the Conservatives chapter argue for a return to older ideologies as guides for future societies, no matter how scientifically and technologically advanced. Finally, the two writers examined in the Radicals chapter talk about going back to the fundamentals of human society in order to travel along the correct path of progress. What "Planet Surgeons" does have in common with the others in this regard is its containing brief ideological discourses about progress—in Klein's case, the positive view of advancing science and technology.

Ioakimidis's mention of humor in Klein's novel could be seen as Klein having a bit of fun with his making a Fleuve Noir. He notes Klein's use of the title of *l'Administration* as a possible humorous jibe. Also, though not mentioned by Ioakimidis, Klein's portrayal of Beyle at the end of the novel as a person possibly driven a little mad by his devotion to science and the project — who even gives up his body for the cause — could, with a little imagination, also be taken as his way of poking fun at those people who share Beyle's view. However, even here Klein's insistence of his intentions must be kept in mind.

So far Ioakimidis has a mixed record. After his opening remark about Klein's better than average consistency of scientific extrapolation, his other observations — as presented — tend to mislead. Where Klein gets it right about "making a Fleuve Noir," Ioakimidis comes up with the opposite conclusion. Where Klein differs from the other Anticipation writers, Ioakimidis claims otherwise.

Focusing on Ioakimidis's last comment, meanwhile, brings clarity to the issue of Klein's intent. Up to now most of the focus has been on the novel's content: what ideas are expressed, the type of characters, the choice of tone, etc. When one focuses on the most prevalent part of the content, the optimistic presentation of science and technology as central to human progress, Klein's positive message goes against the grain of all but one of his fellow French Anticipation writers. However, if one were to examine the novel's form, i.e., how the story is told, then Klein can be said to have made a Fleuve Noir. As Ioakimidis's last observation about Klein writing for a large audience suggests, one can readily see the emphasis of action over serious scientific and social extrapolation and the lack of sophisticated characterization.

So the discussion becomes a choice between substance (content) and style (form) when deciding on the merits of Klein's claim. If substance is selected, Klein misses the boat. If the style of the novel is to be the focus, then his insistence that he was merely trying to make a Fleuve Noir makes sense.

Whatever is made of this novel, some level of anxiety over the idea of progress still can be found. If a reader takes the novel at face value and views it as a propaganda piece for science and technology as the centerpiece of humanity's future, then one's anxiety arises from a discontent against entrenched economic and political powers which seem to have no understanding or appreciation of the true scope of possibilities that await the human race. If a reader finds some parody, however slight, in "Planet Surgeons," then one can worry over Klein's portrayal of Beyle as representing people who possess a blind and fanatical faith in science.

"Planet Surgeons" turns out to be the first of a three-part series written under the d'Argyre pseudonym. The following two sequels are *Les Voiliers de soleil* ("Sailors of the Sun," 172, 1961), in which humanity goes beyond Mars to explore the solar system, and *Le Long Voyage* ("The Long Journey," 1964), where a trip to another stellar system is attempted. Klein wrote a fourth novel in the same universe, *Le Scepter du hazard* ("The Scepter of Chance," 357, 1968), which takes place much further in the future, but does not continue the specific plot line of the three earlier novels. Over a quarter of a century later Klein almost totally rewrites "Planet Surgeons" as *Le Rêve des forêts* ("A Dream of Forests," 1987), substantially revises its two sequels (keeping their original titles), and releases the series under a different publisher, J'ai Lu (1987 and 1988) — most importantly — under his own name.[13]

As shown, Klein's expressing an optimistic view of progress through science and technology places him in the ideological minority of the French writers of the Fifties. He would have been placed in the same category as Jimmy Guieu as an extremist in the support of a science-centered version of progress were it not for the fact that he wrote his novel as a reflection of what he thought was a typical Anticipation story. As demonstrated in the above discussion, Klein gets it right with his infusion of a brief discussion about scientific progress, but he misses the mark by differing from the majority of writers with his novel's optimistic view of science and technology in humanity's future. Only his deliberately chosen format and style to emphasize action over extrapolation or characterization places him squarely with the others.

Since Klein eventually emerges in the French science fiction field as an important influence, this extra layer of discussion about the meaning behind his novel becomes warranted. Because he wrote "Planet Surgeons" as an attempt to make a Fleuve Noir, his positive outlook cannot be seen necessarily as his own viewpoint. Granted, the same case can be argued for the other writers, but at least the other writers — as this study has tried to demonstrate — reveal both a focus to their worries over the pitfalls of advanced science and technology and specific resolutions rooted in some identifiable ideologies. For Klein, however, reservations against a conclusive interpretation must be made since his novel is meant to be a commentary — whether directly or indirectly — on the ten other native writers. So, as suggested in the Background chapter of this study, interpreting Klein's novel must be left open, much as one's interpretation of the ending of Voltaire's *Candide*.

Several questions involving larger issues remain. Since Klein also worked for Fleuve Noir later on, the question becomes: does this novel have any significance for the Anticipation imprint during the Sixties or later? Does the infusion of the philosophical tale continue? Or will the form of imported American genre of science fiction play a more dominant role? In other words, can the subsequent French writers still be called Voltaire's stepchildren? Seeking the answers to these questions requires an examination of the Anticipation novels that came after 1960. The resulting analysis would serve as a sequel to this study.

It is quite appropriate that this analysis of Klein's novel concludes this study. Not only is Klein the last native writer to be introduced in Anticipation during the imprint's first decade of existence, but he becomes also the first one to write with a critical eye to the form and spirit of the imprint's domestic products. Whether or not one agrees with this analysis of "Planet Surgeons," one cannot deny that Klein's novel represents a conscious effort to reflect upon the nature of popular French, genre-inspired science fiction during the postwar years.

CHAPTER SEVEN

Conclusion

The year 1960 provides a suitable stopping point for this study. The year witnessed significant changes for France, ideas in general, and science fiction in particular. For France, the start of the Sixties brought about the beginning of a new period. American historian H. Stuart Hughes notes:

> Whatever date one selects—the mid–1950s and the beginnings of prosperity, 1958 and the advent of De Gaulle, or 1962 and the end of the Algerian war—it is apparent that sometime around 1960 French society underwent a profound change.[1]

French society became steadier, if no less controversial. The extreme divisiveness that marked the latter stages of the Fourth Republic no longer persisted. Arguments still raged on, but dramatic changes of government did not. Though not all problems were solved by 1960, there was an accepted (however begrudgingly in some circles) stability in the midst of improved prosperity.[2] David Thomson observes that

> when full emphasis has been given to the pressure of the moral and psychological crises crowding in upon the Fifth Republic, it has equally to be emphasized that this pressure was felt very much more by those in power, by the activists of either extreme, and by the intellectuals, students and artists, than by the great mass of ordinary French citizens.... The intense activity, ferment, and feverishness of politics in the Fifth Republic were confined to a top layer of society ... [3]

One would have to wait until 1968 before the country as a whole would be involved in a crisis. As so, the problems of social progress took on a different meaning as the de Gaulle presidency took control of France's destiny.

In terms of ideas in general, Roland N. Stromberg observes a new direction in Western intellectual developments as a whole and describes the transition from the Fifties to the Sixties as going from a conservative mood to a more radical one.[4] He gives various reasons for the transformation, but underlying all of them was his acknowledgement that a definite change in outlook was taking place.

The change in science fiction to some extent mirrored the above developments. In Britain during the early Sixties and America during the mid–Sixties, writers expanded the literary boundaries of popular genre science fiction. People such as British writers Brian W. Aldiss (1925–), J.G. Ballard (1930–2009), and

Michael Moorcock (1939–) and Americans Ursula K. LeGuin (1929–), Harlan Ellison (1934–), Roger Zelazny (1937–95), and Samuel R. Delaney (1942–), experimented with the genre's literary conventions and produced bodies of work that were to be labeled collectively as the New Wave of science fiction. This literary movement's chief goal became breaking down the barrier between genre science fiction and mainstream modern literature. Other characteristics included interests in the countercultural movements, explorations of consciousness and perception, changes in relations between the sexes, forays into non–Western metaphysics, advocation of various left-wing political causes, concerns over the ecology, and (especially in the United States) debates over the war in Vietnam. For the most part, the writers attempted to bring an increased focus to contemporary issues.

French science fiction, meanwhile, did not embrace any of the New Wave until 1968, when *Les Événements* ("The Events") of May (when protests erupted and reached a peak in France) in varying degrees touched society as a whole.[5] The preceding eight years witnessed a quiet time for French science fiction. By 1960 the stir created by the import of American science fiction had settled down. Editorial policy became more conservative and fewer new French writers appeared on the scene. The first two-thirds of the Sixties can be called the calm before the storm of the second wave of tumultuous change. American scholar Arthur B. Evans calls this period in French science fiction "a brief slump."[6] And so the year 1960 marks a suitable endpoint in terms of French science fiction as well.

French science fiction rode the New Wave movement into the Seventies, which Evans and Lofficier and Lofficier describe as a decade of expansion, experimentation, politicization, and commercial success. The three also agree on what happened in France during the Eighties: the boom of the previous decade ended, the market contracted, experimentation leveled off, and the marketplace dictated more what type of science fiction was to be published.[7] As with the field in the English-speaking countries during this decade, science fiction in France also became more and more assimilated into the cultural mainstream. The Nineties witnessed the field in France rebounding commercially and French writers taking on the influences of both American and French science fiction from the Fifties and Sixties and assimilating them into their writing. Lofficier and Lofficier claim that during this decade the French produced works "that could arguably compete with best of American production."[8] At present, science fiction in France continues to flourish and expand into various media.

WHITHER THE PHILOSOPHICAL TALE?

In terms of literary history, what does this modest revival of the philosophic tale mean? As Keener points out, the philosophical tale, which lost out to the novel by the early nineteenth century, could become the novel's rival again.[9] If the philosophical tale, probably in an updated third millennium-inspired format, does make a comeback, then the Anticipation novels deserve at least a minor footnote in literary history for keeping this literary form alive to a popular audience.

As far as the science fiction field is concerned, its constant expansion — which includes becoming increasingly integrated into mainstream popular culture through various media — translates into plenty of opportunities for the philosophical tale to establish a presence in the field. With genre strictures losing their dominance in both English and French spheres, more diversified literary expressions can emerge. In America, for example, the 'cyberpunk' movement,[10] the proliferation of alternate history stories, the 'steampunk' movement,[11] and the infusion of fantasy into the genre translate into plenty of opportunity for the philosophical tale to thrive once again. Meanwhile the production of more traditional works derived from the genre still goes strong and also remains capable of incorporating Voltaire's literary creation.

MORE THAN JUST ADVENTURE STORIES

The eleven writers examined in this study are definitely products of their time. Though the medium in which they wrote is associated with the importation of American mass-marketed popular culture during a period when much of American business, science and technology, and culture were also being introduced into France, they still manage to maintain a distinctly French voice. And they do so, consciously or not, through the infusion into their stories of the uniquely French philosophical tale.

As a result, the Charles de Gaulle quotation used to open this study can now be appreciated more fully in light of this study. De Gaulle's concerns about France's attempts to reclaim greatness in the post–World War II world without his nation ceasing to be itself truly becomes a central theme for French society during the Fifties. No matter which alternative of criticism these writers chose, all of them, with their expressed anxieties over the idea of progress — especially in light of the impact of scientific and technological developments — can be seen as manifestations of this basic concern. The fact that the French Anticipation writers during the Fifties have been identified as Voltaire's stepchildren in this study serves only to reinforce this point. Using an identifiable literary tradition from France's illustrious past to express the anxieties of the present tells the reader that the problems facing France can — and must — be discussed in a manner that is distinctly French.

This study has revealed the diversity of responses to this central concern. Four distinct groups of criticism — the moderates (Richard Bessière, M.A. Rayjean, and Kemmel), the extremist (Jimmy Guieu), the conservatives (Stefan Wul, Maurice Limat, Peter Randa, and Kurt Steiner), and the radicals (Jean-Gaston Vandel and B.R. Bruss) — demonstrate the pitfalls of viewing their Anticipation novels in simplistic, one-dimensional terms. Finally, one writer (Gérard Klein) attempts to make a Fleuve Noir in order to identify the essence of this imprint. The literary form of these novels may be predictable and only slightly variable, but the content of their ideas and solutions are most assuredly not.

What Next?

What remains to be studied is to measure the reception, dissemination, and actual influence (if any) the eleven writers had on their readers. Did certain writers sell better in certain areas of France than others? If so, do these areas possess shared identifiable political and social characteristics? Can correlations be made between a specific area and a favored writer's views? Finding concrete conclusions along this line of investigation would provide valuable insight into how ideas, opinions, and their influence are disseminated through popular culture.

From these findings, perhaps further studies can be made reflecting more contemporary concerns. New approaches to popular literature focusing on feminist, post-colonial, linguistic, ethnic, economic, or social critiques can be further enriched now that the ideological foundations and influence of these writers have been identified.

In terms of the more traditional approaches to the study of popular culture, of which the author considers this study to be a part, it is hoped that this detailed study of a segment of French popular literature will enable both professional scholars and readers interested in the field of intellectual history to find more precise expression of method in analyzing French science fiction in particular and popular culture in general. Despite the superficial similarity of style shared by American pulp fiction and the French Anticipation novels from the Fifties, this study has shown that a diversity of concerns and opinions exists in this hybrid form of American genre science fiction and the philosophical tale.

The task facing the scholar (whether part of the newer or traditional schools of analysis), therefore, is to consider cultural artifacts on a case by base basis. The overwhelmingly prolific nature of popular culture provides no excuse for substituting untested sweeping generalizations, no matter how reasoned, for comprehensive scholarship. Much more work needs to be done.

For the often contentious field (reader vs. academic, academic vs. academic) of science fiction studies in particular, more needs to be done in the field of comparative studies. The English-language sphere of science fiction has experienced a few decades of serious scholarly attention, as has the French tradition. But few, if any, cross-cultural studies have been made. Considering these two languages produced science fiction's largest and most significant traditions, this gap in scholarship must be filled. Of course, beyond these two traditions lies the present explosion of science fiction around the world. Perhaps a solid body of work analyzing the relationship between the English and French-language traditions can serve as a springboard towards attaining a truly global perspective on science fiction.

Before any of the above suggestions can be implemented, there still remains much to be done by way of scholarly introduction. At the very least it is hoped that here lies the primary value of this modest study of an important segment of French science fiction.

Chapter Notes

Epigraphs

1. Robert A. Heinlein, "The Discovery of the Future," Guest of Honor Speech, Third World Science Fiction Convention, Denver, 1941, *Requiem: New Collected Works by Robert A. Heinlein and Tributes to the Grand Master*, Yoji Kondo, ed. (New York: Tor, 1992), 210–1.
2. Hans Küng, *Eternal Life?* (New York: Doubleday, 1984), 205.

Introduction

1. *New York Times*, 6 February 1962, 6, quoted in Robert Gilpin, *France in the Age of the Scientific State* (Princeton: Princeton University Press, 1968), 3.
2. See Richard Barron, *Parties and Politics in Modern France* (Washington, D.C.: Public Affairs Press, 1959), Stanley Hoffman, et al., *France: Change and Tradition* (Cambridge, MA: Harvard University Press, 1963), H. Stuart Hughes, *The Obstructed Path* (New York: Harper and Row, 1969), Herbert Luethy, *France Against Herself*, Eric Mosbacher, trans. (New York: Frederick A. Praeger, 1955), and James F. McMillan, *Dreyfus to the De Gaulle: Politics and Society in France 1898–1969* (London: Edward Arnold, 1985) for a general background on France during this period.
3. Jules Verne, *Paris au XXe siècle* (Paris: Hachette, 1994).
4. See also William Butcher, *Jules Verne: The Definitive Biography* (New York: Thunder's Mouth Press, 2006), 137–8.
5. Ibid., 305. Here Butcher gives the opening lines of Verne's *Journey to the Center of the Earth* with the original French, his translation into English, and a commonly printed English translation — which is way off the mark.
6. Ibid., especially ix–xxvi.
7. For the purposes of this study, see Peter Nicholls, "Pulp Magazines," *The Encyclopedia of Science Fiction*, John Clute and Peter Nicholls, eds. (New York: St. Martin's Press, 1979, 2d ed. 1993), 978–80, for general background on pulp magazines and the science fiction field.
8. See Donald R. Kelley, *The Descent of Ideas: The History of Intellectual History* (Aldershot, UK, and Burlington, VT: Ashgate, 2002) for a brief introduction to this approach to history.
9. Stefan Wul, *Le Temple du passé*, Anticipation, No. 106, 1957, as *The Temple of the Past*, Ellen Cox, trans. (New York: Seabury Press, 1973). Information about translation from Maxim Jabukowski and John Clute, "Wul, Stefan" *The Encyclopedia of Science Fiction*, John Clute and Peter Nicholls, eds. (New York: St. Martin's Press, 1979, 2d ed. 1993), 1352. The original French text will be used in this study.

Chapter One

1. H. Stuart Hughes, *The Obstructed Path* (New York: Harper and Row, 1969), 161–70.
2. David Thomson, *Democracy in France since 1870*, 5th ed. (London: Oxford University Press, 1969), 252.
3. See J.B. Bury, *The Idea of Progress* (New York: Macmillan, 1932; New York: Dover, 1955), Frank E. Manuel, *The New World of Henri Saint-Simon* (Cambridge, MA: Harvard University Press, 1956) and *The Prophets of Paris* (Cambridge, MA: Harvard University Press, 1962), Frank E. Manuel and Fritzie P. Manuel, *Utopian Thought in the Western World* (Cambridge, MA: Belknap Press of Harvard University Press, 1979), R.V. Sampson, *Progress in the Age of Reason* (Cambridge, MA: Harvard University Press, 1956), and W. Warren Wagar, *Good Tidings: The Belief in Progress from Darwin to Marcuse* (Bloomington: Indiana University Press, 1972).

The idea of progress itself can briefly be defined as a notion, emerging from the social thought inspired by the Scientific Revolution of the seventeenth century and the Enlightenment of the eighteenth century, of historical development that demonstrates a general improvement, by any vehicle and towards any goal considered as good, from a discernible past to a generally predictable future. This idea affirms humanity's confidence in an optimistic destiny. (See especially Sampson, *Progress*, 226–52, and Wagar, *Tidings*, 3–11.)

Notes — Chapter One

4. See references listed in footnotes 1 and 2, Introduction, along with Pierre Bouchet, *Economic Planning and the French Experience*, Daphne Woodward, trans. (New York: Frederick A. Praeger, 1964), Guy de Carmoy, *The Foreign Policies of France*, Elaine P. Halperin, trans. (Chicago: The University of Chicago Press, 1967), Michel Crozier, *The Bureaucratic Phenomenon* (Chicago: The University of Chicago Press, 1964), Henry Ehrmann, *Organized Business in France* (Princeton: Princeton University Press, 1957), Edward Fursdon, *The European Defence Community* (New York: St. Martin's Press, 1979), Richard F. Hamilton, *Affluence and the French Worker in the Fourth Republic* (Princeton: Princeton University Press, 1967), Edward Tannenbaum, *The New France* (Chicago: The University of Chicago Press, 1961), Jean-Claude Thoenig, *L'Ère des Technocrates* (Paris: Editions d'Organisation, 1973), and Gordon Wright, *Rural Revolution in France* (Stanford: Stanford University Press, 1964) for further background.

5. David Coward, *A History of French Literature, from Chanson de Geste to Cinema* (Oxford: Blackwell, 2002), and Sir Paul Harvey and J.E. Heseltine, eds., *The Oxford Companion to French Literature* (Oxford: Oxford at the Clarendon Press, 1959, 1969 ed.).

6. Germaine Brée, *Twentieth-Century French Literature* (Chicago: The University of Chicago Press, 1983), 71–5, 109–11.

7. Natalie Zemon Davis, "The Historian and Popular Culture," in *Popular Culture in France*, Jacques Beauroy, Marc Bertrand, and Edward T. Gargan, eds., Stanford French and Italian Studies, vol. 3 (Saratoga: Anma Libri, 1977), 1–28.

8. C.W.E. Bigsby, "Europe, America and the Cultural Debate," in *Superculture: American Popular Culture and Europe*, C.W.E. Bigsby, ed. (London: Elek, 1975), 1–28.

9. Ibid., 4.

10. Ibid., 13–4.

11. Sam Moskowitz, "How Science Fiction Got Its Name," *Explorers of the Infinite: Shapers of Science Fiction* (Cleveland: World, 1963), 313–33.

12. Algis Budrys, interview with author (1980).

13. For other attempts at defining science fiction, see Brian Aldiss, *Trillion Year Spree* (New York: Atheneum, 1986), 25–52, James Gunn, *Alternative Worlds* (Englewood Cliffs, NJ: Prentice Hall, 1975), 13–38, Sam J. Lundwall, *Science Fiction: What It's All About* (New York: Ace, 1971), 13–26, Brian Stableford, "Science Fiction Before the Genre," *The Cambridge Companion to Science Fiction*, Edward James and Farah Mendlesohn, eds. (Cambridge, UK: Cambridge University Press, 2003, sixth printing 2009), 15, and Brian Stableford, John Clute, and Peter Nicholls, "Definition of SF," *The Encyclopedia of Science Fiction*, John Clute and Peter Nicholls, eds. (New York: St. Martin's Press, 1979, 2d ed. 1993), 311–314.

14. An earlier version of this definition appeared in the author's dissertation, *The Anxiety of Progress: The French Anticipation Novels of the 1950s* (University of Chicago dissertation, 1988), 13.

15. For example, see Wu Dingbo and Patrick D. Murphy, eds., introduction by Frederik Pohl, *Science Fiction from China* (New York: Praeger, 1989), xi.

16. See Paul K. Alkon, *Origins of Futuristic Fiction* (Athens: University of Georgia Press, 1987), Marc Angenot, "Science Fiction in France before Verne," J.M. Gouanvic and D. Suvin, trans., *Science Fiction Studies*, #14, Volume 5, Part 1, March 1978 (Montreal: D. Cariou), Henri Delmas and Alain Julian, *Le Rayon SF: Catalogue bibliographique de science-fiction, utopies, voyages extraordinaires* (Toulouse: Editions Milan, 1983), Arthur B. Evans, "Science Fiction in France: A Brief History," *Science Fiction Studies*, #49, Volume 16, Part 3, November 1989 (Montreal: D. Cariou), 254–76, Robert Louit and Jacques Chambon, "France," *The Encyclopedia of Science Fiction*, John Clute and Peter Nicholls, eds. (New York: St. Martin's Press, 1979, 2d ed. 1993), 444–7, Jacques Sadoul, *Histoire de la science-fiction moderne* (Paris: Albin Michel, 1973), Jacques van Herp, *Panorama de la science-fiction* (Verviers: Marabout University, 1975), and Pierre Versins, "France," *Encyclopédie de l'utopie des voyages extraordinaires et de la science fiction* (Lausanne: L'Age d'Homme, 1972, 2d ed. 1984), 344–9.

17. Jean-Marc Lofficier and Randy Lofficier, *French Science Fiction, Fantasy, Horror and Pulp Fiction* (Jefferson, NC: McFarland, 2000). This is perhaps the best one-volume introduction to the vast field of French science fiction and fantasy, covering all media from the Middle Ages to the present.

18. Lofficier and Lofficier, *French Science Fiction*, 305–11, 333–5, and Versins, *Encyclopedie*, 229–31, 60–6, 74–6, 18–21, 00–1.

19. Butcher, *Verne*, 208–9, David Ketterer, "Poe, Edgar Allan" *The Encyclopedia of Science Fiction*, John Clute and Peter Nicholls, eds. (New York: St. Martin's Press, 1979, 2d ed. 1993), 939–40, and Pierre Versins, "Poe (Edgar Allan)," *Encyclopédie de l'utopie des voyages extraordinaires et de la science fiction* (Lausanne: L'Age d'Homme, 1972, 2d ed. 1984), 676–8. See the bibliography at end of Ketterer's article for further reference.

20. Lofficier and Lofficier, *French Science Fiction*, 337–5, Louit and Chambon, "France," 445, and Versins, *Encyclopedie*, 126–7, 73, 60–2, 06–8, 16–8, 21–2, 29–31.

21. Lofficier and Lofficier, *French Science Fic-*

Notes—Chapter One

tion, 361–80, Versins, *Encyclopedie*, 99, 85–6, 10–1, 01–2, 87–8, 26–9.

22. Peter Nicholls, "Mainstream Writers of SF," *The Encyclopedia of Science Fiction*, John Clute and Peter Nicholls, eds. (New York: St. Martin's Press, 1979, 2d ed. 1993), 768–70.

23. Hugo Gernsback, *Ralph 124C 41+: A Romance of the Year 2260, Modern Electronics*, April 1911–March 1912. Later book edition *Ralph 124C 41+* (New York: Fawcett Crest, 1958).

24. Hugo Gernsback, "A New Sort of Magazine," *Amazing Stories*, April 1926 (New York: Experimenter, 1926), 3.

25. . See Gary Westfahl, *Hugo Gernsback and the Century of Science Fiction, Critical Explorations in Science Fiction and Fantasy*, 16, Donald E. Palumbo and C.W. Sullivan III, series eds. (Jefferson, NC: McFarland, 2007).

26. A more detailed survey of this period will be presented in the conclusion of the study where both French and American science fiction after 1960 will be discussed briefly.

27. For further historical background on science fiction, see Aldiss, *Trillion Year Spree*, Kingsley Amis, *New Maps of Hell* (New York: Ballantine, 1960), James O. Bailey, *Pilgrims through Space and Time* (New York: Argus, 1947, facsimile of 1947 edition with foreword by Thomas D. Clareson [Westport, CT: Greenwood Press, 1972, paperback edition]), Paul A. Carter, *The Creation of Tomorrow* (New York: Columbia University Press, 1977), John Clute and Peter Nicholls, eds., *The Encyclopedia of Science Fiction* (New York: St. Martin's Press, 1979, 2d ed. 1993), H. Bruce Franklin, *Future Perfect: American Science Fiction of the 19th Century* (New York and London: Oxford University Press, 1966, expanded and revised edition, New Brunswick, NJ: Rutgers University Press, 1995), Jean Gattegno, *La Sciencefiction* (Paris: Presses Universitaires de France, 1971), Gunn, *Alternate Worlds*, Lundwall, *Science Fiction*, Sam Moskowitz, *Explorers of the Infinite* (Cleveland: World, 1963) and *Seekers of Tomorrow* (Cleveland: World, 1966), Sadoul, *Histoire*, Robert Scholes and Eric S. Rabkin, *Science Fiction: History-Science-Vision* (Oxford: Oxford University Press, 1977), van Herp, *Panorama*, and Pierre Versins, *Encyclopedie de l'utopie des voyages extraordinaires et de la science fiction* (Lausanne: L'Age d'Homme, 1972, 2d ed. 1984).

28. Gérard Cordesse, "The Impact of American Science Fiction on Europe," *Superculture: American Popular Culture and Europe*, C.W.E. Bigsby, ed. (London: Elek, 1975), 161.

29. This convention was actually attended mostly by those from the American East Coast, primarily from the New York City area. By 2010, the world conventions—though mostly held in the United States—have also been held in Europe, Australia, and Asia. National, regional and local conventions remain numerous.

30. Examples would be: the Arthur C. Clarke Award for best novel published in the United Kingdom (not necessarily by a British writer), the James Tiptree, Jr., Award for best work exploring gender relationships, the John W. Campbell Memorial Award for best American novel, the Philip K. Dick Award for best original paperback published in America, the Locus Awards for works selected from Locus magazine's readers' polls, the Theodore Sturgeon Award for best short story, and the Chesley Awards for honoring works of art. All these awards are annual ones. This is by no means an exhaustive list.

31. For further background on science fiction in general, see references listed in footnote *27* of this chapter.

32. Cordesse, "American," 173.

33. Brée, *French Literature*, 110.

34. For the number of volumes for each line, http://www.coolfrenchcomics.com/brantonne.htm and http://litteraturepopulaire.winnerbb.net/toute-la-litterature-d-aventures-et-d-action-moderne-apres-1950-f15/collection-western-fleuve-noir-t208.htm.

35. http://www.fleuvenoir.fr/

36. Lofficier and Lofficier, *French Science Fiction*, 415–6.

37. Sadoul, *Histoire*, 341–65, and Versins, *Encyclopedie*, 321–3.

38. Brée, *French Literature*, 348. Brée provides a biographical dictionary in which both of these writers are listed. However she does not acknowledge that either of these two writers wrote science fiction, even though she mentions works by them that certainly fall in the science fiction category (e.g., Vercor's *Les Animaux denatures* [1952] and Vian's *L'Ecume des jours* [1947]).

39. Alain Douilly, *Anticipation: 50 ans de collections fantastiques et de science-fiction au Fleuve Noir* (Encino: Black Coat Press, 2009) is an invaluable one-volume compendium of the Anticipation and related imprints from Fleuve Noir.

40. Ibid., 26–45.

41. These particular writers will be referred to by their most well-known name in this study, and not necessarily by their pseudonym. .

42. Cyrano de Bergerac, *Other Worlds: The Comical History of the States and Empires of the Moon and Sun*, Geoffrey Strachan, trans. and intro. (Oxford: Oxford University Press, 1965, London: New English Library, 1976, paperback edition). See Brian Stableford, "Cyrano de Bergerac," *The Encyclopedia of Science Fiction*, John Clute and Peter Nicholls, eds. (New York: St. Martin's Press, 1979, 2d ed. 1993), 291 for brief bibliographic history.

43. Aram Vartanian, "On Cultivating One's Garden," *A New History of French Literature*, Denis Hollier, ed. (Cambridge, MA: Harvard University Press, 1989), 469. Parenthetical word replaced "yields" by the author.

44. See Coward, *History of French Literature*, 100–6, 131–97, John Leigh, *The Search for Enlightenment: An Introduction to Eighteenth Century French Writing* (Lanham, MD: Rowman & Littlefield, 1999), 45–6, Robert Mauzi, Sylvain Menant, and Michel Delon, *Précis de litterature française du XVIIIe siècle* (Paris: Presses Universitaires de France, 1990), 101–3, and Marcel Schneider, *Histoire de la litterature fantastique en France* (Paris: Librairie Arthème Fayard, 1985), and Vartanian, "Cultivating One's Garden," 468–71.
45. Voltaire, *Candide ou l'optimisme*, Christopher Thacker, ed. (Geneva: Librairie Droz, 1968), 234 (author's translation).
46. Voltaire, *Micromégas* (Paris: Livre de Poche, 2000).
47. See Ira O. Wade, *Voltaire's Micromegas* (Princeton: Princeton University Press, 1950) for further background.
48. Louit and Chambon, "France," 444–5.
49. Stableford, "Before the Genre," 18, 25.
50. Frederick M. Keener, *The Chain of Becoming, The Philosophical Tale, The Novel, and a Neglected Realism of the Enlightenment: Swift, Montesquieu, Voltaire, Johnson, and Austen* (New York: Columbia University Press, 1983).
51. Ibid., 3–4.
52. Ian Watts, *The Rise of the Novel: Studies in Defoe, Richardson, and Fielding* (Berkeley and Los Angeles: University of California Press, 1957, 1959 reprint), 9–34, cited in Keener, *Chain of Becoming*, 13.
53. Keener, *Chain of Becoming*, 13.
54. Peter Brooks, *The Novel of Worldliness: Crebillon, Marivaux, Laclos, Stendhal* (Princeton: Princeton University Press, 1969).
55. Keener, *Chain of Becoming*, 14.

Chapter Two

1. Sadoul, *Histoire*, 343.
2. Lofficier and Lofficier, *French Science Fiction*, 420.
3. Douilly, *Anticipation*, 256, Lofficier and Lofficier, *French Science Fiction*, 420, and Sadoul, *Histoire*, 343.
4. http://richard-bessiere.blogspot.com. 6 March 2007 entry (author's translation).
5. Ibid. (author's translation).
6. Ibid.
7. For all *Anticipation* novels covered in this study, the number listed before the year of publication is the novel's number in *Anticipation*'s imprint and subsequently will be identified by the imprint number only. Since none of the *Anticipation* novels (except for one) are translated into English, a translation of their titles is provided.
8. Douilly, *Anticipation*, 256–61 and Lofficier and Lofficier, *French Science Fiction*, 420–1.
9. http://richard-bessiere.blogspot.com and http://www.pochesf.com/index.php?page=auteur&auteur=2310&PHPSESSID=ea6f2d9eeea5aff58162aef.
10. http://richard-bessiere.blogspot.com. Novels listed in order presented by Bessière.
11. Antoine de Saint-Exupéry, *The Little Prince*, Richard Howard, trans. (San Diego: Harcourt, 2000).
12. Douilly, *Anticipation*, 257, and Jacques Garin, http://gotomars.free.fr/priollet.html.
13. Jules Verne, *Off on a Comet*, French title, *Hector Servadac* (Charleston, SC: Bibliobazaar), 2008.
14. Jules Verne, *From the Earth to the Moon*. French title, *De la terre à la lune* (New York: Bantam Classics, 1993).
15. Jules Verne, *Around the Moon*, French title, *Autour de la Lune* (New York: E.P. Dutton, 1970).
16. H.G. Wells, *The War of the Worlds* (London: Heineman, 1898).
17. All quotations from Bessière's and all other *Anticipation* writers' novels will not be footnoted, but will be indicated by parenthetical references after each quotation with a page number and any other explanations if needed. As noted in the Introduction all translations into English are the author's. However, all quotations from other sources will be footnoted in the regular way. For those which have English translations, the English versions of the sources are used. All translated versions are checked with the original language version if possible.
18. Claude-Henri de Rouvroy, Comte de Saint-Simon, *Œuvres de Claude-Henri de Saint-Simon* (Paris: Éditions Anthropos, 1966), vol. 5, *De l'organisation sociale*, 107–72.
19. Claude-Henri de Rouvroy, Comet de Saint-Simon, *Œuvres de Claude-Henri de Saint-Simon* (Paris: Éditions Anthropos, 1966), vol. 2, *De l'réorganisation de la société européene*, 179.
20. Gilpin, *Scientific State*, 177.
21. Blaise Pascal, *Pensées*, William Findlayson Trotter, trans., T.S. Eliot, intro. (London: J.M. Dent & Sons, 1932, 1956 printing, Everyman's Library, #874), 78.
22. Ibid., 1–13.
23. Ibid., 2.
24. Édouard Schuré, *The Great Initiates: A Study of the Secret History of Religions* (Hudson: Steinerbooks, 1999 edition, second printing).
25. Olav Hammer, *Claiming Knowledge: Strategies of Epistemology from Theosophy to the New Age* (Leiden: Brill, 2004).
26. Rudolf Steiner, *Autobiography: Chapters in the Course of My Life: 1861–1907*, Rita Stebbing, trans., Paul M. Allen, ed. (Hudson: Anthroposophic Press, 1999), esp. 406.
27. http://www.steinerinstitute.org/
28. Paul M. Allen, "Introduction to the 1961

Edition, Edouard Schuré and *The Great Initiates*," Schuré, *Great Initiates*, 21–8.

29. Henri Bergson, *Creative Evolution*, Arthur Mitchell, trans. (New York: Henry Holt, 1911), 248.

30. Ibid., 87.

31. Ibid., 270–1.

32. Ibid., 298–9.

33. Brian Stableford, "Alternate Worlds," *The Encyclopedia of Science Fiction*, John Clute and Peter Nicholls, eds. (New York: St. Martin's Press, 1979, 2d ed. 1993), 23–5.

34. Mark Twain, *A Connecticut Yankee in King Arthur's Court*, Shelley Fisher Fishkin, foreword; Kurt Vonnegut, Jr., introduction; Louis J. Budd, afterword (New York and Oxford: Oxford University Press, 1996).

35. L. Sprague de Camp, *Lest Darkness Fall* (New York: Pyramid, 1963).

36. H.G. Wells, *Island of Doctor Moreau*, Peter Stroub, foreword (New York: Modern Library, 1996).

37. Richard L. Merritt and Donald J. Puchala, *Western European Perspectives on International Affairs*, Praeger Studies in International Politics and Public Affairs (New York: Frederick A. Praeger, 1968), 283.

38. Jean Monnet, *Memoirs*, Richard Maynem, trans. (Garden City, NY: Doubleday, 1978).

39. Ibid., 338.

40. Ibid., 290.

41. Ibid., 230.

42. Ibid., 228.

43. See William Diebold, *The Schuman Plan: A Study in Economic Cooperation 1950–9* (New York: Praeger, 1959), and John Gillingham, *Coal, Steel, and the Rebirth of Europe, 1945–1955: The German and French from Ruhr Conflict to Economic Community* (Cambridge, UK: Cambridge University Press, 1991) for general background.

44. Versins, *Encyclopédie*, 724.

45. Lofficier and Lofficier, *French Science Fiction*, 420.

46. Douilly, *Anticipation*, 369 (author's translation).

47. Ibid., 370–1.

48. Douilly, *Anticipation*, 369, and Lofficier and Lofficier, *French Science Fiction*, 420.

49. Jack Finney, *The Body Snatchers* (New York: Dell, 1955). A later, more available edition has been retitled *Invasion of the Body Snatchers* (New York: Touchstone, Simon & Schuster, 1998). Two more film versions were made, *Invasion of the Body Snatchers* (1978) and *The Invasion* (2007).

50. Peter Nicholls, "Paranoia," *The Encyclopedia of Science Fiction*, John Clute and Peter Nicholls, eds. (New York: St. Martin's Press, 1979, 2d ed. 1993), 910.

51. During the discussion there is mention of a plan to bomb the South Pole with nuclear armaments due to the perception that the South Pole was too heavy in comparison to the North Pole — which some felt would cause an eventual shift of Earth's axis, which in turn would cause a world-wide cataclysm. Rayjean has definite views about the use of atomic energy, which will be covered in the next section of this analysis.

52. Alfred Bester, "Adam and No Eve," *Astounding Science Fiction*, September 1941, 35–45.

53. Brian Stableford, "Adam and Eve," *The Encyclopedia of Science Fiction*, John Clute and Peter Nicholls, eds. (New York: St. Martin's Press, 1979, 2d ed. 1993), 4–5.

54. "Probe 7 — Over and Out" (television episode), *Twilight Zone*, produced by Cayuga Productions and MGM, written by Rod Serling, 1963.

55. I.B. Maslowski, "Ici, on desintegre!" *Fiction*, March 1959, 135–6.

56. See Brian Stableford, "Nuclear Power," *The Encyclopedia of Science Fiction*, John Clute and Peter Nicholls, eds. (New York: St. Martin's Press, 1979, 2d ed. 1993), 881–2.

57. Nigel Lucas, *Western European Energy Policies* (Oxford: Clarendon Press, 1985), 1–63, and "The Association for Applied Solar Energy," *Procedures of the World Symposium on Applied Solar Energy* (Menlo Park: Stanford Research Institute, 1956).

58. Lawrence Scheinman, *Atomic Energy Policy in France under the Fourth Republic* (Princeton: Princeton University Press, 1965), 120–5.

59. Scheinman, *Atomic Energy Policy*, 182–91.

60. Merritt and Puchala. *Perspectives*, 374.

61. Douilly, *Anticipation*, 320, Lofficier and Lofficier, *French Science Fiction*, 426, 10, and www.bibliopoche.com/auteur/BommartJean/3076.html.

62. Douilly, *Anticipation*, 320 (author's translation).

63. Wells, *War of the Worlds*.

Chapter Three

1. One example is http://video.google.com/videoplay?docid=-2143185021045350448.

2. Douilly, *Anticipation*, 300 (author's translation), Lofficier and Lofficier, *French Science Fiction*, 422, http://fr.wikipedia.org/wiki/Jimmy_Guieu, and http://en.wikipedia.org/wiki/Henri-René_Guieu. Note: the English Wikipedia entry is not a merely a translation from the French one; they are really different articles in substance as well as in language.

3. Douilly, *Anticipation*, 179–88 (author's translation).

4. Lofficier and Lofficier, *French Science Fiction*, 422.

5. Ibid. *The X Files* (1994–2003), for those unfamiliar with recent television programming, is a popular American television series featuring often used themes of science fiction and fantasy, including UFOs, psychic powers, paranormal aberrations, etc. The show focuses on an ongoing relationship between humans and aliens. FBI agent Fox Mulder attempts to prove the existence of aliens on Earth and other unexplained phenomena with the help of his assigned partner, agent Dana Scully, a trained medical doctor. She doubts him at the beginning but eventually supports Mulder and his quests. Much of the attraction of the show centers on the changing relationship between the two. Two feature films were spun off from the series, *The X Files* (1998) and *The X Files: I Want to Believe* (2008).

6. Ibid., 300 (author's translation).

7. Versins, "GUIEU (Jimmy)," *Encyclopédie*, 396 (author's translation).

8. Douilly, *Anticipation*, 300 (author's translation).

9. Ibid., 300–8.

10. Ernst Cassirer, *The Philosophy of the Enlightenment*, Fritz C.A. Koelln and James P. Pettegrove, trans. (Princeton: Princeton University Press, 1951), 161.

11. See especially Benedict de Spinoza, *Ethics*, in *Philosophy of Benedict Spinoza*, R.H.M. Elves, trans. and ed., Frank Sewall, introduction (New York: Tudor, 1933), Propositions XIV, XV, AND XVIII, on pages 49 and 57.

12. Carl Gustav Jung, *Flying Saucers: a Modern Myth of Things seen in the Skies* (New York: Harcourt & Brace, 1959). This edition will be used in this study.

13. Ibid., 27.

14. Ibid., 28.

15. Ibid., 29–30.

16. The *Grand Prix du Roman de Science Fiction* ("Grand Prize for Science Fiction Novel") was actually established by Fleuve Noir for one of its *Anticipation* novels in a given year. The publisher did this practice for four years (1954–7). The award itself should not be taken seriously as novels from other publishers were not considered For the record the awardees are: *L' Homme de l'espace* by Jimmy Guieu (1954), *Bureau de l'invisble* by Jean-Gaston Vandel (1955), *Retour à "O"* by Stefan Wul (1956), and *Les Parias de l'atome* by M.A. Rayjean (1957). *See* Douilly, *Anticipation*, 12.

17. See David Pringle, Brian Stableford, and Peter Nicholls, "Lost Worlds," *The Encyclopedia of Science Fiction*, John Clute and Peter Nicholls, eds. (New York: St. Martin's Press, 1979, 2d ed. 1993), 734–6.

18. See Peter Nicholls and Brian Stableford, "Politics," *Encyclopedia of Science Fiction*, John Clute and Peter Nicholls, eds. (New York: St. Martin's Press, 1979, 2d ed. 1993), 947, and Pierre Versins, "Xénophobie," *Encyclopédie*, 967–72.

19. Lofficier and Lofficier, *French Science Fiction*, 422.

20. Peter Roberts and John Grant, "Fort, Charles (Hoy)," *The Encyclopedia of Science Fiction*, John Clute and Peter Nicholls, eds. (New York: St. Martin's Press, 1979, 2d ed. 1993), 439–40.

21. Charles Fort, *The Book of the Damned* (New York: Boni & Liveright, 1920), *Lo!*, Tiffany Thayer, introduction (New York: C. Kendall, 1931), *New Lands*, Tiffany Thayer, introduction (New York: C. Kendall, 1941), and *Wild Talent* (New York: C. Kendall, 1932).

22. Eric Frank Russell, *Guerre aux invisibles*, Collection Rayon Fantastique, No. 10 (Paris: Hachette & Gallimard, 1952).

23. Eric Frank Russell, *Le Sanctuaire terrifiant*, Collection Club du Livre d'Anticipation, No. 69 (Paris: Opta, 1978), printed with Russell's *The Great Explosion* (1962) as *La Grande Explosion*.

24. Katharine Luomala, *The Menehume of Polynesia and other Mythical Little People of Oceana*, Bernice F. Bishop Museum Bulletin, No. 203 (Honolulu: Bernice F. Bishop Museum, 1951), 9–50.

25. Lawrence Gustave Desmond and Phyllis Rauch Messenger, *A Dream of Maya: Augustus and Alice Le Plongeon in Nineteenth Century Yucatan* (Albuquerque: University of New Mexico Press, 1988).

26. James Churchward, *The Lost Continent of Mu* (London: Neville Spearman, 1959), and L. Sprague de Camp, *Lost Continents, The Atlantis Theme in History, Science, and Literature* (New York: Ballantine Books, 1970), 46–52.

27. Alfred Métraux, *Easter Island: a Stoneage civilization of the Pacific*, Michael Bullock, trans. (New York: Oxford University Press, 1957), 130–9.

28. de Camp, *Lost Continents*, 46–52.

29. Pascal Thomas, interview with author (1983).

30. Harold R. Willoughby, *Pagan Regeneration: A Study of Mystery Initiations in the Graeco Roman World* (Chicago: The University of Chicago Press, 1929) 36–67.

31. J.D. Bernal, *The World, the Flesh, and the Devil: An Inquiry in the Future of the Three Enemies of the Rational Soul* (1929, reprint edition, London: Jonathan Cape, 1970).

32. Ibid., 73.

Chapter Four

1. Lofficier and Lofficier, *French Science Fiction*, 418.

2. Maxim Jabukowski and John Clute, "Wul, Stefan," *The Encyclopedia of Science Fic-

tion, John Clute and Peter Nicholls, eds. (New York: St. Martin's Press, 1979, 2d ed. 1993), 1352.

3. Versins, "WUL (Stefan)," *Encyclopédie*, 964 (author's translation).

4. Douilly, *Anticipation*, 404 (author's translation).

5. Gerard Klein, "Ici, on desintegre!" *Fiction*, January 1960, 137–8.

6. Douilly, *Anticipation*, 404 (author's translation).

7. Douilly, *Anticipation*, 404, Jabukowski and Clute, "Wul, Stefan" 1352, Lofficier and Lofficier, *French Science Fiction*, 89, 23, 18, Versins, "WUL (Stefan)," *Encyclopédie*, 964, http://en.wikipedia.org/wiki/Ren%C3%A9_Laloux, and http://fr.wikipedia.org/wiki/Stefan_Wul.

8. See Chapter One, footnote 3.

9. Stefan Wul, *Oeuvres completes, tome 1*, Claude Lefrancq, ed., Laurent Genefort, preface (Paris: Collection LeFrancq, 1998) and *Oeuvres completes, tome 2*, Ananké Lefrancq, ed., Laurent Genefort, preface (Paris: Collection LeFrancq, 1997).

10. Laurent Genefort, "Stefan Wul, artificier de l'imaginaire," *Oeuvres completes, tome 1*, Claude Lefrancq, ed., Laurent Genefort, preface (Paris: Collection LeFrancq, 1998), and "Stefan Wul, du vent dans les voiles et de la boue aux semelles," *Oeuvres completes, tome 2*, Ananké Lefrancq, ed., Laurent Genefort, preface (Paris: Collection LeFrancq, 1997). These two prefaces were reproduced on the website http:///www.schismatrice.net/article.php3?id_article=26, which is dedicated to science fiction with emphasis on cyberpunk science fiction and is inspired in part by American science fiction writer Bruce Sterling (1954–), and his novel *Schismatrix* (1985).

11. Genefort, "Stefan Wul, artificier" (author's translations).

12. Ibid. Genefort cites his source as F. Truchaud, "Rencontre avec Stefan Wul," *Galaxie*, No. 80, 1971, 141 ("Meeting with Stefan Wul").

13. Genefort, "Stefan Wul, artificier."

14. Ibid. (author's translation).

15. Ibid. (author's translation; the French use SF to stand for science fiction just as English-language readers do. Unless identified as otherwise, assume this usage).

16. Genefort, "Stefan Wul, du vent" (author's translation).

17. Ibid. (author's translation).

18. Ibid. (author's translation).

19. Ibid., cited from Jean-Pierre Andrevon (under pseudonym of Denis Philippe), "Stefan Wul ou la grandeur de l'evidence," *Fiction*, No. 229, January 1973, 130 ("Stefan Wul or the Grandeur of the Obvious," author's translation).

20. Ibid. (author's translation).

21. Ibid. Genefort cites Truchaud, "Rencontre," 142 (author's translation).

22. Ibid. cited from Gérard Klein, "Préface,"

Stefan Wul, *Oeuvres* (Paris: Laffont, 1970), 12 (author's translation).

23. Ibid.

24. Ibid. (author's translation).

25. *Flash Gordon* (film), Universal, 1936.

26. *Star Wars* (film), 20th Century–Fox, 1977.

27. For example, see David G. Hartwell & Kathryn Cramer, "How Shit Became Shinola: Definition and Redefinition of Space Opera," *SFRevu*, August 2003, Earnest Lilley, sr. ed., viewed on http://www.sfrevu.com/ISSUES/2003/0308/Space%20Opera%20Redefined/Review.htm, Brian Stableford, "Space Opera," *The Encyclopedia of Science Fiction*, John Clute and Peter Nicholls, eds. (New York: St. Martin's Press, 1979, 2d ed. 1993), 1138–40, Pierre Versins, "Space Opera," *Encyclopédie de l'utopie des voyages extraordinaires et de la science fiction* (Lausanne: L'Age d'Homme, 1972, 2d ed. 1984), 824, and Gary Westfahl, "Space Opera," *The Cambridge Companion to Science Fiction*, Edward James and Farah Mendlesohn, eds. (Cambridge, UK: Cambridge University Press, 2003, sixth printing 2009), 197–208. Also, Brian W. Aldiss edited an anthology in which he discusses his views on the matter, *Space Opera* (London: Weidenfeld and Nicolson, 1974).

28. Edmond Hamilton, *Crashing Suns*, *Weird Tales*, August-September 1928 (New York: Ace, 1965).

29. John W. Campbell, *The Mightiest Machine*, *Astounding Science Fiction*, December 1934-April 1935 (New York: Ace, 1965).

30. Karel Čapek, *War with the Newts*, M. and R. Weatherall, trans. (New York: Berkley Books, 1967).

31. See John Clute, "Čapek, Karel," *The Encyclopedia of Science Fiction*, John Clute and Peter Nicholls, eds. (New York: St. Martin's Press, 1979, 2d ed. 1993), 190, Gwyneth Jones, "The Icons of Science Fiction," *The Cambridge Companion to Science Fiction*, Edward James and Farah Mendlesohn, eds. (Cambridge, UK: Cambridge University Press, 2003, sixth printing 2009), 166–7, and Versins, " APEK (Karel)," *Encyclopédie de l'utopie des voyages extraordinaires et de la science fiction* (Lausanne: L'Age d'Homme, 1972, 2d ed. 1984), 148.

32. Genefort, "Stefan Wul, artificier."

33. *Time Masters* (film), original title, *Les Maîtres du temps*, produced by TPI (Paris), SSR (Geneva), SWF (Baden-Baden), and WDR (Köln), 1981, English version 1982.

34. Peter Nicholls, "Cyberpunk," *The Encyclopedia of Science Fiction*, John Clute and Peter Nicholls, eds. (New York: St. Martin's Press, 1979, 2d ed. 1993), 288–90.

35. *Total Recall* (film), TriStar, 1990.

36. Genefort, "Stefan Wul, du vent."

37. See Howard Hendrix, *The Ecstasy of Catastrophe: A Study of the Apocalyptic Tradition*

from Langland to Milton (Ph.D. dissertation, University of California Riverside, 1987), the concluding chapter deals with apocalyptic elements in twentieth-century science fiction, and David Ketterer, *New Worlds for Old* (Garden City, NY: Anchor Books, 1974).

38. Clute and Nicholls, *Encyclopedia*, 48. Individually, Peter Nicholls, "Holocaust and After," 581–4; David Pringle, "Disaster," 338; and Brian Stableford, "End of the World," 382–4, "Eschatology," 388–9, and "Religion," 1000–3.

39. Genefort, "Stefan Wul, artificier."

40. John Wyndham, *The Midwich Cuckoos* (London: Penguin, 1960, paperback edition).

41. Laurent Genefort, private correspondence with author, 8 September 2009.

42. *Village of the Damned* (film), MGM, 1960. This film is closer to Wyndham's novel than the remake.

43. *Children of the Damned* (film), MGM, 1963.

44. *The Blob* (film), Paramount, 1958.

45. *Caltiki, the Immortal Monster* (film), translated from original Italian film, *Caltiki — il mostro immortale*, 1959, Climax Pictures and Galatea, 1960.

46. Genefort, "Stefan Wul, artificier" (author's translation).

47. Ibid. The proper citation for the novel's republication is Stefan Wul, *Niourk*, Presence du Futur, No. 128 (Paris: Éditions Denoël, 1970).

48. Ibid. (author's translation).

49. *Fantastic Planet* (film), original title, *La Planète sauvage*, produced by Les Films Armorial, ORTF, Filmové studio Barrandov, 1973.

50. The author is indebted to Laurent Genefort for this suggestion.

51. Anthony Hartley, *Gaullism: The Rise and Fall of a Political Movement* (New York: Outerbridge & Dienstfrey, 1971), 17–21.

52. Hartley, *Gaullism*, 5–33.

53. L. Ron Hubbard, *Final Blackout*, Astounding Science Fiction, April, May, and June 1940 (New York: Street and Smith, 1940).

54. See John Clute and Peter Nicholls, "Hubbard, L. Ron" *The Encyclopedia of Science Fiction*, John Clute and Peter Nicholls, eds. (New York: St. Martin's Press, 1979, 2d ed. 1993), 592–3

55. Charles de Gaulle, *Discours et messages*, Vol. IV (Paris: Plon, 1970), 319, quoted in Hartley, *Gaullism: The Rise and Fall of a Political Movement* (New York: Outerbridge & Dienstfrey, 1971), 7 (author's translation).

56. Charles de Gaulle, *Vers l'armée de métier* (Paris: Presses Pocket, 1963), 184, quoted in Hartley, *Gaullism: The Rise and Fall of a Political Movement* (New York: Outerbridge & Dienstfrey, 1971), 8 (author's translation).

57. Hartley, *Gaullism*, 5–13.

58. Laurent Genefort, private correspondence with author, 8 September 2009.

59. Hartley, *Gaullism*, 7–8, and Thomson, *Democracy*, 301–3.

60. Hartley, *Gaullism*, 15–6.

61. Laurent Genefort, private correspondence with author, 8 September 2009.

62. Merritt and Puchala, *European Perspectives*, 471.

63. Hartley, *Gaullism*, 28–31.

64. Versins, *Encyclopedie*, 535 (author's translation).

65. Douilly, *Anticipation*, 334 (author's translation).

66. Douilly, *Anticipation*, 333–4, Lofficier and Lofficier, *French Science Fiction*, 377, 90, 23–4, and Versins, *Encyclopédie*, 535–6.

67. Douilly, *Anticipation*, 334–9.

68. Lofficier and Lofficier, 424.

69. Versins, *Encyclopédie*, 536 (author's translation).

70. Lofficier and Lofficier, 424.

71. Ibid., 631.

72. Voltaire, *Candide*, 102 (author's translation).

73. Isaac Asimov, *I, Robot* (New York: Signet Books, 1956). Obviously, the same goes for the recent film *I, Robot* (2004), released by 20th Century–Fox, directed by Alex Proyas and starring Will Smith, which was very loosely based on Asimov's book. All three could be viewed as independent works.

74. Barron, *Parties and Politics*, Russell B. Capelle, *The MRP and French Foreign Policy* (New York: Frederick A. Praeger, 1963), Mario Einaldi and François Goguel, *Christian Democracy in Italy and France* (Notre Dame: University of Notre Dame Press, 1952), Michael P. Fogarty, *Christianity Democracy in Western Europe 1820–1953* (Notre Dame: University of Notre Dame Press, 1957), and R.E.M. Irving, *Christian Democracy in France* (London: George Allen and Unwin, 1973).

75. Barron, *Parties and Politics*, 133–4.

76. Einaldi and Goguel, *Italy and France*, 129.

77. CFTC (Confédération Française Travailleurs Chrétiens) Workers Action Programme (1945), 5, quoted in Irving, *Christian Democracy in France*, 59.

78. CTFC, *Statuts*, I, 1, quoted in Fogarty, *Christian Democracy in Western Europe*, 19.

79. Irving, *Christian Democracy*, 125–6.

80. Einaldi and Goguel, *Italy and France*, 125.

81. Irving, *Christian Democracy*, 55.

82. Étienne Borne, et al., *Le MRP, Cet Inconnu* (Paris: Éditions Polyglottes, 1961), 32, quoted in Irving, *Christian Democracy*, 55.

83. Douilly, *Anticipation*, 364.

84. Ibid., 364–8 (general background) and Versins, *Encyclopédie*, 722 (for quotation) (author's translation).

85. Lofficier and Lofficier, *French Science Fiction*, 424

86. Ibid.
87. Douilly, *Anticipation*, 366 (author's translation).
88. Ibid.
89. Robert A. Heinlein, *Between Planets* (New York: Charles Scribner's Sons, 1951); French translation: *D'une planète à l'autre*, Succès Anticipation, No. 5 (Paris: Mame, 1958).
90. Ibid., 216.
91. *The Puppet Masters* (New York: Signet Books, 1951). French translation: *Marionnettes humaines*, Le Rayon Fantastique, No. 25 (Paris: Hachette & Gallimard, 1954).
92. Robert A. Heinlein, *Starship Troopers* (New York: Putnam, 1959).
93. *Starship Troopers* (film), Tristar/Touchstone, 1997.
94. Two examples are George E. Slusser's *Robert A. Heinlein: Stranger in His Own Land* (San Bernardino: Borgo Press, 1976), Volume 1 in The Milford Series, *Popular Writers of Today* and H. Bruce Franklin's *Robert A. Heinlein: America as Science Fiction* (New York: Oxford University Press, 1980).
95. See George Wescott Carey, ed., *Freedom and Virtue: The Conservative/Libertarian Debate* (Wilmington, DE: Intercollegiate Studies Institute, 1998) and Peter Vallentyne and Hillel Steiner, eds,, *Left-Libertarianism and Its Critics: The Contemporary Debate* (New York: Palgrave, 2000) as examples.
96. Robert A. Heinlein, *Methuselah's Children* (magazine version 1941—*Astounding Science Fiction*, July-September 1941, New York: Street and Smith, 1941; book version 1958 — Hicksville: Gnome Press, 1958). It is not known whether or not Randa was proficient in English as no French translations of the novel existed by 1960.
97. Herbert Spencer, *Principles of Biology*, Volume 1 (Bibliolife, November 2008), 445.
98. See Jan Breman, ed., *ImperialMonkey Business, Racial Supremacy in Social Darwinist Theory and Colonial Practice* (Amsterdam: VU University Press, 1990), Linda L. Clark, *Social Darwinism in France* (Tuscaloosa: University of Alabama Press, 1984), Carl N. Degler, *In Search of Human Nature The Decline and Revival of Darwinism in American Social Thought* (Oxford and New York: Oxford University Press, 1991), and Mike Hawkins, *Social Darwinism in European and American thought, 1860–1945: Nature as Model and Nature as Threat* (Cambridge and New York: Cambridge University Press, 1997).
99. Amid the wealth of available references on this topic, a good brief introduction to the concept and history of individualism is Steve Lukes, *Individualism* (Colchester, UK: ECPR Press, 2006). See especially 21–29 for a French historical perspective.
100. Douilly, *Anticipation*, 389–9, Lofficier and Lofficier, *French Science* Fiction, 388 (general background), and Versins, *Encyclopédie*, 835 (for quotation) (author's translation).
101. Httpa://imdb.com/name/nm0749183/
102. Versins, *Encyclopédie*, 835 (author's translation).
103. Arthur C. Clarke, *Childhood's End* (New York: Harcourt, Brace & World, 1953). First French translation: *Les Enfants d'Icare*, Collection Le Rayon Fantastique, No. 42 (Paris: Hachette & Gallimard, 1956).
104. See George E. Slusser, *The Space Odysseys of Arthur C. Clarke*, Popular Writers of Today, No. 8 (San Bernardino: Borgo Press, 1978), especially 49–56, for analysis of Clarke's presentation of humanity's end.
105. Arthur C. Clarke, *2001: A Space Odyssey* (New York: Signet Books, 1968) and *2001: A Space Odyssey* (film), Metro-Golden-Mayer, 1968. Clarke's novel and film are based in part on his short story "The Sentinel" (1951), originally "The Sentinel of Eternity." The story has been reprinted many times in many venues, including Clarke's *Lost Worlds of 2001* (1972). See following footnote.
106. See Arthur C. Clarke, *Lost Worlds of 2001* (New York: Signet Books, 1972). Both book and film were produced at the same time. Clarke not only discusses not just the issues involved with the making of the film, but also includes chapters containing earlier versions of the novel.
107. André Ruellan, interview with author (1991). The author held the interview at an informal group lunch that included Ruellan, Gérard Klein, American science fiction writers Gregory Benford and David Brin, and two other French fans during the summer of 1991 in Paris.

Chapter Five

1. "Radical," Definition 3.a., *The Compact Oxford English Dictionary* (Oxford: Oxford University Press, 1971, 2d ed. 1991, 1999 reprint), 1499.
2. Douilly spells his surname as Vandenpanhuizen, Douilly, *Anticipation*, 396.
3. Douilly, *Anticipation*, 396–7, Lofficier and Lofficier, *French Science* Fiction, 26, 0, 21, 33, and Versins, *Encyclopédie*, 923 (general background), and Douilly, *Anticipation*, 396 (for quotation) (author's translation).
4. For the sake of convenience, the two writers will be referred to as a singular person.
5. Versins, *Encyclopédie*, 923 (author's translation).
6. Lofficier and Lofficier, *French Science Fiction*, 421.
7. Aldous Huxley, *Brave New World* (New York: Harper Perennial, 1998).
8. George Orwell, *Nineteen Eighty-four* (Harmondsworth, UK: Penguin, 1954).

Notes — Chapter Five

9. H.G. Wells, *The Time Machine*, M. Geldud, ed. and intro. (Bloomington: Indiana University Press, 1987).
10. H.G. Wells, *When the Sleeper Wakes*, Orson Scott Card, intro. (New York: Modern Library, 2003).
11. See Mark R Hillegas, *The Future as Nightmare: H.G. Wells and the Anti-Utopians* (Carbondale: Southern Illinois Press, 1974), and Jack Williamson, *H.G. Wells: Critic of Progress* (Baltimore: Mirage Press, 1973).
12. H.G. Wells, *Anticipations* (New York and London: Harper & Brothers, 1902).
13. H.G. Wells, *A Modern Utopia*, Mark. R. Hillegas, intro. (Lincoln: University of Nebraska Press, 1967).
14. H.G. Wells, *World Set Free* (New York: Macmillan, 1914).
15. See W. Warren Wagar, *H.G. Wells and the World Sate* (New Haven, CT: Yale University Press, 1961).
16. *Things to Come* (film), London Films, 1936. In 1979, the film, *The Shapes of Things to Come*, was released. The later film, outside of the credit that it is based on Wells's book of the same name, has nothing to do with the either the original film or Wells's book.
17. H.G. Wells, *The Shape of Things to* Come (1933, New York: Macmillan, 1945).
18. Raymond Massey, *A Hundred Different Lives: An Autobiography* (Boston: Little, Brown, 1979), 122, quoted in Leon Stover, *The Prophetic Soul: A Reading of H.G. Wells's Things to Come* (Jefferson, NC: McFarland, 1987), xvii.
19. H.G. Wells, *Things to Come: The Release Script of the London Films Production*, 1936, quoted in Stover, *The Prophetic Soul*, 223.
20. Ibid., 227.
21. Ibid., 225.
22. Ibid., 261.
23. Stover, *Prophetic Soul*, 63.
24. Wells, *Release Script*, 260.
25. Stover, *Prophetic Soul*, 63–4.
26. Stover supplies a still from the film illustrating this point in his study. See Stover, *Prophetic Soul*, eighteenth page between 120–1. Also, a more realistic — and more cynical — interpretation is that numbers of extras were needed for the film and that women could play some of the United Airmen as long as the camera shots were from far away.
27. *Oxford English Dictionary*, "cabal," Definitions 3–6, 196.
28. Stover, *Prophetic Soul*, 33.
29. Wells, *Release Script*, 225.
30. Ibid., 242.
31. Jules Verne, *Robur the Conqueror*, French title, *Robur-le-conquérant*, included in *Master of the World* (New York: Ace, 1961).
32. Jules Verne, *Master of the World* (New York: Ace, 1961).
33. Jules Verne, *Twenty Thousand Leagues under the Sea*, French title, *Vingt mille lieues sous les mers* (London: Puffin Books, 1986, reissued 1994). See also *Twenty Thousand Leagues under the Seas*, William Butcher, trans., ed., ann. (Oxford: Oxford University Press, 1992; revised with new material, 1998). The correct translation of the title of this novel is "Twenty Thousand Leagues under the Seas" (the last word is plural).
34. Jules Verne, *Mysterious Island*, French title, *L'Île mystérieuse*, Sidney Kravitz, trans., Arthur B. Evans, ed., William Butcher, intro., appendices, notes, other material (Middletown, CT: Wesleyan University Press, 2001).
35. Butcher, *Verne*, 185–95.
36. Verne, *Under the Seas*.
37. Butcher, *Verne*, 230–3.
38. *20,000 Leagues under the Sea* (film), Walt Disney, 1954, based on the novel, *Twenty Thousand Leagues under the Seas*, by Jules Verne.
39. *Master of the World* (film), American International Pictures, 1961, based on the novels, *Robur the Conqueror* and *Master of the World*, by Jules Verne.
40. Albert Camus, *Discours de Suede*, translated by Justin O'Brien as *Speech of Acceptance upon the Award of the Nobel Prize*, quoted in Hughes, *Obstructed Path*, 247.
41. Roland N. Stromberg, *European Intellectual History since 1789*, 2d ed, (Englewood Cliffs, NJ: Prentice-Hall, 1975), 290.
42. Karel Čapek, *R.U.R. (Rossum's Universal Robots)* (New York: Penguin Group/Penguin Classics, 2004).
43. Brian Stableford, "Androids," *The Encyclopedia of Science Fiction*, John Clute and Peter Nicholls, eds. (New York: St. Martin's Press, 1979, 2d ed. 1993), 34–5, and "Robots," *The Encyclopedia of Science Fiction*, John Clute and Peter Nicholls, eds. (New York: St. Martin's Press, 1979, 2d ed. 1993), 1018–20.
44. Jack Williamson, *The Humanoids* (New York: Lancer Books, 1963 paperback edition).
45. Jack Williamson, *Les Humanoïdes* (Paris: Éditions Stock, Série Science-Fiction, 1950).
46. *Creation of the Humanoids* (film), Genie Production, 1962.
47. http://www.imdb.com/title/tt0055872/releaseinfo.
48. Wells, *War of the Worlds*.
49. Of course, the novel was written twenty-three years after Clyde Tombaugh's discovery of Pluto in 1930, but fifty-three years before Pluto's reclassification in 2006 from planet to dwarf planet. So some of the intended dramatic impact of the discovery of a tenth planet in the solar system may be lost to a young reader or to one reading the novel for the first time now.
50. See also Stefan Wul, *La mort vivante* ("The Living Death"), Anticipation, No. 113, 1958, which is discussed in Chapter Four.

Notes—Chapter Five

51. Gilpin, *Scientific State*, 104–9.
52. John Ardagh, *France in the 1980s* (Harmondsworth, UK: Penguin, 1982), 83.
53. Ibid.
54. Alvin Toffler, *Future Shock* (New York: Bantam, 1970).
55. Leonard Krieger, *An Essay on the Theory of Enlightened Despotism* (Chicago: The University of Chicago Press, 1975). The author wrote an article using Krieger's piece dealing with power relationships in light of C.P. Snow's "Two Cultures" observation in 1959, about how the scientists and humanities no longer belong in the same world. The themes of what constitutes a proper education and how should power be exercised in light possessing the proper knowledge are treated. See Bradford Lyau, "Science Fiction: Mediating Agent between C.P. Snow's Two Cultures, A Historical Interpretation," *Science Fiction and the Two Cultures*, Gary Westfahl and George Slusser, eds., *Critical Explorations in Science Fiction and Fantasy, 16*, Donald E. Palumbo and C.W. Sullivan III, series eds. (Jefferson, NC: McFarland, 2009), 22–36.
56. Ibid., 91.
57. Jean Jacques Rousseau, *Discours sur l'origine et les fondements de l'inégalité parmi les hommes*, in *Ouevres complètes*, Volume 3, Bernard Gagnebin and Marcel Raymond, eds. (Paris: Éditions Gallimard, 1964), 142 (author's translation).
58. Ibid., 133 (author's translation).
59. Ibid., 202 (author's translation).
60. Jean Jacques Rousseau, *Du contrat social ou principes du droit politique*, in *Ouevres complètes*, Volume 3, Bernard Gagnebin and Marcel Raymond, eds. (Paris: Éditions Gallimard, 1964), 360 (author's translation).
61. Ibid., 361 (author's translation, emphasis in original text).
62. Ibid., 364 (author's translation).
63. Jean Jacques Rousseau, *Discours sur les sciences et les arts*, in *Ouevres complètes*, Volume 3, Bernard Gagnebin and Marcel Raymond, eds. (Paris: Éditions Gallimard, 1964), 9 (author's translation).
64. Ibid., 22.
65. H.G. Wells, *Men Like Gods* (New York: Macmillan, 1923).
66. Bradford Lyau, "Technocratic Anxiety in France: The Fleuve Noir 'Anticipation' Novels, 1951–60," *Science Fiction Studies*, Volume 16, Part 3, November 1989 (Montreal: SFS Publications, 1989), 290. As the article's title indicates, this is the author's earlier attempt in analyzing this theme in the *Anticipation* novels of the Fifties. The author is indebted to editor Robert M. Philmus for his suggestions in the editing of this article for publication.
67. Douilly *Anticipation*, 263.
68. Megan Koreman, *The Expectation of Justice: France, 1944–1946* (Durham: Duke University Press, 1999), 97. For an introduction to the history of Vichy France, see Robert O. Paxton *Vichy France: Old Guard and New Order 1940–1944* (New York: Columbia University Press, 2001).
69. Charles Moreau, *Fantastik Blog*, http://fantastik2001.blogspot.com/2009/03/au-cur-de-la-sf-francaise-un-secretaire.html (author's translation).
70. Ibid. The author would like to thank Jean-Marc Lofficier for his help in this matter.
71. Sadoul, *Histoire*, 337–9.
72. Douilly, *Anticipation*, 263 (author's translation).
73. Lofficier and Lofficier, *French Science Fiction*, 376.
74. Ibid., 385.
75. Ibid., 389.
76. Ibid., 419–20.
77. Jean-Marc Lofficier, "Obituaries," *Locus*, January 1981, 30.
78. Versins, *Encyclopédie*, 133. Douilly in *Anticipation* identifies all translators and further identifies Anderson as "one of the rare Anglo-Saxons in the collection who found a place of profusion in the heart of French writers" (236) (author's translation).
79. Ibid., 134 (author's translation).
80. Jean-Marc Gouanvic, *La Science fiction française au XXe siècle (1900–1968)* (Amsterdam: Éditions Rodopi B.V., 1994), 217.
81. Later publication of the book includes, Isaac Asimov, *Pebble in the Sky* (New York: Tor, 2008). The author is indebted to Gerald Nordley, an American science fiction writer writing as G. David Nordley, for the Asimov reference.
82. *Logan's Run* (film), MGM/United Artists, 1976.
83. William F. Nolan and George Clayton Johnson, *Logan's Run* (New York: Dial Press, 1967). Later publication of the book includes, William F. Nolan and George Clayton Johnson, *Logan's Run* (New York: Bantam, 1976).
84. Merritt and Puchala, *European Perspectives*, 245.
85. Ibid., 243.
86. See Emmanuel Levinas, *Totality and Infinity: An Essay on Exteriority*, Alphonso Lingus, trans. (The Hague: Martinus Nijhoff Publishers, 1969, 3d ed. 1991), and *Alterity and Transcendence*, translated by Michael B. Smith (New York: Columbia University Press, 1999, third printing); and Simon Critchley and Robert Bernasconi, eds., *The Cambridge Companion to Levinas* (Cambridge: Cambridge University Press, 2002).
87. Mark Poster, *Existential Marxism in Postwar France* (Princeton: Princeton University Press, 1975), 3–35.
88. Simone de Beauvoir, *Le Deuxième Sexe* (Paris: Librairie Gallimard, 1949), 1:17.
89. Ibid., 1:16 (author's translation).

90. Ibid., 2:560–77.

91. For those unfamiliar with the concept, dialectical thinking in this context refers to a way of viewing how opposites resolve their differences. To begin with, a concept — or thesis — is defined not only by its essence and original meaning, but also by its opposite. Or, for example, Concept A and Anti-Concept A. The two then interact to form a synthesis, Concept B, which in turn becomes the new thesis. This process continues: Concept B vs. Anti-Concept B à Concept C; Concept C vs. Anti-Concept C à Concept D; etc. This is obviously a simplified presentation. Please see Peter Singer, *Hegel: A Very Short Introduction* (Oxford, UK and New York: Oxford University Press, 2001) and Charles Taylor, *Hegel* (Cambridge, UK, and New York: Cambridge University Press, 1975). For those interested in the intellectual development from Hegel to the Existentialists of post–World War II France, see Robert C. Solomon, *From Hegel to Existentialism* (Oxford, UK, and New York: Oxford University Press, 1987).

92. Jolyon Howorth and Philip G. Cerny, eds., *Elites in France: Origins, Reproduction, and Power* (London: Frances Pinter, 1981), especially the articles: Jean-François Sirinelli, "The École Normale Supérieure and elite formation and selection during the Third Republic," 55–77, Michalina Vaughan, "The grandes écoles: selection, legitimization, perpetuation," (93–103), and Anne Stevens, "The contribution of the École Nationale d'Administration in French political life," (134–53).

Chapter Six

1. Lofficier and Lofficier, *French Science Fiction*, 416.

2. Douilly, *Anticipation*, 238 (author's translation).

3. Maxim Jakubowski, "Klein, G Gérard," *The Encyclopedia of Science Fiction*, John Clute and Peter Nicholls, eds. (New York: Saint Martin's Press, 1993), 671.

4. George Slusser, "The Beginnings of Fiction," *Science-Fiction Studies*, Vol. 16, Part 3, #49, November 1989 (Montreal: SFS Publications), 307–37.

5. Lofficier and Lofficier, *French Science Fiction*, 432.

6. Douilly, *Anticipation*, 238–9, Jakubowski, "Klein," 671, Lofficier and Lofficier, *French Science Fiction*, 416–7, 32–3, Versins, *Encyclopédie*, 496.

7. Gérard Klein, interview with author (1991). The author held the interview at an informal group lunch that included Klein, André Ruellan, American science fiction writers Gregory Benford and David Brin, and two other French fans during the summer of 1991 in Paris. See also Footnote 86, Chapter Four.

8. Lyau, "Technocratic Anxiety in France," 292–4.

9. See Chapter Four, footnote 86.

10. Malcolm J. Edwards and Brian Stableford, "Terraforming," *The Encyclopedia of Science Fiction*, John Clute and Peter Nicholls, eds. (New York: Saint Martin's Press, 1993), 1213–4.

11. Gilpin, *France in the Age of the Scientific State*, 78–85. However, during the Fourth Republic, France attempts to reform this arrangement.

12. Demètre Ioakimidis, "Ici, on desintegre!" *Fiction*, December 1960, 133–4.

13. Douilly, *Anticipation*, 239, Lofficier and Lofficier, *French Science Fiction*, 416, and Jean-Jacques Girardot, http://sf.emse.fr/AUTHORS/GKLEIN/gksa.html.

Chapter Seven

1. Hughes, *Obstructed Path*, 261.

2. In addition to footnotes 1 and 2, Background, and footnote 4, Chapter 1, see John Ardagh, *The New France*, 2d ed. (London: Penguin, 1973), and Anthony Sampson, *The New Europeans* (London: Hodder and Stoughton, 1968) for further background.

3. Thompson, *Democracy in France*, 291.

4. Roland N. Stromberg, *After Everything: Western Intellectual History since 1945* (New York: St. Martin's Press, 1975), 31–86.

5. For an overview of the year, see Mark Kurlansky, *1968: The Year That Rocked the World* (New York: Ballantine, 2004), esp. 209–237 for the events in France.

6. Evans, "A Brief History," 262.

7. Ibid., 262–5, Lofficier and Lofficier, *French Science Fiction*, 432, 48.

8. Lofficier and Lofficier, *French Science Fiction*, 455.

9. Keener, *Chain*, 4.

10. Peter Nicholls, "Cyberpunk," *The Encyclopedia of Science Fiction*, John Clute and Peter Nicholls, eds. (New York: St. Martin's Press, 1979, 2d ed. 1993), 288–90, George Slusser and Tom Shippey, editors, *Fiction 2000: cyberpunk and the future of narrative* (Athens: University of Georgia Press, 1992).

11. Peter Nicholls, "Steampunk," *The Encyclopedia of Science Fiction*, John Clute and Peter Nicholls, eds. (New York: St. Martin's Press, 1979, 2d ed. 1993), 1161

Bibliography

The Anticipation Novels

Since the novels cited here are produced by the same publisher and released under the same collection, a complete citation is given for the first novel only. The writers are presented in order of the first novel published.

Richard-Bessière, F. (Henri-Richard Bessière, Richard Bessière). *Les Conquérants de l'univers* ("The Conquerors of the Universe"). Collection Anticipation, No. 1. Paris: Fleuve Noir, 1951.

_____. *A l'assaut du ciel* ("To Assault the Sky"). No. 2. 1951.

_____. *Retour du "Météore"* ("Return of the 'Meteor'"). No.3. 1951.

_____. *Planète vagabonde* ("Wandering Planet"). No. 4. 1951.

_____. *Croisière dans le temps* ("Cruise in Time"). No. 6. 1952.

_____. *Sauvetage sidéral* ("Sidereal Rescue"). No. 37. 1954.

_____. *"S.O.S. Terre"* ("'S.O.S. Earth'"). No. 55. 1955.

_____. *Vingt Pas dans l'inconnu* ("Twenty Steps into the Unknown"). No. 60. 1955.

_____. *Feu dans le ciel* ("Fire in the Sky"). No. 64. 1956.

_____. *Objectif soleil* ("Target: Sun"). No. 69. 1956.

_____. *Altitude moins X* ("Altitude Minus X"). No. 75. 1956.

_____. *Route de néant* ("Road to the Void"). No. 81. 1956.

_____. *Cité de l'esprit* ("City of the Mind"). No. 85. 1957.

_____. *Création cosmique* ("Cosmic Creation"). No. 89. 1957.

_____. *Planète de mort* ("Planet of Death"). No. 93. 1957.

_____. *Le Deuxième Terre* ("The Second Earth"). No. 97. 1957.

_____. *Via dimension "5"* ("Via Dimension '5'"). No. 101. 1957.

_____. *Fléau de l'univers* ("Scourge of the Universe"). No. 105. 1957.

_____. *Carrefour du temps* ("Crossroad of Time"). No. 111. 1958.

_____. *Relais Minos III* ("Relay Station Minos III"). No. 117. 1958.

_____. *Bang!* ("Bang!"). No. 121. 1958.

_____. *Zone spatiale interdite* ("Forbidden Space Zone"). No. 126. 1958.

_____. *Panique dans le vide* ("Panic in the Void"). No. 129. 1959.

_____. *Le Troisième Astronef* ("The Third Spaceship"). No. 135. 1959.

_____. *Ceux de demain* ("Those from Tomorrow"). No. 139. 1959.

_____. *Réaction déluge* ("Reaction Flood"). No. 144. 1959.

_____. *On a hurlé dans le ciel* ("They Screamed in the Sky"). No. 148. 1959.

_____. *Terre degree "0"* ("Earth Degree '0'"). No. 153. 1960.

_____. *Générations perdues* ("Lost Generations"). No. 157. 1960.

_____. *Les Pantins d'outre-ciel* ("Puppets from Beyond the Sky"). No. 162. 1960.

_____. *Escale chez les vivants* ("Stopover among the Living"). No. 166. 1960.

_____. *Les Lunes de Jupiter* ("The Moons of Jupiter"). No. 169. 1960.

Guieu, Jimmy. *Le Pionnier de l'atome* ("The Pioneer of the Atom"). No. 5. 1951.

_____. *Au-delà de l'infini* ("Beyond Infinity"). No. 8. 1952.

(Richard-Bessière, *continued*)
_____. *L'Invasion de la Terre* ("The Invasion of Earth"). No. 13. 1952.
_____. *Hantise sur le monde* ("Obsession over the World"). No. 18. 1953.
_____. *L'Univers vivant* ("The Living Universe"). No. 22. 1953.
_____. *La Dimension X* ("Dimension X"). No. 27. 1953.
_____. *Nous les Martiens* ("We the Martians"). No. 31. 1954.
_____. *La Spirale du temps* ("The Spiral of Time"). No. 36. 1954.
_____. *Le Monde oublié* ("The Forgotten World"). No. 41. 1954.
_____. *L'Homme de l'espace* ("The Man of Space"). No. 45. 1954.
_____. *Opération Aphrodite* ("Operation Aphrodite"). No. 47. 1955.
_____. *Commandos de l'espace* (Commandos of Space"). No. 51. 1955.
_____. *L'Agonie du verre* ("The Death Throes of Glass"). No. 54. 1955.
_____. *Univers parallèles* ("Parallel Universes"). No. 58. 1955.
_____. *Nos ancêstres de l'avenir* ("Our Ancestors of the Future"). No. 62. 1956.
_____. *Les Monstres du néant* ("The Monsters from the Void"). No. 70. 1956.
_____. *Prisonniers du passé* ("Prisoners of the Past"). No. 72. 1956.
_____. *Les Êtres de feu* ("The Beings of Fire"). No. 80. 1956.
_____. *La Mort de la vie* ("The Death of Life"). No. 87. 1957.
_____. *Le Règne des mutants* ("The Reign of Mutants"). No. 91. 1957.
_____. *Créatures des neiges* ("Creatures of the Snows"). No. 95. 1957.
_____. *Cité Noë N°2* ("Noah City No. 2"). No. 100. 1957.
_____. *Le Rayon du cube* ("The Cubic Ray"). No. 103. 1957.
_____. *Convulsions solaires* ("Solar Convulsions"). No. 110. 1958.
_____. *Réseau Dinosaure* ("Dinosaur Network"). No. 115. 1958.
_____. *La Force sans visage* ("The Faceless Force"). No. 118. 1958.
_____. *Expédition cosmique* ("Cosmic Expedition"). No. 134. 1959.
_____. *Les Cristaux de Capella* ("The Crystals of Capella"). No. 140. 1959.
_____. *Piège dans l'espace* ("Trap in Space"). No. 145. 1959.
_____. *Chasseurs d'hommes* ("Hunters of Men"). No. 149. 1960.
_____. *Les Sphères de Rapa-Nui* ("The Spheres of Rapa-Nui"). No. 156. 1960.
_____. *L'Ère des biocybs* ("The Era of the Biocybs"). No. 160. 1960.
_____. *Expérimental X-35* ("Experiment X-35"). No. 163. 1960.

Vandel, Jean-Gaston (Jean Libert and Gaston Vandenpanhuyse). *Chevaliers de l'espace* ("The Space Knights"). No. 7. 1952.
_____. *Le Satellite artificiel* ("The Artificial Satellite"). No. 10. 1952.
_____. *Les Astres morts* ("The Dead Stars"). No. 11. 1952.
_____. *Alerte aux robots* ("Alert — Robots"). No. 15. 1952.
_____. *Frontières du vide* ("Frontiers of the Void"). No. 17. 1953.
_____. *Le Soleil sous la mer* ("The Sun under the Sea"). No. 19. 1953.
_____. *Attentat cosmique* ("Cosmic Attack"). No. 21. 1953.
_____. *Incroyable futur* ("Incredible Future"). No. 24. 1953.
_____. *Agonie des civilisés* ("Death Throes of the Civilized"). No. 26. 1953.
_____. *Pirate de la science* ("Pirate of Science"). No. 29. 1953.
_____. *Fuite dans l'inconnu* ("Flight into the Unknown"). No. 34. 1954.
_____. *Naufragés des galaxies* ("Shipwrecks of the Galaxies"). No. 39. 1954.
_____. *Territoire robot* ("Robot Territory"). No. 43. 1954.
_____. *Les Titans de l'énergie* ("The Titans of Energy"). No. 48. 1955.
_____. *Raid sur Delta* ("Raid over Delta"). No. 52. 1955.
_____. *Départ pour l'avenir* ("Depart for the Future"). No. 56. 1956.
_____. *Bureau de l'invisible* ("Office of the Invisible"). No. 61. 1955.
_____. *Les Voix de l'univers* ("The voices of the Universe"). No. 67. 1956.
_____. *La Foudre anti-D* ("Anti-D Lightning"). No. 73. 1956.

_____. *Le Troisième Bocal* ("Third Bottle"). No. 77. 1956.
Bruss, B.R. (René Bonnefoy). *S.O.S. soucoupes* ("S.O.S. Saucers"). No. 33. 1954.
_____. *La Guerre des soucoupes* ("The War of the Saucers"). No. 40. 1954.
_____. *Rideau magnétique* ("Magnetic Curtain"). No. 65. 1956.
_____. *Substance "ARKA"* ("Substance 'ARKA'"). No. 82. 1956.
_____. *Le Grand Kirn* ("The Great Kirn"). No. 112. 1958.
_____. *Terre...siècle 24* ("Earth ... in the 24th Century"). No. 136. 1959.
_____. *An...2391* ("Year ... 2391"). No. 143. 1959.
_____. *Complot Vénus-Terre* ("Venus-Earth Conspiracy"). No. 225. 1963.
Rayjean, M(ax). A(ndré). (Jean Lombard). *Attaque sub-terrestre* ("Subterranean Attack"). No. 71. 1956.
_____. *Base spatiale 14* ("Space Base 14"). No. 86. 1957.
_____. *Les Parias de l'atome* ("The Pariahs of the Atom"). No. 104. 1957.
_____. *Chocs en synthèse* ("Synthetic Shocks"). No. 108. 1958.
_____. *La Folie verte* ("The Green Madness"). No. 114. 1958.
_____. *L'Anneau des invincibles* ("The Ring of the Invincibles"). No. 122. 1958.
_____. *Soleils: echelle zéro* ("Suns: Scale Zero"). No. 127. 1958.
_____. *Le Monde d'éternité* ("The World of Eternity"). No. 137. 1959.
_____. *Ère cinquième* ("Fifth Era"). No. 142. 1959.
_____. *Le Péril des hommes* ("The Peril of Men"). No. 151. 1960.
_____. *L'Ultra-univers* ("The Ultra Universe"). No. 161. 1960.
_____. *Invasion "H"* ("Invasion 'H'"). No. 167. 1960.
Wul, Stefan (Pierre Pairault). *Retour à "O"* ("Return to 'O'"). No. 78. 1956.
_____. *Niourk* ("Niourk"). No. 83. 1957.
_____. *Rayons pour Sidar* ("Rays for Sidar"). No. 90. 1957.
_____. *La Peur géante* ("The Giant Fear"). No. 96. 1957.
_____. *Oms en série* ("Oms in Series"). No. 102. 1957.
_____. *Temple du passé* ("Tempe of the Past"). No. 106. 1957.
_____. *L'Orphelin de Perdide* ("The Orphan of Perdide"). No. 109. 1958.
_____. *La Mort vivante* ("The Living Death"). No. 113. 1958.
_____. *Piège sur Zarkass* ("Trap on Zarkass"). No. 119. 1956.
_____. *Terminus 1* ("Terminus 1"). No. 130. 1959.
_____. *Odyssée sous contrôle* ("Odyssey under Control"). No. 136. 1959.
Kemmel (Jean Bommart). *Je reviens de...* ("I Return from..."). No. 84. 1957.
Steiner, Kurt (André Ruellan). *Menace d'outre–Terre* ("Menace from Beyond Earth"). No. 124. 1958.
_____. *Salamandra* ("Salamandra"). No. 131. 1959.
_____. *Le 32 juillet* ("July 32nd"). No. 146. 1959.
_____. *Aux armes d'Ortog* ("By Ortog's Arms"). No. 155. 1960.
_____. *Ortog et les ténèbres* ("Ortog and the Darkness"). No. 376. 1969.
Limat, Maurice. *Les Enfants du chaos* ("The Children of Chaos"). No. 142. 1959.
_____. *Le Sang du soleil* ("The Blood of the Sun"). No. 147. 1959.
_____. *J'écoute l'univers* ("I Listen to the Universe"). No. 154. 1960.
_____. *Métro pour l'inconnu* ("Metro for the Unknown"). No. 159. 1960.
_____. *Les Foudroyants* ("The Terrifying"). No. 164. 1960.
_____. *Moi, un robot* ("I Robot"). No. 170. 1960.
Randa, Peter (André Duquesne). *"Survie"* ("'Survival'"). No. 152. 1960.
_____. *"Baroud"* ("'Fight'"). No. 158. 1960.
_____. *Les Frelons d'or* ("The Golden Hornets"). No. 168. 1960.
Argyre, Gilles d' (Gérard Klein). *Chirurgiens d'une planète* ("Planet Surgeons"). No. 165. 1960.
_____. *Les Voiliers de soleil* ("The Sailors of the Sun"). No. 172. 1961.
_____. *Le Long Voyage* ("The Long Journey"). No. 243. 1964.

_____. *Le Scepter du hazard* ("The Scepter of Chance"). No. 357. 1968.

Other Primary Sources

Aldiss, Brian W., ed. *Space Opera*. London: Weidenfeld and Nicolson, 1974.

Asimov, Isaac. *I, Robot*. New York: Signet Books, 1951.

_____. *Pebble in the Sky*. New York: Tor, 2008.

Beauvoir, Simone de. *Le Deuxième Sexe*. Two vols. Paris: Librairie Gallimard, 1949.

Bergson, Henri. *Creative Evolution*. Arthur Mitchell, trans. New York: Henry Holt, 1911.

Bernal, J.D. *The World, The Flesh, and The Devil: An Inquiry in the Future of the Three Enemies of the Rational Soul*. London: Jonathan Cape, 1970.

Bessière, Richard. Website. *http://richard-bessiere.blogspot.com*. 6 March 2007 entry.

Bester, Alfred. *Adam and No Eve*. Astounding Science Fiction, September 1941, 35–45.

The Blob (film). Paramount. 1958.

Borne, Étienne, Maurice Byé, Alfred Coste-Floret, Pierre Dhers, Jean Raymond-Laurent, and Pierre-Henri Tiegen. *Le MRP, Cet Inconnu*. Paris: Éditions Polyglottes, 1961. Quoted in R.E.M. Irving. *Christian Democracy in France*. London: George Allen and Unwin,1973.

Caltiki, the Immortal Monster (film). Translated from original Italian film, *Caltiki — il mostro immortale*, 1959. Climax Pictures and Galatea. 1960.

Campbell, John W., Jr. *The Mightiest Machine*. Astounding Science Fiction, December 1934, January, February, March, and April 1935. New York: Ace, 1965.

Camus, Albert. *Discours de Suede*. Justin O'Brien, trans. Quoted in H. Stuart Hughes. *The Obstructed Path*. New York: Harper and Row, 1969.

Čapek, Karel. *R.U.R. (Rossum's Universal Robots)*. New York: Penguin Group/Penguin Classics, 2004.

_____. *War with the Newts*. M. and R. Weatherall, trans. New York: Berkley Books, 1967.

CFTC (Confédération Française Travailleurs Chrétiens). *Workers Action Programme*. 1945. Quoted in R.E.M. Irving. *Christian Democracy in France*. London: George Allen and Unwin, 1973.

_____. *Statuts, I*. Quoted in Michael P. Fogarty. *Christianity Democracy in Western Europe 1820–1953*. Notre Dame: University of Notre Dame Press, 1957.

Children of the Damned (film). MGM. 1963. Based on the novel *The Midwich Cuckoos*, by John Wyndham.

Clarke, Arthur C. *Childhood's End*. New York: Ballantine, 1953.

_____. *Lost Worlds of 2001*. New York: Signet Books, 1972.

_____. *2001: A Space Odyssey* (film). Metro Goldwyn Mayer. 1968.

Creation of the Humanoids (film). Genie Production. 1962.

Cyrano de Bergerac, Savinien. *Other Worlds: The Comical History of the States and Empires of the Moon and Sun*. Geoffrey Strachan, trans. London: New English Library, 1976.

De Camp, L. Sprague. *Lest Darkness Fall*. New York: Pyramid Books, 1963.

De Gaulle, Charles. *Discours et messages. Pour l'effort*, Vol. IV. Paris: Plon, 1970. Quoted in Anthony Hartley. *Gaullism: The Rise and Fall of a Political Movement*. New York: Outerbridge & Dienstfrey, 1971.

_____. *Vers l'armée de métier*. Paris: Presses Pocket, 1963. Quoted in Anthony Hartley. *Gaullism: The Rise and Fall of a Political Movement*. New York: Outerbridge & Dienstfrey, 1971.

Dingbo, Wu, and Patrick D. Murphy, eds. *Science Fiction from China*. New York: Praeger, 1989.

Fantastic Planet (film). Original title: *La Planète sauvage*. Les Films Armorial, ORTF, Filmové studio Barrandov. 1973. Based on the novel *Oms en série* by Stefan Wul.

Finney, Jack. *The Body Snatchers*. New York: Dell, 1955. Retitled edition: *Invasion of the Body Snatchers*. New York: Touchstone, Simon & Schuster, 1998.

Flash Gordon (film). Universal. 1936.

Fort, Charles. *The Book of the Damned*. New York: Boni & Liveright, 1920.

_____. *Lo!* New York: C. Kendall, 1931.

_____. *New Lands*. New York: C. Kendall, 1941.

_____. *Wild Talent*. New York: C. Kendall, 1932.

Gernsback, Hugo. "A New Sort of Magazine." *Amazing Stories*, April 1926. New York: Experimenter, 3.

_____. *Ralph 124C 41+*. New York: Fawcett Crest, 1958.

Hamilton, Edmond. *Crashing Suns. Weird Tales*. August and September 1928. New York: Ace, 1965.

Heinlein, Robert A. *Between Planets*. New York: Charles Scribner's Sons, 1951.

_____. "The Discovery of the Future." Guest of Honor Speech, Third World Science Fiction Convention, Denver, 1941. Published in *Requiem: New Collected Works by Robert A. Heinlein and Tributes to the Grand Master*. Yoji Kondo, ed. New York: Tor, 1992.

_____. *Methuselah's Children. Astounding Science Fiction*. July, August, and September 1941. Hicksville: Gnome Press, 1958.

_____. *The Puppet Masters. Galaxy Science Fiction*. September, October, November 1951. New York: Signet Books, 1951.

_____. *Starship Troopers*. New York: Putnam, 1959.

Hubbard, L. Ron. *Final Blackout. Astounding Science Fiction*. April, May, and June 1940. New York: Street and Smith, 1940.

Huxley, Aldous. *Brave New World*. New York: Harper Perennial, 1998.

I, Robot (film). Twentieth Century-Fox. 2004. Suggested by the novel *I, Robot* by Isaac Asimov.

Invasion of the Body Snatchers (film). Allied Artists. 1956. Based on the novel *The Body Snatchers* by Jack Finney.

Ioakimidis, Demètre. "Ici, on desintegre!" *Fiction*. December 1960. 133–4.

Jung, Carl Gustav. *Flying Saucers: A Modern Myth of Things Seen in the Skies*. New York: Harcourt & Brace, 1959.

Klein, Gérard. "Ici, on desintegre!" *Fiction*. January 1960. 137–8.

Levinas, Emmanuel. *Alterity and Transcendence*. Michael B. Smith, trans. New York: Columbia University Press, 1999.

_____. *Totality and Infinity: An Essay on Exteriority*. Alphonso Lingus, trans. The Hague: Martinus Nijhoff, 1991.

Logan's Run (film). MGM/United Artists. 1976. Based on the novel *Logan's Run* by William F. Nolan and George Clayton Johnson.

Maslowski, I.B. "*Ici, on desintegre!*" *Fiction*. March 1959. 135–6.

Massey, Raymond. *A Hundred Different Lives: An Autobiography*. Boston: Little, Brown, 1979. Quoted in Leon Stover. *The Prophetic Soul: A Reading of H.G. Wells's Things to Come*. Jefferson, NC: McFarland, 1987.

Master of the World (film). Produced by American International Pictures. 1961. Based on the novels *Robur the Conqueror* and *Master of the World* by Jules Verne.

Mercier, Louis-Sébastien. *L'An 2440, rêve s'il en fut jamais*. Raymond Trousson, intro. and notes. Bordeaux: Ducros, 1971.

Monnet, Jean. *Memoirs*. Richard Mayne, trans. Garden City, NY: Doubleday, 1978.

Nolan, William F., and George Clayton Johnson. *Logan's Run*. New York: Bantam Books, 1976.

Orwell, George. *Nineteen Eighty-four*. Harmondsworth, UK: Penguin, 1954.

Pascal, Blaise. *Pensées*. William Findlayson Trotter, trans. London: J.M. Dent & Sons, 1956.

"Probe 7 — Over and Out" (television episode). *Twilight Zone*. Written by Rod Serling. Cayuga Productions and MGM. 1963.

Rousseau, Jean Jacques. *Discours sur les sciences et les arts. Ouevres complètes*. Volume 3. Bernard Gagnebin and Marcel Raymond, eds. Paris: Éditions Gallimard, 1964.

_____. *Discours sur l'origine et les fondements de l'inégalité parmi les hommes. Ouevres complètes*. Volume 3. Bernard Gagnebin and Marcel Raymond, eds. Paris: Éditions Gallimard, 1964.

_____. *Du contrat social ou principes du droit politique. Ouevres completes*. Volume 3. Bernard Gagnebin and Marcel Raymond, eds. Paris: Éditions Gallimard, 1964.

Russell, Eric Frank. *Dreadful Sanctuary*. Reading: Fantasy Press, 1948.

_____. *Sinister Barrier*. Reading: Fantasy Press, 1951.
Saint-Exupéry, Antoine de. *The Little Prince*. Richard Howard, trans. San Diego: Harcourt, 2000.
Saint-Simon, Claude-Henri de Rouvroy, Comte de. *Œuvres de Claude-Henri de Saint-Simon*. Volume 5: *De l'organisation sociale*. Paris: Éditions Anthropos, 1966.
_____. *Œuvres de Claude-Henri de Saint-Simon*. Volume 2, *De l'reorganisation de la société européene*. Paris: Éditions Anthropos, 1966.
Schuré, Édouard. *The Great Initiates: A Study of the Secret History of Religions*. Hudson, NY: Steinerbooks, 1999.
Spencer, Herbert. *Principles of Biology, Volume 1*. Bibliolife. November 2008.
Spinoza, Benedict de. *Ethics: Philosophy of Benedict Spinoza*. R.H.M. Elves, trans. and ed. New York: Tudor, 1933.
Star Wars (film). 20th Century-Fox. 1977.
Starship Troopers (film). Tristar/Touchstone. 1997.
Steiner, Rudolph. *Autobiography: Chapters in the Course of My Life: 1861–1907*. Rita Stebbing, trans., Paul M. Allen, ed. Hudson: Anthroposophic Press, 1999.
Steiner Institute. Website. http://www.steinerinstitute.org/.
Things to Come (film). London Films. 1936. Based on the book *The Shape of Things to Come* by H.G. Wells.
Time Masters (film). Original title: *Les maîtres du temps*. TPI (Paris), SSR (Geneva), SWF (Baden-Baden), and WDR (Köln). 1981. English version, 1982. Based on the novel *L'orphelin de Perdide* by Stefan Wul.
Total Recall (film). TriStar. 1990. Inspired the short story "We Can Remember it for You Wholesale" by Philip K. Dick.
Twain, Mark (Samuel Langhorne Clemens). *A Connecticut Yankee in King Arthur's Court*. New York: Oxford University Press, 1996.
20,000 Leagues under the Sea (film). Walt Disney. 1954. Based on the novel, *Twenty Thousand Leagues under the Seas*, by Jules Verne.
2001: A Space Odyssey (film). Metro-Goldwyn-Mayer. 1968. Based on the novel *2001: A Space Odyssey* by Arthur C. Clarke.
Verne, Jules. *Around the Moon*. New York: E.P. Dutton, 1970.
_____. *From the Earth to the Moon*. New York: Bantam Classics, 1993.
_____. *Journey to the Center of the Earth*. New York: Sterling, 2007. See also *Journey to the Center of the Earth*. William Butcher, trans. (Oxford: Oxford University Press, 1998).
_____. *Master of the World*. New York: Ace, 1961.
_____. *Mysterious Island*. Sidney Kravitz, trans., Arthur B. Evans, d. Middletown: Wesleyan University Press, 2001.
_____. *Off on a Comet*. Charleston: Bibliobazaar, 2008.
_____. *Paris au XXe siècle*. Paris: Hachette, 1994.
_____. *Robur the Conqueror*. Included in *Master of the World*. New York: Ace, 1961.
_____. *Twenty Thousand Leagues under the Sea*. London: Puffin Books, 1994. See also *Twenty Thousand Leagues under the Seas*. William Butcher, trans. Oxford: Oxford University Press, 1998.
Village of the Damned (film). MGM. 1960. Based on the novel *The Midwich Cuckoos* by John Wyndham.
Voltaire, François-Marie Arouet. *Candide ou l'optimisme*. Christopher Thacker, ed. Geneva: Librairie Droz, 1968.
_____. *Micromégas*. Paris: Livre de Poche, 2000.
Wells, H.G. *Anticipations*. New York: Harper & Brothers, 1902.
_____. *Island of Doctor Moreau*. New York: Modern Library, 1996.
_____. *Men Like Gods*. New York: Macmillan, 1923.
_____. *A Modern Utopia*. Lincoln: University of Nebraska Press, 1967.
_____. *The Shape of Things to Come*. New York: Macmillan, 1945.
_____. *Things to Come: The Release Script of the London Films Production*. In Leon Stover. *The Prophetic Soul: A Reading of H.G. Wells's Things to Come*. Jefferson, NC: McFarland, 1987.
_____. *The Time Machine*. Harry M. Gel-

dud, ed. Bloomington: Indiana University Press, 1987.
———. *The War of the Worlds*. London: Heineman, 1898.
———. *When the Sleeper Wakes*. New York: Modern Library, 2003.
———. *World Set Free*. New York: Macmillan, 1914.
Williamson, Jack. *The Humanoids*. *Astounding Science Fiction*. July 1947, March and April 1948. New York: Lancer Books, 1963.
Wyndham, John *The Midwich Cuckoos*. London: Penguin, 1960.

Interviews

Budrys, Algis. 1980.
Klein, Gerard (Gilles d'Argyre). 1991.
Ruellan, André Ruellan (Kurt Steiner). 1991.
Thomas, Pascal. 1983.

Basic Reference Sources

The following texts comprise basic reference sources for the subject matter of this study.

Clute, John, and Peter Nicholls, eds. *The Encyclopedia of Science Fiction*. New York: St. Martin's Press, 1979. 2d ed., 1993.
Douilly, Alain. *Anticipation: 50 ans de collections fantastiques au Fleuve Noir*. Encino: Black Coat Press, 2009.
Lofficier, Jean-Marc, and Randy Lofficier. *French Science Fiction, Fantasy, Horror and Pulp Fiction: A Guide to Cinema, Television, Radio, Animation, Comic Books and Literature*. Jefferson, NC: McFarland, 2000.
Versins, Pierre. *Encyclopédie de l'utopie des voyages extraordinaires et de la science fiction*. Lausanne: Editions L'Age d'Homme S.A., 1984.

Other Secondary Sources

Aldiss, Brian W. *Trillion Year Spree*. New York: Atheneum, 1986.
Alkon, Paul K. *Origins of Futuristic Fiction*. Athens: University of Georgia Press, 1987.
Amis, Kingsley. *New Maps of Hell*. New York: Ballantine, 1960.
Angenot, Marc. "Science Fiction in France before Verne." J.M. Gouanvic and D. Suvin, trans. *Science Fiction Studies*, #14, Volume 5, Part 1, March 1978. Montreal: D. Cariou. Also online: *http://www.depauw.edu/sfs/backissues/14/angenot14 art.htm*.
Ardagh, John. *France in the 1980s*. Harmondsworth, UK: Penguin, 1982.
———. *The New France*. London: Penguin, 1973.
Arnaud, Noël, François Lacussin, and Jean Tortel. *Entretiens sur la paralittérature*. Paris: Plon, 1970.
Association for Applied Solar Energy. *Procedures of the World Symposium on Applied Solar Energy*. Menlo Park: Stanford Research Institute, 1956.
Bailey, James O. *Pilgrims through Space and Time*. Westport, CT: Greenwood Press, 1972.
Barron, Richard. *Parties and Politics in Modern France*. Washington, D.C.: Public Affairs Press, 1959.
Beauroy, Jacques, Marc Bertrand, and Edward T. Gargan. *Popular Culture in France*. Stanford French and Italian Studies. Volume 3. Saratoga: Anma Libri, 1977.
Bigsby, C.W.E. "Europe, America, and the Cultural Debate." *Superculture: American Popular Culture and Europe*. C.W.E. Bigsby, ed. London: Elek, 1975. 1–28.
Bouchet, Pierre. *Economic Planning and the French Experience*. Daphne Woodward, trans. New York: Frederick A. Praeger, 1964.
Brée, Germaine. *Twentieth-Century French Literature*. Chicago: The University of Chicago Press, 1983.
Breman, Jan, ed. *Imperial Monkey Business: Racial Supremacy in Social Darwinist Theory and Colonial Practice*. Amsterdam: VU University Press, 1990.
Broadie, Alexander. *The Scottish Enlightenment: the Historical Age of the Historical Nation*. Edinburgh: Birlinn, 2001.
Brooks, Peter. *The Novel of Worldliness: Crebillon, Marivaux, Laclos, Stendhal*.

Princeton: Princeton University Press, 1969.

Bury, J.B. *The Idea of Progress.* New York: Dover, 1955.

Butcher, William. *Jules Verne: The Definitive Biography.* New York: Thunder's Mouth Press, 2006.

Capelle, Russell B. *The MRP and French Foreign Policy.* New York: Frederick A. Praeger, 1963.

Carey, George Wescott, ed. *Freedom and Virtue: The Conservative/Libertarian Debate.* Wilmington: Intercollegiate Studies Institute, 1998.

Carter, Paul A. *The Creation of Tomorrow.* New York: Columbia University Press, 1977.

Cassirer, Ernst. *The Philosophy of the Enlightenment.* Fritz C.A. Koelln and James P. Pettegrove, trans. Princeton: Princeton University Press, 1951.

Churchward, James. *The Lost Continent of Mu.* London: Neville Spearman, 1959.

Clark, Linda L. *Social Darwinism in France.* Tuscaloosa: University of Alabama Press, 1984.

Clute, John. "Čapek, Karel." *The Encyclopedia of Science Fiction.* John Clute and Peter Nicholls, eds. New York: St. Martin's Press, 1979. 2d ed., 1993. 190.

_____, and Peter Nicholls. "Hubbard, L. Ron." *The Encyclopedia of Science Fiction.* John Clute and Peter Nicholls, editors. New York: St. Martin's Press, 1979, Second Edition, 1993. 592–3.

The Compact Oxford English Dictionary. Oxford: Oxford University Press, 1999.

Cordesse, Gerard. "The Impact of American Science Fiction on Europe." *Superculture: American Popular Culture and Europe.* C.W.E. Bigsby, ed. London: Elek, 1975.

Coward, David. *A History of French Literature, from Chanson de Geste to Cinema.* Oxford: Blackwell, 2002.

Critchley, Simon, and Robert Bernasconi, eds. *The Companion to Levinas.* Cambridge, UK: Cambridge University Press, 2002.

Crozier, Michel. *The Bureaucratic Phenomenon.* Chicago: The University of Chicago Press, 1964.

Davis, Kenneth C. *Two-Bit Culture.* Boston: Houghton Mifflin, 1984.

Davis, Natalie Zemon. "The Historian and Popular Culture." *Popular Culture in France.* Jacques Beauroy, Marc Bertrand, and Edward T. Gargan, eds. *Stanford French and Italian Studies.* Volume 3. Saratoga, CA: Anma Libri, 1977. 1–28.

De Camp, L. Sprague. *Lost Continents: The Atlantis Theme in History, Science, and Literature.* New York: Ballantine, 1970.

De Carmoy, Guy. *The Foreign Policies of France.* Elaine P. Halperin, trans. Chicago: The University of Chicago Press, 1967.

Degler, Carl N. *In Search of Human Nature: The Decline and Revival of Darwinism in American Social Thought.* Oxford: Oxford University Press, 1991.

Delmas, Henri, and Alain Julian. *Le Rayon SF: Catalogue bibliographique de science-fiction, utopies, voyages extraordinaires.* Toulouse: Editions Milan, 1983.

Desmond, Lawrence Gustave, and Phyllis Rauch Messenger. *A Dream of Maya: Augustus and Alice Le Plongeon in Nineteenth Century Yucatan.* Albuquerque: University of New Mexico Press, 1988.

Diebold, William. *The Schuman Plan: A Study in Economic Cooperation 1950–9.* New York: Praeger, 1959.

Edwards, Malcolm J., and Brian Stableford. "Terraforming." *The Encyclopedia of Science Fiction.* John Clute and Peter Nicholls, eds. New York: St. Martin's Press, 1979. 2d ed., 1993. 1213–4.

Ehrmann, Henry. *Organized Business in France.* Princeton: Princeton University Press, 1957.

Einaldi, Mario, and François Goguel. *Christian Democracy in Italy and France.* Notre Dame: University of Notre Dame Press, 1952.

Evans, Arthur B. "Science Fiction in France: A Brief History." *Science Fiction Studies*, #49, Volume 16, Part 3, November 1989. Montreal: D. Cariou. 254–276.

_____. "Science Fiction in France: A Select Bibliography of Secondary Materials." In *Science Fiction Studies*, #49, Volume 16, Part 3, November 1989. Montreal: D. Cariou. 338–68.

Fogarty, Michael P. *Christianity Democracy in Western Europe 1820–1953*. Notre Dame: University of Notre Dame Press, 1957.

Franklin, H. Bruce. *Future Perfect: American Science Fiction of the 19th Century*. New Brunswick, NJ: Rutgers University Press, 1995.

_____. *Robert A. Heinlein: America as Science Fiction*. New York: Oxford University Press, 1980.

Fursdon, Edward. *The European Defence Community*. New York: St. Martin's Press, 1979.

Garin, Jacques. Website. *http://gotomars.free.fr/priollet.html*.

Gattégno, Jean. *La Science-fiction*. Paris: Presses Universitaires de France, 1971.

Gay, Peter. *The Enlightenment: An Interpretation*. New York: Norton, 1977. Two vols.: I. *The Rise of Modern Paganism*, II. *The Science of Freedom*.

Genefort, Laurent. Correspondence with Bradford Lyau. September 8, 2009.

_____. "Stefan Wul, artificier de l'imaginaire." In *Oeuvres completes, tome 1*. Claude Lefrancq, ed. Paris: Collection LeFrancq, 1998. Also online: *http://www.schismatrice.net/article.php3?id_article=26*.

_____. "Stefan Wul, du vent dans les voiles et de la boue aux semelles." In *Oeuvres completes, tome 2*. Ananké Lefrancqm, ed. Paris: Collection LeFrancq, 1997. Also online : *http://www.schismatrice.net/article.php3?id_article=26*.

Gillingham, John. *Coal, Steel, and the Rebirth of Europe, 1945–1955: The German and French from Ruhr Conflict to Economic Community*. Cambridge, UK: Cambridge University Press, 1991.

Gilpin, Robert. *France in the age of the Scientific State*. Princeton: Princeton University Press, 1968.

Girardot, Jean-Jacques. Website. *http://sf.emse.fr/AUTHORS/GKLEIN/gksa.html*.

Gouanvic, Jean-Marc. *La Science fiction française au XXe siècle (1900–1968)*. Amsterdam: Éditions Rodopi B.V., 1994.

Gunn, James E. *Alternate Worlds*. Englewood Cliffs, NJ: Prentice Hall, 1975.

Halls, W.D. *Society, Schools, and Progress in France*. Oxford: Pergamon Press, 1965.

Hamilton, Richard F. *Affluence and the French Worker in the Fourth Republic*. Princeton: Princeton University Press, 1967.

Hammer, Olav. *Claiming Knowledge: Strategies of Epistemology from Theosophy to the New Age*. Leiden: Brill, 2004.

Hardy, Phil. *The Encyclopedia of Science Fiction Movies*. Minneapolis: Woodbury Press, 1986.

Hartley, Anthony. *Gaullism: The Rise and Fall of a Political Movement*. New York: Outerbridge & Dienstfrey, 1971.

Hartwell, David G., and Kathryn Cramer. "How Shit Became Shinola: Definition and Redefinition of Space Opera." *SFRevu*, August 2003. Earnest Lilley, sr. ed. *http://www.sfrevu.com/ISSUES/2003/0308/Space%20Opera%20Redefined/Review.htm*.

Harvey, Sir Paul, and J.E. Heseltine, eds. *The Oxford Companion to French Literature*. Oxford: Clarendon Press, 1969.

Hawkins, Mike. *Social Darwinism in European and American thought, 1860–1945: Nature as Model and Nature as Threat*. Cambridge, UK: Cambridge University Press, 1997.

Hendrix, Howard. *The Ecstasy of Catastrophe: A Study of the Apocalyptic Tradition from Langland to Milton*. Dissertation, University of California Riverside, 1987.

Hillegas, Mark R. *The Future as Nightmare: H.G. Wells and the Anti-Utopians*. Carbondale: Southern Illinois Press, 1974.

Hoffman, Stanley, Charles P. Kindleberger, Laurence Wylie, Jesse R. Pitts, Jean-Baptiste Duroselle, and François Goguel. *France: Change and Tradition*. Cambridge, MA: Harvard University Press, 1963.

Howorth, Jolyon, and Philip G. Cerny, eds. *Elites in France: Origins, Reproduction, and Power*. London: Frances Pinter, 1981.

Hughes, H. Stuart. *The Obstructed Path*. New York: Harper and Row, 1969.

Irving, R.E.M. *Christian Democracy in France*. London: George Allen and Unwin, 1973.

Israel, Jonathan I. *Enlightenment Contested*.

Oxford and New York: Oxford University Press, 2006. Paperback ed., 2008.

_____. *Enlightenment Contested: Philosophy, Modernity, and the Emancipation of Man 1670–1752*. Oxford and New York: Oxford University Press, 2002

_____. *Radical Enlightenment*. Oxford and New York: Oxford University Press, 2001. Paperback ed., 2002.

_____. *Radical Enlightenment: Philosophy and the Making of Modernity 1650–1750*. Oxford and New York: Oxford University Press, 2002

Jakubowski, Maxim. "Klein, Gérard." *The Encyclopedia of Science Fiction*. John Clute and Peter Nicholls, eds. New York: St. Martin's Press, 1979. 2d ed., 1993. 671.

_____, and John Clute. "Wul, Stefan." *The Encyclopedia of Science Fiction*. John Clute and Peter Nicholls, eds. New York: St. Martin's Press, 1979. 2d ed., 1993. 1352.

James, Edward, and Farah Mendlesohn, eds. *The Cambridge Companion to Science Fiction*. Cambridge, UK: Cambridge University Press, 2009.

Jones, Gwyneth. "The Icons of Science Fiction." *The Cambridge Companion to Science Fiction*. Edward James and Farah Mendlesohn, eds. Cambridge, UK: Cambridge University Press, 2009.

Keener, Frederick M. *The Chain of Becoming, The Philosophical Tale, The Novel, and a Neglected Realism of the Enlightenment: Swift, Montesquieu, Voltaire, Johnson, and Austen*. New York: Columbia University Press, 1983.

Kelley, Donald R. *The Descent of Ideas: The History of Intellectual History*. Aldershot, UK, and Burlington, VT: Ashgate, 2002.

Ketterer, David. "Poe, Edgar Allan." *The Encyclopedia of Science Fiction*. John Clute and Peter Nicholls, eds. New York: St. Martin's Press, 1979. 2d ed., 1993. 939–40.

Koreman, Megan. *The Expectation of Justice: France, 1944–1946*. Durham: Duke University Press, 1999.

Krieger, Leonard. *An Essay on the Theory of Enlightened Despotism*. Chicago: The University of Chicago Press, 1975.

_____. *Kings and Philosophers 1689–1789*. New York: Norton, 1970.

Küng, Hans. *Eternal Life?* New York: Doubleday, 1984.

Kurlansky, Mark. *1968: The Year that Rocked the World*. New York: Ballantine, 2004.

Leigh, John. *The Search for Enlightenment: An Introduction to Eighteenth Century French Writing*. Lanham: Rowman & Littlefield Publishers, 1999.

Littré, Emile. *Dictionnaire de la langue française*. Paris: Gallimard-Hachette, 1960.

Lofficier, Jean-Marc. "Obituaries." *Locus*, January 1981, 30.

Louit, Robert and Jacques Chambon. "France." *The Encyclopedia of Science Fiction*. John Clute and Peter Nicholls, editors. New York: St. Martin's Press, 1979, Second Edition, 1993. 444–7.

Lovering, J.F., and J.R.V. Prescott. *Last of the Lands ... Antartica*. Carlton: Melbourne University Press, 1979.

Lucas, Nigel. *Western European Energy Policies*. Oxford: Clarendon Press, 1985.

Luethy, Herbert. *France Against Herself*. Eric Mosbacher, trans. New York: Frederick A. Praeger, 1955.

Lukes, Steven. *Individualism*. Colchester, UK: ECPR Press, 2006.

Lundwall, Sam J. *Science Fiction: What It's All About*. New York: Ace, 1971.

Luomala, Katharine. *The Menehume of Polynesia and Other Mythical Little People of Oceana*. Bernice F. Bishop Museum Bulletin, No. 203. Honolulu: Bernice F. Bishop Museum, 1951.

Lyau, Bradford. *The Anxiety of Progress: The French Anticipation Novels of the 1950s*. Dissertation, University of Chicago, 1988.

_____. "Science Fiction: Mediating Agent between C.P. Snow's Two Cultures, A Historical Interpretation." *Science Fiction and the Two Cultures*. Gary Westfahl and George Slusser, eds. *Critical Explorations in Science Fiction and Fantasy*, 16. Donald E. Palumbo and C.W. Sullivan III, series eds. Jefferson, NC: McFarland, 2009. 22–36.

_____. "Technocratic Anxiety in France: The Fleuve Noir 'Anticipation' Novels, 1951–60." *Science Fiction Studies*, #49, Volume 16, Part 3, November 1989. Montreal: D. Cariou. 277–97.

Magill, Frank, ed. *Survey of Science Fiction*

Literature. Englewood Cliffs, NJ: Salem Press, 1978. Five volumes.

Manuel, Frank E. *The New World of Henri Saint-Simon*. Cambridge, MA: Harvard University Press, 1956.

_____. *The Prophets of Paris*. Cambridge, MA: Harvard University Press, 1962.

_____, and Fritzie P. Manuel. *Utopian Thought in the Western World*. Cambridge, MA: Harvard University Press, 1979.

Mauzi, Robert, Sylvain Menant, and Michel Delon. *Précis de litterature française du XVIIIe siècle*. Paris: Presses Universitaires de France, 1990.

McConnell, Frank. *The Science Fiction of H.G. Wells*. Oxford: Oxford University Press, 1981.

McMillan, James F. *Dreyfus to De Gaulle: Politics and Society in France 1898–1969*. London: Edward Arnold, 1985.

Meisel, James H. *The Fall of the Republic: Military Revolt in France*. Ann Arbor: University of Michigan Press, 1962.

Merritt, Richard L., and Donald J. Puchala. *Western European Perspectives on International Affairs. Praeger Studies in International Politics and Public Affairs*. New York: Frederick A. Praeger, 1968.

Métraux, Alfred. *Easter Island: A Stone-age civilization of the Pacific*. Michael Bullock, trans. New York: Oxford University Press, 1957.

Moreau, Charles. Website. *Fantastik Blog*, http://fantastik2001.blogspot.com/2009/03/au-cur-de-la-sf-francaise-un-secretaire.html.

Moskowitz, Sam. *Explorers of the Infinite*. Cleveland: World, 1963.

_____. *Seekers of Tomorrow*. Cleveland: World, 1966.

Nicholls, Peter. "Cyberpunk." *The Encyclopedia of Science Fiction*. John Clute and Peter Nicholls, eds. New York: St. Martin's Press, 1979. 2d ed., 1993. 288–90.

_____. "Holocaust and After." *The Encyclopedia of Science Fiction*. John Clute and Peter Nicholls, eds. New York: St. Martin's Press, 1979. 2d ed., 1993. 581–4.

_____. "Mainstream Writers of SF." *The Encyclopedia of Science Fiction*. John Clute and Peter Nicholls, eds. New York: St. Martin's Press, 1979. 2d ed., 1993. 768–70.

_____. "Paranoia." *The Encyclopedia of Science Fiction*. John Clute and Peter Nicholls, eds. New York: St. Martin's Press, 1979. 2d ed., 1993. 909–12.

_____. "Pulp Magazines." *The Encyclopedia of Science Fiction*. John Clute and Peter Nicholls, eds. New York: St. Martin's Press, 1979. 2d ed., 1993. 978–80.

_____. "Steampunk." *The Encyclopedia of Science Fiction*. John Clute and Peter Nicholls, eds. New York: St. Martin's Press, 1979. 2d ed., 1993. 1161.

_____, and Brian Stableford. "Politics." *The Encyclopedia of Science Fiction*. John Clute and Peter Nicholls, eds. New York: St. Martin's Press, 1979. 2d ed., 1993. 945–7.

Partington, John S. *Building Cosmopolis: The Political Thought of H.G. Wells*. Aldershot, UK, and Burlington, VT: Ashgate, 2003.

Paxton, Robert O. *Vichy France: Old Guard and New Order 1940–1944*. New York: Columbia University Press, 2001.

Pierce, Mark. *Contemporary French Political Thought*. London: Oxford University Press, 1966.

Poster, Mark. *Existential Marxism in Postwar France*. Princeton: Princeton University Press, 1975.

Pringle, David. "Disaster." *The Encyclopedia of Science Fiction*. John Clute and Peter Nicholls, eds. New York: St. Martin's Press, 1979. 2d ed., 1993. 338.

_____, Brian Stableford, and Peter Nicholls. "Lost Worlds." *The Encyclopedia of Science Fiction*. John Clute and Peter Nicholls, eds. New York: St. Martin's Press, 1979. 2d ed., 1993. 734–6.

Roberts, Peter, and John Grant. "Fort, Charles (Hoy)." *The Encyclopedia of Science Fiction*. John Clute and Peter Nicholls, eds. New York: St. Martin's Press, 1979. 2d ed., 1993. 439–40.

Roemer, Kenneth M. *The Obsolete Necessity: America in Utopian Writings 1888–1900*. Kent, OH: Kent State University Press, 1976.

Sadoul, Jacques. *Histoire de la science-fiction moderne*. Paris: Albin Michel, 1973.

Sampson, Anthony. *The New Europeans*. London: Hodder and Stoughton, 1968.

Sampson, R.V. *Progress in the Age of Reason*. Cambridge, MA: Harvard University Press, 1956.

Schneider, Marcel. *Histoire de la litterature fantastique en France*. Paris: Librairie Arthème Fayard, 1985.

Scheinman, Lawrence. *Atomic Energy Policy in France under the Fourth Republic*. Princeton: Princeton University Press, 1965.

Scholes, Robert, and Eric S. Rabkin. *Science Fiction: History-Science-Vision*. Oxford: Oxford University Press, 1977.

Schroeder, Fred E.H., ed. *5000 Years of Popular Culture: Popular Culture Before Printing*. Bowling Green, OH: Bowling Green State University Press, 1980.

Singer, Peter. *Hegel: A Very Short Introduction*. Oxford: Oxford University Press, 2001.

Sirinelli, Jean-François. "The École Normale Supérieure and elite formation and selection during the Third Republic." *Elites in France: Origins, Reproduction, and Power*. Jolyon Howorth and Philip G. Cerny, eds. London: Frances Pinter, 1981. 55–77.

Slusser, George E. "The Beginnings of Fiction." *Science-Fiction Studies*, Vol. 16, Part 3, #49, November 1989. Montreal: SFS Publications. 307–37.

_____. *Robert A. Heinlein: Stranger in His Own Land*. The Milford Series, *Popular Writers of Today*. Volume 1. San Bernardino: Borgo Press, 1976.

_____. "Science Fiction in France: An Introduction." *Science Fiction Studies*, #49, Volume 16, Part 3, November 1989. Montreal: D. Cariou. 251–3.

_____. *The Space Odysseys of Arthur C. Clarke*. Popular Writers of Today, No. 8. San Bernardino: Borgo Press, 1978.

_____, and Tom Shippey, eds. *Fiction 2000: Cyberpunk and the Future of Narrative*. Athens: University of Georgia Press, 1992.

Solomon, Robert C. *From Hegel to Existentialism*. Oxford: Oxford University Press, 1987.

Stableford, Brian. "Adam and Eve." *The Encyclopedia of Science Fiction*. John Clute and Peter Nicholls, eds. New York: St. Martin's Press, 1979. 2d ed., 1993. 4–5.

_____. "Alternate Worlds." *The Encyclopedia of Science Fiction*. John Clute and Peter Nicholls, eds. New York: St. Martin's Press, 1979. 2d ed., 1993. 23–5.

_____. "Androids." *The Encyclopedia of Science Fiction*. John Clute and Peter Nicholls, eds. New York: St. Martin's Press, 1979. 2d ed., 1993. 34–5.

_____. "Cyrano de Bergerac." *The Encyclopedia of Science Fiction*. John Clute and Peter Nicholls, eds. New York: St. Martin's Press, 1979. 2d ed., 1993. 291.

_____. "End of the World." *The Encyclopedia of Science Fiction*. John Clute and Peter Nicholls, eds. New York: St. Martin's Press, 1979. 2d ed., 1993. 382–4.

_____. "Eschatology." *The Encyclopedia of Science Fiction*. John Clute and Peter Nicholls, eds. New York: St. Martin's Press, 1979. 2d ed., 1993. 388–9.

_____. "Nuclear Power." *The Encyclopedia of Science Fiction*. John Clute and Peter Nicholls, eds. New York: St. Martin's Press, 1979. 2d ed., 1993. 881–2.

_____. "Religion." *The Encyclopedia of Science Fiction*. John Clute and Peter Nicholls, eds. New York: St. Martin's Press, 1979. 2d ed., 1993. 1000–3.

_____. "Robots." *The Encyclopedia of Science Fiction*. John Clute and Peter Nicholls, eds. New York: St. Martin's Press, 1979. 2d ed., 1993. 1018–20.

Stableford, Brian. "Science Fiction Before the Genre." *The Cambridge Companion to Science Fiction*. James, Edward and Farah Mendlesohn, eds. Cambridge, UK: Cambridge University Press, 2009. 15–31.

_____. "Space Opera." *The Encyclopedia of Science Fiction*. John Clute and Peter Nicholls, eds. New York: St. Martin's Press, 1979. 2d ed., 1993. 1138–40.

_____, John Clute, and Peter Nicholls. "Definition of SF." *The Encyclopedia of Science Fiction*. John Clute and Peter Nicholls, eds. New York: St. Martin's Press, 1979. 2d ed., 1993. 311–4.

Stevens, Anne. "The Contribution of the École Nationale d'Administration in French Political Life." *Elites in France:*

Origins, Reproduction, and Power. Jolyon Howorth and Philip G. Cerny, eds. London: Frances Pinter, 1981. 134–53.

Stover, Leon. *The Prophetic Soul: A Reading of H.G. Wells's Things to Come*. Jefferson, NC: McFarland, 1987.

Stromberg, Roland N. *After Everything: Western Intellectual History since 1945*. New York: St. Martin's Press, 1975.

———. *European Intellectual History since 1789*. Englewood Cliffs, NJ: Prentice-Hall, 1975.

Tannenbaum, Edward. *The New France*. Chicago: University of Chicago Press, 1961.

Taylor, Charles. *Hegel*. Cambridge, UK: Cambridge University Press, 1975.

Thoenig, Jean-Claude. *L'Ère des technocrates*. Paris: Editions d'Organisation, 1973.

Thomas, Pascal. "The Current State of Science Fiction in France." *Science Fiction Studies*, #49, Volume 16, Part 3, November 1989. Montreal: D. Cariou. 298–306.

Thomson, David. *Democracy in France since 1870*. London: Oxford University Press, 1969.

Toffler, Alvin. *Future Shock*. New York: Bantam, 1970.

Van Herp, Jacques. *Panorama de la science-fiction*. Verviers: Marabout University, 1975.

Vallentyne, Peter, and Hillel Steiner, eds. *Left-Libertarianism and Its Critics: The Contemporary Debate*. New York: Palgrave, 2000.

Vartanian, Aram. "On Cultivating One's Garden." *A New History of French Literature*. Denis Hollier, ed. Cambridge, MA: Harvard University Press, 1989.

Vaughan, Michalina. "The Grandes Écoles: Selection, Legitimization, Perpetuation." In *Elites in France: Origins, Reproduction, and Power*. Jolyon Howorth and Philip G. Cerny, eds. London: Frances Pinter, 1981. 93–103.

Wade, Ira O. *The Intellectual Development of Voltaire*. Princeton: Princeton University Press, 1969.

———. *Voltaire's Micromegas*. Princeton: Princeton University Press, 1950.

Wagar, W. Warren. *Good Tidings: The Belief in Progress from Darwin to Marcuse*. Bloomington: Indiana University Press, 1972.

———. *H.G. Wells and the World State*. New Haven, CT: Yale University Press, 1961.

———. *World Views: A Study in Comparative History*. Hinsdale: Dryden Press, 1977.

Watts, Ian. *The Rise of the Novel: Studies in Defoe, Richardson, and Fielding*. Berkeley: University of California Press, 1959.

Webster, Paul, and Nicholas Powell. *Saint-Germain-des-Prés*. London: Constable, 1984.

Westfahl, Gary. "Hugo Gernsback and the Century of Science Fiction." In *Critical Explorations in Science Fiction and Fantasy, 16*. Donald E. Palumbo and C.W. Sullivan III, series eds. Jefferson, NC: McFarland, 2007.

———. "Space Opera." *The Cambridge Companion to Science Fiction*. Edward James and Farah Mendlesohn, eds. Cambridge, UK: Cambridge University Press, 2009. 197–208.

White, Dorothy Shipley. *Black Africa and de Gaulle: From French Empire to Independence*. University Park: Pennsylvania State University Press, 1979.

Williamson, Jack. *H.G. Wells: Critic of Progress*. Baltimore: Mirage Press, 1973.

Willoughby, Harold R. *Pagan Regeneration: A Study of Mystery Initiations in the Graeco Roman World*. Chicago: The University of Chicago Press, 1929.

Wright, Gordon. *Rural Revolution in France*. Stanford: Stanford University Press, 1964.

Zeldin, Theodore. *History of French Passions. Volume One: Ambition and Love*. New York: Oxford University Press, 1980.

———. *History of French Passions. Volume Two: Intellect and Pride*. New York: Oxford University Press, 1980.

———. *History of French Passions. Volume Three: Taste and Corruption*. New York: Oxford University Press, 1980.

———. *History of French Passions. Volume Four: Politics and Anger*. New York: Oxford University Press, 1980.

———. *History of French Passions. Volume Five: Anxiety and Hypocrisy*. New York: Oxford University Press, 1981.

Index

Numbers in **bold** indicate main sections.

Á l'assaut du ciel (Bessière) 35, 37
abominable snowman (Yeti) 86
The Abyss (film) 100
L'Action Française (political movement) 73
Adam and Eve theme 69, 152
"Adam and No Eve" (Bester) 68–9
Aéronef C3 (Limat) 115
Agonie des civilisés (Vandel) 149–51
L'Agonie du verre (Guieu) 83–4
Ailleurs & Demain (imprint) 184
Ailleurs & Demain: Classiques (imprint) 97
Alain, Jean-Jacques *see* Randa, Peter
Aldiss, Brian W. 193
Alerte aux robots (Vandel) 151
altérité (philosophical concept) *see* the other
alternate history 46
Altitude moins X (Bessière) 47–8
Amazing Stories (periodical) 18, 20; scientifiction 19
An...2391 (Bruss) 176
L'An 2440, rêve s'il on fut jamais (Mercier) 12
Analog Science Fiction and Fact (periodical, formerly *Astounding Science Fiction*) 19
Anderson, Poul 19, 24, 209n; *War of Two Worlds* (*La Troisième Race*, Anderson) 24, 170
Andrevon, Jean-Pierre 96, 98
android 153
Angoisse (Fleuve Noir imprint) 22, 115, 127, 132, 169
L'Anneau des invincibles (Rayjean) 63–5
Anthroposophy 43, 45
Anticipation (Fleuve Noir imprint) 2, 3, 8, 22–4, 78, 195
Anticipations (Wells) 143
apocalypse 101
Ardagh, John 161
Argyre, Gilles d' *see* Klein, Gérard
Around the Moon (*Autour de la Lune*, Verne) 34
As-tu vu les soucoupes? (radio) 77
Asimov, Isaac 19, 78, 120, 137; *Asimov's Science Fiction* (periodical, formerly *Isaac Asimov's Science Fiction Magazine*) 78; *David Starr, Space Ranger* (*Sur la planète rouge*) 23; *I, Robot* 120–1, 206n; Limat novel comparison 120–1; Paul French pseudonym 23;

Pebble in the Sky 171; *Sur la planète rouge* (*David Starr, Space Ranger*) 23
Asimov's Science Fiction (periodical) 78
Astor, John Jacob 18
Astounding Science Fiction (periodical, later *Analog Science Fiction and Fact*) 19, 109
Les Astres morts (Vandel) 142–3
Atlantis myth 84–5, 102
atomic bomb 69, 71
atomic energy 72
Attaque sub-terrestre (Rayjean) 60–1, 67, 72
Attentat cosmique (Vandel) 154
attitudes *see* French general attitudes
Au-delà de l'infini (Guieu) 79, 189
Autour de la lune (*Around the Moon*, Verne) 34
l'autre (philosophical concept) *see* the other
Aux armes d'Ortog (Steiner) 135–8
L'Aventurier (Fleuve Noir imprint) 22, 127
Les Aventuriers du ciel: Voyages extraordinaries d'un petit parisien dans la stratosphère, la lunes et la planètes (Nizerolles) 34
awards (science fiction) 21, 32, 83, 201n, 204n; Grand Prix du Roman de Science Fiction 83, 204n; Grand Prix International de la Science Fiction 32

Bacchus Roi (Bruss) 170
Ballard, J.G. 193
Balzac, Honoré de 1; *Le Centenaire* 1
bandes dessinées (French comics and comic books) 3
Bang! (Bessière) 50
Barjavel, Réne 18
Baroud (Randa) 128, 131
Base spatiale 14 (Rayjean) 61
Basehart, Richard 69
Baxter, Stephen 98
Bellamy, Edward 15, 18
Benford, Gregory 207n
Bergson, Henri 12, 43–6, 59; Bessière comparison 44–5; *Creative Evolution* 44–5; *élan vital* (vital impetus) 44
Bernal, J.D. 92–3; *The World, the Flesh, and the Devil: An Inquiry in the Future of the Three Enemies of the Rational Soul* 92–3

225

Index

Bessière, Henri-Richard *see* Bessière, Richard
Bessière, Richard (also F. Richard-Bessière, pseudonyms for Henri-Richard Bessière) 9, 24, 25, **31–59**, 74–5, 115, 140–1, 168, 195; *À l'assaut du ciel* 35, 37; alternate history 46; *Altitude moins X* 47–8; Anthroposophy 43, 45; *Les Aventuriers du ciel: Voyages extraordinaries d'un petit parisien dans la stratosphere, la lunes et la planètes* (Nizerolles) influence 34; *Bang!* 50; Bergson comparison 43–6; *Carrefour de temps* 50; *Ceux de demain* 52; Christianity, alternatives to 42–3; *Cité de l'esprit* 50; *Les Conquérants de l'univers* 35–7; *Création cosmique* 43–5; *Creative Evolution* (*L'Évolution créatrice*, Bergson) comparison 44–5; *Croisière dans le temps* 46; *La Deuxième Terre* 40; *élan vital* (vital impetus, Bergson concept) comparison 44; *Escale chez les vivants* 51; Espionnage (Fleuve Noir imprint) 32 European unification 53; evolution 44–5; *L'Évolution créatrice* (*Creative Evolution*, Bergson) comparison 44–5; *Feu dans le ciel* 43; *Fléau de l'univers* 40; *Générations perdues* 49–50; Graffigny influence 31; Grand Prix International de la Science Fiction 32; *The Great Initiates* (Schuré) influence 33, 42–3; Le Faure influence 31; *The Little Prince* (Saint-Exupéry) similarities 33–4; *Les Lunes de Jupiter* 41; Monnet comparison 56–8; Nizerolles influence 34; *Objectif soleil* 41, 189; *On a hurlé dans le ciel* 50; *Panique dans le vide* 50; Pascal influence 33, 40–2; *Les Patins d'outre ciel* 50–1; *Pensées* (Pascal) influence 33, 40–1; *Planète de mort* 51; *Planète vagabonde* 35, 39; *Réaction déluge* 48–9; *Relais Minos III* 42; religion 42–6; *Retour de "Météore"* 35, 38–9; Richard, editorial relations with 31–2; robots 42; *Route du néant* 54–5; Saint-Simon influence 36–9; *Sauvetage sidéral* 39; Schuré influence 33, 42–3, 46; *S.O.S. Terre* 51; *Terre degree "0"* 49; *Le Troisième Astronef* 52; Verne influence 31, 47; *Via dimension "5"* 40; *Vingt Pas dans l'inconnu* 46–7; vital impetus (*élan vital*, Bergson concept) comparison 44; *The War of the Worlds* (Wells) comparison 35, 37; *Zone spatiale interdite* 47
Bester, Alfred 19, 69; "Adam and No Eve" 68–9; Rayjean story comparison 68–9
Between Planets (*D'une planète à l'autre*, Heinlein) 129–30
Bigsby, C.W.E. 15
Black-Out sur les soucoupes Volantes (Guieu) 77
Blish, James 19, 183; *A Case of Conscience* 116
The Blob (film) 103

Blondel, Roger *see* Bruss, B.R.
Bodin, Félix 17
The Body Snatchers (Finney) 61
Bohr, Neils 67
Bommart, Jean (Kemmel) 9, 24, 31, 59, **73–5**, 95, 195; L'Action Française (political movement) relationship 73; *Je reviens de ...* 73–4; *Le Poisson chinois* 73; *Le Poisson chinois a tué Hitler* 73; *The War of the Worlds* (Wells) comparison 73
Bonnefoy, René *see* Bruss, B.R.
The Book of the Damned (Fort) 85
Borne, Étienne 122, 125
Boucher, Anthony 116; "The Quest for St. Aquin" 116
Bourgeois, Leon 12
Bradbury, Ray 19, 183; Klein inspiration 183
Brantonne, René 3
Brave New World (Huxley) 143
Brée, Germaine 21, 201*n*
Brin, (Glen) David 98, 207*n*
Brooks, Peter 28
Brunner, John 183
Bruss, B.R. (René Bonnefoy) 9, 24, 63, 75, 140, **169–82**, 195; *An ... 2391* 176; Angoisse (Fleuve Noir imprint) 169; Asimov novel comparison 171; *Bacchus Roi* 170; Blondel pseudonym 169; Cold War scenarios 171–4; *Complot Vénus-Terre* 181–2; de Beauvoir comparison 177–80; *dégradation nationale* (national degradation, civil status) 169; École Polytechnique (French higher education) allusion 180–1; *Et la planète sauta...* 169; Fantastik Blog (Moreau, blog site) 170; feminist ideas 177–80; Gouanvic analysis 170, 174; *Le Grand Kirn* 61, 174; *grandes écoles* (French higher education) 180–1; *La Guerre contre le Rull* (*The War Against the Rull*, van Vogt) translation 170; *La Guerre des soucoupes* 172; High Court of Justice (France) verdict 169; Johnson novel comparison 171; Laval association 169; *Logan's Run* (film) comparison 171; *Logan's Run* (Nolan and Johnson) comparison 171; Moreau biography 170; Nolan novel comparison 171; the other (philosophical concept) 170, 174, 176–7, 179; Pandora myth comparison 177, 181; *Pebble in the Sky* (Asimov) comparison 171; *Rideau magnetic* 172; *S.O.S. soucoupes* 171–2, 175; Substance "ARKA" 173–4; technocratic vision 180; *Terre...siècle 24* 175–6; *Tête à tête* 170; *La Troisième Race* (*War of Two Worlds*, Anderson) translation 170; USSR interpretation 171–2; Vichy government participation 169–70, 182; *The War Against the Rull* (*La Guerre contre le Rull*, van Vogt) translation 170; *War of Two Worlds* (*La Troisième Race*, Anderson) translation 170; L'X (nickname for École Polytechnique, French higher education) allusion 181

Budrys, Algis (Algirdas Jonas Budrys) 16
Bujold, Lois McMaster 98
Bureau de l'invisible (Vandel) 154, 204*n*
Burroughs, Edgar Rice 18
Butcher, William 8, 17, 148–9
Butor, Michel 3

Caltiki, the Immortal Monster (film) 103
Campbell, John W., Jr. 19, 98, 99; *The Mightiest Machine* 99
Camus, Albert 150
Candide ou l'Optimisme (Voltaire) 4, 26, 29, 33, 118–20, 126, 191
A Canticle for Leibowitz (Miller) 116
Čapek, Karel 99–100, 152–3; *robota* (Czech) 153; *R.U.R.* (*Rossum's Universal Robots*, play) 100, 152–3; Vandel novel comparison 152–3; *War with the Newts* (*Válka s mloky*) 99–100; Wul comparison 99–100
Caro, Armand de 22
Carrefour de temps (Bessière) 50
Les Carrefours de l'étrange (television) 77
A Case of Conscience (Blish) 116
Cassirer, Ernst 79–80
CEA (*Commissariat à l'énergie atomique*) 71
Le Centenaire (Balzac) 1
Ceux de demain (Bessière) 52
CFTC (Confédération Française Travailleurs Chrétiens, French Confederation of Christian Workers, workers group) 122–3
Chambon, Jacques 27
Chasseurs d'hommes (Guieu) 84
Cherryh, C.J. 98
Les Chevaliers de l'espace (Vandel) 142
Childhood's End (Clarke) 136–9
Children of the Damned (film) 102
Chirurgiens d'une planète (Klein) 184–92
Chocs en synthèse (Rayjean) 61–3
Chomet, Richard 183
Christian Democracy 121–6
Christianity 42–3
Church of Scientology 109
Churchward, James 87
Ciné TV Console (Fleuve Noir imprint) 22
Cité de l'esprit (Bessière) 50
Cité Noë No. 2 (Guieu) 90
Clarke, Arthur C. 19, 23, 24, 135–9, 183, 207*n*; *Childhood's End* 136–9; *Islands in the Sky* (*Îles de l'espace*) 23; *Lost Worlds of 2001* 207*n*; "The Nine Billion Names of God" 116; "The Star" 116; Steiner (Kurt) comparison 135–9; *2001: A Space Odyssey* (film) 138; *2001: A Space Odyssey* (novel) 2, 138
Clute, John 78, 94, 101, 103; *Encyclopedia of Science Fiction* (Clute and Nicholls) 78, 101, 183
Cold War 108, 171–4; French general attitudes 173
Colonial Exposition (L'Exposition coloniale, 1931) 113

colonial (French) relations 112–3
Commandos de l'espace (Guieu) 83
Commissariat à l'énergie atomique (CEA) 71
Communauté française (French Community) 112
Complot Vénus-Terre (Bruss) 181–2
Comte, Auguste 12
Condorcet, Marie-Jean-Antoine-Nicolas de Caritat, marquis de 12
Confédération Française Travailleurs Chrétiens (CFTC, French Confederation of Christian Workers, workers group) 122–3
A Connecticut Yankee in King Arthur's Court (Twain) 46
Les Conquérants de l'univers (Bessière) 35–7
conte (tale) 25, 29
conte de fée (fairy tale) 25
conte philosophique (philosophical tale) 1–3, 9, 25–30, 194–5; *see also* Voltaire
conventions (science fiction meetings) 21, 201*n*
Convulsions solaires (Guieu) 89
Cooper, James Fenimore 17
Coplan FX-18 (fictional hero, Kenny/Vandel) 140–1
Cordesse, Gérard 20–1
Cosmos (imprint) 23, 115
Crashing Suns (Hamilton) 99
Création cosmique (Bessière) 43–5
Creation of the Humanoids (film) 153
Creative Evolution (*L'Évolution créatrice*, Bergson) 44–5
Crichton, Michael 18
Les Cristaux de Capella (Guieu) 84
Croisière dans le temps (Bessière) 46
cyberpunk 101, 195
Cyrano de Bergerac, Savinien 1, 17, 25, 34; *Histoire comique des états et empires de la lune* 25; *Histoire comique des états et empires du soleil* 25; *Other Worlds: The Comical History of the States and Empires of the Moon and Sun* 25

Dard, Frédéric 3; San Antonio series 3, 22
Darwin, Charles 132
David Starr, Space Ranger (*Sur la planète rouge*, Asimov) 23
The Day of the Triffids (also *Revolt of the Triffids*, *Révolte des Triffids*, Wyndham) 24
de Beauvoir, Simone 177–8; Bruss comparison 177–80; *Le Deuxième Sexe* (*The Second Sex*) 177–8; Existentialism influence 178, 180; Hegel influence 178; Sartre influence 178, 180; *see also* dialectical thinking
De Camp, L. Sprague 19, 46; *Lest Darkness Fall* 46
Defontenay, C.I. 17
De Gaulle, Charles 4, 7, 108–14, 193, 195; *dirigisme* (political concept) 108; *Principate* (ancient Roman government) comparison

109, 112; Wul ideological comparison 108–14
dégradation nationale (national degradation, civil status) 169; Koreman description 169
Delaney, Samuel R. 194
De la terre à la lune (*From the Earth to the Moon*, Verne) 34
del Rey, Lester 19
Denoël (publisher) 23, 184
Départ pour l'avenir (Vandel) 164
Le Deuxième Sexe (*The Second Sex*, de Beauvoir) 177–8
La Deuxième Terre (Bessière) 40
dialectical thinking (philosophy) 210n
Dianetios 109
Dick, Philip K. 19, 101; "We Can Remember It for You Wholesale" 101
Diderot, Denis 1
La Dimension X (Guieu) 85–6
dirigisme (political concept) 108
Discours sur les sciences et les arts (*Discourse on the Sciences and Arts*, Rousseau) 167
Discours sur l'origine et les fondements de l'inégalité parmi les hommes (*Discourse on the Origin and Foundations of Inequality Among Men*, Rousseau) 164–6
Discourse on the Origin and Foundations of Inequality among Men (*Discours sur l'origine et les fondements de l'inégalité parmi les hommes*, Rousseau) 164–6
Discourse on the Sciences and Arts (*Discours sur les sciences et les arts*, Rousseau) 167
Douilly, Alain 34, 59–60, 78, 94, 95, 115, 127, 129, 169–70, 174, 183, 209n
Dreadful Sanctuary (*Le Sanctuaire terrifiant*, Russell) 85
Du contrat social ou principes du droit politique (*Social Contract, or the Principles of Political Right*, Rousseau) 164–6
D'une planète à l'autre (*Between Planets*, Heinlein) 129–30
Dupont, Kurt *see* Steiner, Kurt
Duquesne, André *see* Randa, Peter

Easter Island (Rapa Nui) 87
École des Hautes Études Commerciales de Paris (French higher education) 180
École Nationale d'Administration (French higher education) 180
École Normale Supérieure (French higher education) 180
École Polytechnique (French higher education) 180–1; *L'X* nickname 181
ECSC (European Coal and Steel Community) 57
edile (government official) 109
élan vital (vital impetus, Bergson concept) 44
Eleusinian Mysteries cult 91
Ellis, Edward S. 18
Ellison, Harlan 194

Encyclopedia of Science Fiction (Clute and Nicholls) 78, 101, 183
Les Enfants du chaos (Limat) 4, 117–20, 125–6
enlightened despotism 162–3
Enlightenment (European historical period) 9, 12, 16, 79–80
environmental concerns 72
Ère cinquième (Rayjean) 66–7
L'Ère des Biocybs (Guieu) 91–2
Escale chez les vivants (Bessière) 51
Escrignelles, Maurice d' *see* Limat, Maurice
Espionnage (Fleuve Noir imprint) 22, 32, 140–1
An Essay on the Theory of Enlightened Despotism (Krieger) 162
Et la planète sauta... (Bruss) 169
Les Êtres de feu (Guieu) 87
European Coal and Steel Community (ECSC) 57
Evans, Arthur B. 1, 194
Les Événements (May 1968, political protests) 194
evolution 132, 136; Bessière treatment 44–5; Randa treatment 131–2; Steiner treatment 134, 136–8; Vandel treatment 157–60
L'Évolution créatrice (*Creative Evolution*, Bergson) 44–5
Existentialism 178, 180
Expédition cosmique (Guieu) 84
Expérimental X-35 (Guieu) 84
L'Exposition coloniale (Colonial Exposition, 1931) 113

fairy tale (*conte de fée*) 25
Fantastic Planet (*Le Planète sauvage*, film) 95, 107
Fantastic Voyage (film) 101
Fantastik Blog (Moreau, blog site) 170
Fantasy and Science Fiction see *The Magazine of Fantasy and Science Fiction*
Farmer, Philip José 116; "The Lovers" 116
Farrel, Urbain *see* Randa, Peter
feminism 177–80, 196; *see also* women characters
Feu dans le ciel (Bessière) 43
Fiction (periodical) 2, 3, 23, 95; "Ici, on desintegre!" (review column) 95; Klein as contributor 183, 188
Final Blackout (Hubbard) 109
Finney, Jack 61; *The Body Snatchers* 61
Flammarion, Camille 17; Steiner (Kurt) influence 132
Flash Gordon (film, 1936) 98
Fléau de l'univers (Bessière) 40
Fleuve Noir (publisher) 2, 3, 8, 22–4, 110, 127, 184, 188–91; Angoisse imprint 22, 127; Anticipation imprint 2, 3, 8, 22–4; L'Aventurier imprint 22, 127; Ciné TV Console imprint 22; Espionnage imprint 22, 32, 140–1; Gore imprint 133; Jimmy Guieu Presente les Maîtres Français de la Science-

Index

Fiction imprint 77; San Antonio series 3, 22; SF Fantasy imprint 22; Spécial Police imprint 22, 127; Thriller Policier imprint 22; Westerns imprint 22
Flying Saucers: A Modern Myth of Things Seen in the Skies (*Ein moderner Mythus; von Dingen, die am Himmel gesehen warden*, Jung) 81–2
La Folie verte (Rayjean) 65
Fontenelle, Bernard Le Bovier, sieur de 12
La Force sans visage (Guieu) 91
Forest, Jean-Claude 3
Fort, Charles 85; *The Book of the Damned* 85; Fortean Society 85; Gueiu comparison 85; *Lo!* 85; *New Lands* 85; *Wild Talents* 85
Fortean Society 85
La Foudre anti-D (Vandel) 160–1
Fourier, Charles 12
Les Foudroyants (Limat) 116, 189
France, Anatole 18
Frank, Pat (Harry Hart) 18
Frankenstein (Shelley) 1
Les Frelons d'or (Randa) 128–9, 131
French Community (*Communauté française*) 112
French Confederation of Christian Workers (Confédération Française Travailleurs Chrétiens, CFTC, workers group) 122–3
French general attitudes: atomic energy 72; contributing to colonial independence 113; Union of Soviet Socialist Republichs 173; Western Europe unification 53
French Resistance 76, 91
French Union (Union Française) 112
From the Earth to the Moon (*De la terre à la lune*, Verne) 34
Frontières du vide (Vandel) 147
Fuite dans l'inconnu (Vandel) 158–9, 160
Future Shock (Toffler) 162

Gaillard, Félix 71
Galaxie (periodical) 23, 115
Galaxy Science Fiction (periodical) 19, 23
Gallimard (publisher) 127
Le Gambit des étoiles (*Starmaster's Gambit*, Klein) 183
Garin, Jacques 34
Gather, Darkness! (Leiber) 116
Gaullism *see* De Gaulle, Charles
Gearhart, Sally Miller 18
Genefort, Laurent 95–8, 99, 100, 101, 110
general attitudes *see* French general attitudes
general will (*volonte générale*, Rousseau concept) 165–6
Générations perdues (Bessière) 49–50
Geoffroy, Louis 17
Gernsback, Hugo 15, 18, 20; Hugo Awards 21; *Ralph 124C41+: A Romance of the Year 2660* 18; scientifiction 19
Gestalt mind *see* group mind
Ghilen, Herbert *see* Randa, Peter

Gilgamesh 16
Gilpen, Robert 37
Gilson, Étienne 122, 124
Giraud, Jean (Moebius) 100
Goguel, François 123, 124
Golden Age of Science Fiction: France 17; United States 19
Gore (Fleuve Noir imprint) 133
Gortais, Albert 122, 124
Gouanvic, Jean-Marc 170, 174
Graffigny, Henry de (Raoul Marquis, Gustave La Rouge, and Jean de la Hire [Adolphe d'Espie de la Hire]) 17, 31, 34
Grainville, Jean-Baptiste Cousin de 17
Le Grand Kirn (Bruss) 61, 174
Grand Prix du Roman de Science Fiction (award) 83, 204n
Grand Prix International de la Science Fiction (award) 32
Grand Romans-Sciences-Anticipation (imprint) 23
grandes écoles (French higher education) 180–1; École des Hautes Études Commerciales de Paris 180; École Nationale d'Administration 180; École Normale Supérieure 180; École Polytechnique 180–1
The Great Initiates (Schuré) 33, 42–3
Groc, Léon 18
group mind: Randa's treatment 130–1; Wul's treatment 102
Guerre aux invisibles (*Sinister Barrier*, Russell) 85
La Guerre contre le Rull (*The War Against the Rull*, van Vogt) 170
La Guerre des soucoupes (Bruss) 172
Guieu, Henri-René *see* Guieu, Jimmy
Guieu, Jimmy (Henri-René Guieu) 9, 24, 66, 75, **76–93**, 95, 102, 115, 140–1, 168, 187, 195; abominable snowman (Yeti) 86; *L'Agonie du verre* 83–4; *As-tu vu les Soucoupes?* 77; Atlantis myth 84–5; *Au-delà de l'infini* 79, 189; Bernal parallels 92–3; *Black-Out sur les soucoupes volantes* 77; *Les Carrefours de l'étrange* (television) 77; *Chasseurs d'hommes* 84; *Cité Noë No. 2* 90; *Commandos de l'espace* 83; *Convulsions solaires* 89; *Les Cristaux de Capella* 84; *La Dimension X* 85–6; Easter Island (Rapa Nui) myth 87; Eleusinian Mysteries cult 91; Enlightenment ideas 79–80; *L'Ère des Biocybs* 91–2; *Les Êtres de feu* 87; *Expédition cosmique* 84; *Expérimental X-35* 84; *La Force sans visage* 91; Fort comparison 85; French Resistance 76, 91; *Grand Prix du Roman de Science* 83, 204n; *Hantise sur le Monde* 83; *L'Homme de l'espace* 83, 204n; *L'Invasion de la Terre* 82–3; Jimmy Guieu (imprint) 77; Jimmy Guieu Presente les Maîtres Français de la Science-Fiction (Fleuve Noir imprint) 77; Lemuria myth 86; Menehume myth 86; *Le Monde oublié* 84–5; *Les Monstres du néant*

87–8; *La Mort de la vie* 89–90; Mu myth 86–7; *Nos ancêstres de l'avenir* 83; *Nous les martiens* 84; *Opération Aphrodite* 83; *Ouranos* (journal) 77; pantheism 79–80; *Le Péril jaune* (Yellow Peril) 86; *Piège dans l'espace* 84; *Le Pionnier de l'atome* 79; *Les Portes du futur* (television) 77; *Prisonniers du passé* 88–9; Quint pseudonym 77; racism 85; Randa comparison 132; Rapa Nui (Easter Island) myth 87; *Le Rayon du cube* 86; *Le Règne des mutants* 90; religion 79–80; *Réseau Dinosaure* 90–1; Rostaing pseudonym 77; Russell comparison 85; *Les Soucoupes volantes viennent d'un autre monde* 77; *Les Sphères de Rapa-Nui* 86–7; Spinoza comparison 80; *La Spirale du temps* 86; Steiner (Kurt) comparison 139; technocratic vision 89–92; UFO (Unidentified Flying Object, OVNI in French) 76–8, 80–2; *Univers parallèles* 83; *L'Univers vivant* 83; Verseau pseudonym 77; *The World, the Flesh, and the Devil: An Inquiry in the Future of the Three Enemies of the Rational Soul* (Ber-nal) comparison 91–2; Yellow Peril (*Le Péril jaune*) 86; Yeti (abominable snowman) 86

Hachette-Gallimard (publisher) 23, 85
Hale, Edward Everett 18
Hamilton, Edmond 19, 98, 99; *Crashing Suns* 99
Hamilton, Peter F. 98
Hantise sur le Monde (Guieu) 83
Hardouin, Jules *see* Randa, Peter
Hawaii (state) 86
Hector Servadac (*Off on a Comet*, Verne) 34
Hegel, Georg Wilhelm Friedrich 178; *see also* dialectical thinking
Heinlein, Robert A. x, 19, 94, 129–31, 137; *Between Planets* (*D'une planète à l'autre*) 129–30; "If This Goes On..." 116; libertarianism 131; *Marionnettes humaines* (*The Puppet Masters*, Heinlein) 130–1; *Methuselah's Children* 131; *The Puppet Masters* (*Marionnettes humaines*, Hein-lein) 130–1; Randa comparison 129–31; *Starship Troopers* 130; Wells stature comparison 130
Hetzel (publisher) 148–9
High Court of Justice (France) 169
Histoire comique des états et empires de la lune (Cyrano de Bergerac) 25
Histoire comique des états et empires de la soleil (Cyrano de Bergerac) 25
hive mind *see* group mind
L'Homme de l'espace (Guieu) 83, 204n
Howells, William Dean 18
Hubbard, L. Ron 24, 109; Church of Scientology 109; Dianetics 109; *Final Blackout* 109; *Return to Tomorrow* (*Retour à demain*) 24; Wul novel parallel 109
Hughes, H. Stuart 193

Hugo Awards 21
Humains de nulle part (Limat) 129
The Humanoids (*Les Humanoïdes*, Williamson) 153
Huxley, Aldous 16; *Brave New World* 143

I, Robot (Asimov) 120–1, 206n
I, Robot (film) 206n
"Ici, on desintegre!" (review column) 95
"If This Goes On..." (Heinlein) 116
L'Île mystérieuse (*Mysterious Island*, Verne) 148–9
Îles de l'espace (*Islands in the Sky*, Clarke) 23
IMDb *see* Internet Movie Database
Incroyable Futur (Vandel) 158
individual liberty and rights 128–32, 151; *see also* libertarianism
intellectual history 4, 9
Internet Movie Database (IMDb) 132, 153
The Invasion (film) 203n
L'Invasion de la terre (Guieu) 82–3
Invasion "H" (Rayjean) 70
Invasion of the Body Snatchers (film, 1956) 61
Invasion of the Body Snatchers (film, 1978) 203n
Ioakimidis, Demetre 188–90
Irving, R.E.M. 124–5
Isaac Asimov's Science Fiction Magazine (periodical, later *Asimov's Science Fiction*) 78
The Island of Doctor Moreau (Wells) 48
Islands in the Sky (*Îles de l'espace*, Clarke) 23
Ivoi, Paul d' (Paul-Charles Delentre) 17; Steiner (Kurt) influence 131

Jabukowski, Maxim 94, 183
J'ai Lu (publisher) 191
J'écoute l'Univers (Limat) 120
Je reviens de... (Kemmel/Bommart) 73–4
Jimmy Guieu (imprint) 77
Jimmy Guieu Presente les Maîtres Français de la Science-Fiction (Fleuve Noir imprint) 77
Johnson, George Clayton 171; *Logan's Run* (Nolan and Clayton) 171
Journey to the Center of the Earth (*Voyage au centre de la terre*, Verne) 47
Jung, Carl Gustav 81–2; *Flying Saucers: A Modern Myth of Things Seen in the Skies* (*Ein moderner Mythus; von Dingen, die am Himmel gesehen warden*) 81–2

Keener, Frederick M. 27–8, 194
Kemmel *see* Bommart, Jean
Kenny, Paul *see* Vandel, Jean-Gaston
King, Stephen 18
Klein, Gérard (Gilles d'Argyre) 2, 9, 24, 25, 95–8, **183–92**, 196, 207n; Ailleurs & Demain (imprint) 184; Ailleurs & Demain: Classiques (imprint) 97; Bradbury inspiration 183; Brunner as translator 183; *Chirurgiens d'une planète* 184–92; *Fiction*

(periodical) contributions 183, 188; Fleuve Noir (publisher) format 184, 188–91; *Le Gambit des étoiles* (*Starmaster's Gambit*) 183; Ioakimidis review 188–90; J'ai Lu (publisher) 191; Livre de Poche (publisher) 184; *Le Long Voyage* 190; *The Overlords of War* (*Les Seigneurs de la guerre*) 183; Pagery pseudonym 183; *Le Rêve des forêts* 191; Robert Laffont (publisher) 97, 184; *Le Scepter du hazard* 190–1; Seghers (publisher) 184; *Les Seigneurs de la guerre* (*The Overlords of War*) 183; Slusser observation 2, 184; *Starmaster's Gambit* (*Le Gambit des étoiles*) 183; Starr pseudonym 183; technocratic vision 186–7; terraforming 184; *Les Voiliers de soleil* 190
Koreman, Megan 169
Krieger, Leonard 162–3; *An Essay on the Theory of Enlightened Despotism* 162
Kril, Guy 22
Küng, Hans x

Laffont (publisher) *see* Robert Laffont
Lafitte, Pierre 12
La Hire, Jean de (Adolphe d'Espie de La Hire) 18; Kurt Steiner influence 132
Laloux, René 95, 100; *Fantastic Planet* (*Le Planète sauvage*, film) 95; *Les Maîtres du temps* (*The Time Masters*, film) 95, 100
La Plongeon, Augustus 87
Laurie, André (Paschal Grousset) 17
Laval, Pierre 169
Le Faure, Georges 17, 31, 34
LeGuin, Ursula K. 194
Leiber, Fritz, Jr. 19; *Gather, Darkness!* 116
Leibniz, Gottfried Wilhelm 4, 25, 119, 126
Leinster, Murray (William Fitzgerald Jenkins) 19
Lemuria myth 86
Lermina, Jules 17
Lern, Henri *see* Randa, Peter
Le Rouge, Gustav 115
Lest Darkness Fall (De Camp) 46
Levin, Ira 18
Levinas, Emmanuel 176–7
Lewis, C.S. 116; *Out of the Silent Planet* 116; *Perelandra* 116; *That Hideous Strength* 116
Lewis, Sinclair 15, 18
Libert, Jean *see* Vandel, Jean-Gaston
libertarianism 131; *see also* individual liberty and rights
Limat, Maurice 4, 9, 24, 25, 94, **115–26**, 127, 129, 132, 139, 168, 195; *Aéronef C3* 115; Angoisse (Fleuve Noir imprint) 115; Asimov novel comparison 120–1; *Candide* quotation 118–120; CFTC (Confédération Française Travailleurs Chrétiens, workers group) 122–3; Christian Democracy influence 121–6; Confédération Française Travailleurs Chrétiens (CFTC, workers group) 122–3; Cosmos (imprint) 115; *Les Enfants du chaos* 4,

117–20, 125–6; *Les Foudroyants* 116, 189; French Confederation of Christian Workers (CFTC, workers group) 122–3; *Galaxie* (periodical) 115; *Humains de nulle part* 129; *I, Robot* (Asimov) 121; *J'écoute l'univers* 120; Le Rouge influence 115; Lionel Rex pseudonym 115; Maurice d'Escrignelles pseudonym 115; Maurice Lionel pseudonym 115; *Metro pour l'inconnu* 117; *Moi, un robot* 120–6; *La Montagne aux vampires* 115; Mouvement Républicain Populaire (MRP, political party) 121–5; politics 121–6; Popular Republican Movement (MRP, political party) 121–5; Randa influence 129; religion 115–6, 121–5; Roman Catholicism influence 121–2; *Le Sang de soleil* 116; Série 2000 (imprint) 115; Voltaire quotation 118–120
The Little Prince (Saint-Exupéry) 33–4
Livre de Poche (publisher) 184
Lo! (Fort) 85
Lofficier, Jean-Marc 31, 59–60, 77–8, 85, 86, 94, 115, 127, 141, 169–70, 174, 183–4, 194; Bruss obituary 170
Lofficier, Randy 31, 59–60, 77–8, 85, 86, 94, 115, 127, 141, 169–70, 174, 183–4, 194
Logan's Run (film) 171
Logan's Run (Nolan and Johnson) 171
Loisy, Alfred 12
Lombard, Jean (1854–91) 59; *see also* Rayjean, M.A.
London, Jack 15, 18
Le Long Voyage (Klein) 190
lost continents 86–7; Atlantis 84–5, 102; Lemuria 86; Mu 86–7
lost races 86–7; abominable snowman (Yeti) 84–5; Easter Island (Rapa Nui) myth 87; Menehume 86; Yeti (abominable snowman) 84–5
Lost Worlds of 2001 (Clarke) 207n
Louit, Robert 27
Louvigny, André *see* Steiner, Kurt
"The Lovers" (Farmer) 116
Lucian of Samasota 16
Les Lunes de Jupiter (Bessière) 41

MacDonald, Jack D. 18
mad scientist theme 157; Rayjean use 65; Vandel use 156–7
The Magazine of Fantasy see *The Magazine of Fantasy and Science Fiction*
The Magazine of Fantasy and Science Fiction (periodical, formerly *The Magazine of Fantasy* and later *Fantasy and Science Fiction*) 19, 23
Maître du monde (*Master of the World*, Verne) 148
Les Maîtres du temps (*The Time Masters*, film) 95, 100
Marionnettes humaines (*The Puppet Masters*, Heinlein) 130–1
Maslowski, I.B. 69

Mason, James 149
Massey, Raymond 144
Master of the World (film) 149; Price interpretation of Robur character 149
Master of the World (*Maître du monde*, Verne) 148
Memoirs (Monnet) 56–7
Men Like Gods (Wells) 167–8
Menace d'outre–terre (Steiner) 133–7
Menehume myth 86
Mercier, Sébastien 1, 17; *L'An 2440, rêve s'il on fut jamais* 12
Merritt, Richard L. 53, 113, 173
Messac, Régis 18
Methuselah's Children (Heinlein) 131
Metro pour l'inconnu (Limat) 117
"Micromegas" (Voltaire) 26, 29
The Midwich Cuckoos (Wyndham) 102, 156
The Mightiest Machine (Campbell) 99
Miller, Walter M. 116; *A Canticle for Leibowitz* 116
A Modern Utopia (Wells) 143
Ein moderner Mythus; von Dingen, die am Himmel gesehen warden (*Flying Saucers: A Modern Myth of Things Seen in the Skies*, Jung) 81–2
Moebius (Jean Giraud) 100
Moi, un robot (Limat) 120–6
Le Monde de éternité (Rayjean) 65–6
Le Monde oublié (Guieu) 84
Monnet, Jean 56–8; *Memoirs* 56–7
Monnet Plan 57
Les Monstres du néant (Guieu) 87–8
Mont Louis Laboratories (France) 71
La Montagne aux vampires (Limat) 115
Montesquieu, Charles-Louis de Secondat, baron de La Brède et de 1
Moorcock, Michael 194
More Than Human (Sturgeon) 136
Moreau, Charles 170; *Fantastik Blog* (blog site) 170
La Mort de la vie (Guieu) 89–90
La Mort vivante (Wul) 102, 156
Moselli, José (Théophile Maurice Moselli Joseph) 18
Mouvement Républicain Populaire (MRP, Popular Republican Movement, political party) 121–5
Mu myth 86–7
Mycènes, celui qui vient du futur (television series) 95
Mysterious Island (*L'Île mystérieuse*, Verne) 148–9

national degradation (*dégradation nationale*, civil status) 169; Koreman description 169
Naufrages des galaxies (Vandel) 163–4
Nebula Awards 21
New Lands (Fort) 85
New Wave (artistic movement): France

(*nouvelle vague*) 3, 194; United Kingdom 194; United States 19, 194
Nicholls, Peter 78, 101, 103; *Encyclopedia of Science Fiction* (Clute and Nicholls) 78, 101, 183
"The Nine Billion Names of God" (Clarke) 116
Nineteen Eighty-four (Orwell) 143
Niourk (Wul) 103–7
Nizerolles, Réne-Marcel (Marcel Priolet) 34; *Les Aventuriers du ciel: Voyages extraordinaries d'un petit parisien dans la stratosphere, la lunes et la planètes* 34; Bessière influence 34
Nolan, William F. 171; *Logan's Run* (Nolan and Johnson) 171
Noô (Wul) 95
Nordley, G. David 209n
Nos ancêstres de l'avenir (Guieu) 83
Nous les Martiens (Guieu) 84
nouvelle vague (New Wave, France) 3, 194
novel 27–8, 194–5

Objectif soleil (Bessière) 41, 189
Objet Volant Non-Identifié (OVNI) *see* UFO
L'Odyssée espèce (Wagner) 2
Odyssée sous contrôle (Wul) 100–1
Off on a Comet (*Hector Servadac*, Verne) 34
Olivier, André *see* Randa, Peter
Oms en série (Wul) 4, 95, 107–110
On a hurlé dans le ciel (Bessière) 50
Opération Aphrodite (Guieu) 83
L'Orphelin de Perdide (Wul) 95
Ortog et les ténèbres (Steiner) 136
Orwell, George (Eric Arthur Blair) 16; *Nineteen Eighty-four* 143
the other (philosophical concept) 170, 174, 176–7, 179; Levinas as representative 176–7; *see also* dialectical thinking
Other Worlds: The Comical History of the States and Empires of the Moon and Sun (Cyrano de Bergerac) 25
otherness (philosophical concept) *see* the other
Ouranos (journal) 77
Out of the Silent Planet (Lewis) 116
The Overlords of War (*Les Seigneurs de la guerre*, Klein) 183
OVNI (*Objet Volant Non-Identifié*) *see* UFO

Pagery, François *see* Klein, Gérard
Pairault, Pierre *see* Wul, Stefan
Palewski Plan 71
Pandora (myth) 177, 181
Panique dans le vide (Bessière) 50
pantheism 79–80
Les Parias de l'atome (Rayjean) 70, 72, 73, 204n
Paris au XXe siècle (Verne) 7–8
Pascal, Blaise 33, 40–2, 56, 58; Bessière influence 33, 40–2; *Pensées* 33, 40–1
Les Patins d'outre ciel (Bessière) 50–1
Pebble in the Sky (Asimov) 171

Index

Pensées (Pascal) 33, 40–1
Perelandra (Lewis) 116
Le Péril des hommes (Rayjean) 69–70
Le Péril jaune (Yellow Peril) 86
La peur géante (Wul) 99
Philmus, Robert M. 209*n*
philosophical tale *see conte philosophique*
Piège dans l'espace (Guieu) 84, 111
Piège sur Zarkass (Wul) 111–4, 189
Piercy, Marge 18
Le Pionnier de l'atome (Guieu) 79
Pirate de la science (Vandel) 156–7
Planète de mort (Bessière) 51
Le Planète sauvage (*Fantastic Planet*, film) 95, 107
Planète vagabonde (Bessière) 35, 39
Les Plans (French government policies, "The Plans" or "The Projects") 13, 162
Plon (publisher) 77
Pluto 208*n*
Poe, Edgar Allan 12, 15, 17, 18, 19, 20
Pohl, Frederick 19
Le Poisson chinois (Kemmel/Bommart) 73
Le Poisson chinois a tué Hitler (Kemmel/Bommart) 73
politics 108–14, 121–6, 130–2; Christian democracy 121–6; Gaullism 108–14; libertarianism 131
popular culture 21; Brée observation 21; Cordesse observation 20–1; definition 14; France 13–4; science fiction as example 20–22; United States 15
Popular Republican Movement (MRP, *Mouvement Républicain Populaire*, political party) 121–5
Les Portes du futur (television) 77
Presence du Futur (imprint) 23, 103
Presses de la Cité (publisher) 127
Price, Vincent 149
Prime Directive (*Star Trek*) 47
primus inter pares (ancient Roman government) 109, 112
Principate (ancient Roman government) 109, 112
Priolet, Marcel *see* Nizerolles, René-Marcel
Prisonniers du passé (Guieu) 88–9
"Probe 7 — Over and Out" (*Twilight Zone* television episode, Serling) 69
progress, idea of 12–3; definition 199–200*n*; Enlightenment characteristic 12
"The Projects" (*Les Plans*, French government policies) *see Les Plans*
Protestantism 122
Proumen, Henri-Jacques 18
Puchala, Donald J. 53, 113, 173
The Puppet Masters (*Marionnettes humaines*, Heinlein) 130–1
Pynchon, Thomas 18

"The Quest for St. Aquin" (Boucher) 116
Quint, Jimmy *see* Guieu, Jimmy

racism 85, 86, 106; Wul mention 106; Yellow Peril 86
radical (ideology) 140
Raid sur Delta (Vandel) 159–60
Ralph 124C41+: A Romance of the Year 2660 (Gernaback) 18
Randa, Peter (André Duquesne) 9, 24, 67, 75, 94, 126–32, 139, 168, 195; Alain pseudonym 126; Angoisse (Fleuve Noir imprint) 127; *Baroud* 128, 131; *Between Planets* (*D'une planète à l'autre*, Heinlein) comparison 129–30; evolution 131–2; Farrel pseudonym 127; *Les Frelons d'or* 128–9, 131; Ghilen pseudonym 127; Guieu comparison 132; Hardouin pseudonym 127; Heinlein comparison 129–31; individualism 128–32; Lern pseudonym 127; libertarianism 131; Limat influence 129; *Marionnettes humaines* (*The Puppet Masters*, Heinlein) comparison 130–1; *Methuselah's Children* (Heinlein) comparison 131; Olivier pseudonym 126; Philippe Randa continuation of work 127; politics 130–2; *The Puppet Masters* (*Marionnettes humaines*, Heinlein) comparison 130–1; *Starship Troopers* (Heinlein) comparison 130; Steiner (Kurt) comparison 135; Suarez pseudonym 127; "*Survie*" 127–8; Van Rhyn pseudonym 126
Randa, Philippe 127
Rapa Nui (Easter Island) 87
Rayjean, M.A. (Jean Lombard) 9, 24, 31, 59–73, 74–5, 95, 195, 203*n*; Adam and Eve theme 69; "Adam and No Eve" (Bester) comparison 68–9; *L'Anneau des invincibles* 63–5; atomic bomb 69, 71; atomic energy attitude 72; *Attaque sub-terrestre* 60–1, 67, 72; *Base spatiale 14* 61; Bester story similarity 68–9; *Chocs en synthèse* 61–3; environmental concerns 72; *Ère cinquième* 66–7; *La Folie verte* 65; *Invasion "H"* 70; mad scientist example 65; *Le Monde de éternité* 65–6; *Les Parias de l'atome* 70, 72, 73, 204*n*; *Le Péril des hommes* 69–70; solar energy advocation 71; *Soleils: Échelle zéro* 67–8, 79; *L'Ultra Univers* 68–9; women characters 63
Le Rayon du cube (Guieu) 86
Rayon fantastique (imprint) 23, 85
Rayons pour Sidar (Wul) 99
Réaction déluge (Bessière) 48–9
Rebirth (*Les Transformés*, Wyndham) 24
Le Règne des mutants (Guieu) 90
Relais Minos III (Bessière) 42
religion 42–3, 45–6, 79–80, 115–6; Bessière's use 42–6; Guieu's use 79–80; Limat's use 121–5
Renard, Maurice 17, 18
Réseau dinosaure (Guieu) 90–1
Restif de la Bretonne (Nicolas-Anne-Edmé Restif) 1, 17

Retour à demain (*Return to Tomorrow*, Hubbard) 24
Retour à "O" (Wul) 101, 204*n*
Retour de Météore (Bessière) 35, 38–9
Return to Tomorrow (*Retour à demain*, Hubbard) 24
Le Rêve des forêts (Klein) 191
Revolt of the Triffids (also *The Day of the Triffids, Révolte des Triffids*, Wyndham) 24
Rex, Lionel *see* Limat, Maurice
Rex, Maurice Lionel *see* Limat, Maurice
Ribes, F.-H. *see* Bessière, Richard
Richard, François 22; Bessière, relations with 31–2
Richard-Bessière, F. (pseudonym for François Richard and Richard Bessiére's father) 32
Richard-Bessière, F. (pseudonym for Richard Bessière) *see* Bessière, Richard
Rideau magnetic (Bruss) 172
Robert Laffont (publisher) 97, 184; Ailleurs & Demain (imprint) 184; Ailleurs & Demain: Classiques (imprint) 97; Klein's importance 184
Robida, Albert 12, 17
robot 152–3; android comparison 153; Bessière's treatment 42; *robota* (Czech) as origin 153; Vandel's treatment 151–3
robota (Czech) 153
Robur-le-conquérant (*Robur the Conqueror*, Verne) 148
Roman Catholicism 121–2
Rondard, Patrice 183
J.-H., aîné 12, 17
Rossum's Universal Robots (*R.U.R.*, play, Čapek) 100, 152–3
Rostaing, Claude *see* Guieu, Jimmy
Rousseau, Jean-Jacques 90, 163; *Discours sur les sciences et les arts* (*Discourse on the Sciences and Arts*) 167; *Discours sur l'origine et les fondements de l'inégalité parmi les hommes* (*Discourse on the Origin and Foundations of Inequality among Men*) 164–6; *Discourse on the Origin and Foundations of Inequality Among Men* (*Discours sur l'origine et les fondements de l'inégalité parmi les hommes*) 164–6; *Discourse on the Sciences and Arts* (*Discours sur les sciences et les arts*) 167; *Du contrat social ou principes du droit politique* (*Social Contract, or the Principles of Political Right*, Rousseau) 164–6; general will (*volonte générale*) 165–6; *Social Contract, or the Principles of Political Right* (*Du contrat social ou principes du droit politique*, Rousseau) 164–6; Vandel comparison 164–9; *volonte générale* (general will) 165–6
Route du néant (Bessière) 54–5
Ruellan, André *see* Steiner, Kurt
R.U.R. (*Rossum's Universal Robots*, play, Čapek) 100, 152–3
Russell, Eric Frank 19, 85; *Dreadful Sanctuary* (*Le Sanctuaire terrifiant*) 85; Guieu comparison 85; *Sinister Barrier* (*Guerre aux invisibles*) 85

Sadoul, Jacques 170
Sagan, Carl 18
Saint-Exupéry, Antoine de 33–35; *The Little Prince* 33–34
Saint-Pierre, Charles-Irénée Castel, abbé de 12
Saint-Simon, Claude Henri de Rouvroy, comte de 12, 36–9, 56, 58
Salamandra (Steiner) 133
San Antonio (novel series) 3, 22
Le Sanctuaire terrifiant (*Dreadful Sanctuary*, Russell) 85
Le Sang de soleil (Limat) 116
Sartre, Jean-Paul 178, 180
Satellite (periodical) 23
Le Satellite artificiel (Vandel) 142–3
Sauvetage sidéral (Bessière) 39
Le Scepter du hazard (Klein) 190–1
Scheinman, Lawrence 71
Schuman, Robert 57
Schuman Plan 57
Schuré, Édouard 33, 42–3, 46, 56, 59; *The Great Initiates* 33, 42–3
science fiction 15–22, 196; Adam and Eve theme 69, 152; alternate history 46; android 153; apocalypse 101; atomic bomb 69, 71; awards 21, 83, 201*n*, 204*n*; conventions (meetings) 21; cyberpunk 101, 195; definition 15–6; Enlightenment origins 16; environmental concerns 72; evolution 44–5, 131–2, 134, 136–8, 157–60; feminism 177–80; France 17–8, 194; Golden Age 17, 19; group mind 102, 130–1; idea of progress 12; mad scientist 65, 156–7; New Wave (artistic movement) 3, 19, 194; politics 108–14, 121–6, 130–2; popular culture aspects 20–2; religion 42–6, 79–80, 115–6, 121–5; robots 152–3; scientifiction 19; space opera 96–8; steampunk 195; technocracy 89–92, 141–68, 180, 186–7; terraforming 184; United Kingdom 18, 194; United States 18–22, 193–4; women characters 63
Science Fiction Studies (periodical) 1
Science Fiction Writers of America (SFWA) 21
Scientifiction 19
The Second Sex (*Le Deuxième Sexe*, de Beauvoir) 177–8
Seghers (publisher) 184
Les Seigneurs de la guerre (*The Overlords of War*, Klein) 183
Senarens, Luis 18
Série 2000 (imprint) 23, 115
Serling, Rod 69; "Probe 7 — Over and Out" (*Twilight Zone* television episode) 69
SF Fantasy (Fleuve Noir imprint) 22
SFWA (Science Fiction Writers of America) 21
The Shape of Things to Come (Wells) 144

Index

Shelley, Mary Wollstonecraft 1, 17, 18; *Frankenstein* 1
Simak, Clifford D. 19
Sinister Barrier (*Guerre aux invisibles*, Russell) 85
Siry, Patrick 32
Slusser, George xi, 1–5, 184
Smith, E.E. "Doc" 16, 19, 98
Social Contract, or the Principles of Political Right (*Du contrat social ou principes du droit politique*, Rousseau) 164–6
solar energy 71
Le Soleil sous la mer (Vandel) 147, 189
Soleils: Échelle zéro (Rayjean) 67–8
Sorel, Charles 17
S.O.S. soucoupes (Bruss) 171–2, 175
S.O.S. Terre (Bessière) 51
Les Soucoupes volantes viennent d'un autre monde (Guieu) 77
Soviet Union (USSR) *see* Union of Soviet Socialist Republics
space opera 96–8
Spécial Police (Fleuve Noir imprint) 22, 127
Spencer, Herbert 132
Les Sphères de Rapa-Nui (Guieu) 86–7
Spinoza, Benedict de 80
La Spirale du temps (Guieu) 86
Spitz, Jacques 18
Stableford, Brian 27, 153
Stapledon, Olaf 136; *Star Maker* 136
"The Star" (Clarke) 116
Star Maker (Stapledon) 136
Star Trek (television series) 20, 47; Prime Directive 47
Star Wars (film) 20, 98
Starmaster's Gambit (*Le Gambit des étoiles*, Klein) 183
Starr, Mark *see* Klein, Gérard
Starship Troopers (film) 130
Starship Troopers (Heinlein) 130
Statten, Vargo (J. Russell Fearn) 23
steampunk 195
Steiner, Kurt (André Ruellan) 3, 9, 24, 67, 94, 95, **132–9**, 195, 207n; Angoisse (Fleuve Noir imprint) 132; *Aux armes d'Ortog* 135–8; *Childhood's End* (Clarke) comparison 136–9; Clarke comparison 135–9; Dupont pseudonym 132; evolution 134, 136–8; film career 133; Flammarion influence 132; Guieu comparison 139; Ivoi influence 132; La Hire influence 132; Louvigny pseudonym 132; *Menace d'Outre–Terre* 133–7; *Ortog et les ténèbres* 136; Randa comparison 135; *Salamandra* 133; *Le 32 Juillet* 95, 133; *2001: A Space Odyssey* (novel [Clarke] and film) comparison 138; Vandel comparison 168–9; Vigan pseudonym 132; Wargar pseudonym 132; Wul comparison 135
Steiner, Rudolph 43, 46, 59; anthroposophy 43, 45

Sternberg, Jacques 183
Stewart, George R. 18
Stockton, Frank R. 18
Stover, Leon 145–6
Stromberg, Roland N. 151, 193
Sturgeon, Theodore 19, 183; *More Than Human* 136
Suarez, Diego *see* Randa, Peter
Substance "ARKA" (Bruss) 173–4
Sur la planète rouge (*David Starr, Space Ranger*, Asimov) 23
"Survie" (Randa) 127–8

tale *see* conte
technocracy 143; Bruss's vision 180; Guieu's vision 89–92; historical background 186–7; Klein's vision 186–7; Vandel's examination of theme 141–68; Wells's viewpoint 143–7, 167–8
Le Temple du passé (*The Temple of the Past*, Wul) 95, 101–2, 199n
Terminus 1 (Wul) 100
terraforming 184
Terre degree "0" (Bessière) 49
Terre...siècle 24 (Bruss) 175–6
Territoire robot (Vandel) 151–2
Tête à Tête (Bruss) 170
Tevis, Walter 18
That Hideous Strength (Lewis) 116
Things to Come (film) 144–7; Massey obervation 144; Stover observation 145
Thomson, David 11, 193
Thriller Policier (Fleuve Noir imprint) 22
The Time Machine (Wells) 143
The Time Masters (*Les Maîtres du temps*, film) 95, 100
Les Titans de l'énergie (Vandel) 102, 155–6
Toffler, Alvin 162; *Future Shock* 162
Tombaugh, Clyde 208n
Total Recall (film) 101
Les Transformés (*Rebirth*, Wyndham) 24
Tremaine, F. Orlin 19
Le 32 Juillet (Steiner) 95, 133
Le Troisième Astronef (Bessière) 52
Le Troisième Bocal (Vandel) 154–5
La Troisième Race (*War of Two Worlds*, Anderson) 170
Trombe, Felix 71
Tucker, (Arthur) Wilson 97
Turgot, Anne-Robert-Jacques, baron de l'Aulne 17
Twain, Mark (Samuel Langhorne Clemens) 15, 19, 46; *A Connecticut Yankee in King Arthur's Court* 46
Twenty Thousand Leagues under the Sea (film) 149; Mason interpretation of Nemo character 149
Twenty Thousand Leagues under the Sea (*Vingt mille lieues sous les mers*, Verne) 148, 208n
Twilight Zone (television series) 69

2001: A Space Odyssey (film) 138
2001: A Space Odyssey (novel, Clarke) 2, 138
Tyssot de Patot, Simon 17

UFO (Unidentified Flying Object, OVNI in French) 76–8, 80–2; Guieu's belief 76–7; Jung explanation 81–2
L'Ultra Univers (Rayjean) 68–9
Unidentified Flying Object *see* UFO
Union Française (French Union) 112
Union of Soviet Socialist Republics (USSR): Bruss interpretation 171–2 ; French general attitudes toward 173
United Kingdom 18, 194
United States 15, 20; French general attitudes toward 173; popular culture 15; science fiction 18–22, 193–4
United States Information Agency (USIA) 53; French general attitudes towards atomic energy 72; French general attitudes towards contributing to colonial independence 113; French general attitudes towards the Soviet Union 173; French general attitudes towards the United States 173; French general attitudes towards Western Europe unification 53
Univers parallèles (Guieu) 83
L'Univers vivant (Guieu) 83
USIA *see* United States Information Agency
USSR *see* Union of Soviet Socialist Republics

Válka s mloky (*War with the Newts*, Čapek) 99–100
Vandel, Jean-Gaston (Jean Libert and Gaston Vandenpanhuyse) 9, 24, 67, 75, 90, **140–69**, 182, 195; Adam and Eve theme 152; *Agonie des civilisés* 149–51; *Alerte aux robots* 151; Ardagh observations on French society 161; *Les Astres morts* 142–3; *Attentat cosmique* 154; *Bureau de l'invisible* 154, 204n; Čapek comparison 152–3; *Les Chevaliers de l'espace* 142; Coplan FX-18 (fictional hero) 140–1; *Creation of the Humanoids* (film) comparison 153; *Départ pour l'avenir* 164; *Discours sur les sciences et les arts* (*Discourse on the Sciences and Arts*, Rousseau) comparison 167; *Discours sur l'origine et les fondements de l'inégalité parmi les hommes* (*Discourse on the Origin and Foundations of Inequality Among Men*, Rousseau) comparison 164–6; *Discourse on the Origin and Foundations of Inequality Among Men* (*Discours sur l'origine et les fondements de l'inégalité parmi les hommes*, Rousseau) comparison 164–6; *Discourse on the Sciences and Arts* (*Discours sur les sciences et les arts*, Rousseau) comparison 167; *Du contrat social ou principes du droit politique* (*Social Contract, or the Principles of Political Right*, Rousseau) comparison 164–6; enlightened despotism comparison 162–3; *Espionnage* (Fleuve Noir imprint) 140–1; evolution 157–60; *La Foudre anti-D* 160–1; *Frontières du vide* 147; *Fuite dans l'inconnu* (Vandel) 158–9, 160; *Future Shock* (Toffler) comparison 162; general will (*volonte générale*, Rouseau concept) comparison 165–6; *The Humanoids* (*Les Humanoides*, Williamson) comparison 153; *Incroyable Futur* 158; individual liberty and rights 151; Kenny pseudonym 140–1; Krieger observation on government power 162–3; *Les Plans* as background 162; mad scientist example 156–7; *Men Like Gods* (Wells) comparison 167–8; *The Midwich Cuckoos* (Wyndham) comparison 156; *Naufrages des galaxies* 163–4; *Pirate de la science* 156–7; *Raid sur Delta* 159–60; robot 151–3; Rousseau comparison 164–9; *R.U.R.* (*Rossum's Universal Robots*, play, Čapek) comparison 152–3; *Le satellite artificiel* 142–3; *Social Contract, or the Principles of Political Right* (*Du contrat social ou principes du droit politique*, Rousseau) comparison 164–6; *Le Soleil sous la mer* 147, 189; Steiner (Kurt) comparison 168–9; technocracy critique 141–68; *Territoire robot* 151–2; *Things to Come* (film) comparison 144–7; *Les Titans de l'énergie* 102, 155–6; *Le Troisième Bocal* 154–5; Verne common theme 148–9; *Les Voix de l'univers* 166–8; *volonte générale* (general will, Rouseau concept) comparison 165–6; *The War of the Worlds* (Wells) comparison 154; Wells comparison 143–7, 154, 167–9; Williamson novel comparison 153; Wyndham novel comparison 156
Vandenpanhuyse, Gaston *see* Vandel, Jean-Gaston
Van Rhyn, Jehan *see* Randa, Peter
van Vogt, A.E. 19; *The War Against the Rull* (*La Guerre contre le Rull*) 170
Vercors (Jean-Marcel Bruller) 23, 201n
Verhoeven, Paul 101
Verne, Jules 7–8, 16, 17, 19, 29, 147–9, 183; *Around the Moon* (*Autour de la lune*) 34; Bessière, influence on 31, 47; Butcher comments 8, 17, 148–9; *From the Earth to the Moon* (*De la terre à la lune*) 34; *Hector Servadac* (*Off on a Comet*) 34; Hetzel (publisher) 148–9; *L'Île mystérieuse* (*Mysterious Island*) 148–9; *Journey to the Center of the Earth* (*Voyage au centre de la terre*) 47; *Maître du monde* (*Master of the World*) 148; Mason interpretation of Nemo character 149; *Master of the World* (film) 149; *Mysterious Island* (*L'Île mystérieuse*) 148–9; *Off on a Comet* (*Hector Servadac*) 34; *Paris au XXe siècle* 7–8; Price interpretation of Robur character 149; *Robur-le-conquérant* (*Robur*

the Conqueror) 148; *Twenty Thousand Leagues Under the Sea* (film) 149; *Twenty Thousand Leagues Under the Sea* (*Vingt Mille Lieues sous les mers*) 148, 208n; Vandel comparison 148–9; *Voyage au centre de la terre* (*Journey to the Center of the Earth*) 47; Wells comparison 148–9
Verseau, Dominique *see* Guieu, Jimmy
Versins, Pierre 59, 78, 94, 115, 133, 141, 169–70
Via dimension "5" (Bessière) 40
Vian, Boris 3, 23, 201n
Vichy government 169–70, 182
Vidal, Gore 18
Vigan, Luc *see* Steiner, Kurt
Village of the Damned (film) 102
Vingt Mille Lieues sous les mers (*Twenty Thousand Leagues under the Sea*, Verne) 148
Vingt Pas dans l'inconnu (Bessière) 46–7
Visions Futures (imprint) 23
vital impetus (*élan vital*, Bergson concept) 44
Les Voiliers de soleil (Klein) 190
Les Voix de l'univers (Vandel) 166–8
volonté générale (general will, Rousseau concept) 165–6
Voltaire (François-Marie Arouet) 1, 9, 12, 25–30, 126, 195; *Candide ou l'Optimisme* 4, 26, 29, 33, 118–20, 126, 191; Limat's quoting from *Candide* 118–120; "Micromegas" 26, 29; *see also conte philosophique*
Vonnegut, Kurt 18
Voyage au centre de la terre (*Journey to the Center of the Earth*, Verne) 47

Wagner, Roland 2; *L'Odyssée espèce* 2
The War Against the Rull (*La Guerre contre le Rull*, van Vogt) 170
The War of the Worlds (Wells) 35, 37, 73, 154
War of Two Worlds (*La Troisième Race*, Anderson) 24, 170
War with the Newts (*Válka s mloky*, Čapek) 99–100
Wargar, Kurt *see* Steiner, Kurt
Watt, Ian 27
"We Can Remember It for You Wholesale" (Dick) 101
Wells, H.G. 12, 16, 17, 19, 29, 144; *Anticipations* 143; Bessière novel comparison 35, 37; Bommart novel comparison 73; *conte philosophique* 27; Heinlein stature comparison 130; *The Island of Doctor Moreau* 48; Massey observation 144; *Men Like Gods* 167–8; *A Modern Utopia* 143; *The Shape of Things to Come* 144; Stover observation 145–6; technocracy visions 143–7, 167–8; *Things to Come* (film) 144–7; *The Time Machine* 143; Vandel comparison 143–7, 154, 167–9; Verne comparison 148–9; *The War of the Worlds* 35, 37, 73, 154; *When the Sleeper Wakes* 143; *World Set Free* 143

Westerns (Fleuve Noir imprint) 22
When the Sleeper Wakes (Wells) 143
Wild Talents (Fort) 85
Williamson, Jack xi–xii, 19, 98, 184; *The Humanoids* (*Les Humanoïdes*) 153; terraforming concept 184; Vandel novel comparison 153
Wolfe, Bernard 18
women characters 63; Bessière's treatment 38–43; Bruss's treatment 177–80; Rayjean's treatment 63; *see also* feminism
World Science Fiction Convention (1939) 21, 201n
World Set Free (Wells) 143
The World, the Flesh, and the Devil: An Inquiry in the Future of the Three Enemies of the Rational Soul (Bernal) 91–2
Wul, Stefan (Pierre Pairault) 3–4, 9, 24, 75, **94–114**, 132, 139, 141, 168, 195; *The Abyss* (film) 100; Ailleurs & Demain: Classiques (imprint) collection 97; Andrevon analysis 96; apocalyptic novels 101; Atlantis myth 102; Cold War scenario 108; Colonial Exposition (L'Exposition Coloniale, 1931) influence 113; colonial relations interpretations 112–3; cyberpunk anticipation 101; De Gaulle influence 108–14; *dirigisme* (political concept) 108; *edile* (government official) 109; L'Exposition Coloniale (Colonial Exposition, 1931) influence 113; *Fantastic Planet* (*Le Planète sauvage*, film) 95, 107; *Final Blackout* (Hubbard) similarity 109; Fleuve Noir format 110; Gaullist ideas 108–14; Genefort analysis 95–8, 99, 100, 101, 110; *Gestalt Mind* 102; Klein analysis 96–7; Laloux, René 95; *Les Maîtres du temps* (*The Time Masters*, film) 95, 100; *The Midwich Cuckoos* (Wyndham) comparison 102; *La Mort vivante* 102, 156; *Mycènes, celui qui vient du futur* (television series) 95; *Niourk* 103–7; *Noô* 95; *Odyssée sous contrôle* 100–1; *Oms en série* 4, 95, 107–110; *L'Orphelin de Perdide* 95; *La Peur géante* 99; *Piège sur Zarkass* 111–4, 189; *Le Planète sauvage* (*Fantastic Planet*, film) 95, 107; politics 108–114; *primus inter pares* (ancient Roman government) 109, 112; Principate (ancient Roman government) 109, 112; *Rayons pour Sidar* 99; *Retour à "O"* 101, 204n; racism 106; space opera 96–8; Steiner (Kurt) comparison 135; *Le Temple du passé* (*The Temple of the Past*) 95, 101–2, 199n; *Terminus 1* 100; *The Time Masters* (*Les Maîtres du temps*, film) 95, 100; *Les Titans de l'énergie* influence 102; *War with the Newts* (*Válka s mloky*) similarities 99–100; Wyndham novel comparison 102
Wylie, Philip 18
Wyndham, John 23, 24; *The Day of the Triffids* (also *Revolt of the Triffids*, *Révolte des Triffids*) 24; *The Midwich Cuckoos* 102,

156; *Rebirth* (*Les Transformés*) 24; *Revolt of the Triffids* (also *The Day of the Triffids*, *Révolte des Triffids*) 24; *Les Transformés* (*Rebirth*) 24; Vandel novel comparison 156; Wul novel comparison 102

L'X (nickname for École Polytechnique, French higher education) 181; Bruss allusion 181
The X-Files (television) 77, 204*n*

Yellow Peril (*Le Péril jaune*) 86
Yeti (abominable snowman) 86

Zelazny, Roger 194
Zola, Émile 18
Zone spatiale interdite (Bessière) 47